Praise for *The Map Across Time*:
"The novel is fast-paced and tightly plotted, which means that the reader will quickly be drawn into the complex twists and turns of the story and, in fairy tale tradition, led toward a surprising yet satis-fying conclusion."

—Publisher's Weekly

"*The Map Across Time* is a fairy tale in the classic sense of the term. As J.R.R. Tolkien pointed out, fairy stories serve to draw the reader into a mythical world that conveys the joy of the gospel. Lakin's tale meets this noble task head-on. Her novel is not only interspersed with the Bible (including biblical Hebrew!), it is a retelling of the Bible's over-arching narrative. Not many Christian novels manage to blend great storytelling and scriptural truth—but here is a book that does!"

—Bryan Litfin, author of *The Sword* and *The Gift*

"[*The Map across Time* and *The Wolf of Tebron*] are set in a mythi-cal world that is permeated with a sense of both good and evil—a world in which the leading protagonists are required to battle not only external forces that seem to be beyond their control, but also their own inner demons of fear, anxiety and self-doubt. The tales are most definitely coming-of-age novels, in which the well-rounded characters come increasingly into their own as they both literally and metaphorically navigate their way across a landscape that is lovingly, though at times fearfully, depicted."

—Lois Henderson, Bookpleasures.com

Praise for *The Wolf of Tebron*:
"The Gates of Heaven promises to be one of the best fantasy series to come along in quite some time. One of the signs of this potential is its ability to hook you into its world at page one and leave you saying, 'just one more page' or 'just one more chapter.' That has happened to me before with C. S. Lewis's The Chronicles of Narnia,

J.R.R Tolkien's *The Lord of the Rings,* and Susan Cooper's The Dark is Rising sequence. Now C. S. Lakin has done the same with The Gates of Heaven."

—**Jonathon Svendsen,** Narniafans.com

"Much richer and deeper than traditional tales from fairyland . . . what Lakin does so well with her fairy tale is to provide images which remind us of what God has done for us."

—**Mark Sommer,** Examiner.com

"*The Wolf of Tebron* is a grand, sweeping tale of one man's journey to the truth and to rescue his true love. This fanciful, whimsical, wild tale can truly inspire you to perseverance—highly recommended."

—**Grace Bridges,** Splashdown Reviews

"It's a thoroughly enjoyable adventure story, with exotic settings, unpredictable turns, a terrifying enemy, and unexpected humor. Lakin's work is stylistically beautiful. The exotic locales are vivid, from dark north to burning desert to misty jungle. I found myself looking forward to each leg of Joran's journey just so I could experience another part of her story world."

—**Rachel Starr Thomson,** Little Dozen Press

"This book is filled with beautiful literary allegory and symbolism. I enjoyed the fairy tale world C. S. Lakin created for her characters to navigate. I love how the story unfolded in the end and look forward to more in The Gates of Heaven series."

—**Jill Williamson,** author of *To Darkness Fled*

"Lakin has masterful control of the writing craft, developing her characters and drawing the reader to see the world through their eyes."

—**Phyllis Wheeler,** *The Christian Fantasy Review*

THE MAP ACROSS TIME

A FAIRY TALE BY
C. S. LAKIN

LIVING INK BOOKS
Writing Worth Reading

The Map Across Time
Volume 2 in The Gates of Heaven® series

Copyright © 2011 by C. S. Lakin
Published by Living Ink Books, an imprint of
AMG Publishers, Inc.
6815 Shallowford Rd.
Chattanooga, Tennessee 37421

ISBN 13: 978-0-89957-889-7
First Printing—February 2011

Cover designed by Chris Garborg at Garborg Design, Savage, Minnesota, and Megan Erin Miller.

Cover Illustration by Gary Lippincott
(http://www.garylippincott.com/).

Interior design and typesetting by Reider Publishing Services, West Hollywood, California.

Edited and proofread by Rich Cairnes, Christy Graeber, and Rick Steele.

C. S. Lakin welcomes comments, ideas, and impressions at her Websites: **www.cslakin.com** and **www.gatesofheavenseries.com**.

Look for *The Land of Darkness*—the next book in **The Gates of Heaven** series, releasing spring 2011

Printed in Canada
16 15 14 13 12 11 –T– 7 6 5 4 3 2 1

With utmost gratitude to the true Keeper of the Promise, who keeps safe in heaven "an inheritance that is imperishable, undefiled, and unfading." (1 Peter 1:4, ESV)

• PART ONE •

NE̦ 'BUAH

(PROPHE̦CY)

ONE

"HURRY, CHILDREN."

Reya squeezed the twins' hands tighter and pulled them across the great hall. She couldn't blame them for their hesitancy. Dread sat heavy on her heart, since she knew what she would find behind the closed doors. She imagined how the Queen's children would react when they saw their mother in such a state.

Their footsteps echoed off the cavernous stone walls as they walked in solemn procession. There would be no more banquets here for a long while, Reya thought with bitterness. Adin snuffled as he trailed behind her, making Reya's heart clench in her chest. She glanced left. Aletha wore a stoic face; only her red, puffy eyes gave away her ruse. Reya gave them both a reassuring smile, although an empty gesture.

As they climbed the massive stone staircase, Aletha reached into her tunic pocket and handed her brother a rag. "Here, Adin. Wipe your nose."

He took the cloth, catching her eye for a moment, then stared back at his feet, careful not to trip on the irregular steps.

Reya instinctively adjusted her pace to Adin's faltering one, listening to the uneven rhythm of his soft shoes as they marked a beat characteristically his own. She knew what effort it had taken the young prince to give up his cane and stand erect. Each time he fell, stabs of pain coursed through her own gut. Yet Adin was, if anything, a determined ten-year-old boy, and—heaven bless him—no one could stop him once he set his mind to something.

Aletha. So like her brother in so many ways. They both had their mother's wavy copper hair and green eyes but had inherited the King's olive complexion and stubbornness to boot. Yet it was nature's cruel joke that Aletha embodied perfection in every way—an angelic face, strong stature, and graceful posture—all gifts denied Adin. Not that the young prince ever resented Aletha or wished his miseries on his sister, for he doted on her, even more so in the recent months of the Queen's illness and subsequent seclusion. No, Adin carried the full weight of the Queen's infirmities on his own delicate shoulders, adding to the already unbearable strain of his defects.

They crested the stairs, then walked across a balustrade that spanned the banquet room. Sunlight spilled through the long row of tinted windows, casting splashes of color over the floor. Aletha's skirts swished along the planking. Smells of meat pies cooking in the kitchen wafted in the air, mingling with the sooty, stale aroma of the smoldering fireplace below. Reya ignored the grumblings in her empty stomach.

In the warmth of the afternoon sun, Reya realized she had overdressed. Of course, coming to court always required layering the proper tunics and cloaks, even if she was practically family. And although this effort was more for the benefit of observers than for royalty, she had no desire to provoke the King.

Below her, Reya caught glimpses of the servants as they went about their tasks, their occasional whisper drifting up to her ears. Scissors snipped, cutting flowers from early blooms overflowed from golden vases. Diligent hands rubbed silver urns with soft cloths. Reya recognized the palpable tension and worry as servants dusted and mopped distractedly. Eyes filled with sadness dared cast a fleeting look up at the twins as they approached the latched door.

Reya turned and knelt before the children, taking a deep breath and fumbling with their clothing. Usually the twins wore loose, simple garments designed for play. But today she had helped them dress, picking out what she deemed suitable—nothing austere and depressing, but elegant and cheerful—hoping to give the Queen any reason to smile.

She chided herself for stalling and steeled her emotions. Aletha, mirroring Reya, lifted her chin in an attempt at bravery, clearly more for Adin's benefit than her own. Reya stroked their heads with weathered fingers, luxuriating in the softness of their hair. The huge oak door opened behind her, and a servant dressed in the court blues and browns ushered them in, then retreated silently into a corner.

A warm wave of humidity and pungent odor drenched them; the twins made a sour face, but Reya was all too familiar with the scent of impending death. Sunlight filtering through the ceiling panes illuminated the wisps of candle smoke as they swirled like hovering ghosts, waiting. Reya shuddered.

The pallor of death stretched like a gauze over the Queen's features. Reya sent the twins a reproving look, and they closed their gaping mouths and retreated cautiously behind her skirts. She climbed the stair to the massive bed and ushered the children to her side, where they gazed down at the face of their mother.

With her eyes closed, the Queen looked small and lost under mountains of blankets. Adin's hand touched his mother's clammy face carefully, as if she were as brittle as glass. The Queen's bronze hair spilled across the pillow, framing her face, lit up by the dozens of tapers glowing on the sideboard. Aletha stood beside Adin, clenching her brother's hand, unusually quiet.

The Queen forced her lids open and looked at her children, her expression that of one whose heart has relinquished its futile grasp on hope. Aletha and Adin reflected back that same look. Reya sensed her own grip slipping as well, but while the Queen still had breath in her Reya would not succumb to despair.

Why have I not been able to produce a cure? In all her many seasons she had treated every known illness and handily counter-acted poisons from noxious plants mistakenly ingested or, on rare occasion, purposely administered. There was no plant she could fail to identify; cite uses for its seed, leaf, and root; and use to prepare at least half a dozen infusions to treat every known ailment in this kingdom.

But this! For months this illness had baffled her. The symptoms of the Queen's ailment were like fenweed poisoning, but she had the fever and chills caused by harrowbane. Nothing Reya tried had elicited a positive reaction. She could almost sense a magical binding but could not suss it out. There were none of the obvious markers, and yet when she laid her palm on the Queen's neck she met with an odd sensation, a resonance both strange and chillingly familiar. If magic was the culprit, then it was masterfully masked. Reya had not wanted to admit the possibility, but seeing the Queen now in her final hours—the horrible reality of something evil at work, something beyond her wisdom to cure or even name—and it sent a shiver up her spine.

Reaching into the pouch slung across her chest, Reya extracted a small lidded jar. She gently placed her hand under the Queen's head.

The Queen stiffly turned her face toward Reya, her eyes straining to focus. "Reya." Her gaze alighted on the twins, then back on her gray-haired nursemaid, her most trusted friend. "You brought . . . the children." Her words came on papery breath, fragile and faint.

"Majesty, I am going to help you sit up. I have something for you to drink."

The frail queen struggled to comply, then shook her head in a slow motion of dismissal. "No more, please. Too many . . . tired."

As the twins nervously shifted beside Reya, she ignored the Queen's protests. How she longed to spare them this pain, but she was at her wick's end—just like the candles pooling in their trays before her. She had little faith this tonic would prevent the inevitable. She needed more time!

Carefully, she helped the Queen sip the bitter tea and watched as she made a half-hearted attempt to smile. "You don't ever . . . stop brewing these . . . *sha'arurah* . . ."

Reya took the jar and set it down on the step. Of course it tasted horrible, but there was nothing to be done for that.

She found it odd the Queen had taken to using the ancient speech more and more as she grew weaker. The old tongue was nearly extinct; few words had survived through the centuries to become integrated in daily conversation. Reya knew many more than most, handed down to her through family lore, and gleaned from reading old decaying texts that advised how to gather and prepare herbs. Even then, the words had been translated and reshaped from their original form. Apparently, the Queen's illness was unleashing her mind, causing her to dredge up half-buried words and images.

"Here, children, come close to your mother so she can see you." Reya stepped away from the bed and watched as Aletha helped Adin maneuver from the stair to the mattress. Once she got him settled, she sidled up next to him, where they drew close to hear their mother's fluttering words.

Reya fretted in the dim light as she waited in an overstuffed, ornately upholstered chair. Huge velvet drapes were drawn across the large windows that looked out on the orchard, barricading the room from the sunlight that recklessly shined everywhere else in Sherbourne. She searched her mind for the ancient word, one she had not used in a very long time. What was it? *Cha'mas*. A cruelty, an injustice with the overlay of violence. Like most of the many-layered words of the ancient tongue, no modern word captured the gist of *cha'mas*. But at this moment in time, in this room, no other word would suffice.

As the Queen spoke haltingly, Reya could make out snatches of sentences as they hung in the still, heavy air. She watched the twins cry as the Queen weakly gathered their hands in hers. From time to time Aletha wiped her face, and Adin's too—Adin so intent on his mother that he took no notice. Reya sighed; she found it hard to tell where one child ended and the other began.

The Queen recounted the story of their birth, a story told countless times until it had almost become a tale from a picture book. How Aletha had been born feetfirst, as if ready to stand and take on the world.

Reya remembered that night, and turned up the palms of her hands as if she could still see the perfect little body cradled there. The smell of birth, that sweet, sickly smell of fluids and sweat. Her own legs shaking with exhaustion from hours of worry over a difficult breech delivery. Watching Aletha as she emerged out of a warm sea, first toes, then belly, then head, the cord trailing alongside her wet face, up along her upraised arms, and then—stopped. Reya had tugged gently, mystified by the sudden halt of birth, wondering what the cord might have caught on or what *yo'shana* was at work. But as Reya pondered the mystery, the Queen's sharp and sudden cry startled her.

Once more, contractions racked the Queen and she howled. Reya noticed Aletha's hands grasping tightly to something. With a ferocious push, the Queen expelled a second child—an unexpected son—who gripped his sister's hands in his tiny ones. Reya quickly gathered up the twins and gently disengaged their fingers, but not without much effort. Who knew how long they had been that way, floating peacefully together, undisturbed until the violence of birth meant to rip them apart?

Adin, clearly, had been cramped in the womb, for whereas Aletha had emerged robust and energetic, kicking and sprawling in Reya's arms, Adin was small and fragile, hunched over, breathing weakly, his skin a pale gray. Upon further exploration, Reya's heart sank. Adin's right foot and leg were twisted a quarter-turn, and his face brought tears to Reya's eyes. She did not allow herself to think of the King's predictable disappointment, only the realization of what a hard road lay ahead for this unfortunate babe.

And now that hard road was going to be even harder, Reya thought, watching Adin's heart break as he drank in every word his mother spoke. With the Queen gone, Adin would have no one but Aletha to insulate him from the cruelty of the King. A king who had every reason to be proud of this sweet, kindhearted boy, but who made no attempt at hiding his disgust—a disgust that had grown into contempt after the Queen had given birth to a perfectly formed stillborn son two summers ago.

Reya sighed, despair entering her like a flood of water, lifting and carrying her to an unknown shore. She raised herself, ignoring an old pain in her hip that shot down her leg as she approached the bed. The Queen looked over and pointed to a small pouch on the side table. Reya brought it to her.

"Here," the Queen whispered to the children, her breath nearly gone, "wear it and remember . . ." With shaking hands she slowly withdrew two silver lockets on chains: simple, plain, with a tiny latch on the face of each circle. The twins turned them in their hands, puzzled. Aletha popped open the locket door and found inside a single strand of copper hair. Adin traced his finger over the tiny engraved marks on the back. Reya leaned over Adin's shoulder and, on closer

scrutiny could see the scribbles and curves of the ancient language—
the *law'az*—but no one, not even she, knew how to read it.

The Queen fell back on her pillow; the exertion of talking with
her children had emptied her. Reya gathered the twins to her as
she so often had. Adin reluctantly released his grip on the Queen's
gown and Reya was stung anew by the poignancy of the repeated
gesture. Adin again grasping, trying to hang on to a life being
wrenched away from him.

Reya leaned over and gave the Queen a gentle kiss on her
clammy forehead. As she turned and took the children in hand,
the Queen tugged on Reya's sleeve. Her words, like the rustle of
a leaf, lingered in the stillness of the room. Reya was not sure she
heard them correctly until the Queen repeated herself with an
unexpectedly steady voice and an almost peaceful look spreading
over her face.

"*Ahabah 'az ma'veth.*"

The words stabbed Reya's heart, words that had not been
uttered for centuries. Words that came welling up through her
memory like a spring pushing its way through softened soil.

Ahabah 'az ma'veth.

Love is as strong as death.

TWO

IN THE darkened dining hall, the King slumped in his chair, unnoticed by the servant tiptoeing across the polished floor. Only when he coughed did his startled attendant spin around, then fumble to catch the slipping tray, muttering under his breath. The King's head lifted, his eyes squinting in scrutiny at the cowering man who kept his head low and his gaze just far enough ahead to see the table. Vacantly, he watched the servant place the covered dishes, steaming in their silver containers, on the inlaid wooden table in front of him. Slowly, and with meticulous attention, the flustered man lined up silver utensils with precision and poured wine from the decanter into the chalice. When the servant leaned over to light the tapers, the King spoke, his voice puncturing his own oppressive mood of despair.

"No candles."

The servant set down the flint box and waited.

The King waved his hand across the food before him. "Why do you keep bringing me food?" He sighed in exasperation, then raised his voice in anger. "No more food. No more candles. Go!"

The young man scurried toward the door, bowing profusely, and then turned and fumbled with the door latch. Once the door was secure, the King gritted his teeth. A low growl rumbled from his throat, and in a rage he let his arm fly across the table, sending dishes crashing to the floor. He grew still, listening to the spinning of silver on stone as plates wobbled to a stop. He clenched his fists.

Never before in his life had he felt such fury. Such complete powerlessness. He was a king used to getting what he wanted, when he wanted it. Did he not have a palace filled with everything his heart desired? Did he not have a legion of men at the ready, to fight and even die for him if need be? Did he not rule a kingdom where his every word was law and his every whim fulfilled? Then why, for heaven's sake, with all his power and influence, could he not save his wife?

The King jumped out of his chair. He threw off his robe and mopped his forehead with a dinner napkin, then began pacing the floor like a caged beast. He should be at the Queen's side, but he did not want to endure one more moment of that agony. What more could he do? The question ate at his heart.

For months he had sent riders out to the far reaches of the land, summoning healers to his court—worthless, useless idiots who wasted his time and money on impotent remedies. He should have thrown the lot of them into the dungeon to rot! He watched miserably as day after day the Queen wasted away before his eyes, his beautiful queen suffering in silence, the carefully masked look of pain and fear only evident to him. How he suffered with her!

Lately he had been thinking back to earlier days, to when he first married her. A cloud draped over his mind; he picked at images that failed to inspire any feeling. He knew a time existed, long ago, when he seemed happy. When he was content, not driven by this insatiable need for something else, something more. Was there a time, even briefly, when he had sat with her, looking out at the gardens, holding her hand and happy in that simple pleasure? If that moment had ever existed, it was lost to him now. Contentment eluded him, teased and taunted him, and now jeered fearlessly in his face.

He threw down the napkin and stormed out the door. Servants backed quickly out of his way, dropping to their knees as he strode across room after room until he reached the library doors. Flinging them open he stood like a drowning man gasping for air, on the threshold of the courtyard. A slight breeze cooled his neck and forehead. He composed himself, straightened his clothing, and ran a sweaty hand through his matted hair. He knew he smelled rank. He had lost count of the days since he'd taken a proper bath.

Across the yard, the spring in the fountain bubbled softly. The orchard bloomed profusely with snowy bunches of flowers, giving off a thick perfume. There was something about the perfect beauty of the courtyard—the planters overflowing with hyacinth and narcissus; the sprawling, manicured lawn of deep green that flowed down the hill like a carpet; the fruit trees in their neat little rows, trimmed and bursting with life—that broke him utterly. The King fell to his knees and wept.

He had no idea how long he remained hunched over, sobbing. Numbly, he stumbled over to the fountain, his legs weak and unresponsive. He sat on the smooth rock ledge encircling the pool and stared at the water as it spilled from the crevice in the black obsidian rock. Long ago, centuries ago, this spring had flowed freely down the knoll, unbound by castle walls. He knew the city of Sherbourne had started here—built around this spring of life-giving water. And for strategic reasons, the first rulers had built the palace on the same knoll, for it was the highest point in the kingdom, which spread as far as the eye could see. The location provided an unmatched vantage point.

He lifted his eyes and looked out upon his kingdom. The high walls of the courtyard had once held a row of thick wooden doors, arching to peaks ten feet tall. Now, with the old wood long rotted away, gaping vistas opened to the world outside. From where he sat he could see the sprawl of the city below. Cottages and shops lay choked together, randomly divided by winding cobbled streets. Smoke from hundreds of chimneys lingered over rooftops. Horses and carriages crossed the bridge over the great river Heresh at the edge of the city. People as small as crickets bustled about, busy with their daily tasks. And ringing the entire city for many miles were the remains of the great wall.

Parts of it were still intact, but in most places rubble littered the boundary of the city; huge boulders lay in piles where the wall had been attacked and breached in the battle centuries ago. The stones rose up thirty feet, with a parapet on the inside, designed for soldiers to be able to stand without being hit by arrows. The King imagined a night of battle—the smoke and yelling, the towers with their signaling fires, skirmishes against the ramparts, men attacking the walls with weapons in hand.

But now, straining his ears, all the King could hear was the clang of a bell, faint and soft. He was too far away to hear voices, too removed to hear conversation. This was his kingdom, yet he rarely entered into that throng of humanity. For most of the year, the only reminder the peasants had of royalty was the looming presence of the palace atop the knoll. A melancholy smile crept across the King's face as he recalled the rare occasions he and his queen had attended an important function, making a necessary but brief appearance, reminding his subjects of his authoritative presence. He tried to imagine himself in the royal procession with all its fanfare—palace guards dressed in livery, riding horses in neat formation; trumpeters marching behind, sounding clear brass tones that brought excited children pushing through the crowds to listen; he and the Queen atop the magnificent carriage, pulled by a team of six white horses decked in silver trappings, waving to the bystanders as they passed. A trembling sigh escaped his throat at the thought of his beautiful queen, who would never sit beside him like that again.

So intent was his gaze over the city, he did not hear or see the councillors approach until they stood beside him.

"Sire." The tall, lean man, robed in dark brown, spoke in a deep, flat voice. He waited, hands clasped in front of him, his head cocked slightly. A shock of straight black hair fell over one gray eye; the rest of his head lay buried under the hood. His face, pale and wrinkled, held eyes like glass beads set above the hook of his nose. Two others in similar garb flanked him, their faces hooded in shadow.

The King stood and looked into Rasha's face. It held the same expression it always had, one the King could never read. Even in rare moments when the councillor's words were encouraging, the King sensed cynicism and condescension. Maybe his imagination misled him, for the bony old man never gave anything away in his features, except for his eyes, which seemed to laugh at the King.

The King sighed. "What is it now, Rasha?"

He would wave the men away if he could, but he knew better. Rasha, a most skilled advisor, had served the former king, his father. He was the head of the Council, an institution as old and established as the monarchy itself. One could not exist without the other. The Council took care of all the tedious details of running a kingdom; the King could not be bothered with the grumblings, disputes, and demands of the commoners. Especially not now.

"Certain pressing matters need to be brought to the King's attention."

The King mustered an air of authority, trying to focus. But, as Rasha spoke, he found it difficult to listen; his eyes kept veering to the second floor window, where drapes blocked the view of the Queen.

Rasha tilted his head and followed the King's gaze. "The children are with their mother."

The King muffled a sound in his throat. The councillors stood like silent sentinels, their eyes fixed on their sovereign.

"Sire, we apologize for the intrusion." Rasha paused until the King wrested his eyes from the window. "Your subjects grow tired of delays in funding and there have been some riots in the streets . . ."

The King spun around, wiping his face. "Why do you trouble me with these senseless problems? If the sewers need fixing, then fix them! If the jail is full, then build another!"

"Sire, you know we only have so much jurisdiction. If you would like to see to it that the Council tends to these particular matters—"

"Yes. Take care of these matters." He barely reined in his fury. He worked at calming down, breathing deeply. "Please." After a moment of silence, the King adjusted his attire and walked toward the palace doors as the councillors stood and watched, unmoving.

Rasha strolled along the courtyard wall, away from the palace, his two associates on either side. He kept his head low and glanced around, his eyes drawing the others to come closer. He stopped at the far end of the courtyard, at the last row of apple trees, and spoke in a raspy whisper.

"So, things are better than I had predicted."

The tall, wiry figure on his right nodded. "The city is in disarray, m'lord."

A smile grew on Rasha's face. "The King is distracted." He snorted in disgust. "The Queen will be dead by morning." He walked a few steps over to one of the archways and leaned against the wall. His eyes surveyed the city.

The smaller man spoke, still hidden under his hood. "You were wise to slow the *ro'osh*. Dragging out the illness has proved beneficial. Look how the King has steadily fallen apart."

Rasha spat and cocked his head. His hair fell once more into his eyes. "The King is a fool. Humans are such weaklings. They are obsessed with love; it blinds them to everything else. He does not know what he is fighting. There is no *ga'haw*, no cure, for this *keh'ber*. No potion in this world has the power to undo it."

The others joined him at the archway. Rasha pointed to the city spread out below him. "See. The King is tumbling toward ruin. His queen will die and he will be consumed by it. Little by little, his precious city will suffer from neglect. Heavy taxes will be levied; revolts will break out. Famine, disease, and unrest will plague Sherbourne. This 'Crown of the East' will tarnish and decay. And, true to prophecy, will one day only exist in memory. If it exists at all. The *ne'buah* cannot fail."

The taller associate leaned in to his commander. "M'lord, what about the prince?"

Rasha laughed deeply. "That *na'baal*? In time the King will grow to believe his son plots against his life."

"But the prince is but a child."

"We will bide our time. You see how the King detests his son. And that . . . unfortunate incident with the stillborn child . . ."

The small man chuckled. "A work of genius, m'lord. There is no greater bitterness than losing what could have been."

"Yes," Rasha muttered. "Yes."

He turned, squeezing his eyes shut in thought, and clasped his hands together. "And in time, slowly, the King will suspect his son, and the son's anger and humiliation will fester. It is . . . inevitable."

"Then you need not do more than put the knife in his hand."

Rasha met the eyes of his associates. At his nod, the two joined him as he walked back to the palace with a confident, easy stride.

With their backs turned, they had not noticed the cloaked man standing outside the courtyard wall, his face pressed against the warmth of stone. They did not know he had been there, just steps away, hiding behind a shrub, as they held their private discussion. They did not hear him, because he had been careful not to utter a sound or even think a thought that might attract their regard.

He had been very careful not to be detected, for he knew his detection would mean the end of his kingdom.

THREE

RAIN FELL lightly on the twins as they sat by the fountain. Clouds swollen with water hung over their heads, matching the gloom in their hearts. Aletha was too shocked to cry. She and Adin had been roused from their beds at dawn, dressed hurriedly, and rushed to the library. They had stood by the blazing fire, staring at the walls of books for an interminable time, until the head servant came and broke the news. The Queen had passed on in the night. Adin had squeezed Aletha's hand so tightly he drew blood with his fingernails. Even though this moment had been inevitable, hearing the words linger on the air gave it an unexpectedly harsh edge of reality.

Leaving with a brief, sincere apology, the servant had been kind enough to close the library doors and give them some privacy in their grief. But Adin had fled the room as fast as his twisted legs could carry him, as if he could leave the horror behind him there in the library and find a place where the world was safe and sensible again.

Aletha had rushed after him, afraid he would fall in his recklessness, but he made it to the fountain ledge, where he threw himself down in a heap. Aletha stroked his head while he heaved and wailed, but she felt oddly unable to tap into her own sadness. She knew it would come to haunt her in late night hours, but now all that mattered was Adin.

As he buried his head in his hands, Aletha fell into her familiar role as comforter. All her life she had been watching over Adin, for as long as she could remember. A sickly, weak boy, Adin could not keep up with Aletha's pace, running through the orchard and climbing trees, hiking for long hours under a hot sun, or building miniature castles out of blocks of snow. As much as Aletha had wanted to spend her childhood in play with other children, she felt forced to grow up quickly and assume a mantle of responsibility for her brother. He did not make friends easily. Children were cruel, even when they were warned pointedly not to tease the prince. Children naturally single out and snicker at those who are different and don't fit in.

From an early age Adin knew he was laughed at, that he would always be taunted, and so he carried his humiliation and shame like a boulder in his gut. His hunched back was the brunt of jokes; his oddly shaped face, with its twisted mouth drawn up on one side, caused other children to make faces back at him, pulling at their cheeks and mouths with their fingers and sticking out their tongues. Their cruelty hurt Aletha as much as it did Adin.

On more than one occasion the young princess had thrown her royal manners aside and smacked a tormenter in the nose with her fist. She was not above pulling hair and kicking shins either, behaviors she was subsequently punished for, but she took her stripes with honor. Unlike Adin, she made friends easily, seeking out the children of the servants who lived in the residences, since her nearest relations lived in the wealthier part of town that rose up the eastern ridge. Part of Aletha's secret mission was finding appropriate friends for Adin. Fortunately, she had stumbled across Merin, the head cook's son, a year younger than she and Adin.

Merin was a chubby, jovial boy who was shy around adults but entirely mischievous out of their sight. The best thing about Merin was his kind and warm nature. Never once did he look at Adin with disdain, or mention anything about her brother's deformities—if he even noticed them. Merin was also the target of heartless remarks, from children who called him names such as "Porkpie" and "Melonball."

In this way, Adin and Merin became partners in humiliation. Relieved, Aletha could deposit Adin at the kitchen door, knowing he and Merin would fast be up to some minor infraction of the rules, usually in the form of lifting meat pies off the cooling racks when no one was around. She would then go for long hikes alone in the hills, practice shooting her bow and hunting quail, and have tea parties with her girlfriends and their dolls in one of the many unused chambers of the palace.

As they sat in the dripping rain, Aletha drew deep into her thoughts. The steady patter of the drops hitting the surface of the pond droned a mesmerizing rhythm. Two ravens swooped down next to her to drink—big black irritating birds. She waved them away with her hands, sending them squawking into the trees. Through the windows of the palace she could make out movement. Now the preparations would begin.

Would there be an elaborate funeral, attended by rich merchants and landowners, by nobility from far away? Would Aletha be called on to appear in Sherbourne and sit with her visiting cousins and aunts as they all cried and mourned her mother? Would this end up like any other affair of state, an event where Aletha had to be composed and regal, pretending she was oh, so grown-up? And what about Adin? Would the King shunt him off into some hidden room where he would not be noticed?

Aletha gritted her teeth at the all-too-familiar image. In moments like these she wished with all her heart she was just an ordinary child, living down in the city, away from all the privileges and expectations that came with nobility. Away from all the watching eyes and wagging tongues. She could almost hear the whispering going on in the palace—voicing the pity that people felt for her and Adin. And she knew rumors had spread throughout the city.

Everyone had heard how the healers had failed to save the Queen from a mysterious and strange illness. Not even Reya had been able to cure her, and that disturbed Aletha the most. Reya had always had just the right medicines for Adin, drawing heat from his lungs and chills from his bones. From her earliest memories, Aletha recalled Reya always at the ready with her remedies, making sure she and Adin grew up as strong and healthy as they could. Reya had never failed until now, and this realization shattered Aletha's world.

Aletha adjusted Adin's cloak so the hood covered his hair. He was already drenched through, and she worried for him. Out of the corner of her eye she saw someone walking toward her from the library doors. She instinctively wrapped her arm around Adin and raised her head to meet the councillor's eyes.

Rasha. How she despised this man! He was always so carefully polite to her, so complimentary. But she saw something in his face she could not make out. If she stared long and hard she noticed a pale wash come across his features, almost erasing his nose and mouth and turning his eyes black and empty. It gave her the shivers. She watched how he lingered around the palace, melting into corners, his stiff posture so inflexible, his attention so penetrating. She was sure he was sneaking around, up to no good. She did not like the way he spoke to her father in that measured voice, and she did not like the way he had always spoken to her mother, with sappy words as if he were talking to a three-year-old. Aletha might be only ten years old, but she was no dummy. She could tell when someone was phony, and when he wanted things he did not voice.

"What do you want?" Aletha did not bother to mask her irritation.

A polite smile rose to his lips as his eyes bore down on her. Aletha looked away. "I am worried about Your Majesties. Perhaps you would like to come back inside and get warm."

She scoffed at his pretense of concern and forced herself to meet his eyes. "When can we see Mother?"

Rasha pursed his lips. "I am sorry, Princess. That will not be possible."

Aletha jumped to her feet, but Adin kept his head buried in his cloak. She heard Adin renew his sobbing. "I demand we be taken to her at once." She waited for a response that was not forthcoming. "Where is my father?"

"He is . . . indisposed at the moment."

"I want to see the King."

The councillor's eyes remained unchanged. Aletha pinched her lips together. *Nothing ever ruffles him.*

After a long moment of silence he gave a slow nod. "I will see what I can arrange." He moved to turn away, and then, cocking his head, faced Aletha once more. "I suggest, Princess, that you face the facts." His voice grew thick and low. "The Queen is dead. Life will go on. The sooner you accept this truth, the easier things will be for you."

Aletha wanted to spit in his face. She glanced over at Adin, who stared at Rasha with pained eyes. She controlled her voice, collected her pride. "Leave us. And go find my father and tell him we want to see him. We want to see our mother."

Aletha's throat clenched tight and tears pooled in her eyes. It took all her will to stand there facing him without flinching.

Without a reply, Rasha quickly turned and marched toward the palace. Aletha collapsed on the ledge next to Adin, her hands trembling as if she had been in a fistfight.

Adin's chilled hand grabbed her own. She felt him shiver from the cold. She looked at him as he tried to bring a crooked smile to his face. A warm glow replaced the pain in her gut. At least she had her brother. Her sweet, kind brother who loved her with all his heart. Aletha sighed. Now that their mother was dead, Aletha would have to be doubly watchful over Adin. The King was rarely around; he had never given much time to either of them, being so busy with his duties as king. She doubted whether that would change. But she was certain their mother's death would change Adin.

Their mother had doted on him. She had been the encouraging word in his ear. Her love for Adin had been poured out on him and coated him each day, protecting him from the harsh world. Even on her busiest days she had always taken time to listen to him, reassure him, make him feel special and loved. Single-handedly she had kept Adin safe—safe from the outside world, but, more importantly, safe from his inner world of pain. And now the task fell to Aletha—and she worried deep in her heart that she might not be up to it.

As she collected her thoughts and stood, trying to roust Adin from his stupor, Aletha noticed movement at the end of the orchard. She strained to see past the rows of trees to the far wall, where someone appeared to be waving at her. She watched and he waved again, then slipped from view. Her curiosity was piqued.

"Come, Adin. There is someone who wants to see us."

Adin said nothing, but took Aletha's hand and trudged at her side. Rainwater made the grass slick and Aletha stepped carefully. They traversed the length of the courtyard, making such slow progress that Aletha wondered if the strange visitor would still be waiting for them. When they reached the last row of trees, Aletha leaned her head around the wall that widened to the left and discovered a man in a dark brown cloak hunched over on a bench, his knees pulled up to his chest. His hood partially hid dark rust-colored hair and a thick beard that covered his chin. Aletha noted that he was a young man, with friendly and inviting eyes. He patted the bench and Aletha approached with Adin in tow.

Try as hard as she could, Aletha did not recognize him, but there was something strongly familiar about him. Especially his eyes. She could not tear her gaze away, and the man seemed mesmerized by her eyes as well. It was more than a little unsettling. Before Aletha could ask the obvious questions, the man spoke. The compassion in his voice evoked a strange sensation in Aletha.

"Princess, I am a friend of your mother's. I cannot speak for long." His eyes shifted to Adin's; Aletha noticed her brother start to focus and become alert. Adin looked the man over and listened.

"Adin, this is a desperate time for you. All seems hopeless." Aletha could swear she saw the man catch his breath and choke up. She watched as he locked eyes with Adin, and, suddenly, time stopped. She no longer felt the rain dripping on her head or the wind brushing her face. Adin's shivering ceased as he grew unusually attentive. For the first time that day, her brother spoke.

"You have something to tell us." It was a statement, not a question.

The man nodded and looked around cautiously. He leaned closer to the twins, and Aletha could smell traces of smoke on his clothing and feel his warm breath on her skin. His cloak was torn and dirty, and there were cuts on his hands and face. Normally Aletha would never allow such a stranger to get this close to her; usually her hackles would rise, ready to defend her brother against any hint of a threat. But for some reason she trusted this strange man with the kind eyes. There was no malice about him, no deception. He had the truest face she had ever seen. And she wanted to hear what he had to say.

"Can you keep a secret?" he whispered.

The twins nodded in unison. The man pulled back and looked at them intently—first at one, then the other. "You must not tell anyone what I tell you now. Not a soul, not ever. Not even Reya."

Now Aletha held her breath in anticipation. Adin's eyes widened at the mention of Reya's name. "Who are you?" Adin pleaded.

"A friend. One of the few you can trust. I know you may not believe what I have to tell you, but even if you do not, keep these words locked in your heart and let them give you hope."

The man stood and walked to the corner of the wall, limping slightly, as if injured. He peeked around the wall, then returned to the bench. Without hesitation, he took the twins' hands in his own and squeezed them gently. His hands were calloused but gentle. Aletha was surprised at how safe she felt with him.

Adin could not contain himself. "What is it? What have you come to tell us?"

The man looked at Adin and smiled, the warmth melting Aletha's aching heart. "Your mother lives!"

Aletha startled and drew back. "No, sir, you are mistaken. She died last night."

"And you have seen this?" The man waited as Aletha shook her head. "And you will not be able to. By the time you make your way into the Queen's chamber, she will be gone. They will say . . . she has died. But, by heaven's grace, she lives!"

"Where did she go?" Adin asked. Aletha heard the tinge of hope in his voice.

"Somewhere safe. Where no one can harm her." At those words, Adin's countenance dropped.

"But she will return."

"When?" Adin demanded.

The man put his hand on Adin's shoulder. "Adin, you must be brave. It will be many years before the Queen returns, but you must not lose hope. Keep this *mik'vah* hidden in your heart and let it give you strength. And do not speak a word of this!"

The man shifted his attention to Aletha. "Take care of Adin. *Shaw'kad*—be watchful! Not everyone in the palace is your friend."

These words sent a shudder through Aletha's body, and she jumped at a noise in the branches near her. Two huge ravens alighted on the tree at the end of the row, and as soon as the man saw them, he rose quickly from the bench. He took Aletha's hand once more, this time squeezing it in urgency. His hot breath whispered in her ear.

"There is a proverb: *yesh 'achar'ith tiq'vah k'rath.* 'Surely there is a future, and your hope will not be cut off.' I must go. Never forget!"

Aletha and Adin watched as the man gathered his cloak around him and hurried out of the courtyard through one of the archways. They stared at the wall in silence for a long time, then Aletha turned to Adin and spoke softly, one eye on the ravens, which had grown strangely quiet.

"We will never speak of this."

Adin nodded in agreement, his eyes full of wonder and possibilities. Aletha hugged him tightly, then grasped his hand and started the long, deliberate walk back to the palace.

FOUR

ADIN SCRUTINIZED himself in the mirror that hung in the great hall. Mirrors had never been kind to him, and when he was a child, he had fantasized grabbing one of his father's fancy goblets and using it to smash every mirror in the palace. As the years dragged along, he learned to distance himself from the reflection staring back at him. He told himself what he saw was just an image, a disguise, masking the real person inside. He was in there, hiding, but no one—apart from maybe Aletha and Reya—could see him.

The face staring back at him was no longer a boy's. Now, at eighteen, his features had sharpened, hair grew on his face, and his skin was scratchy. Mercifully, the deformity on his face—the way his cheek pulled up the right side of his mouth—had softened over the years. As his face grew, his cheeks had lengthened, and although he felt far from handsome, at least he didn't look like a freak. Deep green eyes penetrated back at him, but they were indecipherable. What was this young man thinking?

Adin wanted to laugh, for the image was laughable. Here he was, all dressed in royal colors, fine attire made by the court seamstresses. From the cap on his head to the intricately detailed leather boots, his appearance announced wealth and privilege. His full head of copper hair had recently been trimmed and styled in order to be presentable to his father. If he had been any other

King's heir, he would be paraded through the streets of the city and shown off proudly as the future king. But not this misshapen disgrace of a son!

Adin felt bile rise in his throat. It was no secret what his father thought of him; the King took a special pleasure, it seemed, in humiliating Adin whenever the opportunity presented itself. And for that reason, Adin had little reason to find himself in the King's presence; he hadn't seen the King in months. Ever since he could remember, he would cringe when he had to face his father. Today was no different.

Adin grunted and turned from the mirror to survey the opulence around him. Dozens of animal heads hung from wooden posts, their glassy, vacant eyes staring at him. Strange beasts from even stranger lands, bounty from expeditions made across the known world. Treasures of gold and silver, studded with gems, rested on shelves and in glass display cases trimmed in filigreed silver. Room after room was cluttered with ancient and rare finds, procured at great cost, from archaeological digs.

Cost, apparently, was no concern of the King. From what rumblings Adin had heard, tucked away in his safe and protected palace, his father was milking his subjects with oppressive taxes—taxes on imported goods, taxes on food and ale. Each time his father heard news of another valuable oddity, he had to have it. If no gold remained in the coffers, then the people of Sherbourne would have to come up with the means. Adin walked over to a cabinet that held small ceramic figurines of animals, glazed in pastel colors. He shook his head in astonishment. What was the point of all this? To show off to visitors? His subjects needed bread and medicines, and all the King cared about was amassing wealth.

Adin recalled how, after his mother died, the King went into seclusion for months. And then suddenly he became consumed with his "collection." Collecting every valuable, rare thing known in the world. The more dangerous and difficult the venture, the greater the thrill. The King had all but forgotten his responsibilities, passing them on to others, and had just as easily all but forgotten he had children. So Adin was curious why the King demanded his attendance today. He had planned to dress in his usual "commoner" clothing—for he resisted the trappings of the court, not wishing to resemble his father. Then he thought there would be some poetic irony in playing the part of royal prince, since it was a part his father refused to acknowledge. Let the King see what ugliness his own loins had produced—paraded before him in a mockery of elegance!

Adin turned at the sound of steps hurrying his way. He smirked. His sister had found him out. Aletha came to him, breathing hard, and fingered his collar.

Adin touched her hand and frowned. "Don't you dare laugh."

Aletha pulled back and took in the sight. "Laugh? I would never laugh at you, Adin! You look splendid!"

Adin couldn't resist giving her a courteous bow, and just seeing the look on her face made him glad he had chosen to dress up. At least his sister appreciated the effort. Coming from anyone else, the comment would have sounded vacuous and insincere, but he could trust Aletha to be truthful. If something was out of place, she would not hesitate to straighten it. And if he was making a fool of himself, she would make sure he knew. He breathed a sigh of relief.

He took a long look at his sister and couldn't help notice how Aletha grew more beautiful day by day. Her face was an angel's; her hair, braided down the back of her gown, shone like spun gold. She had grown tall and elegant, no longer a child. Aletha was now a woman, and she looked so much like their mother. A small stab of pain pinched his heart. Even after these many years, he could not think of his mother without pain. He tried not to let it show, knowing Aletha would become distraught as well, yet there it was. Adin pushed the sadness away and embraced her.

"I looked for you upstairs," she told him. "I thought we were hunting rabbits today."

"The King has summoned me."

Aletha's face showed panic. "Why? What does he want?"

"How should I know? You see him more often than I. What do you think?"

If Aletha thought anything, she hid it well. One thing Adin did know—his father was not inviting him to a tea party. "I have to go," he said.

"And I'm coming."

Adin sighed as he walked toward the Council chambers. After a lifetime with his sister, he knew better than to try to dissuade her from anything. Secretly, Adin was relieved. When he had received the summons, his first thought was to find Aletha and make her come along for moral support. But he knew he needed to be brave and face his father alone. The thought of standing before the King made his knees shake, but how was he ever going to feel like a man if he couldn't act like one? Well, maybe today was not to be the day. Aletha would temper the King's mood, whatever it was. And for that he would be glad to postpone his manhood awhile.

When the twins entered the large, round room, they found the King bent over his work table, a giant heavy slab of polished red wood, with dark lines ringing in concentric circles. Adin guessed: another one of the King's unusual acquisitions—from a forest far to the west.

How could a tree grow this wide? In the forest of Sherbourne grew birch, maple, beech—all small trees with leaves that turned golden in the fall. The wood of this table made Adin want to run his hand along it, but he resisted the urge as he stood with Aletha at attention. Obviously, their father had heard them enter the room, but many minutes passed before he deigned to acknowledge them. He fussed over an unrolled parchment, weighted down at the corners by luminous stones. He raised his head and a stern expression spread across his broad face, directed at Aletha.

"Why are you here?"

"Father." She curtseyed politely and dropped her eyes. "I haven't seen you for so long. I wanted to know how you were faring."

The King harrumphed and drummed his fingers on the table. Adin noticed his father had not even glanced his way. Adin looked around the Council chamber. He thought it the most beautiful place in the palace with its high corniced domed ceiling, and the brilliant multi-tinted windows encircling the whole room. Each window pane depicted a scene from Sherbourne's history, set up high above the ring of chiseled stone chairs that protruded from the wall. On his left, the first pane showed the knoll with its bubbling spring. As Adin's eyes continued around the room, images of the early barricade wall, the building of the palace, and the line of regents—beginning with the first down to his grandfather—were portrayed in color. Adin had heard the next window was already in progress, the one with his father on the throne. He doubted very much that one day his own image would beam down from the wall.

If anyone should rule, it was Aletha. She was older, if only by moments. And she was well-loved already. Adin thought of Aletha's confidence, how she comfortably presented herself to both royalty and peasant. She made important visitors feel welcome and attended to. She inspired trust from the common people because she took the time to visit them, attend their public forums, and listen to their complaints. That was more than their father did these days. And as much as Adin truly cared for the people of Sherbourne, his deformities made him self-conscious and awkward, always doubting he would be taken seriously. No, the throne would pass to Aletha, and Adin would gladly stand by her side.

Funny, he and Aletha had never spoken about this. Maybe because it seemed their father would rule forever; it certainly looked as if he intended to. Their entire lives they had been groomed for ruling. Tutors had worked diligently to make sure they not only knew their letters, history, and numbers, but also etiquette and all the manners and protocol of the court.

Adin held no interest in weapon work or archery, but Aletha excelled in swordplay and loved using her bow and arrows. Adin knew she had first taken her training in order to defend him, but then grew to love the discipline. She had pushed him to learn as well, telling him he needed to be able to stand up against his enemies. She spent hours with him in the training yard, poking him with swords and goading him with friendly jeers. Maneuvering around with his uncooperative leg frustrated him, and he had often fallen down, eventually heading back to his room humiliated and bruised. Aletha had shown him no mercy and worked him hard, yet he knew she did it for his own good. Dear Aletha! What would he do without her?

"What are you smiling for? Wipe that stupid grin off your face."

Adin's attention snapped back to his father. The King stood and strode over to them. Adin noticed the creases on his father's face had deepened since he last saw him. His brown hair had thinned and was now streaked with gray, as was his beard. Adin straightened as best as he could, but he knew it would never be enough for his father. His back remained bent at the shoulder blades, forcing him to stoop forward. His neck strained from the effort of trying to raise his head upright. In his father's presence, he felt the full burden of his deformity, and he now regretted his attempt to dress the part of a prince. He was a mockery and an imposter. If Aletha had not been at his side, he would have fled the room.

The King circled Adin, and the prince felt like some prey being cornered, knowing death was imminent. Adin's breath caught in his throat and the room spun. His father said something, but Adin could not focus on the words that boomed in his ears. His mind wandered to a memory and unlocked it—Adin, a small boy, struggling with his cane to walk across the courtyard. His mother, radiant and smiling, arms outstretched to urge him toward her. And his father standing at her side, patient and encouraging. Adin squeezed his eyes shut. Was this a fabrication of his imagination, or was there truly a time when his father had felt something for him other than disgust? Was he just rewriting his own history to make it bearable?

Suddenly, a slap across the face jolted Adin from his reverie. So unexpected and forceful was the blow that he stumbled backward and fell to the hard marble floor. Aletha gasped and ran to him, putting her protective arm around his shoulder.

She fumed as she knelt by Adin's side. "What was that for? Adin has done nothing to deserve your wrath!" Adin could hear his sister's breath panting through her nostrils, like a horse readying itself for battle. His cheek stung, and he rubbed it with his hand. He tried to stand but Aletha held him down. Her eyes challenged the King's, meeting his harsh gaze.

"Aletha," Adin said, "please." Aletha would understand what he was trying to say. Please stop trying to be my champion, my defender. Please let me find a way to stand up against the King on my own. Please stop protecting me.

Aletha, he knew, was reacting instinctively. What she didn't know was that the time had come to let him do his own defending. He squeezed Aletha's hand and looked at her sternly. She withdrew her arm from his shoulder and pulled back, letting him gather himself together and slowly, awkwardly, rise to standing. Aletha also rose to her feet, smoothed out her gown, and retreated behind Adin, watchful as a hawk.

"Your brother is conspiring against me. He means to wrest the throne out from under me." The King spat out the words and shoved a hand in Aletha's face when she opened her mouth to speak. "And do not try to defend him. I have eyes all over this palace—nothing goes unnoticed." The King huffed and looked at Adin. "And no act of treachery will go unpunished."

Aletha clenched her mouth shut and turned to Adin. Her eyes pleaded with him. For if he would not speak in his own defense, then she certainly would.

But all Adin could do was laugh. He chuckled, shaking his head, and then the laughter brought tears running down his cheeks. The more the King fumed—his ruddy face turning a deep red—the harder Adin laughed. Finally, catching a breath, Adin spilled out his words.

"What . . . makes you think I would ever want to be king? That I would ever want your throne?" Adin waved his hand to the hallway behind him. "That I would want all this useless . . . stuff with which you clutter the palace?"

"You lie!" the King accused, pointing a stern finger in Adin's face. "I know you plot against me. And stop laughing! Do you not know I can have you exiled? Or thrown into the dungeon?"

Adin wiped his wet face with the back of his hand, still chuckling and catching his breath. "Why don't you just hack off my head and have it stuffed? Then you can mount me on the wall between the lion and the rhinoceros—just another one of your worthless conquests you can show off to your guests."

The King held a trembling hand inches from Adin's face, but Adin didn't flinch. Somehow he had broken through his fear to a place where a calmness washed over him. His hurt subsided and a feeling of pity replaced it, pity for this man who had recklessly traded love for greed. It was his father—he lucidly saw in this frozen moment of time—who was truly deformed and crippled. But the King could not see it.

Adin looked over at Aletha, who was staring at him with puzzled eyes. Then he turned and limped out the Council chamber doors, with a steady stride and head held as high as he could manage.

"Why? Why do you torment him like this?" Aletha blurted out.

The King visibly relaxed; with composure, he returned to his desk and fingered one of the stone weights resting on the map. Without looking at her he said, "My dear Aletha, why do you spend so much time with that fool?"

"How can you accuse him of treason? He has only longed for your approval his entire life. Why can't you just love him?"

The King laughed bitterly. "Love him? He is unworthy of love—he is ugly and weak. He should have never been born. And he will never be king."

"Didn't you hear him? He has no desire to be king. He is not plotting against you. All he wants is a little encouragement—not your criticism and accusations!"

"Come here, my child." The King waved her over, and Aletha reluctantly obeyed. When she came to his side, he reached to stroke her hair. Aletha stood stiffly, not meeting his eyes. "You look so much like your mother . . ." His hand moved to her face, where his fingers grazed her cheek.

He shook his head slowly in cold amusement. "Aletha, you are young and naive. You have no idea what it means to run a kingdom. Someday you will wear the crown, but before you do, you need to learn how to separate your friends from your enemies. You will learn you can trust no one—not even those closest to you."

"If that's what it means to be a ruler, then I want none of it. Find someone else to manage your empire." Aletha started to turn away, but the King firmly stopped her with his hand. Aletha felt a shiver race up her back as she looked into her father's face. His smile appeared affectionate, but what Aletha saw in his eyes frightened her. In the dark recesses she saw something shift, and his pupils grew vacant and birdlike. His complexion wavered from dark to pale and his features softened and blurred. As Aletha drew back, shaking, her father gripped her shoulder more tightly. Her words came out no louder than a whisper.

"Father, please. Let me go."

The King gripped tighter, then with his other hand drew back the hair from her face. His eyes searched beyond her, as if he were looking through her. He mumbled, more to himself than to Aletha, "So beautiful . . . perfect, just perfect."

A sickly feeling washed over Aletha as her father's hands stroked her hair, as if he were hypnotizing some quarry. His face transformed and what she saw terrified her. Without another moment's hesitation, Aletha pulled herself from her father's embrace and ran out the door, nearly colliding with Rasha, who stood just steps outside the Council chamber, leaning against the wall.

In her haste, she almost failed to notice the smug expression on the councillor's face, an expression that seemed to smack of pleasure.

FIVE

REYA SENSED the arrival of her unexpected visitor before she heard the sound of branches cracking under footfalls. She wiped her floury hands on a kitchen towel and pushed the curtain aside as Adin came through the coppice of trees, kicking up fallen leaves in his tracks. As she watched him through the window, she tried to assess his mood—and it was hard to read. Her small cottage was nestled down in a draw, beside a winding creek, so Adin had to wend around rocks and planting beds to reach the front door. She was surprised to see his formal court dress hanging in a soggy mass over his thin frame. Even though the rain held back, the fog was thick with moisture and had done a thorough job of transforming her young friend's appearance into that of a wet rat. She hurried to open the door and ushered him in, tossing him a towel for his hair, at the same time removing his cloak. "Well, here's a pretty sight."

Adin panted hard; she could tell he had run most of the way from the palace to her sequestered haven—a place in which the twins had spent a good portion of their childhood. While Adin plopped down in the comfy chair near the fire, Reya stoked the coals, adding logs to her smoldering fire and creating a new blaze of warmth that illuminated the small, open-beamed room. Adin removed his woven cap and wrung it out.

Reya ruffled his damp hair. "You have impeccable timing—pear tarts are in the oven. How do you always know?"

Adin reached down and felt for a cold nose, finally finding one. "I thought I saw Yo'fi. She always looks like part of the floor. And you're the one who said I had a special sense. I could smell your tarts all the way from the palace."

Sprawled out at Adin's feet was a dark-brown wolf, small and sleepy. Stretched across the wooden floorboards, she did look camouflaged. She gave a short sigh and raised her head, sniffed Adin, then lowered it back down and closed her eyes. Next to the fire, on the stone hearth, a pair of hedgehogs lay curled up together, their fur steaming. A mouse ran over the mantle and sniffed at a dish of flower petals, then scurried down the wall to a hole.

"You have a gift of sight, not smell, young prince. My tarts were not the reason for your visit, so don't try to fool me. I am not *bah'ar*." Reya took the towel from Adin's hand and hung it from a hook by the fire, below a nest of cooing doves. The cottage was more cluttered than usual; fall was gathering time, and Reya was always diligent to collect the herbs, bark, and roots she would need throughout the winter to have enough stock on hand for the ill and weak. Plants dried in bunches, hanging from the rafters near the fireplace. Seeds and roots covered Reya's workbench in the living room, and the three long wooden shelves mounted on the wall over the bench displayed dozens of labeled jars of herbs.

Adin reached over and gently picked up a young raccoon that pawed at his lap. "Hey fella, did I take your chair?" He called back to Reya. "And I didn't say you were stupid."

Reya smiled and went to open the oven door. Using a cloth, she removed the clay rack loaded with fragrant tarts. Outside, thunder cracked and rain pelted the roof and filled the woods with crackling sounds as drops bounced off the mat of autumn leaves. She looked at Adin, who seemed perfectly content with a musty raccoon on his lap. She smiled. How much more like a son could Adin be to her? She had raised him and Aletha from infancy, feeding them their first bottles and teaching them to walk. She had been by their side through every season, every illness, every disappointment.

The Queen may have been their mother, but she had been busy with the court and overseeing the inner workings of the palace. There had always been visitors to prepare for and entertain, engagements of State, dinner parties. She had made time for the twins, and took them on outings—to the abbey, into the countryside, and to the city to distribute clothing to those in need. But Reya knew that when something bothered them, the twins came to *her*, to this cottage, where they could forget they were royalty and behave like other children.

Adin, even more than his sister. So many days he had spent here, helping her look for plants; separating seeds from leaves; or sketching flowers at her kitchen table, rubbing the eraser intensely over his lines, perfecting his drawings, his lips pressed together in concentration. Everything he did had to be just so. And he had the patience and determination to see to his tasks at hand.

Reya warmed to the memories—there were so many. She used to tuck the twins into the small bed in the alcove, burying them under warm blankets, telling bedtime stories she spun from her imagination. Stories of fairies, dragons, and magical beasts that lived eons ago. Sometimes snow would pile in drifts as they slept, and in the morning Aletha and Adin would throw on coats and grab shovels and clear a path through the woods. They made snow angels and candy icicles, pouring boiled treacle into shapes in the snow. Spring saw them off on adventures, with a list of plants to gather into their pouches, returning at supper with shirts full of chervil and pennyroyal that they dumped on the table. On rainy nights they all lay on the rug by the fire, with animals sleeping across their legs and in the hollows of their backs as they tossed the dice and played games until they couldn't keep their eyes open any longer. In summer they built dams in the creek and made small pools to lie in, floating on their backs and watching the sunlight sparkle through the leaves in the trees overhead.

And now, as Reya looked over at the man sitting quietly in the chair, she wondered what had happened to the little boy she had often carried to bed. How time had sped by! She fingered the choker around her neck as she stood lost in nostalgia. The twins rarely visited anymore. And as adult responsibilities started making demands on their time, Reya surmised she would see them even less. Already she felt the pangs of parting.

Adin looked over at her. "What is it, Reya? You look sad. Is something wrong?"

Adin stood and carefully placed the raccoon on his warmed seat. "I have just the thing for you." He led her to a kitchen chair and sat her down, at the same time deftly scooping up one of the tarts and stuffing it in his mouth. He filled the kettle and placed it on the stove, then rummaged through the row of jars on the shelf, finally settling on one filled with green and lavender leaves.

Reya let herself be pampered. That was something that always made Adin happy, busying himself with things that made *her* happy. Making himself useful in a world where he was treated as useless. "Nothing's wrong, Adin. Except you've grown up. And what brings the royal prince here to the home of a peasant? And in this weather?"

Adin poured hot water into the pot of herbs, releasing a minty-fresh smell that permeated the room. The fire snapped and crackled heartily as the rain pounded the roof. The familiar warmth of the cottage assuaged Adin's aches and worries. The peace he found there had always proved a more powerful medicine than many of her strongest potions. That feeling of being safe; of enjoying familiar, comforting tastes and smells; of having a place where he could leave his fears at the door. She watched as Adin poured two cups of hot tea, piled tarts on a plate, and sat across from her at the table. As if on cue, Yo'fi came trotting over and promptly positioned herself at Adin's feet, her coal-black eyes fixed on the plate. Mindlessly stroking her fur, he handed the wolf a tart that she greedily munched down.

"Reya, you should be proud of me. Today I stood up to the King." Reya's eyebrows rose. "He called me into the chamber and accused me of some ridiculous plotting against him. I thought I would completely fall apart, but I surprised myself."

Reya sipped her tea thoughtfully. Adin reached for the honey jar and spooned a big glob into his cup and stirred. "I've hated him for so long, Reya—because he's always hated me. But now I think I just feel sorry for him. He's a miserable man."

"The King doesn't hate you, Adin. He is just suffering."

"Suffering? So that means he can take out his misery and disappointment on others?"

"I'm not justifying what he does, Adin. I'm trying to make a distinction. He lashes out at you because you embody his own failures. He cannot see you for the trees. And don't forget the *qa'lal.*"

Adin scoffed. "There you go again with that old widows' tale." Adin made a scary face and hunched in his chair. "The evil, ancient curse. You used to tell us stories about that—to scare us at bedtime."

"Adin, it is not just a story. Evil is a real, tangible thing. You have seen it with your own eyes. How it takes hold of a man and makes him do unthinkable things. Your own history is one of continual bloodshed, murder, and treachery. Remember the violence that formed your kingdom? You were born into that heritage, Adin."

He tipped his cup, drinking down the last drop of tea. Another tart made its way into his mouth. "People are greedy, selfish. They always have been and they always will be. Even you said it. Remember? 'The heart is treacherous—who can know it?'"

Reya nodded. "Evil is from ancient times, from before humans walked this world. It brought to the world *kho'shek*: darkness, spiritual darkness. The course of evil is to annihilate all that is good and decent. But there was a time, here, in this world, before evil polluted the hearts of men, before the *Sha'kath*—the Destroyer—came. Here, to this place, and other places."

Adin's smile told Reya he was not taking her seriously. He had heard this tale before, many times; to him it was just a story. Reya pointed to the pot. "Adin, would you please pour me another cup? Oh, and one for Aletha, too."

"Aletha?" He glanced out the kitchen window through the driving rain and into the woods. Branches blew and waved, but his sister was nowhere in sight. He knew better than to question Reya's abilities, though. By the time he filled another cup and prepared a place for Aletha, the door flew open.

"There you are," she said, her voice bursting with accusation. "I've been looking everywhere for you."

Aletha tossed her cloak onto the hearth, narrowly missing the sleeping hedgehogs. Her eyes took in the cottage and its occupants. "I see the whole neighborhood has come in out of the rain." She shook her hair, and water flew.

"And you as well," Reya added. "Come, Adin has brewed tea and there are still a few tarts your brother has yet to eat. Grab them while you can."

Aletha pulled a chair up to the table.

Adin handed her a plate. "You should have known I would come here."

"I did. That's why I came."

"So, why are you upset?"

"Worried. There's a difference."

Adin sighed. "Aletha, you spend too much time worrying about me." His eyes were warm with love. "I'm a big boy now. You can stop worrying."

"Never," she replied defiantly, then laughed. Reya and Adin laughed with her.

"Umm, good tarts. I was thinking about an almond tarte tatin. Can we make that next?"

Reya laughed again. "May as well, since it is not even noon and these will be gone long before teatime."

"Reya was just telling me the story of the evil curse," Adin said, watching as her sister sipped her tea.

"What about it?" Aletha replied.

"I was reminding Adin about the curse, the *qa'lal.* How it was said centuries ago that the *Sha'kath* brought evil to this realm. That it became attached to a place, this place, somehow. So that the evil that men do is not just from their own hearts but spurred on by something more potent. I have been trying to explain to your brother that all humans face temptation to sin, to do harm, and that such inclinations can—and should—be overcome and mastered. But it is not possible when evil binds with it."

Adin leaned back in his chair, eyeing the last tart on the plate. He looked at Aletha. "Do you want another?" She shook her head. He looked at Reya with a hopeful expression.

Reya held her stomach. "Take it; I am full, too. I don't know where you find the room in that small body of yours."

Adin smirked. "Looks are deceiving."

He, of all people, should know that painful truth. Reya patted Adin's shoulders, stirring him from his chair. "You should sit by the fire and get your clothes dry—both of you." She led the twins into the den, gathering up thick blankets and placing them in a heap on the floor.

After wrapping up in their warmth, they sat on the rug watching the flames, falling into a familiar quiet amid the sounds of soft wolf snores and pattering rain on the thatched roof. The hedgehogs shifted and, noticing the twins, waddled over and burrowed under their covers. Occasionally, drops of water ricocheted down the chimney and hissed on coals. Reya could tell contented stomachs and the warmth of the fire were causing the twins to grow drowsy.

"So, if you want a tale, let me tell you one," she said.

Adin snuggled up close to Aletha and rested his head on her shoulder. They both stared dreamily at the flames as Reya, sitting across from them, poked the fire with an iron rod.

Reya began to speak quietly, reaching back into her memory. "Long ago, when evil started ravaging the realms of this life, heaven decreed there would be sacred places set aside, sacred sites that would be established as the gates—the *sha'har*—between heaven and earth. Seven sites were chosen and the *ra'wah ten'uah*—the Keepers of the Promise—were appointed to watch and protect the sites, to prevent evil from gaining a stranglehold in man's world. It is not known how, but somehow, long ago, the evil infected this land, and the *qa'lal* was set in motion. The site had somehow become desecrated; protective spells no longer held. And the thing you need to understand is that the curse has a direction, or a determination, attached to it."

Reya closed her eyes and muttered words in the ancient tongue. Adin and Aletha looked at her curiously. After a moment of silence, Reya opened her eyes. "The curse will be locked until it is fulfilled. 'How long, oh, how long? Until cities lie waste without inhabitants and houses without people and the land is utterly desolate.' That is the determination of the curse."

Adin spoke up. "If that is what will happen to us, to Sherbourne, then what can be done? If we are bound by fate and inevitability, then why should we concern ourselves? It is out of our hands."

Aletha turned and stared at her brother. "Don't you care? If it's true, then someday Sherbourne will be gone, destroyed. You sound so fatalistic." She turned to Reya. "Isn't there anything that can be done to reverse the curse, or stop it, so that these things won't happen?"

Reya shrugged. "There is a prophecy that has been whispered down through the ages—of the *pa'lat*, the Deliverer. Over the centuries that prophecy has been lost. Even the greatest seers throughout time have been unable to penetrate the mystery of the *qa'lal*, how it began, what started it. And how, if possible, to stop it before it runs its full course. But know this—whatever evil was done must be undone or the curse will be fulfilled."

She paused in thought. "That is why I say the King is not an evil man; he is poisoned by evil. Whatever good is in him does not have the *ko'akh*, the inner strength, to win out over the *qa'lal*. And why you two need to be very careful to resist evil in all its forms. Why you need to develop your 'sight.' The more you train your inner eyes to detect evil in all its many shapes and disguises, the safer you will be."

Over the years Reya had reminded Aletha and Adin about their gift of sight. They had a vestige of a disappearing power, a power that people had enjoyed centuries ago, enabling them to join in with the magical world that was more prevalent in those early days. She guessed it had been passed down through their royal line somehow, for in the past, those with extraordinary powers usually became rulers of their lands. The twins didn't understand how this sight worked, but they knew they saw things others didn't. Reya explained that the gift of sight acted like a knife that stripped away the outer layers of appearance, revealing truth that lay underneath.

Sometimes, she explained, what they saw was *ma'hath'alaw*—an illusion meant to deceive. As the twins grew older, the frequency of these "sightings" increased, and they found the images disturbing, not to mention bewildering. But, as she had often reminded them, having this sight was a useful gift, and not to be ignored.

Adin and Aletha exchanged looks; Adin was about to laugh, and Aletha's eyes scolded him in warning. Reya reached over and put a hand on each of theirs. "Mock me, Adin, if you like. But, I believe the *pa'lat* will come."

She sat back and spoke, this time to the fire. "I believe it with all my heart. For I have seen it."

SIX

THE HORSES stood huffing, hot and lathered, in a small grassy hollow. Even though the autumn day grew cool in the late afternoon, a balmy warmth enveloped them in the close thicket of trees and undergrowth. The King, flanked by a half-dozen riders, rested his stallion on the mountainside in the last remaining forest of Sherbourne. Two attendants rode up next to him with the bodies of small red deer draped behind their saddles. After a minute of listening, the King gave the signal, and the entourage resumed their trek back toward the palace. Leaves crunched under hooves, and the hunters kept silent as they let the horses find their footing on the familiar path. When the King was in a foul mood, they all knew the price of making small talk.

They'd headed out before daybreak, but it wasn't until midday that any game was spotted. And what they found was hardly worth shooting. The King tightened his grip on his reins, feeling his ire rise. Years ago the woods were brimming with game—not only deer, but bear, elk, and wild pig. When he was a boy, the woods seemed to go on forever; it would take him and his father days to traverse the forests to the base of the mountains, and even then they could scramble up the cliffs and find sheep and mountain goats to track.

Not any more. No doubt it was because of the insolent villagers—expanding their farms, stealthily poaching game, cutting down trees for building and for firewood. By the time the King had passed decrees forbidding entrance into the woods on penalty of death, little game could be found. What was the point in hunting if this was all he could show for his efforts? In fact, hunting in recent years had become tedious and unfulfilling. He had lost the excitement, the thrill of tracking down quarry. There was nothing to kill that hadn't been killed before. Boring—it was all so boring.

The King thought about his palace and his collection of treasures, his trophies mounted on the dark wooden walls, their glazed-over eyes, vacant and lifeless, staring at nothing. Creatures from so many strange lands—all vanquished under his bow and knife while he subjected himself to danger, to tiresome journeys in filth and discomfort, to oppressive heat and torrential rain, all to bring him some kind of victorious satisfaction. But the more he hunted and conquered, the emptier he felt. At first there had been a thrill that spurred him on, the challenge of the task at hand, feeding him like a fire and igniting his soul with an unmatched passion. But, over time, that thrill had faded. He attempted greater challenges, riskier adventures. As his walls became filled, his heart drained. He searched deep in his soul to recall the excitement, to awaken it from slumber, but to no avail.

So what if he had the most beautiful, the most exotic, collection in the world? Still, it could be bigger, better. He had a nagging feeling that something was missing, that it wasn't impressive enough. His collection should be legendary, the envy of every other kingdom to the ends of the earth.

As he shifted in his saddle to come he imagined what it would be like to have the rulers of all the known world come and pay tribute to him, to bow at his feet in amazement and awe. He needed to leave a legacy such that generations would declare him the greatest king who ever lived. This desire ate away at his gut—this need for fame and, yes, worship. *Kings will come and worship at my feet.*

A sudden thrashing in the underbrush—not thirty feet in front of the hunters—jolted the King out of his musings. Guards suddenly reined in horses, and the King sat up abruptly. Immediately, eight bowstrings were taut with arrows that pointed to the shape that stumbled toward them. One of the King's bodyguards shouted, holding up a hand.

"Wait," he instructed the archers. He urged his horse forward three steps. "Sire, it is a man."

Emerging from the dense thicket was indeed a man, with leaves and twigs tangled in his wild hair and beard. His tunic, muddy and ripped, hung over a pair of woolen trousers with cuffs rolled up to expose the man's bare feet. The King stared at this intruder, who seemed youthful and disoriented. The man, trembling, darted his head as if confused, and it was then that the King realized the intruder was blind.

The bodyguard addressed him. "Sir, you are trespassing in the King's forest. Identify yourself!"

The man scrunched up his face, turning toward the voice. Horses pawed the dirt as the hunters kept their arrows aimed. "King's forest? Where, what land?"

The King sat back in his saddle and scrutinized the man who spoke with an unusual accent. His bodyguard addressed him more harshly.

"You stand before the King, man! Answer!"

Taken by fright, the man fell to his knees. His voice came out in stammered spurts. "I am sorry, Your Highness. I fear I have lost my way. Pray tell, where am I?"

The King spoke, his curiosity engaged. "You are in the kingdom of Sherbourne. Tell me your purpose and how you came to be bumbling through my woods."

Realizing the King was speaking to him, the man lowered his head to the ground. "Sherbourne? I have heard of this place, but it is far from my home. I come from Wentwater, in the east. I was on an expedition but got separated from my party."

"An expedition? To what end?"

"To find the firebird, sire."

The King laughed, and chuckles arose from the mounted men. He signaled his hunters to lower their bows. "The firebird? Then you went on a fool's errand, young man." The King reflected on the legend of the fabulous, mythical creature. In the Queen's own chamber in the palace hung an ancient tapestry of the bird, alongside others depicting unicorns, manticores, and griffins—all imaginary creatures. The firebird tapestry was one of the King's unusual acquisitions. From what he had been told, it had hung in an abbey for centuries, in a forgotten room. Later, it ended up in a small, abandoned cottage on the east end of the kingdom, outside the old walls. One of his royal purchasers had seen the tapestry for sale in the open market, buried beneath a pile of drapes, and had gleefully carted the worn and faded item back to the palace after paying only three silvers. No doubt it was a rare and unique find.

The tapestry depicted a tall, elegant bird of gold. According to legend, so brilliant were her wavy feathers and long draping tail that she radiated a light brighter than the sun, which paled insignificantly behind her. It was said that the firebird was born of the sun itself and that no man could ever catch her. She was the only one of her kind, immortal and indestructible. And she had the power to bestow either life or death upon any she chose. The King could not believe this meager specimen of a man had set out on so outrageous a quest.

He frowned. "Do you dare lie to me? Do you really expect me to swallow such a ridiculous story?" He signaled his guards, and two dismounted with ropes in their hands. "Who sent you, and upon whom are you spying?"

The man responded in agitation. As he felt the men grab him and start to tie him, he scurried to his feet, pushing them away.

"Wait, please. You must believe me. I am no spy—how can I be a spy—I cannot see!"

The King once more halted his men and let the man continue.

"There had been reports in my land of the firebird. At first I did not believe them, but they persisted, and I, and two of my friends, set off west, following the trail of rumors." The man paused and turned his head to the sky as if he could see what he described.

"M'lord, we were taking lunch by a stream when suddenly the sky lit up as if on fire. I heard the rustle of huge wings, like those of an eagle, and the air shook and shimmered, and heaven strike me if I did not see an enormous creature, nearly the size and weight of a man, descend from the skies like an angel. So breathtaking was she, stretching her wings as she floated down to light in a tree across the water! Thousands of gold feathers covered her—from head to tail, and her tail feathers trailed like a golden skirt around her, hanging from the branches, so long they touched the ground. The sight of her aroused in me such a longing—a craving—a need—to possess her for my own. I could think of nothing save capturing her and taking her back with me so I could spend the rest of my life staring at her beauty."

He took a breath and continued, a smile lighting up his whole face. "Sire, she is the most magnificent creature in the world! And I was determined I alone would have her. My two friends saw her, and they, too, were smitten, and we began to fight and push each other as we ran into the icy water and forded the current."

His face fell at the memory. "Being the strongest, I knocked my companions hard, and they tumbled into the stream. I do not even remember what came next, or how they fared, I was so mesmerized by the creature before me. I took a rope from my sack and slowly made my way toward the tree. But as soon as I reached her, a bright shock of light blinded me. I jumped toward her and she flew away, leaving my heart in shreds.

The man turned to where the King sat, his eyes looking long-ingly beyond the monarch, as if seeing the firebird in his mind, in all her splendor. "Sire, once you see her, you will never rest until you have her. I have been wandering these many weeks, the image of her burned into my thoughts, neither desiring food nor drink, only her. And I will never stop until I find her again."

The King shook his head and waved his hunters over to the man. They once more grabbed his arms and joined his hands to bind them together. "No, no! You must let me go. I must find the firebird!" He fell to the ground and began weeping. "Please, I must have her!"

"You have told us an entertaining tale, man, but that will not spare you punishment. You have trespassed in my forest, and the penalty is death." He turned toward his head guard. "Lead him to the palace and throw him in the dungeon." The King reined his horse to the right and began heading down the hill toward the north gate.

"Wait! Let me prove it!" He spoke to the man holding the rope that bound his hands. "Reach under my shirt—behind me," he pleaded.

The attendant stopped and patted the man's back, feeling something under the cloth. He pulled up the shirt and produced a tapered feather, the length of a man's arm. Upon releasing it from its hiding place, the clearing lit up with a magical light, causing the King to yank his horse to a stop and spin around. What he saw made his mouth drop open. For there stood his attendant, with his hand raised in front of him, an expression of disbelief on his face. And there crouched the prisoner, lost in admiration, as if the luminosity of the feather were piercing his blindness.

As for the feather—there were no words to describe its beauty, a beauty unmatched by any in this world. Through the pulsing radiance, which lit up every leaf on every tree in spectacular detail, the King feasted his eyes on liquid gold. Gazing upon it quenched the deepest thirst he had ever suffered. He had not known his need until this instant. For, now, the greed that festered in his heart spread with a fury, and without hesitation the King leaped down from his horse and ran over and snatched the feather from the attendant's hand.

"Where?" he demanded, shaking the blind man's shoulders forcefully. "Where did you see her? Tell me!"

The man shook his head, terrified. "I do not know. East. Somewhere between here and Wentwater."

The King stared at the feather, unable to tear his eyes away.

The man reluctantly spoke again, his voice impassioned. "Sire, even if you find her, you cannot catch her. She will blind you as well."

Carefully placing the feather inside his vest, the King patted it and stood deep in thought. The hunters waited for his instructions. Finally, he spoke, his voice charged with emotion.

"Take the prisoner to the dungeon. The rest of you—back to the palace—make haste!"

The King quickly mounted his horse and kicked it hard, spurring it into a run. With his hunters' horses galloping behind, he headed toward his palace with the greatest speed, kicking up clods of dirt and sending leaves spinning in whirlwinds. He would find this firebird, oh, yes! He would bring all his resources to bear upon this one task—to capture her and keep her for his own. He would not be denied, and he would not stop until she was in his clutches.

"Do you know what all this commotion is about?" Aletha pressed her face against the library window, watching the King ordering his men. In the courtyard, morning fog muted the voices, but Aletha could tell from the flurry of activity that her father was agitated. Servants bowed and hurried, and a scribe followed at the King's heels with pen and parchment, trying to keep up with a barrage of words.

Adin busied himself at the huge table, his paints and charcoal spread out before him. He held a slender boar-hair brush poised over a canvas of bleached hide. "Haven't a clue. Aletha, how am I supposed to capture your face if you keep turning away from me? You're too curious for your own good." He dipped the tip of the brush in a jar of brown ink and made a tentative stroke. "I suppose I can just work on the shrubbery for now." He looked up when a servant came into the room carrying a feather duster.

"Amanda, what is going on out there?" Aletha asked. "The King looks flustered. Has something happened?"

The young girl went to work dusting the rows upon rows of books in the library. "Your Highness, some say the King is plannin' t' make a proclamation. Rumor has it he's discovered a magic-like creature and plans to send all his best hunters off to capture it."

Adin made a disgruntled noise but said nothing.

"Creature?" Aletha sighed. "The whole city is falling to shambles and this is what he gets excited about?" Aletha sat on a window seat overlooking the courtyard. Adin lost himself in his art, tuning out the noises around him.

The previous afternoon, when the two had returned from Reya's cottage, Aletha retired to her room hoping to read. But the conversation they'd had about the *qa'lal*, and the image of Sherbourne in ruins, nagged her heart. She changed out of her wet clothes and, seeing that the clouds had blown away, revealing a crisp blue sky, impulsively threw on riding clothes and hurried unnoticed to the stable. She rode out the south palace gate down to the city, making her way through the cobbled streets, past shops and houses, and stopped at the Swan's Tavern, where she handed her horse over to be tended. With her hair wound and stuffed in a cap, and dressed in common garb, she knew no one would recognize the princess of

Sherbourne. No one except the barkeep at the tavern, and he knew to keep her secret under wraps.

"Well, we haven't seen the little miss around here for the longest time," the stout, bald man said, pouring her a glass of dark ale. Aletha removed her cloak and set it on the seat beside her at the bar. "How are things up on the hill?" he whispered, leaning over to inquire of her in confidence. "The King still filling the palace with more stuff while we little folk foot the bill?"

Aletha knew that, joking aside, conditions were getting worse. While Sherbourne was not tottering on the brink of ruin, the last eight years had taken a hard toll on those trying to run an honest business. Seeing few customers in need of attention, she convinced her confidant to sit and share an ale with her—and tell her what people were saying about the King.

He leaned over and put a finger to his lips. "You know the old saying: 'Do not curse the King, even in your thoughts, for a bird of the air may carry your voice or some winged creature tell the matter.' So what I tell you now is confidential-like."

She smiled and looked around. "No birds or winged creatures in here. Come, you can trust me." She knew he took a risk in grumbling to royalty, but he was always honest with her. Aletha had proven as good as her word in the past, and always left him a few extra silvers on the counter.

For more than an hour the barkeep shared stories of floundering businesses, black-market thievery, and violence; rumors of rebellions, gangs, and conspiracies against the King. Things were worse than Aletha had imagined. She needed to help these people, to circumvent her father, but she had no say in the Council. Even to her young eyes it was apparent that while her father grew more and more obsessed with acquiring treasures, the kingdom was being slowly wrested from his control by the councillors. And Aletha had no authority or influence over them. They seemed blind to the troubles in the city, and unless her father made a concerted effort to regain control and make drastic changes, the situation looked bleak for Sherbourne.

When she had finished her ale and put on her cloak, the man said something that sounded more like a warning than a proverb: "Remember, miss, the wealth of the rich is their strong city, and is like a wall—*in their imagination.*"

As she walked her horse through the neighborhoods on the way to the river, she thought of another proverb she had read long ago in *The Book of Kingly Sayings*: "Greed takes away the life of its possessors." It seemed a paradox—the more one accumulated out of greed, the more one lost. Perhaps each thing hoarded cost the precious coin of security and peace of mind. How much effort it took for the upkeep and protection of treasures that would only one day rot and return to dust!

Wasn't there a much greater treasure in things that were not tangible—things like honor and goodness? Maybe those things could not be weighed and measured, but their value, to Aletha, was greater than all the gold in the world. And what about family? How precious that was, and how fragile. Another proverb came to her mind: *"Where your treasure is, there your heart will be."*

Aletha thought of Adin and her heart swelled with love. He was everything her father was not. If he ruled as king, he would make sure his subjects were well treated. He would put their needs ahead of his own and make Sherbourne a place of prosperity and joy. And here was her father, neglecting his family in search of perfection. If only her mother were still alive. She would have prevented this downfall.

Aletha stopped her horse at the bridge and looked down at the river, wide and slow-moving at this time of year. In spring, the banks overflowed, water inching up to the pathways and flooding the park. Wide wooden planks spanned the Heresh, supported by massive stone columns. The elaborately scrolled wooden rails were carved from wood harvested from the black oak forests west of Sherbourne and ran the length of the bridge. Even though traffic over the river was heavy—horses, carriages, peddlers pushing carts to and from their favorite selling spots—Aletha felt alone. Thinking of her mother brought tears to her eyes. She wanted to believe what the man in the garden had promised her and Adin—that their mother lived. Yet in the eight years since that promise was made, she had heard no word that lent credence to his declaration.

A gravestone outside the abbey bore the Queen's name, but from what Aletha gathered from the abbey monks, no one had seen a body interred there. Each time she and Adin visited the grave, they had a heated argument about their mother. Adin insisted the man in the courtyard had known some secret truth; he refused to believe their mother was buried there and threatened to dig up the grave and uncover the ruse. Then he would confront the King with his proof and demand an explanation. Aletha was horrified by the idea; the grave was sacrosanct. He couldn't just dig up her casket without suffering the consequences.

How could he think their father was behind the deception? Look how much he had loved his wife! They would finally stop arguing and fall to wondering who that strange man in the orchard could have been. Aletha often looked for him in town, hoping she would recognize his kind face and warm eyes. She was sure she would know him if she saw him.

But her search proved empty, and when she asked around, describing him, no one remembered seeing him. Perhaps he had left Sherbourne, or died. In either case, whatever secrets he had carried were lost with him. She told Adin it was futile to hold on to the hope that their mother was still alive, that he was only torturing himself. But, secretly, she couldn't help but hope—hope against hope—that what the stranger had told them was true.

Aletha's thoughts were interrupted by the loud boom of the King's voice in the drawing room next door. She glanced over at Adin, but he hunched over his painting, pretending not to hear. The library doors flew open, and a man dressed in a dark, full-length robe came in. His head was shaved, and Aletha recognized the abbey insignia on the chain around his neck.

"Excuse me, Your Highness." He nodded at her, and then at Adin, who eyed him curiously. Aletha watched as the agitated monk perused the book titles on the shelves, evidently searching for something in particular. After a few moments he stopped and turned around. "Do you know if the King keeps any books on the ancient writings?"

Adin spoke. "There *are* no books that teach the ancient writings, unless you keep such a book at the abbey. They have all been lost to fire and decay. Why are you asking?"

"The King wants to know what the writing on the tapestry hanging in the Queen's chamber says. Do you know, by any chance?"

"Which tapestry?"

"The firebird. There is a line of writing across the bottom of the cloth."

Aletha remembered seeing the squiggly lines stitched in black thread under the image of the bird. "Ask Reya—she may know."

"Reya?"

"Our nursemaid," answered Adin. "But, Aletha, she doesn't know the writing, only some of the spoken language." He stopped and thought. "Why, pray tell, does the King need to know what some old writing on a tapestry means?"

The monk came over to Adin and smiled at his painting. "It appears the King wants to find the firebird. And he hopes the writing will tell him how."

Adin put down his paintbrush and laughed. "Now it's the firebird—a mythical fabrication! What will he hunt for next—a basilisk? A dragon?"

The monk put a hand on Adin's shoulder; his eyes lit up in his flushed, round face. "Oh, but the firebird exists! A young man was caught in the forest yesterday with one feather from the firebird. You must see it—an amazing, beautiful thing that lights up the whole room. The brilliance of the bird was so powerful, it blinded the poor man." He lowered his voice and Aletha drew closer. "Your father has thrown the unlucky fellow in the dungeon and plans to execute him. For trespassing!" His eyes pleaded with her.

"Excuse me," Aletha said, hurriedly gathering her wrap and signaling the cleaning girl to follow her.

As she left the library, she heard Adin speaking to the monk, and her brother's voice expressed incredulity. What madness was her father up to? Throwing poor blind men into the dungeon and chasing myths? As she ran down the hall to the far end of the castle she thought back to yesterday morning, in the Council chamber, when her father had stroked her hair. Aletha shuddered. Was her father losing his mind? Was he truly infected with some sort of evil poison, as Reya believed?

She exited the west side of the palace and followed the wall until she came to a bolted door. Thankfully, no one was around, but she wasn't surprised. She knew that once the melodrama of tossing a prisoner into the dungeon was over, the King cared little what followed. Nine parts bluster and one part insouciance. She doubted he'd given the poor man a second thought.

Instructing her servant to wait, Aletha lifted the torch from the wall and bounded down the dozen steps that led to a heavy wooden door, with a bolt unreachable from inside the cell. With a hefty pull, she managed to slide the iron bolt and free the door. A man in filthy, torn clothing sat on the small bench in the tiny dank cell. She winced at the smells lingering in the dark, cold space. The man was shivering.

"Sir, I apologize for your treatment."

The prisoner cocked his head. "Who are you?"

"A friend. Please, take my hand and let me lead you out and to freedom."

"Oh, thank heavens. You are an angel of mercy!" he whimpered.

Aletha took hold of the man's cold hand and led him up the stairs to the foggy morning outside. She placed her woolen wrap around him, which he clenched tightly, nodding in gratitude. "I wish I had something to give you for your kindness, but alas, I have nothing," he said.

"We have a proverb in our kingdom: 'Those who are kind reward themselves.' I am just glad to know you are unharmed." She turned to her servant. "Amanda, take him to Reya's. Tell her I sent you. He needs a hot bath and some strong tea before she sends him on his way. Mum's the word." Aletha put a finger to her lips, and the girl smiled and nodded.

Aletha watched as the two walked quickly around to the north gate, the bedraggled man in Amanda's tow. With that taken care of, Aletha returned to the palace and made her way to the kitchen to wash her hands. She shook the memory of the stench from her thoughts as she filled a basin of hot water from the huge stove. Servants busied themselves preparing platters for lunch, slicing meats and arranging fruit. They nodded respectfully at the princess and offered her something to eat. She realized she was starving, having skipped breakfast.

She asked one of the cooks for a snack, and in moments a plate was set before her, piled with aged cheese, smoked pork, and a handful of fat berries with a dollop of clotted cream on top. She could hear a crowd of people out in the courtyard, voices yelling and cheering. From where she sat in the kitchen, she had no view of the yard, but one of the cooks listened intently at a window next to the cold storage. The heavy woman, with her hair up in a net, pushed the transom open wide and leaned her head out. The large south window faced down the breezeway to the courtyard, and the cook reported that from there the King could be seen standing on the raised dais, his arms outstretched.

Aletha ate everything on her plate, skimming every drop of cream off the bottom. As she lowered her spoon, she heard the woman gasp.

"What is it?" Aletha asked. The other cooks and kitchen helpers gathered over at the window, trying to get a look. The cook, her pudgy face in a fret, threw up her hands and ran over to Aletha. She grabbed Aletha's hands in her own, squeezing and kneading them mindlessly.

"Why, m'lady, a huge crowd is gathered around the King. And he's just declared he will give half his kingdom to anyone who will capture the firebird alive!" She gulped and raised her eyes to heaven. "And, m'lady—he says that to the man who does this, he will also give the hand of his daughter in marriage. Why, that's you, m'lady!"

Aletha felt a rush of blood fill her cheeks as she swooned and fell off her chair to the hard stone floor while a dozen servants looked helplessly on in surprise.

SEVEN

ADIN WAS cleaning his paintbrushes in the library when one of the cooks came running in, panting and babbling hysterically. She dragged him toward the kitchen by his sleeve, all the while wiping her eyes. He found Aletha on the kitchen floor, a bundle of towels propped under her head, and a crowd of aproned servants bent over her, fussing and fretting.

The sea of bodies parted to let the prince come to her side, and when his weak attempt to lift her failed, the head cook, Darcy, graciously hefted Aletha's back, using her strong arms to bring the princess upright. Adin managed to support Aletha's legs, and with the assistance of a few more concerned servants, they carried her down the hallway and up the stairs to her chamber, an effort that fomented a stabbing ache in his bad leg and a strain in his back. After dismissing the other servants, he turned to Darcy, who was making the princess comfortable in her bed.

While the concerned cook dabbed Aletha's forehead with a cool cloth, she explained the events leading up to the injury. Shocked by the news, Adin grabbed Darcy's hand and asked her to stay with his sister, and upon getting her assurance she would not leave the princess's side, ran out of the room as fast as his clumsy legs could carry him.

He found the King sitting in the small antechamber of his bedroom, a space used as an office of sorts. With his back to Adin he growled in a low voice, "I thought I ordered that no one disturb me!" Adin waited, but the King never turned around to see who stood behind him, never even moved his head.

Slowly, Adin walked toward his father and realized the King was staring at something on the table before him. Mounted on a golden stand was a feather, long and delicate, a soft yellow shade, like butter cream. Apart from its size, Adin saw nothing special about it, nothing that merited his father's adoration. Adin was baffled; hadn't the monk said the feather shone with a blinding brilliance? And how was it that the King did not even acknowledge Adin's presence?

Adin walked over to the feather and reached out his hand to touch it.

"Stop! You fool—what are you doing?" The King leaped from his chair and shoved Adin with such fury he knocked his son to the ground. He cradled his hands around the feather as if protecting it. Finally, he turned and glared.

"What are you doing here? You cannot have this—it is mine!"

Adin stood and backed away to a safe distance. "I don't want your feather. I want to talk to you about your proclamation." Adin mustered strength in his voice. "You cannot promise to give Aletha away like that. She is not one of your collectibles. You must change the proclamation."

The King tipped his head in mockery. "Or what? You'll go through with your secret plans to take the throne? So then, this is your big opportunity to make your move. Well, go ahead and try! You will fail. I know how you conspire against me, and those who are with you."

"I have no idea what you're talking about." Adin checked his anger. He watched as the King sat back down in his chair and once more fixed his attention on the feather. "How can you do this to Aletha? She's your daughter, she loves you . . ."

Adin's mind reeled with the ramifications of the King's announcement. His emotions—anger, outrage, and fear—tumbled over the thought of Aletha being given away like some prize. Then, he let his words diminish; he could tell his father was no longer listening. He leaned closer and looked into the King's eyes, and all Adin could see was a vast wilderness, an emptiness like that of a bottomless well. This vacant expression did something to Adin's resolve. His father was clearly gone; it was as if someone else inhabited the body sitting in the chair. The man before him was a stranger.

Suddenly, all the warnings Reya had spoken to him crystallized into one succinct vision—that of a man possessed by an undetectable force, a force bent on squelching every last remnant of his father's dignity, conscience, and—yes—his basic humanity. This evidenced more than the King's succumbing to greed. Could it truly be the effect of the *qa'lal?* And would it also be *his* fate—as Reya had implied—if the curse was left unhindered? Bewildered, he took one long, last look at his father and then left the room.

Upon entering Aletha's chamber, he waved Darcy out of the room and sat in the chair beside the bed, entangled in his musings. He couldn't shake the memory of his father's empty eyes.

Adin's thoughts were interrupted by movement in the bed. Aletha moaned as she touched the back of her head and tried to sit up.

"Hey," Adin said, helping her, "easy now. You smacked your head on the floor. Should I send for Reya?"

Aletha slowly shook her head. "I think I'm all right. Just throbs a bit."

"Here." Adin placed the cloth back on her forehead. She held it as she lay back against the pillow. Adin took her hands and let out a big sigh.

"How'd I get up here? You didn't carry me, did you?" she asked.

Adin shrugged. "I had some help."

Aletha's face filled with worry. "Adin, do you know what Father did? What he said?" Worry turned quickly to anger. "How can he think I would marry someone just because he tells me to? And to announce it to the whole kingdom without even consulting me?"

Adin stood and went over to the window and looked out across the orchard. The fog had lifted and was now blowing in wisps down the knoll toward the city. The courtyard below had emptied, the morning's commotion apparently ended. Darcy had told him that notices were being posted throughout the city, calling for hunters to seek the firebird and receive the reward. The elusive, magical firebird.

"Aletha," he said, turning toward her, "do you really think anyone will catch this bird? And if the bird blinds those who come near, why would anyone try?"

Aletha snorted. "Half the kingdom is why. And a free princess thrown onto the pile, to boot. Strong motivation for plenty, I would venture to guess. Surely some poor soul will get his hands on the bird and bring it back for Father to gloat over. Then I'll be forced to marry some blind, greedy idiot."

Adin thought about the blind man his father had captured in the forest. "I feel terrible for that man in the dungeon."

"Don't. I set him free."

Adin's eyes widened. "You what? And when Father finds out? He'll have your head!"

"Adin, it is not the first time Father has left some poor sod to rot in the dungeon. And not the first one I helped release. Trust me—he'll never notice." Aletha's anger grew more forceful. "And I don't care about his decrees. This mad proclamation to capture the firebird is wrong. It's foolhardy! Why doesn't the King go catch his own firebird? How does he expect to keep her in a cage and gaze upon her if he too will go blind? It is madness." Aletha shut her eyes tightly, but tears fell to her cheeks despite her effort to remain composed. Adin sat on her bed and held her hand, thinking.

Finally, he spoke. "I will go and capture the bird."

"What? Are you mad as well?"

"If I can capture her, then you will not be forced to marry anyone. You should be allowed to choose your own husband as other women do. Out of love, not obligation."

"Adin—"

Adin put his hand out and stopped her. "Aletha, I will not stand by, helpless, and watch the King ruin your life. Do you really think you will be able to oppose him on this matter? He has already given his word to the entire kingdom—you will not be able to back out and shame the throne. You will have to marry. Or run away."

Aletha grabbed Adin's shoulders. "Then run with me! Why not leave this palace and travel far away? Disguise ourselves and start a new life somewhere."

Adin shook his head. "That will mean certain ruin for Sherbourne and all our people. One of us, at least, must stay and keep Father and his councillors honest."

The truth of Adin's words dampened Aletha's spirit. They both knew what would happen if the only heirs to the throne suddenly vanished. Chaos and violence would break out in the city, since very little was now holding the discontented populace in check. The King would be furious, and he would take out his wrath on those least deserving it. No, there had to be another solution.

Adin's eyes pleaded with Aletha. "Please, don't you see? I should go. I know I can find a way to capture the firebird—there has to be a way. Maybe there is a secret to it; somewhere there must be a book or scroll that will tell how. Everyone else will be seeking her out of greed, and greed is what blinds men to their folly. Don't you see—the firebird doesn't blind men! She only reflects back what is in their hearts, of that I am sure."

Aletha frowned. "How do you know? You know nothing about this creature. Just what you learned in stories."

Adin stood and rubbed his leg. He was suddenly aware of his hunched back and twisted face more keenly than ever. Aletha was staring at him, and the familiar feelings of weakness and helplessness washed over him. He sensed her pity, and disgust filled his heart like the worst of all poisons. Disgust at himself, at his deformities, at his purposeless life. All the years of humiliation lay piled at his feet. The continual looks of disappointment and repulsion on his father's face. The sneers and taunts of strangers who pointed at him in the streets, laughed at him, made him feel like a worm. He'd had enough. He clawed his way out of the suffocating pile of shame and worthlessness and raised his head to face Aletha with a fierce determination.

"I will find the firebird, Aletha. I love you with all my heart, and I will not let the King trade you away so easily. He will give me half the kingdom, and I will take those treasures and give them to the poor and needy of Sherbourne. Then you can marry whomever you choose. And more importantly, I will win back Father's love. He will see I am not a useless, worthless man!" Adin's voice cracked with emotion and his breath came out in spurts.

"Adin, don't, please. You can never win Father's love. Reya was right—his heart is poisoned. Even if you do this thing, he will never love you. He will only want more and more—it never ends, don't you see? Please, Adin, you are being foolish. Think!"

"I have been thinking for too long. Now it's time to act." He leaned over and kissed Aletha on the cheek, then hobbled to the door. He turned and gave his sister a crooked, sincere smile. "Do you remember the last words Mother said to us, before she died?"

Aletha, speechless, just stared at her brother.

"Love is as strong as death," he said.

He closed the door to the sound of Aletha sobbing her heart out.

Adin stuffed his satchel with clothes, food, and a bag of gems and coins. Strapped to the satchel were a woolen bedroll and a heavy blanket. He would take no rope or knife. Deep in his heart, he knew the only way he could capture the firebird was with weapons of honesty and pure motives. He did not have much of a plan, other than to scour the old book stalls in the marketplace and bury himself in the deepest catacombs of Sherbourne's library on the east side of town. He would take no horse, but would walk at his own maddeningly slow pace. That way he could sleep where he chose and not be burdened with feeding and stabling the animal. He really would love to take Yo'fi along—Reya's little wolf—as he so often did on his jaunts through the woods. She was a comforting companion, and great to cuddle up to on cold nights. But she would be another responsibility he didn't need right now.

And what if he failed to find any writings on the firebird? He would just have to trust his instinct and follow whatever leads presented themselves. And head east, to where the bird was last seen.

By mid-afternoon Adin was ready. He couldn't bear saying good-bye to anyone in the palace. He certainly didn't want to explain his decision. And he couldn't bear to see Aletha again, for it would tear at his resolve and he had little enough as it was. He chided himself; he had wrestled for too many years with self-doubt and skirting confrontation. He would be determined—and single-minded. He had a task before him, and he would see it through—no whining, no turning back.

As he slipped out the library doors into the courtyard, the chill of the autumn afternoon struck his face with a biting breeze. Water rising from the spring in the fountain caught in the wind, spraying the ledge of rock. Adin stopped and pulled a water jug from his satchel. Leaning over the fountain, he let the clear, cold liquid fill his container as he mentally mapped out his journey. Distracted, he did not notice the water overflowing his jug until it spilled onto his hand and soaked his sleeve.

He abruptly stood and pushed in the cork, then something curious caught his eye. He looked closely at the jug, his hand, and his sleeve. For a moment he thought he saw something odd—the water turning black and fizzing, like an acid eating away at iron. He shook his head to clear his vision and examined the fabric. For a moment, a dark stain seeped up his arm, then it faded, leaving a slightly damp mark. He turned his hand over, and a shadow passed across it. When he uncorked the jug and poured a drop into his palm, the water appeared clear and untainted. He knew he had just seen something with his gift of sight, but what did it signify?

Adin felt a strange sensation come over him and his hands shook. He was more unsettled than afraid. As if something inside was pressing him—to do something, to go somewhere. But where? What was it? A rush of urgency filled his heart, and he knew he must hurry.

Mindlessly, he touched the silver locket around his neck, the locket his mother had given him eight years earlier as she lay dying in her chamber. As he limped his way down the grassy slope to one of the southern archways, a strong sense of her presence enveloped him, as if she were right beside him. He spun around, searching the hillside, but he was alone. The air grew strangely calm; not even a bird could be heard in the fruit trees. Time slowed to a crawl, and then stopped. Adin braced himself in anticipation.

Suddenly, a gust of air, heavy and thick, brushed against him so hard he nearly lost his footing. The sensation was like the slow, steady beat of giant wings.

Merin hadn't meant to listen in. It wouldn't be eavesdropping, would it, if all he was doing was gathering wood from the bin for the cookstove—minding his own business, as it were?

The portly young man with branches weighing down his apron stood at the back kitchen entrance and thought hard. His mum'd always told him to stay out of trouble. The servant's place was to see nothing, hear nothing—be invisible around nobility. But Adin was his friend—had been since they were young'ns. And they'd always made it a point to help each other and look out for one another. And although in recent years they'd spent little time together—usually it was Adin dropping 'round for a snack and a chat on any odd day—there was still loyalty to think of, and if his mum'd taught him anything, it was to be true to a friend. "A true friend is loving all the time," she'd say. "And is a brother born for when there is trouble."

Well, if this wasn't trouble, now, then what was it? Merin felt a nervous twitch in his stomach, and he knew it wasn't from the giant platter of eggs and ham he'd had for breakfast. That man, Rasha, gave him shivers, what with his smooth talking and these eyes that grabbed you like a pair of hands. For that matter, all those councillors made him uneasy, huddled together, moving silently through the palace halls. Merin could always tell when one was around, watching. He'd be off fetching something from the storage room and feel something creep along his neck. There'd be one of 'em, standing still as a statue, eyeing him like he was up to no good.

But now! They'd been talking about the prince, and Merin had been stooping just outside the chamber window, hearing how they couldn't find Adin anywhere. Rasha had told the others to search the palace, and when they found him, to throw him in the dungeon! What mischief were they up to? One thing he knew about Adin was that the prince was a kindly, good-hearted fellow, not like that father of his. Merin well knew of the way the King treated Adin and he didn't like it one bit, king or no. But what to do?

No way would he duck his head while the prince was in trouble. Adin has come to his own defense more times than he could reckon—so what if his meddling now got him into hot water? Merin exhaled hard. Trouble was not something he looked for or particularly wanted in his life. He was content to just do his work without grumbling and keep his nose clean. But "friends is friends," he reminded himself, and hurrying into the kitchen, he dumped the pile of wood next to the stove and shook out his apron.

An idea struck him. He would go to the princess; she would know what to do. Merin quietly left the kitchen and hurried down the long hall, glancing around for signs of the councillors. But as he climbed the stairs to Aletha's chamber, he was stopped by her attendant, who took him aside and explained that the princess was distraught. How the prince had left Aletha in a state of tears only an hour ago, and now the princess wanted to be left alone; no one was to disturb her. With her hands, the attendant shunted him back, away from the door.

Merin grew even more upset, but just nodded his head and said nothing. As he trudged down the stairs, feeling helpless and defeated, another idea popped into his head. What about Reya? Merin knew how much the old nursemaid cared for the twins, and, oh, how upset she'd be to hear what trouble was brewing! It had been years since he had gone with Adin to play at the cottage, a place Merin remembered fondly. Reya had always been kind to him, and fed him the most wonderful pies and tarts. Merin's mouth watered at the thought, then he berated himself. This was no time to think about food! But now that he had a plan, he walked back to the kitchen with a spring in his step. At the end of the day, when his chores were done, he would head out the north gate and through the woods and find Reya.

Merin grunted as he bent over to open the stove door and stoke the coals. Reya would save the prince; if anyone could help him, she could. And, he couldn't help imagining, she would no doubt have something freshly baked on her table to offer him for all his effort.

EIGHT

FOR THREE days Adin traversed every street of Sherbourne. He visited every book stall and spent hours combing through stacks of manuscripts and scrolls. By the end of each day his leg screamed in pain from the hours of standing and browsing, even though he managed to find places to sit and read tomes that had caught his interest. He kept quiet about his search, and he didn't need to keep much of a disguise, for few people in Sherbourne had ever seen or heard of him. He could thank the King for that anonymity, which at the moment it served him well; the last thing he wanted was recognition. From time to time he caught people eyeing him as he limped along, his hunched back an oddity, but they politely turned their eyes away.

Evenings he spent at a quiet inn on the east side of the city, across the river. Situated in the wealthier part of town, the lodgings were comfortably simple and the meals substantial. The innkeepers were polite and left him to his reading, as he perused his day's findings while filling his stomach.

The fourth day he spent in the library, a sprawling stone building that took up two city blocks. One of the oldest structures in Sherbourne, the library dated almost as far back as the abbey. Rooms had been added piecemeal over time, with random steps that led up and down to different levels, and long hallways that opened into vast chambers of plank shelving reaching up two stories to a glass dome.

Adin shuddered at the thought of climbing the steep ladders up to the highest stacks to scan the titles. Fortunately, a librarian came to his aid—a fidgety, wiry man not much older than himself, who spoke continually, his words following random thoughts and skipping around on subjects as he led Adin through the puzzling corridors. Adin watched as the librarian darted up the ladders as quickly and steadily as a spider; retrieved books and scrolls, and, tucking them under his arms, managed to scurry gracefully down to the ground without even a bead of perspiration breaking out on his brow.

He led Adin to a table, and after depositing him and all his books there brought him tea and biscuits from some hidden kitchen Adin had failed to notice in his wanderings around the library. He also lit a bright oil lamp so Adin wouldn't strain his eyes in the dim room. Adin had been turned around so many times he was sure he would become lost trying to navigate his way out at the end of the day. But the librarian must have had experience with that very scenario, for once he was sure Adin was settled in, he handed him a small silver bell, instructing him to ring it when he was finished.

Hours went by and he learned little. In an encyclopedia of mythical beasts Adin found a short description of the firebird with an accompanying illustration similar to the depiction on the tapestry. No mention was made of its supposed origin or of any sightings. None of the other writings spread across the table gave any indication that the firebird was, or had ever been, a real creature. So where did that leave him? Either the firebird was rare and secluded, living far from human habitation, and had only recently entered the world of men, or it belonged to another world, one of magic.

In past seasons, Adin would have quickly discounted magic. But Reya had warned him in many lectures that magic was indeed a real power to be reckoned with, and now, after his last encounter with the King, Adin was beginning to agree. She taught that just because he couldn't see magic at work, that did not mean it wasn't there. Just like the wind, she'd say. You don't see it, but you see the things it moves. Magic was much the same way. She'd spoken of a time, long ago, when the world was drenched in *la'at*—enchantment—during the early days of man, before kingdoms spread across the lands. According to Reya, magic, then, was so commonplace that nothing appeared odd or unexpected; amazing and wonderful things would happen without explanation, yet no one would be surprised. Adin remembered stories of those who had parted great seas with just a staff in hand, who had torn lions apart with their bare hands, changed rivers into blood, and even walked on water!

Now, though, what magic was left was like the wisps of fog that lingered after a rain. They were frail threads that wove through nature, losing power as men expanded their cities and cut down forests. Magic that had pooled in pockets of the earth had drained away, leaving an emptiness that could be felt only by those who had the "sight."

Adin rubbed his tired eyes and rang the little silver bell. The librarian appeared at his side so quickly it seemed he had materialized out of thin air. Adin clearly had spent too many hours pondering mysteries he could not unravel. He left the library weary and discouraged, and comforted himself with a hot bath and a huge dinner of vegetable stew and brown bread slathered with butter.

The next morning dawned clear, with a cold, shining sun lighting up the stones of the city walls. A fresh breeze coming off the river ruffled Adin's hair, and for some reason he felt happy and invigorated. Maybe just getting away from the walls that enclosed his life was what he needed to get a fresh perspective. With a determination anchored in his heart, he pushed aside his doubts about the enormousness of his task and walked briskly toward the east gate.

In the quiet morning hours few people shared the road. Adin traveled along the wide cobbled street as it exited the city under the tower. Carved, crumbling steps rose steeply alongside the street to the tower entrance. Adin looked up at the slate-tiled roof of the tower, and his eyes followed the length of wall as it stretched behind the dozens of small cottages with their grassy yards and garden plots. A few chickens pecked the dirt; mourning doves cooed in their cages. He realized he had rarely explored this city, his kingdom; he knew little of the people here. Hiding away in the palace all these years may have protected him from embarrassment and humiliation, but now he saw he had missed out on so much.

As he exited the gate, the cobbled road turned to dirt, and before him the sun rose over hundreds of thatched cottages that dotted the rolling hills in all directions. Turning to look back, he could make out the palace perched on top of the knoll, and he thought of Aletha sleeping in her comfortable bed. He already missed her so much and knew she must be angry and afraid. Leaving her to fend for herself with the King discomfited him greatly. He turned and quickened his step. He would not dawdle, for the sooner he found the firebird, the sooner he could return to Aletha.

Heading east, he passed droves of people on their way to the city. From peasants in shabby clothing to those with coin to spend, all seemed driven with purpose and determination. The dirt road was muddied from horse hooves and cart wheels, and Adin kept to the side of the wide road to let all pass. After an hour, the dwellings thinned out, and occasionally he would wave to a woman hanging laundry or sweeping a porch. Children could be seen busy at their morning chores, dumping out buckets in the yards or gathering eggs in their aprons. As the sun climbed in the sky, patches of clouds cast patterns on the road, and the morning chill dissipated.

Coming upon a stretch of empty countryside, Adin heard a distressing sound. He looked around and saw open fields bordered by tall elderberry bushes. He crossed over to the meadow littered with autumn leaves from the small coppice of beeches. He heard what sounded like a shrill cry and followed the sound until he was surprised by what looked like a pig's head protruding from a muddy hole. He was more astonished when he heard the pig speak.

"Now there, my good lad, could you see to it to help me out of my predicament?"

Adin came over to the pig, who was indeed buried to the neck in mud. He set down his satchel on the side of the road and squatted near the animal, who did not seem awfully distressed, considering his circumstances.

"What's the problem?" Without hesitation, Adin removed his cloak and tunic, setting them aside as the pig grunted in a humorous manner.

"Well, I seem to have caught my back trotter in a root, imagine that, and am havin' the dickens of a time trying to wrest it free, so there you have it." He grunted again; this time Adin was sure he was laughing.

The pig squirmed and then yowled. "Oh, fuss and bother! I have tried to turn the blasted thing every which way, lad, but it's locked in good 'n' tight. Would you be so kind . . .?"

Out of the corner of his eye, Adin saw a couple of men dressed as laborers coming down the road toward him. He was about to signal them for help, but they quickly crossed to the other side and averted their eyes. Adin sighed. The pig nodded his head, spraying Adin with specks of mud. "Tha's the way it's been all morn, lad. No one wants to help out a pig in distress, imagine that. Might get their fine trimmings all amuss."

"In for a pence, in for a pound," Reya used to say. Adin unlaced his boots and set them aside. Wading into the mud, he was struck by how thick and gooey it felt. The morning sun had warmed it, and with each step he took toward the pig, he sank deeper. His feet mired, and it became difficult to move any closer; pulling against the suction required all his strength. Sweat streamed down Adin's face.

Finally, he reached the pig, whose head showed bits of white patches under all that goo. The pig offered words of encouragement, sounding like the cheering section at a jousting tournament. "Tha's a boy, you're making excellent headway, just a wee bit more, there you have it."

The pig wasn't exceptionally large, but he was plenty stout. His beady brown eyes glinted and bristly gray hairs covered his head. "Name's Winston, my lad. Do you have a name?"

Adin gave his name, then reached an arm down into the muck and followed the pig's flank until he could find the hooves. He was up to his shoulder in mud. "Not the front—the back, lad. There, you see?"

The pig grunted again and let out a little squeal. Adin stopped. "Did I hurt you?"

The pig laughed in spurts. "No, no, my lad, just tickles is all. Go on, then. Right about yer business." The pig raised his snout in the air with a look of concentration. "I'll try not to wiggle."

Adin felt around in the mud until he came across the trapped hoof and fingered the root that entangled it. Mud was now seeping down his neck, and in order to reach around the hoof he had to lay his cheek in the mire. Trying to keep his nose clear so he could breathe, Adin strained and stretched his arm as far down as he could, finally edging two fingers between the root and the hoof. Getting a grip, he carefully pulled and twisted the hoof, trying to ignore all the pitiful sounds coming from the pig.

"Ah, there you have it, lad!" The pig flailed excitedly, striking Adin carelessly with all four feet as he scrambled out of the mud puddle. Sharp hooves scratched Adin's arms and face. Adin pushed the pig from behind, where the animal's cycling legs set up a steady spray of mud into his face and hair. By the time Adin had extricated himself from the mudhole and collapsed onto the dirt road in a heavy pant, not an inch of him was unsullied.

The pig, now standing on solid ground, shook his body in delight. He turned to Adin and grunted loudly, a wide smile spreading across his jowls. "Jolly good effort, lad. Brilliant of you." The pig took a step toward Adin and squealed, falling flat on his belly, legs splaying in all directions. "My, my, that still smarts. Dona think I'll be able to walk, lad."

Adin took a deep breath and stood. He wiped his face and hair, then tried to squeeze and scrape as much mud from his clothing as he could, forming a puddle at his bare feet.

"You are quite the sight, my boy."

Adin came over to the pig and felt the back hoof. "Your foot's swollen. You'll need to stay off it awhile. Do you live around here somewhere?"

"Oh, my cottage's just down the lane a piece. You'll be welcomed with a towel, no doubt, and a hot meal. But I'm afraid you'll have to carry me there. Up to it, lad?"

Adin looked incredulously at the pig, who must have weighed at least three stones. The pig winked at Adin, who became aware of the eyes of travelers upon him. He could hear snickers from those walking by and doubted any would be willing to get their hands and clothes dirty to assist him.

Adin was aware of the pig's watchful eyes as he laced up his boots over his muddy feet. He put his outer clothes in the satchel he slung over his back. "Which way?" Adin asked.

The pig nodded his head toward a lane leading left, into a dark, wooded hollow where Adin could make out the thatching of a roof and smoke rising from the chimney. Taking a deep breath, Adin reached down and wrapped his arms around the pig's ample girth and, with a grunt of his own, hoisted the pig to his chest. He readjusted his load and wobbled to standing, knowing without a doubt he would never be able to carry the pig that distance.

The pig huffed, and turning his head to meet Adin's eyes, said, "You can do it, lad. You'll see. Small acts of kindness do not go unnoticed, my boy. *Pe'ree tsa'diyq.*"

Adin tried not to groan with each small step. Catching his breath, he asked, "What does that mean?"

"'Tis an old saying. 'Truly there is a reward for the righteous.' Takes a special person what would stop to help the helpless, lad. You'll have your reward."

Adin kept his gaze on the ground, careful not to trip on rocks and sticks. Somehow the pig stayed in his slippery arms, and with each step his burden felt more manageable. "I don't want any reward. Those who are kind reward themselves."

The pig laughed in a way only pigs could—with a series of rapid snorts. "Ah, you would say that, lad. But a *sa'kar* you will have, nonetheless."

"The only reward I want is a hot bath."

"Oh, and that you shall have, my boy. But, pray tell, lad, what'll it be, eh? You get to choose, you know. Tha's how it works, haven't you heard?"

Adin took a few more faltering steps and ventured a look ahead. The cottage inched closer, but now his nose itched. The dried mud on his clothing pulled him down as if his pockets were loaded with rocks, but he kept focused on putting one foot in front of the other. His back ached miserably. The pig, on the other hand, thoroughly enjoyed his ride and kept up his patter of talk with animated expression.

"Well, my boy. How would you like to be fixed proper-like? *Naw'ame*—made beautiful? Have that troublesome leg of yours straightened out? And that awful bit of work on yer face? Be able to stand tall and have all those lumps in yer back gone—on long holiday as we say?"

Adin had no idea what the pig was talking about; how could anyone make him whole? Just the idea of it filled him with a longing he quickly squelched. How many times he had stared at himself in the mirror and begged heaven to change the image that glared at him! The thought was only a cruelty that led him down the dangerous spiral of self-pity. He tried to shut out the pig's words and concentrate on his steps. One thing was uncanny—the closer they got to the cottage, the lighter the pig felt. Adin shook his head in wonder. He managed the small stone steps toward the door with more ease, the pig still carrying on.

"Now, tha's a tempting choice, I'll grant you. And there's no shame in going that way, so there you have it. Wouldn't blame you a smidgen for going that route, eh? And then there's the usual gold and jewels and such, but I imagine you wouldn't be a-wanting those, since I can tell ye're a man of some means. On t' other hand there's wisdom. Oh, I know tha's often highly over-rated in diverse times and places, but we always throw that into the mix, you see? Wisdom helps you make decisions proper-like, make sense of wha's confusing, keeps you out of trouble. All that stuff and whatnot."

Adin looked up. The cottage was made of dark plank wood and seemed old but well kept. On the right, a quiet creek spilled over rocks and disappeared into the dense woods. Adin stopped and deposited the pig on the front porch, straightening out the kink in his back. The pig did pose an intriguing consideration—albeit hypothetical—Adin had to admit. Which would he choose? Which would serve him best?

Adin thought of Aletha and what she would say. She would want him to be rid of the burden of his deformities, but for her happiness, not his. Then he thought of the King, and the state of Sherbourne, and all the troubles that plagued his kingdom. How he wished he knew what to do, to make life better, to bring his father to his senses. It seemed the weight of all Sherbourne rested on his shoulders, and he longed desperately to know how to prevent its ruin. Would catching the firebird solve all his woes, make the King finally love him as he so deeply wanted? Aletha's words replayed in his head. He hadn't wanted to admit it, but she was probably right. His father was never going to love him just for capturing the firebird.

Adin sat on the porch next to the pig, who looked like a large piece of cracked ceramic. Chunks of mud had fallen off his skin, revealing patches of white. The pig scratched at his flank with a hind hoof and groaned.

Adin sighed. "If I could have the wisdom to find my way through this life, I would want that more than all the treasures in the world. Even more than a sound body." He looked in the pig's face, and the pig stopped scratching and cocked his head. "They say, 'Wisdom is better than gems, and all things that may be desired are not to be compared to it.'"

The pig pinched his lips together and snorted. "I see, lad, you've been taught yer proverbs. But, there's this one, too: 'For in wisdom is much grief, and he who increases knowledge increases sorrow.' Scares some people away, that does." The pig stared thoughtfully at Adin, who sat quietly for a moment.

"The price one pays, I suppose. Still." Adin stood and pain shot through his hip. The day was getting on, and he knew he should be, too. But now the thought of finding the firebird had lost its urgency. In fact, he questioned whether it was a wise course after all. Was his quest folly, as Aletha had declared? What if he spent weeks chasing after an elusive creature and, upon his return, the palace and all he held dear had fallen to chaos? Should he just hurry home and fight for change on the home front? Suddenly Adin was struck with doubt and confusion. The determination that had spurred him on these last few days deflated, leaving him with a sense of despair.

Without knowing where to go, he turned to leave.

"Where do you think you're going, lad?" The pig scratched a hoof at the front door and it cracked open. "Say, let's get you out of those filthy clothes and into a bath, righto?"

Adin hesitated. How could he continue on in this state? At the very least he could go down to the creek and wash out his clothes and scrub the caked mud from his skin. He started to strip off his clothing.

"Dona worry 'bout that, lad. Come on inside." With that the pig disappeared into the cottage, leaving Adin bewildered. He shrugged and followed the pig.

Once inside, the pig sat with a grunt on an old oval rug before a hearth where a large iron cauldron steamed. Adin could tell the fire had recently been stoked, and he could hear the soft sound of water boiling. The room lacked a woman's touch; there were no curtains or pretty coverings over the table or chairs. Just a sparse room with a few simple but well-built pieces of furniture, and shelves full of books. Little brown mice ran over the tops of the tables and shelves, and one of them ran up to Adin and rose up on two legs to have a better look. Adin carefully stepped around the mouse and surveyed the room.

What instantly caught Adin's eyes were the drawings and paintings covering all the walls. A wooden easel stood in one corner with a stretched canvas resting upon it. The partially finished painting, like the others in the room, was a depiction of the countryside. Adin recognized some of the scenery captured in the paintings—the city walls, villages, shops. Other pieces were more disturbing, depicting scenes of fighting, bodies lying on the ground, smoke filling the air. One painting showed men stacking stones, assembling what looked like the walls around Sherbourne. Whoever painted these had talent, and Adin assumed that person probably earned a livelihood by this talent. In addition to the mounted art, Adin noticed piles of sketches on the floor and rolled-up parchments stacked behind the easel. Before he could ask about the cottage, he heard a man's voice speak from another room in the back.

"Right on schedule. Adin, your bath will be ready momentarily."

Adin's eyes grew wide at the man's words. How did this man know his name—or that he'd be needing a bath?

From around the corner came a man dressed like some kind of hermit, with a floppy hat and funny garb. He wore a long tan tunic that almost touched the floor, with a white tailored shirt draped over it, the sleeves rolled up in bunches on his arms. He carried a wooden bucket in one hand, which he set down next to the cauldron. Adin noticed he was not very tall or remarkable in any way, except for his exceedingly long, ruddy hair and beard, both at least a foot in length. The man's olive complexion was free from wrinkles, but his age was hard to tell, his face was so buried in hair. Overall, he did not seem very old at all. His pale eyes were bright and penetrating, and when he turned and looked at Adin he smiled cheerfully.

"Oh my, you really do need a bath! Come." Adin found himself speechless as he followed the man into a small, warm bathing room. He noticed the man walked gracefully, with a poise and stature that bespoke nobility. Peasants didn't carry themselves that way.

"And Winston," the hermit gently called out, "please find a moment to throw yourself into the creek and get *ta'hore* before you track mud over every inch of the house." Adin heard the door opening and the tapping of trotters over stone outside. He smirked. The pig didn't seem to have any trouble walking now.

Adin didn't know what to say. "Is he your pig?"

The hermit laughed and shook his head, his amiable face lighting up. He handed Adin a towel. "I think it is more that I am his human." Adin tried to get a feeling for this stranger who seemed to know much about him. Could he be some sort of wizard or magician? Adin stared at the hermit and was abruptly overcome by dizziness.

The room faded in and out of focus, giving Adin the sensation he was dreaming. With a softened gaze he watched the walls grow transparent, and through a mist he saw the outline of the woods and rocks—even the small creek behind the house. He placed a steadying hand on a large wooden tub. The essence of magic permeated everything around him. Adin lifted his hand and moved it through air thick as pudding.

"What is happening? How do you know my name—and that I was coming to your home? I don't understand." Adin set his satchel down next to the tub and waited as the strange vision passed and all returned to normal.

The hermit eyed him calmly. "Oh, we will have plenty of time to talk. I'm going to brew some tea and round up something to eat. Here, throw all your messy things in that sack over there and enjoy your bath." He pointed at the little stool next to the tub. "There's soap, and a blade and mirror if you shave." He stroked his long, thick beard. "Haven't used those for a while. I'll be in the other room if you need anything. Just come out when you've finished."

As Adin lowered himself into the wonderfully hot water, he could hear the man singing quietly to himself as he moved about the kitchen. The song sounded familiar, but Adin could not put a name to it. How in heaven's name had this hermit known he was coming? The question ate away at him, making him scrub quickly so he could get out and have his questions answered.

Adin dunked his head over and over, picking at the caked mud until he could run his fingers through his hair. The water in the tub turned a dark gray, but he stood and gave himself one more thorough rinse with the full bucket left next to the tub and, once he had toweled off, he felt tingly clean.

Adin pulled out a shirt and trousers from the satchel and dressed. He hesitated, then picked up the hand mirror and looked himself over. His lopsided mouth, his hunching shoulders, the way his head sank into his neck—all glared at him. Always the same face reproaching him. Sometimes these moments washed over him, making him feel ugly and awkward. He set the mirror down and combed his hair.

His eyes caught on a small painting next to the bathing room door, one he had not noticed before, as it faced away from the tub. In it, a woman looked out over a garden, an orchard. Around her gentle face a tumble of coppery red hair fell, lighting on her shoulders. The painting was made with wide implying strokes, not as detailed as the others Adin had seen adorning the cottage walls. But Adin was still awestruck as he stared, unmoving, at the painting.

There was no doubt this was a portrait of his sister, Aletha.

NINE

ALETHA WAS restless and upset. Adin had been gone only three days and it felt like three years. She tried to pass the time reading and playing her small flute, but she could not concentrate. Even stitching failed to calm her; she felt about to burst out of her skin. So, the following morning, she rose before dawn and left a note for her attendant. After rigging the carriage with her two favorite mares, she headed north, alone, out the gate with a wave to the guard on watch.

The abbey was a half-day's journey, and she hadn't been there for many months, but she felt a strong need to visit her mother's grave and spend time in silence in the chapel. Just getting away from the palace cleared her head. As the hours passed, she began to unwind and observe the scenery. The King's forest was secluded; apart from the beasts and birds, she knew it was hers to enjoy. Leaves blanketed the well-trodden path; most of the trees were already bare from the approach of winter.

Aletha knew that her heart was filled with worry. Worry for Adin and worry over her father. Worry for Sherbourne. And what Aletha hated even more than worry was feeling useless. She needed something to do, but what? Somehow the confines of the palace numbed her brain, made her indecisive. Hopefully, this trip would help her refocus, give her a plan of action. Who knew how long Adin would be gone, and worrying about him would not make him return any sooner. She would have to find a way to tackle the many problems piling up on her. She owed it to her brother—and to the people of Sherbourne.

After three hours the forest thinned to open prairie, where an occasional massive oak spread its boughs to provide shade for sheep. A few farms could be seen in the distance, but as Aletha traveled she encountered no one until she ascended the road toward the abbey. Old stone houses dotted the side of the red clay road as Aletha drove the horses on. An old man poked at a herd of sheep, moving them out of the carriage's way.

As she came over the first rise, she could make out the ring of pointed mountains in the west, and a grove of dark green trees that lay at their feet. Someday she would make the trip across the vale to those mountains. She and Adin had talked about it but had never found the time to go. Just seeing the majestic crags pierce the deep blue sky took her breath away, but now, with the way things were going, she feared she would never get her wish.

Upon cresting the second rise in the road, the abbey came into view. Made of a pale yellow stone quarried in these hills, the abbey stood like an ancient, sacred relic, with moss growing up the sides of the beautifully carved and scalloped walls. Ornate scrollwork trailed up columns that rose fifty feet to meet the domed roof. A woven pattern, a braid of imprinted green tile, encircled the entire building like a ribbon tied on a package. The huge domed windows were all beveled, rising to a peak, painted panes of greens and blues, and they looked out all four sides of the abbey down the hill to the vale below.

On one side of the abbey was the small cemetery, enclosed by a wooden gate and low stone wall. Behind the abbey was the garden where the monks grew medicinal herbs and vegetables in large quantities to provide not only for the needs of the monks, but to give to the needy. As she drew the carriage to a stop at the entrance, she knew there would be monks busy digging potatoes and harvesting winter squash and onions. In the summers, Aletha had often picked tomatoes and snow peas, helping herself to handfuls of grapes and cherries—whatever was ripe. Some of her fondest memories were kneeling in the dirt with Adin and their mother, the rich, loamy smell filling the air.

However, the last summer she had spent here with her mother she would rather forget. Aletha and Adin had worked silently, thinning carrots, while their mother sequestered herself in the chapel. Only a month earlier the Queen had given birth to Aletha's new baby brother at the palace. Aletha still remembered the horror of that night—the screaming and crying, the blood-stained sheets carried out by sad-faced attendants, and Aletha, only eight, hiding down the hall behind a chair, terrified at the mayhem and noise. She never did get to see the body of the baby, although as they rode in the carriage to the abbey, Aletha was aware of the small casket stacked on top of their baggage. Once at the abbey, she and Adin had slept together in a small room each night by themselves and could hear the sobs coming from the room next door. The Queen had rarely spoken to them the week they remained there, and after that pivotal event, everything in their lives had changed.

Upon returning to the palace, an aura of sadness and tension had hung in the air and affected all who entered. Some nights Aletha could hear her father raise his voice in anger while her mother cried. At first her mother would argue back, and to Aletha's dismay, the quarrelling often centered on Adin. Her mother could not understand why the King was opposed to Adin as heir, why he treated the young boy so contemptuously. And her father would hear none of it; he wanted her to produce another son, and the Queen would be at his mercy until he got what he wanted.

Over time it seemed her mother had grown more withdrawn, and even through Aletha's young eyes she saw how the Queen had silently given up her will to the King. Whatever he had wanted his wife to do, she did with a nod and detached air of complacency. And then the King began ignoring her, turning his attention to his hunting expeditions. Aletha didn't understand it at the time, but now that she was older she grasped how her father had blamed his wife for the baby's death, and how her mother had suffered so under that guilt.

Aletha sighed and stepped down from the carriage. A caretaker in a brown robe greeted her and then led the horses to a large barn. Her heart felt heavy as she walked to the cemetery and opened the wooden gate. Beyond the enclosed yard grew a large, stately oak, a place where Aletha, Adin, and their mother had picnicked on warm afternoons. She could picture Adin stomping on acorns while their mother looked on and laughed.

Where had all the joy gone, the simple joy of celebrating life? Finding her mother's stone, she knelt down beside it and let her tears flow. She reached her hand out and ran it slowly across the chiseled letters, feeling, for the first time in her life, utterly alone.

As she huddled over the grave, a breeze tickled her hair, sending a shiver down her back. A sensation came over her—that someone was watching her—but upon rising she found no one. She wiped her eyes, preparing to leave and visit the chapel, yet the feeling persisted. This presence nudged her, like a finger tapping her shoulder.

Aletha spun around. Was her grief unlatching her imagination? She stopped and took a deep breath, willing her mind and heart to empty. Then, a clarity seeped into her heart, and turning slowly and with purpose, she walked to the far wall and looked over at the oak—and waited.

At first all she saw were a few branches swaying in the windless afternoon. She let her gaze soften and calmed her heart. Color and shape blended, and gradually emerging from the swirl of gold and the swish of movement was a huge graceful creature, lighting on a heavy limb. Aletha held her breath in wonder, listening as a beautiful strain of song drifted toward her, sounding like a thousand tiny bells tinkling in a breeze. A sense of peace flooded Aletha's heart, and all her sadness and worry seeped away.

As the firebird raised her wings and became airborne, catching an updraft and rising high over the fields, Aletha felt her spirit soar, as if she were that beautiful bird, winging in the exhilaration of freedom.

Of this she was now certain—the firebird never could, and never would, be captured.

At the hermit's urging, Adin sank into a big, comfortable chair next to the hearth and told him about his quest to find the firebird. Despite the warnings in his heart, Adin felt compelled to pour out his story to this calm and curious man. With a cup of hot tea in his hand, he shared his fears about Sherbourne and the King, and his worry over Aletha. The hermit listened quietly as he stood, staring into the air and nodding his head in concentration. As Adin spoke, he realized he yearned for someone to confide in; he'd always had Aletha to talk with when he felt confused. Without her, his thoughts wandered aimlessly; he couldn't hear himself think.

As Adin recounted his episode with the King and the feather, the front door creaked open. The pig, now white as snowberries, trotted over to Adin and plunked down on the rug.

"Ah, now, shining as a pig in a pot!" the pig said. "And you, lad, I see you're all spit and polished as well. Having a spot of tea does the trick, eh? What about those scones?"

The hermit chuckled and went into the kitchen. "Thank you, Winston, I nearly forgot. Adin, you must be starving." He set a plate on Adin's lap and tossed a scone to the pig, who snuffled and chewed happily. He pointed at the floor. "Don't leave a pile of crumbs."

"Oh, would never do," the pig answered, sucking up the few remnants of scone from the rug. "Well, tha's been more'n enough excitement for this pig for one day. Now, if you'll pardon me . . ." With that, the pig turned a few circles and finally plopped down with a huff and a grunt. Within minutes his eyes closed and a quiet little snort escaped from his mouth with each exhale.

Adin ate quietly, enjoying the snack. Lugging a pig down the road had worked up his appetite, and his stomach growled audibly. Just what did the hermit want from him? He must have been brought here for a reason. "Now that I've told you my tale, would you please tell me who you are and why I am here?" Adin realized he hadn't bothered to mask the irritation in his voice. "And why do you have a painting of my sister in your bathing room?"

Removing his floppy hat, the man gave a little bow and offered his hand. "You may call me Ta'man. And I am here to send you on a journey, a *ma'gur*. More accurately, the word means 'pilgrimage.' Do you know what a pilgrimage is, Adin?" He pulled up a chair next to the prince and sat down.

"Not really. A religious quest?"

"A pilgrimage is a journey to a sacred place, with a purpose in mind. In your case, you will be traveling not just to a sacred place, but to a sacred time." Before Adin could speak, Ta'man reached over to the corner and retrieved a scroll. He unrolled a tattered parchment of what looked like a map of the kingdom, and pointed to a drawing in the corner. It was a silver five-pointed star, unevenly shaped so that one arm and one leg were longer than the others. Set within the star was another smaller golden one, and in the center of that star was a pale blue circle, which Adin assumed was a gemstone.

"Have you seen this before?" he asked Adin.

"No. What is it?" Adin shifted in his chair and leaned closer.

"It is called a pentacle."

"What sacred place are you talking about? Is that where I can find the firebird?"

The hermit laid the map on the floor and looked Adin in the eyes. "Adin, you will not be seeking the firebird." Ta'man held up a hand to stop Adin's protests. "You have a different *makha'sha'bah,* a special path to follow. That is why you came here. You do not need to pursue the firebird; you have something much more important to do."

Adin's heart pounded hard in his chest. Part of him wanted to dismiss the hermit's words as those of a lunatic. But, for some odd reason, he found himself drawn to them like a thirsting man to a well. "What path is that?"

"Think back to what you have been taught about Sherbourne's history. Tell me what you know about the sacred site, the *qa'lal,* and the Keepers of the Promise—the *ra'wah ten'uah.*" Ta'man sat back in his chair to let Adin talk.

Adin gasped. Could it really be a coincidence that this stranger brought up the curse? Throughout his entire life, no one but Reya had ever mentioned it, and now—this! A talking pig, a cottage held together by threads of magic, a hermit who painted portraits of his sister! Clearly, some power wanted Adin to see this was no coincidence. Every nerve in his body alerted him to pay attention, that he was meant to be here, right now, in this place and no other.

Adin met the hermit's eyes and found only friendly encouragement. If some evil magic hid there, it was not manifest. He took a deep breath and words spilled out.

"Reya—that's our nursemaid—taught us that long ago there were special places set aside as sacred. That these Keepers were supposed to protect these sites, to prevent evil"—he thought for a moment—"the *Sha'kath*—the Destroyer—from bringing ruin to the world of men. Somehow a curse, a *qa'lal,* was set in motion, and it poisoned the site. Because of the curse, Sherbourne is doomed. Unless something can be done about it." Adin stiffened. "But aren't these just old tales? What proof is there?"

The hermit smiled. "Adin, what would you say if I told you there existed a map, a very unique map, that was made to take its possessor back in time, to the beginning of the curse?"

"That's impossible. Maps show you where to go—from one place to another. A map is just a guide to show you the way across land."

"Well, I know of a map that leads across time. Adin, it is a very ancient, magical map, and it has been kept safely hidden for centuries. Whoever uses this map will find their way back in time to Sherbourne's infancy. Once there, they should be able to see what or who caused the sacred site to be desecrated, and how the *qa'lal* came to pass."

Adin looked at the hermit incredulously. "Are you serious?"

"Adin," he said, with a firm, solemn tone. "You have no reason to trust me or believe me. But, know this—if you want to save your kingdom and bring your father back to his senses, you must follow the map to the past and learn how to undo the curse."

"Me? Why me? If you know so much about it, why don't you do it?"

Ta'man chuckled and stroked his long beard. "Trust me, I cannot. The map is meant for you, Adin." Ta'man paused in thought. "Someone once told me this proverb: 'It is the glory of God to conceal things, but the glory of kings to search things out.' You are destined to be king; it is your task to search out the mystery."

Adin made a cynical face. "You are mistaken—I will never be king. But tell me then, where is the map? Do you have it? That's something I'd like to see."

"It is locked in a trunk in the labyrinth below the abbey, and only you have the key that can open it."

Adin's mind reeled in confusion. "The abbey? What labyrinth?"

"This is what you will need to do; it is very important that you listen carefully. In the lower chambers of the abbey, there is a maze of tunnels. When you arrive at the abbey, tell the head abbot you have come to seek the map. Take the stairs that lead underground and follow the corridor until you get to a place where you will have to choose left or right." The hermit went over to the table and brought back a small wooden box.

"In this box will be three mice. When you get to the first intersection, let one of the mice loose, then follow it as it winds through the tunnels and corridors until it vanishes. As long as you can continue on a single path, keep going. When you get to the next place of decision, set another mouse down and follow it, the same as the first. And so with the third. That last mouse will lead you to the correct door."

The hermit set the box down on the floor and knelt next to Adin, his eyes meeting the young man's. "Adin, you will see many doors, but if you open the wrong one you will be forever lost in the tangle of corridors and never find your way out. No matter what you see or hear in the labyrinth, do not open any door but the one the mouse leads you to."

"I don't understand. Why is the map hidden in such a complicated place?"

"Adin, many have tried to find that map. Over the years rumors have leaked of its power and importance. Can you imagine what could be done—for ill or good—with a map that could move you across time? For that reason the map is laid within a trap, and those with evil intent have been caught in it like flies in a spider's web. And, as a further precaution, the map can only be attuned once, to one individual, so if the map is ever lost or stolen, it will be useless to any other who claims it."

"How do you attune the map?" Adin asked. He didn't know whether he felt excitement, fear, or just blatant disbelief.

"Wait. When you open the correct door to this *keh'der*, this chamber, you will see a large trunk sitting on the floor in a large, empty room. Open the lock of the trunk with the *maf'tay'akh*—the key—and remove the map. But do not unroll it inside the room or it will crumble to dust in your hand and your *ma'gur*, your quest, will be over and your kingdom destined for ruin. Instead, seek a loose stone in the wall across from the door and press it. Take the set of stone stairs up and out of the abbey. Right away, find a secluded place, away from prying eyes, and unroll the map, holding it with both hands, like this."

The hermit picked up the parchment he had placed on the floor, unrolled it, and grasped the sides. "As you stand there, you will see how the map will attune to you and your location. After you attune the map, you can rest easy, for then it will belong to you and you alone. Each time you unroll the map it will redraw to the place and time you find yourself in."

"How do you know all this?"

"I have spent a long time, young prince, gathering bits and pieces of this story." The hermit smiled at Adin. "I know this is a lot to digest and you have had a tiring day, what with Winston and all." He reached over and scratched the head of the pig, who was sleeping soundly and contentedly. "Perhaps you would like to rest, take a nap, while I prepare a proper meal for us and get your muddy clothes washed. Then tomorrow, fresh and well-rested, you can be on your way."

Adin's face creased with worry. Somehow this tale did not seem as silly as it once had. Was this man casting a spell over him, making him believe this madness? How could he tell?

"Ta'man, everything you say is amazing. And I want to believe it is true—that it is possible to use this magical map and go back in time. To go back and find the cause of the curse. But, if it really did work, how would I know where to go, or what to do once I got there?"

"The map will take you to the right time. You will find the right place. Look for the pentacle, that star I showed you. The Keepers use it as a symbol of their appointment. Are you familiar with what we call the 'morning star'?" Adin nodded and Ta'man continued.

"This orb we see in the sky before dawn travels this exact star-shaped pattern around the constellations every eight cycles. To the Keepers it is a symbol of hope, for the promise of the morning star is the promise of each day dawning anew." Ta'man raised his head and closed his eyes. "*Shemesh tsa'daq zar'ach marpé ka'naph.* 'The sun of righteousness will rise with healing in its wings.'"

Ta'man's words struck Adin to his heart, the ancient *law'az* flowing into him like a stream of clear water, washing away all his doubts. Healing. That is what was so desperately needed in his kingdom—and in his family. Words caught in his throat.

"Ta'man, why me? I am young, inexperienced. I can barely walk and people treat me as if I'm a freak. How in heaven would I ever be able to do all this?"

The hermit again stroked his beard thoughtfully. "Heaven is not impressed with power and strength, but favors those with a true heart. Let your heart lead you, Adin, for love is what will drive you and protect you. Think of Aletha, your mother—even your father, Adin. The solution to all your troubles lies in your past. I believe if you do this for them, then you will not fail."

He sighed and smiled again, and that smile struck Adin like a ray of warm, healing light. The hermit added softly, "I believe it with all my heart. For I have seen it."

When the first light of dawn seeped through the bedroom window, Adin dressed and laced up his boots. Quietly, he tiptoed out to the den, only to find Ta'man and Winston already bustling about the kitchen. The hermit wore the same odd clothes and stood at the iron stove, feeding pieces of kindling in through the hatch. Warmth emanating from the stove erased the morning chill from the air. The pig snuffled at a huge clay bowl in the corner.

"I asked Winston to be polite and wait to eat with our guest . . ."

A loud snort erupted from the pig. "If friends and relations can't see to it to rise at a decent time, well, there you have it. A pig's belly can't be put off, you see, lad? Must be punctual about some things, eh?" Once the pig was sure he had thoroughly licked the bowl clean, he ambled out the door.

"Where's he off to so early?" Adin asked.

"Who knows? Snuffling in the dirt, I imagine." Ta'man broke some eggs into a heavy pan and stirred, tossing in a pinch of herbs and some dashes of liquid from a dark bottle on the shelf. "Do you like mushrooms?"

Adin's mouth watered. "Oh, yes. Thank you. And thank you for the bath—and the bed. I feel strangely at home here."

The hermit picked up the hot pan with a cloth and scooped the eggs onto two plates. "Good, I'm glad to hear it." He sat beside Adin at the table. Warm bread, butter, jam, and milk were spread before them. "You have a long and difficult journey ahead of you. But there are a few more things I need to tell you."

Adin chewed thoughtfully and listened. Last night, for several hours, he had lain in the bed, looking at the stars through the window. Ta'man's words had replayed in his mind, over and over, and Adin had tried to make sense of it all. Could a map really move a person across time? The idea was outrageous—and yet somehow seemed feasible. The urgency Adin had been feeling for so long drew him toward the thought of that map, gathering all his attention, as if summoning him. He knew, now, he could not turn aside. The firebird no longer compelled him.

Could it be that all the experiences he'd had during his life had been meant to lead him here—to this hermit's cottage? Something deep inside him answered yes, and it frightened as well as intrigued him. Oh, if only Aletha were here—she would be able to tell him if this hermit was trustworthy or not!

Ta'man slathered butter on his bread. "Like any map, Adin, there are boundaries and directions. Be sure to orient the map so that you walk toward your past. Keep your eyes on the map as you walk, for it will show you the path you are taking through time. Do not get distracted by anything you happen to see."

He took fast bites and the slice of bread disappeared. "When you get to the point on the map that marks the end, stop walking and you will have arrived. You will land in exactly the same location where you started your journey, for, remember, the map only moves through time, not space. Stay on the path and do not detour, or you will end up somewhere—or rather some*time*—you should not be."

"How long will it take—to go back that far?"

"Time loses its coherency. You may leave in one moment and arrive the next—who knows? Just be sure that when you return, you follow the map exactly to your starting point. That way you will arrive around the same season you left in. But know this, Adin: you must take great care. For time is a strange and fluid thing, and there is no telling when the stream of time will drop you. Even though the map will lead you to and from your destination, you may arrive weeks before the event you seek. This is not an exact science." Ta'man pursed his lips in thought, then jabbed his eggs with his fork. "And when you return, if you should step even one hair past your starting point, you may find yourself weeks beyond the day you left."

Ta'man grew quiet, as if pondering whether to say something. "Don't forget what I told you about the labyrinth!" He polished off his eggs, then pushed his plate away and retrieved the wooden box. Adin watched as the hermit gathered up three mice from the floor and stuffed them in, then latched the lid with the clasp and handed the box to Adin.

Adin got up from the table, his stomach full. He picked up his satchel from the floor and looked at Ta'man with puzzlement. "One thing I don't understand. Who made this map?"

The hermit walked with Adin to the door, stroking his beard and thinking hard. "You know, I have often wondered that myself. But I really have no idea. Perhaps you will find out when you get back to the beginning. For, no doubt, the map is centuries old, and whoever made it clearly knew of all we've been speaking about. Look for the pentacle, Adin. Find the Keeper and be careful and observant. Guard the secrets of your quest, but don't turn your back on those who offer their friendship. You will need allies."

Adin opened the door, and the crisp air stung his face. He turned to the hermit and saw the concern in his eyes. The hermit laid a hand on Adin's shoulder. "You asked me about the painting in the bathroom—the one that resembles your sister."

Adin had nearly forgotten. Ta'man seemed to know much about his family, more than just the usual town gossip. As much as Aletha was loved by many in the kingdom, Adin doubted her admirers went to the trouble of painting her likeness.

"Adin, hers is the face that comes to me in my dreams. A face that comforts and haunts me. Suffice it to say, I cannot tell you more." A rich sadness filled Ta'man's eyes, a sadness that corresponded with the one in Adin's own heart, unmistakably linking their destinies. That realization shook Adin profoundly.

The hermit took Adin's hands and squeezed them tenderly. "Good-bye, Adin, and safe journey. May heaven guide you wisely on your *ma'gur*." The door gently closed with a click.

A lump formed in Adin's throat as he looked down the path that led back to the road. What if everything the hermit had told him was a hoax, meant to manipulate him? If so, to what end? Why not just go back to the palace and forget this whole foolish quest? And then what? The thought of pursuing the firebird now seemed as silly as chasing a dream with a net. And the thought of returning home to his useless, meaningless life was unbearable. There was one way to determine the truth of Ta'man's words, and that was to go to the abbey and ask for the map. What did he have to lose?

It would take him at least two days to reach the abbey. Rather than retrace his steps through the city, he decided he would stay outside the walls and go through the countryside. There he could think without distraction. North, then west through the King's forest, then down to the prairie. Strange that his path should lead him to the abbey. All these years! Had the map been hidden there while he played in the fields and worked in the garden—a world of magic beneath him, in a strange, dangerous labyrinth?

Adin turned at the sound of a snort.

"Well, lad, you're off then?" The pig trotted briskly alongside Adin as he approached the road. "By the way, you made the right choice, you see. Wisdom and all. Will serve you in good stead, my boy. Cheerio!"

With that the pig returned to his snuffling and turning up dirt with his snout. Adin adjusted the satchel on his back, and, taking one limping step after another, set his face to the road turning north.

TEN

THE JOURNEY to the abbey afforded Adin time to reflect. He walked at an easy pace, stopping to sit and drink from his jug. He spoke to no one apart from giving an occasional polite greeting. He busied his mind trying to remember what he had learned in his lessons about the early days of Sherbourne. If the map truly existed, how far back would it take him? The curse could have been placed at any time in his kingdom's history. If he found himself centuries in the past, would he stand out strangely in the clothes he wore, and would he be able to understand the speech of that era?

At the end of the first day, he reached the boundary of the King's wood. Adin ignored the posted warning on the barred gate and, seeing no one around, slid back the bolt and entered the forest. From time to time he glimpsed deer stepping softly over branches and around rocks. Squirrels chattered and scurried up and down trees. Knowing his way around every inch of the wood, he sought out shelter in a place he and Aletha had discovered years ago—a huge hollow in a mountain of rock. A fire ring of blackened stones still marked the entrance, and Adin set down his satchel with relief as dusk colored the sky. While he lay in his bedroll inside the hollow, a fire crackled and sent sparks into the air, and the sweet aroma of burning wood eased his mind like a tonic. He fell into a deep, undisturbed sleep, with a cloudy, chilly morning waking him.

After a meager breakfast, he started out again. The biting cold compounded with the long days of walking made Adin's back and leg throb. His pace slowed as he wrapped his cloak around him. He pulled out a cap Aletha had stitched for him and tugged it down over his ears. Keeping his eyes to the ground, Adin was unaware how many hours passed, but finally he arrived at the eastern gate of the wood, and below him spread the vale, with a dusting of frost coating the prairie grass.

A cool wind accompanied him down the road; the day grew a little warmer from the weak sun peeking through a mat of clouds overhead. Thankfully, an old man and woman driving a mule cart stopped and helped Adin up, giving him a ride across the vale to the foot of the lane leading to the abbey. There they parted ways. As Adin slowly trudged up the hill and took in the panoramic views around him, his thoughts dwelt more on a bowl of the monks' vegetable soup and a hot bath than on the mysterious map hidden in the labyrinth.

A beautiful sunset spread out over the vale below, coating the horizon in brilliant orange and indigo. Adin stood in front of the abbey and took a deep breath. He had reached one destination, but a door was now opening to another completely unknown to him. Would he soon take a step out of the world he knew and into mystery? The thought twisted his gut in a knot.

He unlatched the wooden gate and sat beside his mother's gravestone, thinking of her sad face and how beautiful she had been. He missed her so much. Once more the question plagued his heart. Was her body really interred there? What really happened that night? Did she die, or had that stranger told the truth—that the Queen lived and would one day return? More than any of the things he feared to hope for in his heart, he hoped his mother still lived. Whether his *ma'gur* would reveal answers to these puzzles, he did not know. But he felt that somehow everything that had taken place in his short life was intertwined with a greater thread of destiny. He, Aletha, the King, and the Queen were part of some greater story, one that began centuries ago and perhaps would continue for centuries longer. Adin felt a sweep of ageless time brush over him, and it made him feel small and overwhelmed.

"Young prince," a voice announced from behind him. Adin turned to find a bald monk reaching out his hands to greet him. "What a surprise to see you! You just missed your sister."

Adin jumped to his feet. "Aletha! When?"

Taking Adin's arm in his, the monk led Adin toward the gate. "Why, Adin, she just left yesterday; didn't you know?"

"I have been traveling. Is she well; how did she seem?"

The man laughed as he walked. "Do you always worry that much about her? The princess seemed chipper, actually. And her appetite was as I remembered. She polished off two huge bowls of soup and a small loaf of bread."

"Oh, excellent! I am glad to hear it." A huge weight lifted from Adin's heart. As long as Aletha was managing, he was happy. And he was glad she had left the palace to come here for solace and to lift her spirits. The monk closed the gate and led Adin toward the abbey doors just as the bell rang in a low, steady clang.

Adin's step lightened. "Just in time. I'm starving, and I can assure you I will be able to match Aletha's appetite any day!"

As Adin sat with the other monks at the long dining tables, finishing off the last heel of bread, the head abbot came over and sat across from him. The older man's face was round as a plate, and full of wrinkles from many years of laughter. No matter how hard times seemed, the abbot found a way to be cheerful. Just seeing those crinkly eyes and that shiny bald pate made Adin smile.

"Ah, Adin, my young friend, this is a pleasant surprise! What brings you to our abbey so unexpectedly?" The abbot poured wine into Adin's empty glass. "Taking a bit of holiday from all your royal obligations?" He reached for an unused glass and poured wine for himself, then sipped joyfully. "What do you think of our last season's vermillion? Not bad, eh?"

"Actually, Father, I'm here to get the map."

The abbot nearly choked on his wine. A blush of red filled the old man's face as his countenance dropped. Slowly, with a slight shake of his hand, he lowered his glass and set it on the table. A hush came over the once-boisterous group in the dining hall. A younger monk touched the abbot on the shoulder. "Father, are you not well?"

Ignoring the concerned men around him, the abbot reached across the table—just missing the wine decanter—and grasped Adin's tunic in a flash. "Come with me," he whispered, looking around at the worried faces. He spoke to those assembled and forced a smile. "I am fine, just swallowed wrong. Please, everyone . . ." With a sweep of his hand, he encouraged them to finish their meal, and the din in the room resumed. With Adin in tow, he walked briskly out of the dining hall to the vestry. As soon as they were inside, he latched the door.

"My, my, please tell me I did not hear you correctly." The abbot stood facing Adin, waiting, his eyes almost pleading. His thick, bushy eyebrows scrunched together in one long line and his hands nervously played with the cord around his ample belly.

"I have been sent here to retrieve the map."

He threw his arms in the air as if frightening away a flock of birds. "Heavens, son, by whom? Do you have any idea what you are doing?"

Adin sank down in a chair by a case of old books. So, it was true!

The abbot sighed and sat beside him. He drummed his fingers on a trunk that served as a low table and sighed again.

"Father, before I tell you my story," Adin began, "perhaps you should tell me what you know about the map. I believe the one who sent me is trustworthy, but I have known you since I was a small child. I know you won't hide the truth, or try to lead me astray."

The abbot sank into his chair and rubbed his eyes. For the first time in Adin's memory, the abbot lost his smile.

"My, my, Adin, you have grown wise and cautious, and I applaud this. No one here knows about the map but me, and it has been many long years since anyone came seeking it." He leaned close to Adin and his cheeks flushed red.

"You see, lad, when I received my appointment as a young man, the head abbot who chose me as his successor told me what I am about to tell you. But, oh, my dear boy, know this—I took an oath not to speak a word of the map to anyone and I have kept that oath my entire life. But for you, Adin, I will break that oath—I must. Not because I know you to be good and true, because that is of little concern. It is because of this."

The abbot jumped up and hurried over to the desk and, reaching into his coat pocket, brought out a ring of iron keys. Adin watched as he unlocked a drawer and withdrew a small gold-trimmed pouch, which he presented to Adin with trembling hands.

With his eyes, the abbot urged Adin to look inside. Slowly, Adin reached his fingers into the pouch, and what he withdrew caused his breath to catch.

He would know that locket anywhere. He held it in his hand, and then turned it over to find the same ancient scribbling engraved on the back. Immediately, he felt for the chain around his neck and fingered it thoughtfully. "Is this Aletha's?" he asked.

The abbot sat back down and spoke quietly, his face animated. "Ah, no. Adin, this abbey was built centuries ago, as you know. A wealthy patron from a distant land provided the means and the land this abbey was built upon. The construction took many, many years, and this person often came and watched the progress until its completion. It is said that the patron provided the plans for the building, which were followed in secrecy, and . . ." The abbot cleared his throat. "I am guessing you have been told about the unusual layout of the structure underground."

Adin nodded but said nothing. The abbot continued. "When the abbey was completed, the patron—by that time very old— visited one last time. Supposedly, the patron gave this locket \ to the head abbot, making him promise to keep it secret, telling him about the map that had been placed in hiding in a chamber below. He was to pass on the locket—and the secret—to the next head abbot, and so on down the line. He was told many would come and try to steal the map, and that it had been secreted away because of its power and importance. But—listen! He was also informed that one day a special man would arrive, the one the map was meant for." The abbot pointed to Adin's neck. "That man would be wearing the identical locket around his neck. Only he would possess the key, and only he could find the map."

Adin's mouth fell open. "Heavens! The key! I know nothing of a key—I forgot to ask Ta'man for it." Adin sighed in frustration and clenched his teeth. He jumped to his feet. "I have been so stupid and have made this long journey in vain. I am sorry, Father, I must leave . . ."

The abbot stopped him with his hand. He picked up the locket and opened it. Adin looked over at the abbot's hands.

"It's empty. I don't understand," Adin said.

"The one who keeps the locket keeps the key. Or so it is said." He pointed again to Adin's neck. Adin, confused, unclasped the chain around his neck and showed the locket to the abbot. "But, look," he protested, "there is nothing inside but one hair from my mother's head." He carefully unlatched the hook and, upon opening the locket, revealed the small strand of copper hair. The hermit's words came to mind, that he must use the key to unlock the trunk.

This hair was the key! And Ta'man must have known, must have seen Adin's locket around his neck. No wonder he sent him off with such assurance. But how could he have known about his mother's strand of hair? Only he and Aletha knew what the lockets contained. And for that matter, had their mother known something about the locket in the abbey, and the map? Or was all this just coincidence—again?

Adin slowly closed the ornament and placed it back around his neck. The abbot waved Adin to his seat. "Only the one with the locket was to be shown the secret stairs down to the labyrinth—the real stairs. For there are numerous false entrances."

The abbot pondered long and hard. "Adin, you mentioned someone—Ta'man, was it? Is he the one who sent you, and what did he tell you?"

As Adin recounted his story, the abbot listened, nodding his head and wringing his hands. He asked no questions, and when Adin was finished, he closed his eyes in thought. Adin waited quietly as night fell and the room grew dark.

Finally, the abbot opened his eyes and, finding a flint, lit the oil lamp on the desk. The room brightened, giving an intimacy to the space that ensconced them. "Well, then. What you have been told is true and proves the fellow trustworthy. Although I was never informed that the map could transport one through time. Imagine that. And I know nothing about a curse. My, my, makes one's head spin, it does."

The abbot picked up the locket that rested on the table. "I do know one thing you may find of interest. The writing on the back. A scrap of parchment used to be in the pouch, but it has long since crumbled to dust. Fortunately, one of the first abbots wrote down the ancient writing—and its translation."

Adin stared as the abbot rummaged through his mind and recited the words he had committed to memory. "*Soom kow'tham leb; ahabah 'az ma'veth.* The first part means 'Set me as a seal upon your heart,' and the second means . . ."

Adin closed his eyes and mouthed the words silently as the abbot spoke, for these were words the prince would never forget as long as he lived.

"'. . . Love is as strong as death.'"

ELEVEN

"HERE YOU ARE, my dear boy." The abbot stopped at the fourth door, which was identical to the other three they had passed. The lantern he held cast a bright light down the rough stone floor of the hallway. All was quiet in the abbey; most were still asleep. Earlier, Adin and the head abbot had found three of the monks in the kitchen preparing breakfast, and they had eaten their fill in silence, along with a strong pot of tea. Darkness still shrouded the world, so as Adin followed the abbot through the abbey, he could barely make out the shapes of the trees outside the windows. A slight wind whistled down the hall from a drafty door, causing the lantern's flame to flicker.

Adin's satchel was slung across his back, and in his arms he carried the box of mice. With a worried look, the abbot handed Adin the lantern and then put his hands on the prince's shoulders. "Heaven guide you, Adin. Use caution, and be brave."

"Thank you, Father. I hope we will meet again. Soon."

The abbot nodded his head vigorously and wiped a tear from his eye. He waved Adin toward the door and hurried down the hallway. Just then, the morning bell started chiming, awakening the monks to start their day. Adin paused a moment, then placed his hand on the latch. The door opened and a cool, stale air blew upon his face. Old broken stairs led down into blackness, but Adin mustered his will and, with the lantern held out in front of him, cautiously put one foot in front of the other, descending into nothingness.

Down he went; Adin lost count of the stairs. The air grew cooler and acrid and the steps more steep. At one point the stairs twisted in a spiral, the passageway so low that Adin had to bend and duck his head. Finally, he arrived at a landing with three openings. Holding up the light, he could see that each doorway led down a long corridor into more darkness. Adin took a deep breath and hoped these mice were not very fast. Already his leg throbbed with pain from navigating the steps.

He unlatched the box and pulled out a mouse. Stroking it gently, he whispered, "All right, I'm going to follow you. Show me the way." He set the mouse on the rough stone floor and watched as it sniffed curiously at its surroundings. It lifted its head and twitched its whiskers, its eyes darting as it looked around. Finally, it put a tiny nose to the ground and scampered through the opening to the left. Adin kept his eyes on the mouse, which stopped and sniffed in spurts, allowing Adin to limp steadily behind it. Cold seeped into Adin's bones, and he fastened his cloak tighter. He paid no heed to the many twists and turns he took, or the many closed doors he passed. All his concentration was on the mouse.

Suddenly, Adin heard a noise, and he stiffened. A pitiful moan came from behind, sending a chill down his back. He spun around to see who or what was following him, but the blackness revealed nothing. And then he realized the mouse was gone!

In a panic, Adin hurried around the corner and let out a breath of relief. The rodent was there, about to go through another passageway, and Adin pressed hard to catch up. After a while, Adin heard other sounds that froze his heart: voices muttering in the air, muted sobs, cursing, yelling. Sometimes the voices sounded as if they were right next to him, on the other side of a door he was passing. Other times he could swear they were inside his head. He fought every instinct in his heart that pleaded with him to answer the cries of the lost. His chest clenched when he saw the shape of a man, just a shadow, cross the tunnel up ahead. His breath caught in his throat when the shape stopped for a moment and turned to face him, but Adin forced himself to look away and follow the mouse's lead.

After what seemed like hours, Adin entered a large room. Doors lined both sides, and only one corridor leading out the other end. Adin waited and watched as the mouse sniffed at a door and then, unexpectedly, squeezed itself flat and slid under it. Adin was about to open the door and follow, then caught himself. He stopped suddenly, then collapsed onto the floor. In his weariness he had forgotten there were still two more mice in the box. What was he thinking? He needed to rest; and at least now he could stop awhile and catch his breath. His throat was parched, and he clenched his teeth to keep them from chattering.

As he drank some water and ate a muffin from his satchel, he could hear footsteps approaching, but nothing appeared. Rubbing his leg and back helped ease some of the pain, but Adin was already exhausted. This task was taking a long time, and anxiety was wearing him down. He turned his thoughts to Aletha and what she would do if she were here. Smiling, he remembered her poking him with a sword, telling him to quit complaining and get on his feet. Her eyes sparkled and her boisterous laugh rang in the air. She would even find this adventure exciting, no doubt—chasing mice down hallways and running from scary sounds. Adin chuckled and got to his feet. He put the satchel back on and withdrew another mouse from the box.

After mumbling a few encouraging words to the creature, he set it down, and off it went. Again, Adin trudged in pursuit, passing more doors until he felt he must certainly be retracing his steps. The mouse led him up a dozen stairs, then down twice as many. He was sure he had stumbled through the same passageways and was going in circles. Upon reaching the large room with the two rows of doors, his fear was confirmed. Would he be stuck in this maze forever, or was there truly a way out? He watched as the second mouse slipped under the same door as the first, and now he grew more worried. Maybe that mouse was just following its friend. How could he be sure they were showing him the way to the map? This whole task suddenly seemed ludicrous and futile.

Once more Adin slumped to the floor. His eyes were drawn to something moving at the end of the corridor leading out of the room. Adin strained to see what looked like a man—a man gesturing excitedly for Adin to draw closer. A feeling of lassitude came over him, and without thinking Adin stood and started down the hall. In the lantern's glow, the man took shape. He was dressed as one of the monks, with a dark robe and friendly face. He smiled at Adin and kept waving him along with his hand. Maybe one of the monks had come to help him, to get him out of the confused circling he found himself in. Maybe he knew the mice were not doing their job. With a sigh of relief, Adin turned the corner after the monk, but when he met the man's eyes in the bright light of the lantern, the hair on his neck stiffened.

What he saw frightened him to the bones. What had appeared to be a benevolent, encouraging face turned into a pale, vacant mask overlaying features that blurred and shifted as Adin stared. A darkness rippled under the skin, like small, crawling beetles. Adin shuddered. He shook the stupor from his head and quickly ran back to the large room and fell to the floor, hiding his head with his arms. Eventually, his breath slowed and his heart stopped pounding against his chest. Gathering up nerve, he lifted his eyes and looked around. All was quiet and the hallway empty. Every muscle in his body screamed and the putrid air made him gag. He knew he needed to end this quickly or he would lose his wits.

Setting the last mouse on the ground, Adin concentrated hard, shutting out distracting sounds and sights. Without allowing a thought to enter his mind, he kept his eyes pinned on the mouse as it sniffed and wandered its way through the maze. Hours dragged on, and Adin ignored the aches and fatigue. Finally, to his chagrin, he veered right through an opening and found himself once more in the large room. He wasn't surprised.

He stood and watched. Minutes went by as the mouse sniffed under each closed door, lingering a long while at the one the other mice had scurried under. Then it raised its little head and shook it. Glancing around, it rose on its hind legs and sniffed again. Then, without delay, it ran past Adin to the other side of the hall and in a flash scooted under the door at the end.

Adin left the box on the floor and unlatched the door. As he shone the lantern in front of him, he saw he had entered a large, high-ceilinged room, empty except for the small wooden trunk resting on the ground before him. He sighed deeply and set down the lantern. Unclasping the locket, he warily lifted out the strand of gleaming hair and, leaning over the trunk, inserted it in the keyhole. With a startling hissing sound, the hair glowed and disappeared, and then Adin heard a soft click as the top of the trunk popped slightly open. He lifted the lid to find a small, rolled-up parchment, aged and brown. Yet he was surprised when he picked it up that it felt soft and pliable, not brittle as he expected. Remembering Ta'man's warning, he carefully placed the map into his satchel and walked across the room to the wall. He ran his hands along the surface, found the loose stone, and pushed, and to his right a wall of stones parted to reveal a narrow passageway leading upward.

As he ascended the stairs, the air grew warmer and smelled cleaner, which dispelled some of Adin's chill and achiness. By the time he arrived at the top, where he saw a small wooden door, his head had cleared as if he had just awoken from a dream. How long had he been down there, wandering miles through those endless hallways?

He realized he would never know, for when he slid the bolt open and stumbled out onto the field alongside the abbey garden, the sun was barely coming up in the east. And the morning bell, waking the monks in the abbey, clanged three last somber rings.

The morning air refreshed Adin. He took deep breaths and looked out on the peaceful hillside spread before him. Sheep nibbled grass, the bells on their collars tinkling quietly. As Adin walked over to the large oak, he noticed a monk go into the garden to gather something. Finding a secluded place out of sight, Adin set down his satchel and took out the map. The hermit had told him to attune it right away, before anyone else could do it, and this was as good a place as any.

Upon unrolling the parchment, he could see faint lines but could not make them out. They looked like pencil sketching that had faded over time. He held the map as Ta'man had shown him and watched as a small image materialized in the center of the parchment. Adin recognized the pentacle with its five points and inset star. The outline was drawn first, and then silver and gold filled it in like a spreading dye. The blue gemstone in the center grew luminescent. And then the image completely faded. Adin stood and waited.

Suddenly, a strange tingling came over him. From his toes, up his back, until it filled the top of his head. He watched as his hands, shaking, gripped the edges of the map as if they were glued there. Fear took hold of him and, instinctively, Adin tried to drop the map, but his fingers stuck to the parchment. Helplessly, he watched as the blank surface filled, as if an invisible hand held a paintbrush.

First, broken lines appeared, then they joined to form shapes, and the shapes solidified into trees, fences, a garden—and then the abbey. Colors filled in spaces like a paint wash, and by the time the drawing stopped, Adin held in his hands a beautiful rendition of his surroundings. There were the abbey and garden, and in the center of the map a glowing dot marked the spot under the oak tree where he stood. Instantly, the tingling vanished from his body, and Adin could move his fingers. A strange shudder passed through him, and somehow he knew he had finished the attunement. He quickly rolled up the map and stashed it in his satchel.

A wave of fatigue engulfed him, now that he had gotten this far. He felt sleepy, as if he had been awake for days on end. He knew he would need to recover from this morning's adventure before going any farther. And he needed to return to Sherbourne, or somewhere near it, before he tackled this journey, this *ma'gur*. It wouldn't do to make the trek back in time this far from the city walls and the sacred spring. What if he arrived when there were no roads, no clear path to lead him there? No, it made more sense to position himself close to the city, since the map would only move him through time, not space.

Adin couldn't think of a safer, more comforting place to rest than here, under his favorite tree, in this place drenched with so many treasured memories. He unrolled his bedroll behind the oak, where no one would stumble upon him, and wrapped himself in his thick woolen blanket. There was no hurry now, for what did time matter?

He had all the time in the world.

TWELVE

LATE MORNING sun streaked through the branches of the oak, warming Adin's face and nudging him awake. Feeling as rested as if he had slept a week, he stood and stretched the kinks from his back. Sounds from the abbey carried on the breeze as the monks busily went about their daily tasks. As Adin gathered up his bedroll and satchel and headed for the back entrance of the abbey, a monk in the garden noticed him and hurried inside. In moments, the head abbot ran through the rows of corn toward Adin, his face beaming with relief.

The abbot grabbed Adin's shoulders and shook him energetically. "My, my, Adin, my dear boy, Adin! Why, you've made it out of the maze, and none the worse for wear, as far as I can tell."

Before Adin could speak, the abbot entwined an arm through his and led him toward the abbey. He leaned close and in a harsh whisper asked, "Did you find what you were seeking?" When Adin nodded, the abbot grasped the emblem hanging around his neck and kissed it. "Ah, thank the heavens that business is done. And now where will you go?"

When Adin explained his need to return to Sherbourne, the abbot offered to drive him back in one of the produce carts. Adin gratefully accepted the offer; just the thought of walking that long way back made his leg twinge. So, after a hearty lunch and a trip to the pantry to fill his satchel, the two hitched the mules and headed down the road. During the trip, the abbot asked about Adin's ordeal, and couldn't help making noises of astonishment and horror as Adin related his story. When they arrived at the entrance to the King's wood, Adin reassured the abbot they would be safe traveling through the forbidden forest. It would take hours to circumvent it on the commoners' road, and Adin didn't want to waste another day. With some trepidation the abbot acquiesced, and despite his calm demeanor, Adin noticed the abbot startling at every small noise, his eyes darting from side to side.

They passed without incident through the gate that led down to the north wall, and at the crossroads they said their farewells, the abbot giving Adin a big hug and a pat on the head. Adin watched as the cart moved off west along the commoners' road, passing a few midday travelers. A soft autumn wind tickled his hair as he stood and thought.

He was maybe a half-league from the palace. He could make out a guard walking outside the gate. The broken walls of the city stretched out in both directions and, behind them, the palace rose from the knoll. He walked a short distance off the road to one of the huge slabs of stone that lay half-buried in the dirt. Just like the pieces of bluestone in the orchard, this was one of the ancient stones that had, for some reason, been hauled off the knoll and had ended up discarded, partially buried in lichen and moss, with patches of grass and plants fastened on its face. Surrounding the stone, a few red-leafed maples hung on to the last stubborn leaves of fall, and their fat trunks afforded a partial barricade against curious eyes.

Wanting a good vantage point but needing to stay secluded, Adin determined this spot would do. He hoped the spot would remain isolated when he arrived at the other end of the map. He shuddered to think what might happen to him if he arrived inside the stone wall of a house. Here he had a good chance of the ground remaining unchanged; he could find no evidence of old building foundations.

Adin cringed at the overwhelming idea of moving through time. What would it feel like? Surely if it was dangerous, Ta'man would not have encouraged him to go—and return. And if the map had been made by someone hoping to save Sherbourne, then could it be evil? Adin was just going to have to trust this *ma'gur*. It was his destiny—or so it seemed. Ta'man's words rang in his ears: "It is the glory of God to conceal things, but the glory of kings to search things out." *So then*, Adin told himself, *let the search begin.*

After taking the map from the satchel, Adin looked around. The midday sun was westering, and fast-moving blankets of clouds cast shadows that skimmed over the land in shifting patterns. A peddler's cart headed toward the gate, pots and pans banging against the sideboards, the driver urging on a stubborn black mule. All else was quiet; not even a bird alighted nearby. Now was as good a time as any.

Adin adjusted the satchel on his back and stepped into the small clearing behind a large maple. He unrolled the map and held it as before, and a tingling started up his fingers and spread to his arms. His eyes were transfixed on the lines as they miraculously materialized from the parchment, piecing together a picture of the landscape in which Adin found himself. Brown trees sprouted leaves; withered grass multiplied in a series of brush strokes. The large slab of rock appeared before him; even the lichen and weeds were depicted in detail. Spreading outward, the scenery emerged like a spill across a table. Now his whole body prickled as if a thousand pins were poking him. The map was now a part of him, not just stuck to his fingers, but more like an extension of them. He and the map were joined.

Finally, color spread to the edges of the map. The palace on the knoll, the wall, the north gate, even the peddler's cart had a place in the painting he held in his hands. And in the middle was a small bright dot, not gold or yellow or any color, but like the flash of fire when it first ignites tinder. At the far end of the map was another mark, a tiny pentacle that glowed dully. This would be his destination—and now only one thing remained for Adin to do: walk.

Adin was unprepared for what followed. Holding the map before him, he lifted a foot and the map exploded in a swirl of color. And not just the map—the world around him swiftly disintegrated, and Adin found himself in a whirlwind of chaos. A deafening noise, incoherent and many-layered, hurt his ears—as if a cacophony of a thousand voices and daily noises of years were crushed together.

Adin ventured a fearful glance to his side, and dizziness assailed him. Gone were the familiar shapes of his world; instead, patterns tumbled, rose, and fell, with such speed as to make them unrecognizable. He stepped slowly, watching as the glow of fire made a trail across the page. Mesmerized by the path of the flame, Adin did not look at his feet until he had walked many steps. Then, with a glance down, he cried out, but his voice was swallowed by the din surrounding him.

Below him, his footstep glowed with a tiny outline of fire, hanging upon nothing. The world underneath was gone, giving way to a dark chasm that sucked light and form to its depths. Adin swooned and felt as if he were falling, but he found nothing to hold on to, and his hands remained frozen to the parchment. Yet he didn't fall, and with that realization he caught his breath and looked again to the map. Shaken, he walked on, and light flickered all around, like night and day alternating every second.

Water flowed across his boots, then receded. Out of the corner of his eye he saw what looked like hills rising, then falling, trees thickening, then gone. A flash of fire and a smell of choking smoke passed quickly, flashes of thunder and lightning, blue and black skies spinning overhead. A strange thud hit his body full force, then passed through him. *What in heaven was that?* Adin kept up his pace.

Cold and heat took turns washing over him; he passed through a downpour of rain, the aroma of turned earth, falling snow, sewage; and he noted the sound of water falling, tumbling, flooding to his left. A rivulet expanded into a huge river, then gradually thinned, meandering like a snake at his side. A blast of wind, howling, and mountains withering in the distance. Then sand and dust filled his nose and mouth, causing Adin to cough.

Adin looked at the glowing trail on the map; it touched the border of the parchment, but where was the star? Confused, he slowed his steps. The moon wheeled fast over his head, waxing and waning every few seconds. As he slowed, stars exploded like sparks from a fire, then the hot ball that was the sun raced from one horizon to another. Adin swooned again, his head spinning. Now the noise lessened; there were no voices shouting and pounding his ears. Only animal sounds—buzzing, humming, calling—puncturing the air in fits and starts.

A large patch of green coalesced in front of him, and the swirling shapes alongside him settled into brown and gray, shrinking down as if melting to the ground. Then came the smell of snow, and white filled the spaces around him, then a single cry, a bird wheeling in the sky, emerging from a funnel of blue that spread wider and wider until it filled the horizon before him. Adin stopped, and looking down, saw his boot standing on solid ground, an outline of dazzling light seeping out from underneath.

The day settled down around him like a flock of birds landing on a fence.

Quiet.

Far off in the distance, a sound of shifting rocks drew Adin's attention from the map. The maple trees were gone; there were none as far as the eye could see. Through a thinning haze Adin could barely make out a small piece of the slab that was buried in front of him. Now, under a hillock, only one edge of the bluestone peeked out. Still holding the map, Adin tried to peer through the glare and dust. He could see nothing as light filtered out across the countryside and revealed rolling hills rising to a barren knoll. Adin froze in shock.

Barren it was. The city walls were gone; only mossy boulders dotted the line where it had once stood. Rubble littered the ground as far as his eye could see. There were no houses, no buildings, no palace at all. A weak sun shone overhead.

Adin caught movement in the distance. A pack of wolves moved in unison, heads lolling as they made their way down the hill. Adin looked down at the map in terrible recognition of what he had just done. The trail he had taken across the map, now fading and faint, led to the boundary edge of the parchment. But now he understood why he couldn't find the pentacle marking his destination. It sat on the opposite end, in the opposite direction Adin had walked! He had landed, not in his past, but his future!

Adin rolled up the map, stuffed it in his satchel, and ran as fast as he could, his heart pounding so hard he thought it would burst in his chest. Scaling a huge rock, carelessly banging his legs and scraping his hands, Adin panted and clawed until he reached the top. Breathless, he forced himself to stand and look out over the remains of the city of Sherbourne. But, even before he saw it, he knew in his heart what lay before him.

The words of the *qa'lal* came storming into his mind. *"Until cities lie waste without inhabitants and houses without people and the land is utterly desolate."*

Utterly desolate. There was nothing at all left of the great city—no houses, no shops, no bridge, no people. Nothing. Only piles of stones overrun with weeds, and a trickle of water running through the land—what was left of the river Heresh. Adin slumped down on the rocky promontory and sobbed. The curse had run its course and Adin had been powerless to stop it. How could he have made such a foolish mistake and gone the wrong way? This was his future, and there was nothing he could do to prevent it.

He lifted his eyes to the devastation. Or was there?

Adin looked out over the wasteland, calming his heart. What if he went back the other way, the right way? He had the map; he had just gone in the wrong direction. Wasn't there still time to go back to the beginning? Could he then prevent this future from occurring? Who was to say whether this outcome was inevitable, or if it could be changed? Regardless, he had no choice—whether or not all was lost he still had to try. The star still appeared on the map, so as long as he followed it, why wouldn't he arrive at the right time?

Adin forced himself to look one last time out over the land, to set the sight to memory. This had been the great kingdom of Sherbourne, his home, Aletha's home. This was a future he would do all in his power to prevent.

He turned and set his face to the past, climbing down the rocks one step at a time and hobbling weakly to where he first arrived at this heaven-forsaken place. When he reached the bluestone rock, he saw his footprint—glowing with a dazzling light. Maybe he could retrace his steps and then continue to his destination. All he had to do was step into that print and put one foot in front of the other. How hard could that be?

The lonely desolation of his surroundings brought tears streaming down his face. *Oh, Aletha, there has to be some hope. How can I do this without you?* Adin wiped his eyes and drank water from his jug—clean, pure water he wished could wash away the bitter sadness he felt.

As he opened the map and lowered a foot into the print etched in the dirt, he heard a voice, the voice of a kind, reassuring stranger who, many years ago, had looked into his eyes and made him a promise.

"Surely there is a future, and your hope will not be cut off."

If only Adin could believe that as deeply as the stranger had.

THIRTEEN

ALETHA COULD HEAR her father's angry voice echoing down the hall, but she pushed aside the trepidation she felt. Just this morning she had gotten wind of another riot in the city; this time black marketeers were forcing bread prices up, and those trying to run their family businesses were receiving threats. Sherbourne was at the mercy of sinister, greedy gangs squeezing illicit profits from every corner. Just yesterday she had ridden down to the town hall to listen to grievances and tried to assure the throng of frightened citizens that the King would step in and restore order. Though they wanted to have confidence in her words, their hopeless, pleading eyes belied that, and Aletha felt literally sick to her stomach over the plight of her people.

Resolute, she tried to call for an emergency meeting of the councillors, but Rasha reacted to her fervor as if she were hysterical and needing mollification. With his emotionless gray eyes he dismissed her, making her blood roil. It took all her self-control not to spit in his face. Aletha realized she had been bottling up her frustration for months now. Maybe the councillors had been overseeing Sherbourne's affairs long enough; she would confront the King and persuade him to remove their authority. Something must be done—and quickly!

A servant hurried past her, a man close to her own age, with an ashen expression on his face. He briefly met Aletha's gaze and dropped his head in sorrow. Aletha stopped and watched as he slinked away. What in heaven's name was happening in the palace? Her home had always been a pleasant, peaceful place for the servants, who were always treated with respect and appreciation. Now, everywhere Aletha turned, she encountered looks of fear and sadness. If her father's raging temper did not subside soon, there would be no servants left for him to yell at.

Quickening her pace, Aletha took a deep breath and threw open the doors to the Council chambers. The King sat at his desk; sunlight filtering in through the colored window panes streaked across the parchments laid out in front of him. Even before she could make out words, she knew he was researching the firebird. His finger ran over an illustration of the bird as if caressing it; his eyes glazed over as he stared mindlessly at the image. She could tell the parchment was old, and the drawing was a simple representation of the creature, depicting the long, flowing feathers and the regal turn of its head. But, Aletha thought wryly, the King would never be able to see the firebird's true beauty; his voracious greed trapped him in the deception of appearances.

Adin had been right—the firebird was only a mirror, a mirror of your heart. Whatever longing entrapped you, whatever weakness imprisoned you, she would reflect a hundredfold. Aletha grimaced. This obsession was leading her father to *ho'lay'la*, to madness, but Aletha felt helpless to prevent the King's downfall. She feared he would wither away, and that she could do nothing but just stand there and watch.

The King tore his eyes from the firebird. "Close the doors," he said calmly. Aletha was aware of the King's stare as she did as he asked. She came back and stood before him, aware of the quiet filling the chamber. The King wore his heavy robe in the cold room; Aletha noticed that the fire had not been lit and her breath came out steamy. She wore only a simple gown, and soon the chill air seeped into her bones.

The King motioned her over and stood. "Here, you're shivering." He removed his outer robe and offered it to her. Aletha went to his side, and her father draped the heavy wool around her shoulders. She could smell his mustiness on the fabric as she clutched it around her. She felt small and vulnerable by his side, a feeling she tried to dismiss.

"Father, we need to talk. Sherbourne needs help, and I want to sit down and make some suggestions of what should be done."

The King chuckled and patted the chair beside him. "Oh, by all means, my daughter. We can let you play queen awhile. Tell me—what is bothering you?"

Aletha sat in the chair, but scooted far enough away to face her father and see his eyes. "You are not taking me seriously. Do you have any idea what is going on in the city? Do your councillors tell you anything?"

The King reached over and took Aletha's hands in his. "Aletha, sweet child, why do you worry your pretty head about all this business? You are young—and so beautiful. You should be out attending balls and parties, enjoying yourself. Not worrying about the plight of peasants."

"I *wouldn't* worry if you were doing your job!" Aletha pulled back her hands. "I care for the people of Sherbourne—and they are suffering because of your neglect. What happened to you? Once you cared for your people. You used to go down to the city and listen to them—now you never leave the palace, or have any of the merchants in to report to you. You are completely out of touch."

The King leaned back in his chair and scowled. A strange look came over his face and he spoke to the wall. "Do you know, when I met your mother, I nearly fell down at her feet. She was the most beautiful, the most perfect thing I had ever seen. Things of beauty are rare in this world, Aletha. I knew the moment I met your mother that I must have her. She would be mine to gaze upon day and night." Aletha noticed her father's fingers tremble. "And then she withered away, day by day, her beauty draining out of her until there was nothing left . . ."

Aletha felt her throat close up and tears well up in her eyes. She would never forget the last time she saw her mother, lying helpless on the bed. The King cleared his throat and turned to Aletha.

"When she . . . left . . . nothing could fill that space. I could find nothing in this world to match her beauty, to erase this longing that eats away at me. And then I learned of the firebird." He squinted his eyes in determination. "Aletha, how can I make you understand? I must have that creature; I will do anything to possess her, for she alone will make me happy. I know this deep in my heart. Once I have the firebird, all will be well. She will be the pride of my kingdom, and people will come from the ends of the earth to see her and pay tribute to me. So do not worry your head about these trifles."

Aletha was speechless. She watched as her father's gaze drifted back to the drawing of the bird, the parchment pulling him like a magnet. As his eyes stroked the bird, the King forgot Aletha was in the room. Aletha sat and stared at her father in amazement. He was so mistaken. If the firebird was brought to the palace, he would lose himself in her magnificence and never find his way back. Even now, he was so far gone down that path that he did not hear a word his own daughter said. The kingdom and all its troubles were like a murmur on a faraway shore.

She thought of all the hunters off after the firebird, spurred on by dreams of riches and power. She thought of Adin, poor Adin, wanting so much to win a father's love, a love he would never have. How could she have let Adin go on that futile quest? She was *kes'eel*, a complete fool! Why hadn't she tried harder to stop him? Aletha berated herself. What if something happened to him; what if he got hurt?

Suddenly, fear washed over her, and she knew she couldn't stay in the palace a moment longer. She had to find Adin and stop him! Sherbourne needed him here; between the two of them, she and Adin could try to stop this insanity and impose some order. Aletha knew she couldn't tackle this alone.

She stood and handed the King his robe. He lifted his eyes and looked at her.

"Aletha," he whispered, taking a long look at her. "You have grown to be so beautiful, so radiant . . ." The King dropped the robe to the floor and went over to his daughter. He ran a hand through her wavy hair. Aletha shuddered, unmoving.

"Father," she said sternly, "I am going to find Adin. He is off seeking your firebird, thinking foolishly he might win your favor."

The King kept his hand on her head and laughed. "He is a fool; he will never catch the firebird. He is worthless and spineless." His voice shifted abruptly, anger rising in his throat. "He is a traitor; he is not seeking the firebird, but allies—to rally against me! But I am prepared for him. The moment he returns, he will be caught and executed! I will not stand for treason in my own household!" He laughed, and Aletha, stunned, saw a shadow drift across his features. The King's eyes grew vacant and his skin paled. Aletha sought to pull away, but his hand grabbed her hair more tightly. He clenched his teeth and cocked his head. In a harsh whisper he breathed into Aletha's ear. "You, my stunning daughter, will be queen. You have so much to learn, and I, I have so much to teach you." He buried his face in her hair and breathed deeply. "Every beautiful thing is mine, and once the firebird is captured, she will be mine as well. Nothing will be denied me, nothing!"

"You are mad! Let go of me! What are you doing?!" Aletha pulled harder, but the King kept gripping her hair. With his other hand he grabbed her waist and jerked her tightly to his chest, and Aletha could smell his sweat and feel the scratchiness of his beard against her face. She flailed in his arms, horrified, as the King laughed at her struggles. As he lifted her chin, she managed to free an arm and slap him hard across the face. The King laughed harder.

Aletha shook her head in shock and wriggled out of his clutches. As she fled through the chamber doors, he called out after her in anger, his voice booming down the hall.

"I will not be denied!"

With the map in his hands, Adin retraced his steps slowly through the pandemonium of time. This time he did not look down at the crevasse below, but watched his trail blaze across the parchment in the direction of the pentacle. He longed to cover his ears and muffle the screeching wind with its fell voices and incessant moaning. Summer and winter, day and night tumbled him like a rock in an avalanche, causing his stomach to wrench. He shut his eyes against the flickering lights that stung his head, peering out only enough to glance at the map and make sure of his direction through time.

A huge tremor nearly knocked him down. Once more he felt a hard thud as something crashed into him, then passed through him like a ghost. He fought the urge to turn around and look back. Out of the corner of his eye he could make out the glowing footprints at his feet, and he could see the fainter outlines of his former steps leading into the future. Once he reached the point on the map where he had begun his journey, he continued on without stopping, this time in the right direction.

Time moved strangely as he traversed the map. For ages, a clamoring assaulted his ears, and smells of cook fires, roasting meat, wet grass from rain wafted by. Chills racked his body as cold and heat washed over him; one moment he was soaked through, another moment he sweltered from the heat of a blue sun. A bolt of energy shook him senseless, and for a moment he blacked out, the world screeching to a halt around him. Quickly, he resumed walking, and watched the flare of light trickle across the map, nearing the star.

What seemed like hours dragged on, and Adin wondered how much more he could take with his head spinning and stomach knotting. He suddenly grew very thirsty and yearned for the water jug in his satchel. But there was no way to let go of the map until he stopped, so he ignored his dry mouth and pressed on.

He could make out nothing around him except a flurry of movement as shapes rose and fell. Soon the area near him thickened with shadow, and Adin felt the panic of claustrophobia. His skin tingled from a thousand tiny touches, things brushing him, pushing at him, and leaning against him. He kept walking, breathing hard. His back hurt and he tried to straighten, but nothing alleviated the pain stabbing his back and leg. Snow buried him, but he walked through the drifts into bitter cold. All light vanished, leaving him in absolute darkness. He could see nothing, not even the map—only the pinprick of light as it snaked across the parchment, and the bright outline of his footstep etched in nothingness below him.

Then fear gripped him. He could make out a wavering shape, a person walking toward him while the world around him teetered in chaos. How could this be? Adin slowed as the shape came at him. He knew he must not stop until he reached his destination, yet the person approaching was about to collide with him. He steeled his nerves for the impact, but right before he felt it, he got a glimpse of a man in a ragged dark cloak, a beard on his chin, and strangely familiar eyes. Glaring light obscured Adin's vision, but it seemed the man was just as surprised by the encounter, and before Adin had time to react, the man staggered to avoid a collision and was gone.

Adin limped on, badly shaken. Every muscle screamed with fatigue. If only he could stop and rest, drink some water, and rub his leg. He checked his trail; he was almost there. With a renewed determination he walked faster, which made him grow dizzy. Colors spun all around him in a frenzy, and Adin had long since lost feeling in his toes. Energy seeped away from his limbs; it took all his effort to keep lifting one foot after the other.

Finally, he reached the boundary of the map, and Adin was relieved, for he could go no farther. The tiny flame of light entered the pentacle on the map, and Adin slowed to a stop. As he stepped one last time, the blue gemstone in the center of the silver star flared brightly, then faded.

Adin sighed deeply and waited while the swirling calmed and the noise abated. Recognizable sounds returned to the world: birds chirping and rustling, a bell ringing far away. Still surrounded by darkness, Adin waited for his eyes to adjust and found himself in a dense thicket of trees, tangled in branches and leaves. The rich loamy smell of earth filled his nostrils and, looking down, Adin saw the bright glowing outline of his footstep on top of a forest floor of rotting leaves. Exhaling, he rolled up the map and stuffed it in his satchel. Without a moment's hesitation, he pulled out his water jug and drank in huge gulps.

Inching his way out of the branches, Adin realized the trees went on as far as he could see. He looked for the bluestone slab but could not find it. Weaving through the forest, Adin finally found a way out. Morning was breaking over the horizon, and the air was smoky and cool. He walked through a damp meadow thick with grass that came to his knees, and wading through it, like fording a stream, he came to a rise—and what he saw took his breath away.

Before him stood a newly built wall, stretching for leagues in both directions. Two towers inset in the wall stood tall, their roofs recently tiled. A rampart of dirt had been mounded against the outside of the wall, and there were wooden scaffolds and heavy equipment lying on the ground at intervals. Already, men were arriving to work, lifting and leveraging the quarried stone to fit into the gaps in the wall. As the morning sun hit the towers, they lit up in a blaze of silver. Adin looked beyond the wall to the knoll and his mouth dropped open.

The palace was not there; it hadn't yet been built. Instead, at the top of the hill stood dozens of the huge slabs of stone, and Adin could tell they had once, long ago, been erected in a circle around the spring, just as Reya had described. Some of the tall slabs stood four times the height of a man, and some were capped with a lintel across the top. How these heavy stones had been lifted into place boggled Adin's imagination.

Sunlight spilled over the knoll, lighting up the rocks, exposing their mossy faces in detail. Near the standing rocks were piles of smaller pieces, and even from where Adin stood he could tell these had once been part of the circle, but had been broken up and were being used to construct a building near the knoll, rectangular with a thatched roof. In fact, this was the only building Adin could see that was being built with rock.

Adin let his eyes wander over the hundreds of small shacks, built of wood logs, with posts of tree trunks as support. All these looked like homes, their roofs also thatched grass, with smoke drifting from their chimneys. Outside the north wall where he stood, there were no villages or homes, only dense woods covering the hillside. A dirt road encircled the walls, and as Adin approached the north gate, he saw a portcullis blocking the entrance. He hesitated, then wrapped his cloak tightly around him and approached the entrance to the city.

Two guards noticed Adin and pulled the ropes to raise the gate. They wore no uniforms, but each had a sword at his side. They eyed him carefully, but waved him through without a word.

Adin wondered about the time he found himself in. If the walls were just being completed, then this was early in Sherbourne's history—before it was even called by that name. Up until the siege, people had lived in scattered settlements across the countryside, and many groups had been nomadic. Some had settled down and farmed, while others had traveled with their goods, trading across the lands. But with war threatening, they were no longer safe from vicious raiders who left a swath of destruction in their wake. These attackers from the south burned homes and murdered those who resisted them.

Adin didn't know what land the assailants hailed from, but they were strong and menacing enough to force the people to unite—and to build a huge wall to enclose their city so they could defend themselves. With the walls intact, Adin guessed the decisive battle had yet to be fought, but when would it be? Today, next week, next year? History was unclear. He only knew that it would be a violent fight and many would die, but Sherbourne would emerge a strong city because of it. Adin shuddered. He prayed he would be able to find the Keeper and uncover the curse before he wound up fighting for his life in a bloodbath.

Adin kept his head down as he walked along the cobbled road through the gate. Fortunately, the plain cloak he wore drew no attention, although he did attract stares as he passed. But he was familiar with the looks in their eyes—they only saw a pathetic, deformed man limping down the lane, no one who would pose them any threat. Those he encountered were bundled against the chill of the morning, their clothes simple woven shirts and trousers, boots made of sheepskin. Few were out this early; some seemed on their way out the gate to help with constructing the wall, as they carried iron tools and pushed empty wooden carts. Adin moved on past the sentry shacks and into what were the beginnings of the city.

He was surprised to see so many trees inside the walls; they had been cleared only to make room for the houses and gardens. Adin guessed it was late fall, since the branches had lost most of their leaves. The cobbles soon ended, and dirt lanes ran in all directions. Every cottage he came upon was newly built, and the dwellings were close together, affording little privacy. These were not of quality construction; evidently, these structures had been erected in haste—for functionality and for warmth against the impending winter. Piles of chopped wood lay outside the doors; sheep grazed freely between the cottages, and a dog barked in the distance.

The dirt lanes had been muddied by recent rains, and as two guards on horses rode by, Adin pressed against the wall of one cottage, barely avoiding their splashing as the horses trotted through the shallow puddles. Smells of crowded conditions assaulted Adin's nose: breakfasts cooking over open fires, pigs rooting through the weeds, human waste dumped in the streets. He could feel a tension in the air as he walked along, unsure of where he was going. Was there a town center somewhere? Did people shop for food or goods? Adin had no clue, but he did not want to bring attention to himself by asking questions that would mark him as a stranger.

He thought of one place that would afford him a view of the city, and that was the top of the knoll. His curiosity prompted him to start climbing the hill; he wanted to see the giant rocks up close and the spring that would one day become the centerpiece of his courtyard.

Adin trudged up the muddy road as it wound around the scattering of houses until he caught sight of the stone building at the top of the hill. At least a dozen guards milled around, some talking together as others scanned the land below. He came to the last house and stopped, wondering if he should go farther. He imagined the building held some importance. Perhaps it served as the fortress for the city, where the guards lived and where weapons were kept.

Adin watched awhile, resting on a log, rubbing his forehead. Traveling through time had taken a toll on him; he could sorely use a hot bath and a hot meal, if either was to be found in this place. As he drank water and ate a piece of fruit from his satchel, he noticed men hauling crates into the "fortress." Two stood guard as goods went inside, then the doors were bolted and locked when the delivery was complete. Not wanting to step into trouble, Adin decided he would make his way back down—and save his sightseeing for another time.

As morning progressed, the lanes became crowded with people, most with olive skin and dark eyes. A busy, harried feeling seemed to drive them, and their tension was obvious, shown in the manner of their exchanges. Within a short distance Adin witnessed not a few arguments and grumbling between neighbors, and those he passed on the road did not smile or greet him but scowled or kept their heads bowed. What few children he saw went about chores with serious faces. Even they did not wave at Adin but stared at him with suspicion.

Without knowing many of the strange words, Adin recognized the sound and tone of the *law'az*, the ancient language. He could make out some of what was said, although the accent was wholly strange and their sentences were structured differently. He feared he would have a difficult time trying to speak as if he belonged there. The best thing for him to do was to say as little as possible and listen hard and learn. It would take time, but he was sure he could imitate the accent and pick up the right words. He just needed time.

In the midst of a section of cottages, Adin came upon a field crammed with squatters. Makeshift shelters of branches provided room for one or two to get protection from the elements, but all these little hovels rested on the mud, and the faces of those tending their cookfires displayed misery. In one area, large cauldrons of water steamed, and women dunked and squeezed clothing, then hung them to dry on lines of rope. Others picked through woven baskets of withered vegetables, selecting what was salvageable and tossing it into pots. The stench of crowded conditions nearly made Adin gag.

Few men lingered, and those he saw were either old or bandaged up; Adin wondered if the able-bodied ones were off seeking work—or helping with the battle preparations. As he walked along, he sensed the hopelessness and despair. Had they just arrived, having abandoned their family homes—for this?

Adin tried not to be disheartened. He let the throngs of people be his guide, for most headed east, around the base of the knoll. Squalor met his eyes wherever he looked, poverty evident in the scant and worn clothing and the meager plots of ground where residents dug in the soil, trying to pull up a few roots for soup. This was the beginning of the great city of Sherbourne—and he found it hard to believe. As much as he worried for the people of his time, his heart went out to these poor souls, knowing that when the siege fell upon them, their horrors would multiply. Famine, disease, grief—all these followed in the wake of battle, and even though Adin had never experienced war, it took little to unleash his imagination. But he reminded himself: he was not here to stop a war, or to fight a battle, but to prevent an even worse outcome— the attachment of the *qa'lal* to this once-sacred ground. All the struggles of this newborn city would come to naught if he failed in his *ma'gur*. His only task was to seek the Keeper, to look for the sign of the pentacle. But how—and where?

As the sun neared its apex, Adin grew fatigued. He had been walking down roads that all looked the same. Off in the distance was the east wall, and Adin could make out shapes of men walking the battlement. Crowds pushed past him as he limped along, and at one point he was knocked down to the ground without as much as a simple apology. Claustrophobia agitated him and suddenly he felt the impossibility of his task bearing down on him like a boulder. Here he was, in the midst of his own city, in a mob of people, and he had never felt so alone in his life. This was not his time, not his home; he had nowhere to go, knew no one. He had been mad to think he alone could accomplish this impossible undertaking. If only Aletha were with him—she would see him through this.

Adin wormed his way out from the crowd and into a tiny lane that was more like an alleyway. He caught his breath as he stumbled along, his throat choking with emotion. He tried to brush thoughts of home from his head, reminding himself he could go back anytime he wanted. Home was only, literally, steps away. Aletha's face came to him, and he wondered how she was faring without him. His mind filled with images of the King, of Reya, of the hermit and the pig—of a life that seemed so far off.

Adin followed the lane as it turned a corner, relieved to be free of the jostling mob. On both sides, the backs of the cottages crammed together. There were no lawns or gardens here, only rank-smelling trash piled up against the walls. He looked for a break in the buildings, thinking that at some point he would see evidence of the city center. But the rows of houses went on, and Adin was exhausted. And even if he was willing to take a chance and ask for help, he saw no one coming his way.

As he leaned against a wall and dropped his head, he did not notice the two men come up quietly behind him until they grabbed his arms and threw him to the ground.

Adin pushed against the men and tried to pull free, but they were big and strong, and for a quick moment Adin saw a dark, mean face and the flash of metal. He heard more than felt his head crack as one man lifted him and threw him against the wall. And then an excruciating pain in his gut made him slump to the dirt. As he began to black out, he felt a jerk as his satchel was wrenched from his back.

Adin clutched his hand to his waist and felt a hot, sticky liquid spreading over his shirt. A moan escaped his mouth as his head reeled. In his dimming vision, he saw legs running down the lane, and his satchel with everything he carried—his clothes, gems, and the map!—swinging above the ground and then fading out of sight.

Fourteen

A LETHA BRUSHED aside the voice nagging at her heart. As she galloped down the hill toward the city, she knew her chances of finding Adin were ridiculously slim. She had no idea where her brother had gone; it was now nearly a week since he'd left. That little voice told her she was wasting her time on a wild goose chase; Adin could be a hundred leagues away by now, tracking a bird he would never catch. But her determination squelched that voice, and as she spurred her horse, she considered which direction to take.

Dressed in her warm riding clothes, with her hair tucked in a cap, she knew she could pass for a commoner. She had chosen a plain saddle and bridle, rigging her mare for what she guessed would be a long trip. Saddle bags filled with food and clothing were draped behind her, topped with a blanket and a sack of grain. She had considered riding first to see Reya but didn't want to endure the scoldings and warnings that would no doubt be issued. Instead, she left a sealed note with her attendant, instructing her to deliver it to her nursemaid. At least Reya would know where the twins had gone off to, and hopefully that would curtail her worry. Aletha doubted very much whether the King would even notice her absence, and frankly, she didn't care.

As she neared the edge of town she slowed her mare's gait, for there were many walking on the road this warm late morning.

Winding through the crowds of people, Aletha pondered her choices. She knew Adin had headed east, but would he have stopped anywhere? She imagined him asking questions, inquiring about the firebird—but of whom? The only place she pictured Adin visiting was the old library, a stop along her way.

She paused at a market stall where a young girl and her mother displayed a rack of steaming-hot pasties filled with meat and potatoes. She was in a hurry, but not so much as to pass by her favorite treat. Dismounting, she led her horse to the stall and pulled her cap down farther over her ears. She couldn't help a smile when the older woman handed her the doughy treat and said, "My, Princess, 'tis an honor to be graced with your presence. We haven't seen Your Highness for a long time." The woman and her daughter curtseyed and lowered their eyes.

"I apologize; I would come more often if I could. Be assured, I would be here every day if I could manage it. Not even the palace cooks make a pasty this delicious." Aletha offered her coin, but the woman shook her head, then handed her the fattest pasty on the rack.

"Oh, no, Highness! Our treat." Mother and daughter exchanged looks of agreement. "We all 'preciate so much what you try to do for us common folk."

Aletha's heart warmed. "Nevertheless, we must make sure you can afford to buy the best ingredients or those pasties will suffer now, won't they?" She took the woman's hand in her own and squeezed it, leaving three silvers in her palm. Before the woman could protest, Aletha mounted her horse and waved farewell. By the bright shine of the woman's eyes, Aletha knew she had just made her day. How she wished she could see that look in every face in Sherbourne!

By midday Aletha reached the library, where, after much searching, she found a young librarian who remembered the hunchbacked, limping gentleman who was researching mythical beasts. From what Aletha gathered, she was at least three or four days behind her brother, who was last seen walking toward the bridge. She continued her brisk ride through the city and across the river. Finally she reached the east gate and clicked to her horse to pick up speed. She trotted under the archway and as soon as the cobbles ended urged her mount into a gallop. One main road led east and that would be the one to follow. Hopefully, at some point she would find someone who had seen Adin and could send her in his direction.

She passed through one village, paying little attention to the scenery as she rode. Houses thinned and eventually the road straightened out along a meadow of elderberry bushes and open fields. Her mare frothed at the mouth, needing water, so Aletha glanced around, hoping for a creek.

As she slowed by the edge of the meadow, her horse started and reared back, nearly throwing Aletha from the saddle. She got her mount under control and stared curiously as something rustled and snorted in the tall grass right next to the road. With one hand on her knife, she leaned down for a better look and was surprised when a large white pig came charging out at her.

"Whoa now, what's your hurry?" Aletha asked.

The pig screeched to a stop, but slid on its rump along the wet dirt until it collided with the horse's front leg. Aletha backed up her horse and dismounted, then came around to see if the pig was hurt.

"Now there—tha's a fine sight. What's the princess doin' traipsin' about in these parts, I wonder?"

Aletha stared at the pig with interest. "Why is a pig running headlong into my horse? I wonder." Aletha stood holding the reins and watched as the creature shook bits of grass from his body. "And how do you know I'm the princess?"

The pig snorted as if offended. "Weren't born yesterday, my good lass. And my business is yer business, so there you have it."

The pig stretched his snout back, straining his neck to reach his tail. "Would you be so kind, I've an itch something fierce. Right there, you see?"

Aletha snickered and removed her riding gloves. She squatted down next to the pig and scratched his back near the tail.

The pig rolled his eyes in ecstasy. "Ah, there you have it. How glorious to be able to reach those difficult spots, eh?"

As Aletha scratched she asked, "And just what is your business, dear pig?"

"Oh please, dear lass, call me Winston. What yer brother calls me, so it's a name for you as well."

Aletha stopped scratching the pig and stood abruptly. "My brother? You've seen Adin?"

"Oh, and had a jolly good meal or two with him. He's such a polite young lad, and so very helpful. Why only just the other day . . ."

"Dear sir—"

"Winston." The pig nodded humbly.

"Winston, please, can you tell me where he has gone?"

The pig sat back on his haunches and raised his head. "Why, of course, dear lass. Haven't yet taken leave of me wits. 'Twas my master who sent him off after the map. Right on schedule, as it were."

"What map? To find the firebird?"

The pig laughed. "Oh heavens no, Princess. No more about that bit o' business. Mythical creatures and all that rot. Your prince went to fetch the map, hidden under the abbey."

Aletha cocked her head. "The abbey? I don't understand."

"Of course you don't, my dear lass. But, you see, the prince has much more important doings, and he's set about doing them. So, there, you see?"

Aletha let the pig's words sink in. What could have been so urgent as to cause Adin to abandon his quest for the firebird? "Tell me about the map. Where will it take Adin?"

"Ah, so many questions, and the day is speeding along. My, could the princess be anxious about her brother?"

"Of course I am. Please . . . Winston." She smiled kindly. "Do you know where Adin has gone?"

The pig snorted, then turned and waddled down the road. Aletha walked alongside him, leading the horse, who took advantage of the nearness of grass to grab a clump with her mouth. "Where are you going?" she asked.

"Well, I'm not one for inviting strangers, but I s'pose you're not really a stranger, being the princess and all. My stomach is making unpleasant noises and I know there is a plate of warm biscuits waiting at home. Care to join me in a spot of tea?"

Aletha's face dropped. "Thank you for the kind offer, but I really must find Adin." She put a foot in the stirrup and lifted up onto her mare. She made sure her words sounded respectful. "Thank you, sir, for your helpful information. I will look for him at the abbey."

"Oh, I imagine he's long left there by now, don't you reckon?"

Aletha huffed and threw her arms in the air. "Well, then, how am I supposed to know where he's gone?"

"Not where—when."

"What?"

The pig repeated. "Not what, either—when."

The princess shook her head in confusion. "I don't understand."

The pig stopped and turned to look at Aletha. "You asked *where* the prince had gone, and, my dear lass, it is not *where* but *when* that merits our concern. *When* is the operative word, for yer brother is following the map across time. It's a magical map, imagine that!"

"A what?"

"Of course, that also depends on whether he was able to find the map in the labyrinth. A bit of tricky business, there. Of course, the prince has a good, clever head on his shoulders, and no doubt he has managed swimmingly to fetch his prize. Why don't you go to the abbey and find out? Up to it, then? Seeing that you're bowing out on my offer of tea."

"Please forgive any disrespect I've shown. Perhaps I can take you up on your invitation another time?" Aletha put on her best apologetic face.

The pig grunted in satisfaction. "Well, then, we'll plan on a future date. Be off with you then, and lass . . ."

The pig came alongside the horse and strained his neck to see Aletha. "Look for his footprints. You may not have a map to follow, but being twins, I fancy you're of the same blood. Tricky to spot the prints; no one else can see 'em, but, yes, there's a special bond a'tween you two. Takes a special sight to see 'em. Can't miss 'em, then. But, they may not last long—time and tide, and all that rot—so best be about your way quick-like. Heaven bless!"

Aletha watched the pig trot vigorously down the road, then veer into a shaded glen off to the left. After finding a creek of fresh water and resting her horse, she headed back west until the way branched north. Wind blew warm on her face as she galloped along, her mind preoccupied with the pig's words.

All the way to the King's forest, and late into the night as she camped under the rustling boughs, she wondered about the map and its purpose. A map that could move one through time? She had heard of magical things, but nothing as outrageous as that. Why go back in time? What did Adin hope to accomplish, if something as fantastic as a magical map *could* exist? Was it a trap, a deception? If so, who would want to lead Adin to harm?

Aletha scowled. Rasha, for one. If that evil man had anything to do with this strange quest, he would answer to her! She knew without a doubt he was responsible for discrediting Adin with her father, and for spreading lies about his loyalties.

The pig had said his master sent Adin after the map. Who could that be? As odd as she found the pig, he seemed harmless—not that she'd encountered any other talking pigs in her life. But this one had been sincere, and exhibited friendly feelings toward Adin. Surely he wouldn't answer to a master as horrible as Rasha. But, whoever the pig's master was, he must have been convincing, for Adin had been quick to change course and follow his suggestion. Aletha now wished she had taken the pig up on his offer of tea. Then she could have questioned his master about this baffling map.

The next day she met with the head abbot, who told her, in confidence, all he could about the map and Adin's quest. Aletha listened, absolutely flabbergasted. When he mentioned the curse, Aletha held her breath. Could they possibly be true—the stories Reya had told them about the *qa'lal* and its beginnings long ago? Apparently Adin thought so, for now he was using this map to try to find the answers to all those mysteries.

She thought about Adin, alone in a strange place and time. After all these years of living with him, knowing him as well as she knew herself, Aletha could easily imagine Adin trying hard to be brave and capable, but being beaten down by his own self-doubt. At times Adin was his own worst enemy. As much as he protested that he was grown up and could stand alone, Aletha knew how little it took to make him fall. If this quest was as vital and danger-ous as she guessed it to be, then Adin needed all the help heaven could grant.

She thought of a verse her mother used to recite to her from the *Book of Kingly Sayings*, reminding Aletha to be a support for her brother. "Two are better than one, because they have a good reward for their labor. For if they fall, one will lift up his companion. But woe to him who is alone when he falls, for he has no one to help him up." Yes, it would be woe to Adin without anyone there to comfort and support him. She must find her way to her twin, to help him in any way she could. She would not rest easy until she knew he was safe, even if it meant chasing him across the centuries.

Following the abbot's directions, Aletha returned to Sherbourne, stopping at the northern crossroads where the abbot said he had parted ways with Adin. She had no way to tell where Adin had gone from here, but the abbot said that as he drove the wagon back toward the vale, he glanced back and saw her brother walking into the woods north of the intersection. Well then, she would start searching there, looking for a magical footprint—one that neatly matched her own.

She unpacked her mare, stuffing all she could into a small bag she slung over her shoulder. With an encouraging word and a pat on the rump, she sent her mare trotting toward the palace gates, knowing the horse would easily find her way back to her stall where fresh hay and a bucket of rolled oats awaited her.

Without another moment of hesitation, Aletha brushed aside branches and leaves, adjusting her sight to detect anything magical on the ground around her. Her task didn't take long, for just a few yards in front of her, atop a blanket of dead leaves, rested a single footprint etched in bright light, clear as the morning star on the horizon at the break of dawn.

Aletha touched the print with her finger, then pulled her hand back in surprise. The fiery line burned to the touch. She took a deep breath, and before she could change her mind, placed her soft boot inside the line of her brother's print and, in an instant, the world disappeared.

• PART TWO•

SHA 'HAR SHA 'MA 'YIM

(THE GATES OF HEAVEN)

FIFTEEN

CAPTAIN JERED TEBRON ducked down the tiny lane, his usual shortcut across town. Not because he was in a hurry to deliver the regent's instructions to the outpost on the eastern wall, but because the crowds were so maddeningly slow and the roads obstructed with wagons and horses and all manner of filth under his feet. Most made way for him upon recognizing his silver vest and helmet, identifying him with the *tsa'ba*—the militia—but fewer knew him by his face. With the population burgeoning inside the walls these last months, he encountered more stares from faces of people he did not know.

And this itself had been the subject of the regent's concern at the morning's conference. How could one say no to the steady influx of *z'ur* seeking safety within these walls? And at what point does one decide to turn needy people away and into the cruel hands of those *ghed'ood* from the south?

The captain walked briskly past the dwellings jammed together along the alleyway. Smells of rotting food assaulted his nose as he sidestepped the piles of refuse. Even from this secluded street, the noises of the throng carried loudly to his ears. Nothing good could come of all this crowding.

When they had started erecting the walls nine months ago, no one would have imagined this squalor, a city nearly bursting at the seams. Who could have predicted so many families and stragglers from all corners of the land would seek refuge here? And now trouble brewed like a simmering kettle, for when neighbors became crowded like too many badgers caught in a cage, violence was sure to follow. That was why, despite the risk, Jered often took to riding outside the north walls into the forest, just so he could breathe deeply and clear his head. Too often he felt he was pacing the cage.

Especially now, with word from the southern patrols that a large army was heading for the city, gearing up for *mil'ka'ma*, and ravaging the land like a cyclone, uprooting all in its path. Rumors told of a powerful ruler swallowing up lands on all sides. Well, let him come!

These *ghed'ood* were moving too slowly for the captain's taste. His men were ready. As much as he hated the thought of battle descending upon his fortress, a bloody *mil'ka'ma* was better than this interminable waiting. His own *tsa'ba*, granted, were not experienced fighters, but they knew what they stood to lose—their families and friends, and a way of life they cherished. The *tsa'ba* were not a large enough force to mount a head-on confrontation; they accomplished more in clandestine skirmishes and sabotage, hoping to reduce the numbers of their *o'yab* before they closed in. Whether that strategy would make a difference in the end, only time would tell.

Jered grunted in disgust. What was the world coming to? Only three years ago he had been off exploring mountains and charting unknown territories. How he missed the freedom of those wild spaces! Nothing gave him greater joy than listening to the world quietly spinning under a web of stars. And, almost overnight, that sense of peace had been shattered.

While he was up in the western peaks, word had come to him that his village had been destroyed. Raiders had burned the houses and shops, stolen livestock, and even killed one of his neighbors who had dared resist. The people of his village'd had no warning and no experience with hostility. They succumbed like all the other villages, unprepared to meet with violence in their peaceful land.

By the time Jered arrived home, the remains of his village had been abandoned. Only the charred posts of his own cottage stood in the ground. He panicked with worry over his father and younger brothers. Where had everyone gone—and were they safe?

Finally, he located a settlement close to the center of the kingdom, groups of the displaced who gathered together for comfort and answers. Gratefully united with his family, Jered looked upon the faces laced with distress and knew his exploring days were over—for now. Outrage filled his heart, and even though he'd had little experience with weapons other than the bow and knife he used for hunting, he took charge, knowing that with passion and leadership he could help rally and organize these settlers to resist the intruders. And he had no plans to quit until he saw this through, until the land was rid of terror and life could return to the simple ways of the past.

Unbeknown to Jered, a man his father's age named Kah'yil had already seen the need for unity and defense. While Jered had still been off in the mountains, this visionary planned a fortressed city, and had already started the layout of the *ma'ak'eh*, the battlement walls. From what Jered heard, the man had no aspirations to be a leader of a kingdom, but he had lost his wife and child to those *o'yab*, and that loss fueled his fierce determination and single-mindedness.

Jered sought Kah'yil out, and upon meeting him felt instant admiration and awe for this gentle, quiet-spoken man. In short time, those under Kah'yil's direction rallied in support of making him regent, despite Kah'yil's protests. But the people wanted a ruler, a banner to gather under, a figurehead of unity in these treacherous times. And Jered found himself appointed as captain of the militia at the new regent's insistence. Kah'yil made it clear he valued the counsel of each and every man, and over the last two years, both Jered and his regent had relied heavily on each other—for advice and moral support, forming a bond of friendship that Jered valued more than all the treasures in the world.

As Jered rounded a corner, he stopped abruptly. A man in a dark cloak lay against the wall among the piles of trash. The captain's eyes locked on the pool of blood in the dirt, and he rushed to the poor man's side. What *oro'bah* was this?

Quickly, Jered turned the man over and assessed his wounds. The man was alive, but the wound in his side was deep, and he groaned in pain as Jered tried to lift his back. As Jered placed his hand behind the man's neck, blood dripped from the back of his head onto Jered's shirtsleeve.

Out of the corner of his eye Jered saw movement on the street and looked up to see two young men staring from a doorway.

"You there! Get over here and help. What's wrong with you? Can't you see this man is hurt?" He watched the men hesitate, no doubt weighing whether to keep their noses out of trouble or answer to the captain of the militia. But Jered gave them no time to ponder.

"Get your *a'khore* over here before I throw you both in *keh'leh!*" Jered cursed under his breath. Just another symptom of this city's disease—people abandoning decency and human kindness in the midst of fear. Didn't they understand?—when times are hard, that's when those qualities are needed the most.

"Hurry," he barked at them, hoisting the injured man with their aid. As they carried him down the lane, Jered got his bearings and decided on a direction. The only healer he knew lived too far away. But Brynn's tavern was close. There he could at least get the man stitched up and prevail upon Brynn to put him up in the spare room—if it wasn't currently being rented. What other choice did he have? He couldn't take him to the barracks to see the medic. So Brynn's it would be.

Jered ignored the grunts of the men as they stumbled down the street under the weight of their load. They were thin, not brawny like Jered, but the captain pressed them hard until they found the cross street leading to the main thoroughfare. Only two blocks more and they arrived under the wooden sign that portrayed a sheep and a large tin mug.

Brynn's tavern, a large wood-planked building rising two stories, sat in the heart of the market district. Many of the shops in this part of the city had been built early on, when the mills outside the walls were still operational. So, rather than the log construction seen in the cottages across town, these buildings were of a finer quality, with beveled-glass windows and wood beam supports. Even the roofs were tiled rather than thatched, and for at least a mile the wide street retained the old ruddy cobbles that had been inset at the arrival of the first settlers to the region.

At Jered's urging, the two conscripted men helped bring their awkward load in through the front door as onlookers cleared a path. After depositing him onto the top of a long wooden table that Jered deftly cleared of dishes with the sweep of an arm, they slunk away, clearly not wanting to be inducted into more service.

"What poor *na'baal* have you rescued this time, Jer?" The aging, hefty innkeeper in a stained apron came over to look, her dark hair pulled back under a scarf and her black eyes shining. After a quick glance at the mess strewn on the floor, she put her hands on her hips. "You'll be upsetting my customers with this commotion, you know."

Jered pulled off his helmet and went to work, tearing away the bloodied shirt and grimacing. The woman came closer and whistled through her teeth. "Oh my, that's not a pretty sight, there. I'll fetch you hot water and cloths." She hurried off, oblivious to the staring eyes of the few customers drinking ale at the other tables. Jered called after her.

"I'll need needle and thread, too, Brynn." With his knife, the captain cut away matted hair from the head wound. Brynn came with a bucket of hot water and a stack of clean rags.

"Who is he, Jer? Looks to be a foreigner, by his dress."

Jered gently washed the wounds as blood continued to seep out. "Here, hold this." She reached over and pressed the warm cloth against the man's stomach. He left her, circling around the hewn-wood counter and reaching underneath. Bringing a sewing box over to the table, he said, "Have no idea. I found him down the *na'thib*. Some thieves, no doubt."

Brynn whistled again. "What in *shama'yim* is happening to this city? A person can't even take a stroll without fearing for her life. Never used to be like this. Like the regent says, 'When the wicked multiply, trouble increases, but the righteous will see their fall.' I'll be one to thank the heavens on that day."

With her work-worn hands she replaced the compresses and cleaned the man's face. "He's young, Jer, maybe still in his teens. Has a funny face, there." She looked closer. "And his back is strange, bent. But not from an injury, from what I can tell."

Jered threaded the needle and stitched closed the stomach wound. "Good thing he's knocked out. He'll be hurting some when he comes to."

Brynn pursed her lips. "And I'm supposing you probably want to keep him in the upstairs room until he recovers."

Jered tied a knot in the thread and threw Brynn a charming smile. "You know I'm good for it. If he wakes, feed him, give him ale—whatever he wants. Just keep him warm and comfortable." Jered cut the thread at the knot with his sharp hip knife and examined his handiwork. It would do. Unfortunately, with all the injured coming back from the skirmishes, he'd been getting a lot of practice stitching men up. After rechecking the head wound, he cleaned off the sewing needle and placed it back in its case. "His head wound seems to be closing up on its own. I'll check it later today."

Jered stepped back and looked at his charge. The poor fellow. Hopefully he had family here, someone searching for him. But, for now, Jered, who never abandoned those in his care, was all he had.

With the aid of Brynn's strong back, he managed to lug the man up the narrow stairs to the landing, then down the hall into a small room at the end. They set him gently on the bed, and Brynn covered him with a blanket. "This room'll get the afternoon sun. He'll be plenty comfortable. I'll send the boy along in a bit to check on him, but I should get back to my customers."

Jered followed Brynn down the stairs and handed her a fistful of coins. "This should do for now, but keep track and I'll pay you in full—however much it comes to."

"You've a kind heart, Jered Tebron. Too kind for your own good, I think." Brynn tousled Jered's coal black hair; she always treated him more like a son than the captain of her brother's army.

"Well, you know the saying: 'Do not withhold good from those to whom it is due, when it is in your power to do it.'"

"Still," she responded, gathering mugs and flatware from the floor, "you've others to care for, an army to manage. You can't go acting the *yasha* with every poor fool you meet. Times are evil."

Jered faced her squarely. "Fool or no, he's lost whatever he had. And if we don't help those in need during evil times, then where's our humanity? Brynn, we can't give up even one small shred of decency; that'd be like the crack in the dam. Kindness, like evil, is not measured by quantity. One small lie can be as destructive as a big lie, and one small act of kindness the same as rescuing a king-dom." The captain washed up in the bucket, splashing his face and wiping his dripping beard.

Brynn laughed. "You've been around Kah'yil too long—you're starting to sound like him with his string of sayings."

Jered smiled, thinking of the regent always scribbling his clever phrases in his little handmade book. "I'll be back in a while to check on our patient."

After giving Brynn a quick kiss on the cheek, the captain left the tavern, heading toward the east wall. The sun rode high overhead, banishing the chill from the air. His thoughts lingered on the man in the upstairs bed. This was just one more indication how bad things were getting in the city, one more reason to bring this *mil'ka'ma* to a head. In three days he would ride south and assess the *ghed'ood*, those men bent on destroying everything he loved. And he would do what he could to strengthen the hearts of those fighting to protect the city. He only hoped the words of the proverb carried truth: "What the wicked dread will come upon them." Then he thought of another clever saying of Kah'yil's: "Wisdom is better than weapons of war." Jered surely hoped so, for he feared that where weapons were concerned, his *tsa'ba* were vastly outnumbered.

"Well now, it looks like we've come back from the dead."

Adin tried to adjust his eyes to the stabbing light. Just moving his head toward the voice sent a wave of pain through his skull. He grimaced, becoming aware of an even worse feeling in his side. He felt around with shaky hands and happened upon bandages. A large woman, holding out a cup, stood beside the bed Adin found himself in.

"Here's some *sha'qah*. Do you think you c'n manage a sip, here, luv?"

Very slowly, Adin tipped his head forward. His mouth was severely dry. Soothing water dripped down his throat. He tried to find his voice. "Where am I?" He squinted as he surveyed the room. The woman set the cup down and closed the curtains enough to temper some of the glare.

"There, is that better?"

Adin nodded and let his head fall back against a soft pillow. The woman smoothed her black hair out of her eyes and looked him over with sharp eyes. "Name's Brynn. You're upstairs at the Sheepshead Tavern. Know the place?"

Adin tried to shake his head but stopped when a stabbing twinge shot across his scalp. He tried to make out her words mired in the thick, lilting accent. The woman clucked her teeth.

"You were beat up something bad. The captain stitched you right—you should heal just fine in a few days." She watched him for a moment. "I've given you one of my husband's nightshirts. Your shirt's being mended and your trousers washed. C'n you eat anything, you s'pose?"

Adin could not tell if he was hungry. When had he last eaten? Slowly, he pieced together the last things he remembered. Walking down the lane—in Sherbourne's past—two men attacking, his head hitting the wall.

Adin's eyes widened in the horror of understanding. His satchel containing his clothes, his gems, and the map had been stolen! How would he be able to survive here—and how would he ever be able to return to his own time? He panicked at the thought of being trapped in this place and time, and not having the means to procure food or lodging.

"Please," he begged, "I had a satchel, with all my things . . ."

The woman laid a hand on his shoulder. "There, there, don't get yourself in a fret. I don't know anything about a satchel. Captain says you were robbed, and if that's the case, luv, your things're long gone."

Hopelessness engulfed Adin, smothering him in despair. How could this have happened? He'd not even been here one day and already his quest had failed. He was stupid—stupid! He'd been so sure he could just waltz into history and solve all the mysteries single-handedly. He thought of the hermit's confidence in him—his *misplaced* confidence. Why hadn't that fellow sent someone else—someone with more sense? Hot tears pooled in his eyes; he didn't even care if this woman watched him flail in his misery.

Her voice was tender. "Captain'll be here soon. Maybe he can help you track down your things. Do you have a name?"

Adin tried to get words out through the lump in his throat. "Adin." He gestured at the room. "Thank you." He closed his eyes in resignation.

Brynn spoke softly. "Tell you what, I'll have Hadar bring 'round a bowl of soup, how's that? I'll just tell the boy to come in quiet and set it down. You eat when you like." Adin heard her walk over to the door. "You rest. You c'n stay as long as you need, till you get well. You have any family, someone I can fetch?"

Adin kept his eyes closed but shook his head, this time ignoring the sharp pain. "No. No one. I'm all alone."

"All right," she said, her voice filled with pity. "You rest."

Adin heard the soft click of the door. His body hurt terribly. He reached and felt the cloth binding the back of his head, then he touched his face. On his chin were the scratchy beginnings of a beard. Just how long had he been lying here?

From his bed he could hear sounds from the street below: voices, wagon wheels turning, the clop of horses' hooves on stone. He barely opened his eyes. The tops of roofs spread out before him through the window, and smells of food lingered on the air, mixing with the scent of freshly laundered sheets. A wash basin and a pitcher of water sat atop a small dresser, and next to the bed was a metal chamber pot. Adin's heart sunk deep into his chest like a heavy rock. He sensed his motivation draining as he lay listless for hours. What was the point—of anything? Even if he could find the Keeper, even if he somehow managed to uncover the curse, what could he do about it? Unless he had the map, he wouldn't be able to return to the palace—to Aletha—with the remedy.

His chest heaved with bitter sadness. He would never see his sister again. That thought caused him more pain than all his injuries put together. He had to find the map! Somewhere in this huge city, among thousands of people, was his map—a map that, to anyone else, would look like a useless piece of parchment. And what would his thieves do with a map they couldn't use? No doubt toss it—or burn it. Adin cursed his fate. By the time he would be well enough to try to track down the map, it would be too late. Impossible . . . hopeless, all of this. What he really needed was a map to guide him through the confusing labyrinth of this life, to make sense of what lay before him and give him clear direction around the potholes and pitfalls. Why didn't anyone make *that* kind of map?

Adin's thoughts were interrupted by a gentle knock at the door. A head peeked in; a man not much older than Adin, with thick black hair and a trim beard, looked him over with compassion. Adin waved him in, and the tall, muscular man came over to his bedside. Adin saw he was dressed in something resembling a uniform, with an insignia or design sewn on the front of his silver vest. He brandished a sword at his side, and his dark woolen pants were clean and pressed.

His visitor smiled with encouraging eyes. "I'm Jered. Glad to see you're awake. How is your *kheel*? Not too bad, I hope."

"Are you the captain—the one who stitched me up?"

Jered nodded. "You're not from around here—Adin, is it?"

Adin nodded. "Just arrived."

The captain frowned. "And got a warm welcome for it." He pulled a chair over from the corner of the room and sat alongside Adin. "I apologize for the state of our city. Times are . . . difficult, and trouble reduces some men to *ghen'ay'ba*, rather than working for an honest wage. May I ask what brought you here, to our *makh'as'eh*?"

"What is that—*makh'as'eh*?"

"Shelter, refuge. I imagine you have come seeking a safe place, away from the marauders. Although, now, I suppose you are regretting your decision."

Adin knew the captain was trying to cheer him up, but he wanted none of it. He closed his eyes and fell back on his pillow. He mumbled an effort at gratitude. "Thank you for coming to my aid."

The captain put a hand on Adin's shoulder. "What can I do to help? Brynn says a *ga'nab* took your bag. Was there anything of value in it?"

Adin sighed. "More valuable than you can imagine. But not to anyone but me." Adin opened his eyes and looked at the captain, who waited patiently. "A rolled-up parchment, a map. It will show nothing of interest." Adin's voice weakened. "However, I must find it. All my hope rests on finding it."

The captain smiled. "Then we will do all in our power to retrieve that map, Adin. Being the captain of the militia, I have eyes all over the city, and I will put them to work for you. What else can you tell me about your bag?"

Adin wanted to be encouraged by the captain's optimism, but he knew better than to hope. He described the contents of his satchel, knowing that the gems would surely disappear. Who knew what their value would be in this time—but Adin did not doubt someone would recognize their rarity and find them useful in trading. At least, that was what Adin had hoped to do with them. Now he would have to rely on strangers to help him. He hated being so helpless, so at the mercy of others' kindness, but what choice did he have?

Adin's words came out in shallow breaths. It hurt to talk. "Sir, you have shown me extraordinary kindness. I am in your debt, and

Brynn's. Yet I have nothing with which to repay you. There must be something I can do to make this up to you, some work I can help you with."

Jered laughed. "Right now you are in no shape to do much but sleep and eat and get well. In the meantime, I will think of how I can put you to good use. For I am always in need of men, and this city, I fear, is in great trouble. War is coming—no doubt you have heard—and every able-bodied man will be needed to fight this *mil'ka'ma*." The captain's face grew strained, and Adin lay quiet. Through the window, he could see the evening spread out across the sky in bands of pink and orange, the sunset coloring the haze of smoke lying like a blanket over the city.

"There is one other thing, sir."

"Please, Adin, call me Jered."

"Jered. I have been sent to look for someone here. I know nothing about this person, just that I could identify him or her by a symbol—a five-pointed, silver star, inset with a smaller gold star. In the center lies a blue gemstone—the color of your eyes."

Jered pursed his lips. "A piece of jewelry, perhaps? Or maybe something on a garment?"

Adin shrugged. "I do not know. Have you ever seen a thing like that?"

Jered thought for a moment. "Nothing comes to mind. But I will ponder your mystery and ask around."

"Oh, no. Please do not mention this to anyone." The captain's eyebrows lifted in curiosity. "What I tell you is spoken in confidence," Adin told him, adding, "if you don't mind."

Once more the captain patted Adin on the shoulder and stood up. "You are a puzzle, Adin, a *yo'shana*. You seek someone you do not know, and chase after a strange symbol. You lost a map that has meaning only for you. You wear unusual clothes and have an accent I have never before encountered." His smile warmed Adin's heart. "But I will keep your mystery a secret, and do what I can to help you recover your lost map. Try to cheer up. There is always hope. As we say around here, *yesh 'achar'ith tiq'vah k'rath.* 'Surely there is a future, and your hope will not be cut off.'"

Adin's breath caught in his throat; he knew these words!—the words of the strange man in the courtyard echoed through his skull. Could that man have come from this time, from the past? If not, how had he known a common saying that would perish into obscurity centuries later? The idea made his head spin.

The captain searched Adin's eyes. "Adin, are you all right? Maybe you need some fresh air." He walked over to the window and unlatched it, letting in a cool breeze. "I must be off; I'm needed at the barracks, but I will be by tomorrow and we will talk some more. And I will bring you some clothes and other necessities. Get some *ya'shane*—sleep—and recover, and we will look for your mysterious map."

After the captain left, Adin lay in the quiet room, the evening traffic noises a backdrop to his thoughts. He remembered what the hermit had said, to be willing to seek allies in his quest. Well, it appeared he had found one in the person of Jered Tebron, captain of the militia. Thinking of the captain's reassuring smile took the edge off Adin's despair. He imagined he would not find a better ally than this—a man willing to help a stranger in distress. Not many people Adin had ever known would have performed such a generous deed; lifting him from the street, stitching his wounds, and providing him a bed and food and care. This captain was a rare man, and Adin was glad to know, in the midst of such turmoil, that a man with such honor would lead Sherbourne's army to victory.

Later that evening a boy came to his room to collect his dishes. The boy looked about ten years old and wore a big white apron around his small waist. Adin introduced himself and learned that Hadar was Brynn's nephew, earning a few coins a week washing dishes and chopping vegetables. The boy's father had lost a hand in one of the skirmishes last year. Between his mother's doing laundry for hire and Hadar's work at the tavern, his family was getting by.

Adin saw that the boy worried for his father, now incapacitated and frustrated. At Adin's urging, Hadar sat and told Adin all he knew about the war, the enemies coming toward the city, and his fears for his future. Adin's eyes widened when Hadar proudly told him about his uncle, the newly appointed regent of the land. The first regent of Sherbourne! Adin hoped to meet this man he only knew from his history lessons.

Through Hadar he learned more about the city, about the streams of new people coming through the gates each week, and the fact that limited supplies were beginning to run out. Supply wagons continually met with ambush, and fewer merchants from other areas dared travel to the city for fear of getting robbed— or worse. He'd heard Brynn complaining to her brother—the regent—about the worrisome lack of grain, potatoes, and barley. How were they supposed to keep up with the demand for ale if the brewery ran out of hops? Brynn was sure the people could do without a few potatoes, but run out of ale and you'd have a riot on your hands, she had warned.

"You talk funny," the boy said. "Where are you from?"

"Oh, a long way from here. But maybe you can help me." The boy nodded with eagerness.

Adin continued. "Do you think you can find me something to write with—parchment, pen?" Again the head bobbed. "Because I am a stranger here, I don't understand much of what people say; their words are confusing. So I thought I would write down a list of all the words I don't understand, and maybe you can tell me what they mean."

"Kind of like I'd be a teacher and you a student. We had a school—back in the place I used to live."

"Right, and that would be a great help. I am sure once I get on my feet and find some work I can pay you."

Hadar's eyes lit up. "I'll get you those things right away!" The boy gathered the plates and cups into his arms and left.

Adin lay awake late into the night, watching through the window a sickle moon rising, and wondering if this city would now become his home. Maybe, in time, he would get used to the idea, but for now the thought caused only grief. Maybe the map was lost for good, and once he healed, he would have to find some employment. But what was he good for—with his misshapen back and useless leg? Who would hire him? Would he sit in some kitchen peeling potatoes while, outside the city walls, a war raged? Would he even survive the impending attack on Sherbourne? Did it matter?

Was it only yesterday he had looked out upon the ruins of the once great city? Not a stone left upon a stone; it was utter waste and desolation. Maybe the future *was* fixed, and Adin was doomed to fail in his *ma'gur*. Maybe all this was an exercise in futility. Only heaven knew for certain. For now, the matter was out of his hands. All he could do was rest and recover. Nothing more.

With that depressing thought, Adin closed his eyes and shut out the sounds of an agitated and uneasy city outside his window, the words of the *qa'lal* lapping against his mind, rocking him into a fitful sleep.

SIXTEEN

IN THE CHURNING maelstrom of noise and color, Aletha searched the ground for the next footprint but saw nothing but a black, gaping chasm. About to step into nothingness, she gasped and retracted her boot. Weary and nauseated, she tried to calm her breath, willing the dizziness to subside. How long had she been journeying through this madness? Her legs ached as if she had walked twenty leagues, and now, without a footprint to show her the way, she slumped to what felt like soft ground.

Suddenly, all the spinning and roaring diminished, and Aletha watched in astonishment as the mass of shapes and colors gelled into recognizable patterns of tree and rock and sky. Dozens of thin maple branches hemmed her in, and at her feet a blanket of leaves displayed the dark hues of fall. The sky above cleared to a deep blue, punctuated by clouds heavy with rain. From the quality of the light, Aletha guessed it was late afternoon. She stood and took a step and glanced back at the footprint, which glowed softly. Looking around, she took in her surroundings, committing this place to memory.

Aletha brushed off her skirt, straightened her vest and blouse, and put a small hat on her head. She could only assume this was where—or when—Adin had arrived, and she saw no other choice but to venture out and look for her brother. But how long had he been here? Days, weeks, months? There was no telling how the twist of time worked. She only hoped he was safe and that she would be able to find him.

Pushing her way through the woods, Aletha tried to get her bearings, but all she could see were trees. Only after she stumbled out into a clearing could she tell where she was. A muddy road and fields of high grass stretched out to her right, and just beyond were the city walls. The sun, beginning to set, shone brightly against the gray stone, lighting up the wall with a stunning brilliance. The sight took her breath away. Not even in her imagination had she envisioned how imposing and finely crafted this battlement had been at its creation. Surely just the people's ability to construct such a work would give an advancing enemy pause.

Keeping out of view, Aletha positioned herself so she could watch the activity at the northern gate. Guards were posted at the entrance, although they didn't seem unduly interested in the occasional person entering or leaving the city. She could make out a group of men stacking stones to the left of the gate, working on an unfinished section of wall. Up along the parapet, a half-dozen others patrolled, walking a steady pace while they scanned the distant hills.

Aletha found it unsettling to look up to the crest of the knoll and not see the palace. And even more unsettling to see her beautifully erected city of stone replaced by a sprawling mass of wooden shacks covered by a thick mantle of smoke. Even where she stood, the acrid scent of burning wood reached her nose, different from the coal fires of her Sherbourne. And trees as far as she could see. Aside from the riverside park and occasional backyard fruit trees, her city was almost barren of vegetation. All the major farms spread outside the city walls, although flower boxes adorned many a window and added color to the cold stone. But—sheep grazing in the middle of town? She had never imagined Sherbourne ever having looked like this.

Once Aletha was on the open road, a cold wind whipped her neck and face. She pulled her gray cloak from the bag slung across her shoulder and wrapped it tightly around her as she entered the gate. She tried not to gape at the amazing beauty of the rockwork— so new and imposing. It saddened her to think that most of these walls would end in rubble after the great siege, never to be rebuilt. Not that Aletha wished for more war—for that would probably be the only reason such a reconstruction effort would ensue—but to be able to walk along the parapet in a time of peace and gaze out over the land, stretching for leagues on end—that would be a joy.

No one hindered her entrance, and with her eyes lowered she scrutinized the people she passed, taking in their clothes, listening to their conversations. So many odd words came from their mouths, although occasionally Aletha thought she understood a phrase or two of the ancient language. What she found most upsetting was the sadness etched on their faces. She certainly had not arrived at a time of joy and prosperity.

As she followed the main road, the crowd thickened—apparently people heading home to supper after a day's work. She looked up at the knoll, where the tall slabs of stone stood sentinel, and decided to climb the lane to the top. Strange, even though so much around her appeared different, she felt oddly at home, knowing she had walked this hill a thousand times.

As she trudged along the lane, avoiding puddles, she tried to think of where Adin would have gone. He knew no one in this time—how would he know what to look for, whom to ask for help? At some point, something significant was supposed to happen to trigger the curse—but what if it wasn't obvious? And how in heaven would Adin know the remedy? Fueled by frustration, Aletha neared the top of the hill and caught sight of a handful of men standing in front of a large stone building. Not far off, the huge stones rose majestically to the heavens, the evening sun glancing across their mossy faces and illuminating them with a magical aura.

Aletha stopped and stared in wonder. She had often tried to re-create in her mind how the giant slabs had once looked, encircling the spring. And now she knew. Reya had once told her that the spring had been chosen as one of seven sacred sites, but what did that mean? Why seven—and where were the others? What made this place sacred and how would the curse contaminate it? She could picture a time, long ago, when the first people arrived in this land and discovered the spring pouring forth water from the heart of the earth. It took little imagination to see why they chose this as a sacred site—whoever "they" were.

Aletha veered away from the stone building, not wanting to attract attention. But she felt conspicuous, being the only one at the top of the knoll, apart from the guards who watched her as she headed for the spring. On the ground next to the pool were piles of broken slabs and stacks of wooden buckets for carrying water. She'd heard that at one time an aqueduct had been built to carry the delicious spring water down the hill into the city, but it had been dismantled later. As the population had grown, the spring could no longer provide enough water for the city dwellers, and instead, men had tapped into the river Heresh with underground iron pipes, and so were able to distribute water to all the districts. By the look of things, this spring was just for the use of the men stationed at the stone building.

Her boots squished in the wet grass as she made her way over to the spring. From here she could follow the entire battlement wall with her eyes as it enwrapped Sherbourne in stone. Down below, the strange city was buried in smoke. She could only make out the river and a few of the buildings in the center of town.

She stopped next to the spring. Water gurgled from the black rock into a large, natural pool, and Aletha felt as if she were in a dream. Mindlessly, she knelt before the pool, dipping her hand in the refreshing liquid. As she splashed her face she heard someone yell and, turning, she realized two guards were running toward her. Quickly, she dried her face on her sleeve and stood and watched as the men moved toward her.

One man, hefty with a broad face and wide-set eyes, grabbed Aletha by the arm. He stood tall above her, and the strength of his grip pinched her cruelly. The other man took a defensive stance between Aletha and the spring. Like his partner, he was dark-skinned, with wavy brown hair and sharp features. They wore the same uniform and carried both a sword and a knife at their sides.

Before Aletha could speak, the one holding her said, "What do you think you are doing? This place is *ko'desh*, it is not *tsa'diyk* to be here, or touch the water! Have you not been warned? The *mowt'sa* is not to be touched."

"I am sorry—I did not know," Aletha said. "Please, let me go."

The man standing behind her came around and grabbed her chin with his gloved hand. "What is a young *na'kee* doing here, alone?" He smiled, and Aletha felt a chill race up her spine.

"I . . . I am looking for my brother."

The man holding her laughed and readjusted his grip. "Well, you will not find your *ach* here. Come, Bat'sa, take her arm." He and the other man pulled Aletha along, making for the stone structure. Bat'sa walked closely at her side, and she felt his eyes upon her. She tightened her grip on her shoulder bag. "We will see what *kha'ta'aw* is in store for you, for your *iv've'leth* in touching the *mowt'sa*." They came to the building, where three men watched their arrival.

One of the guards called out, "There's a fine catch, Ka'zab. Did you fish her out of the water?"

Ka'zab replied with a guttural laugh, "Yes, and don't you think she'll make a nice meal?" He stopped in front of the men and pulled Aletha close to his chest.

She squirmed and tried to free her arms, but the man held her pinned. "I demand you release me at once!"

Ka'zab threw back his head, chuckling. "I see. Or you'll what—go off crying to your brother?"

Bat'sa came over and pulled the cap off Aletha's head, throwing it to the ground. He buried a hand in her thick hair as it tumbled down her shoulders. "It is not fair, Ka'zab. I spotted her first. Surely there is enough here to share?"

Aletha tried to yank away from Bat'sa's hand, but he held her fast and Aletha screamed. Ka'zab, still holding her tightly, pressed his hand against her mouth, hoping to shut her up. Aletha's eyes widened in fear as she realized the men standing guard were laughing; no one was coming to her aid!

With a lunge, Aletha bit down hard on the man's hand, and as he pulled it back in pain, she screamed, "Let me go! Help, someone!" Ka'zab, angered by the blood dripping from his fingers, shook Aletha hard and raised a hand, ready to slap her across the face.

The door to the stone building swung open and a tall, trim man in a black tunic and silver vest came storming out. The men standing guard quickly drew back, and the instant Ka'zab and his partner saw him, they dropped their arms and stepped away from Aletha as if she were infected with plague. With a stern look, he sized up the situation with his dark, brooding eyes, and a fury crossed his face. Aletha, rattled, smoothed out her hair and clothes and watched as the formerly cocky men shriveled under the man's gaze. She reached down and brushed the dirt off her hat.

A long moment of silence hung heavily over the men. Now that Aletha could distance herself, she looked in the faces of her two assailants. Despite their humble, regretful expressions, Aletha saw that they were not ashamed, only annoyed at being caught. Clearly they answered to this man but held him in no regard.

She could see nothing but evil in their eyes, yet when the one in authority faced her, his eyes were a well of compassion and concern.

Aletha guessed him to be in his fifties. By the way he moved, she could tell he had once suffered injury. A recent scar fell across his right cheek, just above the trim graying beard on his chin. As he walked silently around his men, he carried himself with confidence, but without arrogance. Aletha could tell he was a thoughtful man, but the lines in his face revealed too many months of worry. Had she encountered this man in any other circumstance, she would not have guessed at the authority he wielded. But when he spoke, there was no doubt of his position.

He turned to the men, meeting each pair of eyes. "Leave. Finish your work. And you two,"—he pointed at Bat'sa and Ka'zab—"inside, right now, or you will face the brunt of my *khayma*." He stood calmly and watched as the men dispersed. Once the door closed, Aletha breathed a sigh.

"My name is Kah'yil; I am the regent here. How might I apologize for the misbehavior of these men? They will be severely punished." Kah'yil's face showed his anger. "There is no excuse for such acts of *keli'ma*." He searched her face, standing at a respectful distance. "My lady, are you all right? Have they harmed you?"

"No, I am fine, thanks to your timely intervention. I did not know it was forbidden to touch the water. I am . . . new to this place." Aletha shook uncontrollably and, without warning, her knees buckled. The regent took her arm.

"Here, come sit down in here." He led Aletha to a small wooden hut a few steps away. A heavy brown cloth hung over the entrance, which the regent pulled aside and hooked onto a nail. The room was sparsely furnished, with only a table, two stools, a small cabinet, and a cot with a folded wool blanket neatly tucked around a thin mattress.

The regent gestured her inside. "My home away from home. Not much in the way of comforts, but it serves its purpose." Aletha sat, and Kah'yil brought her a glass of water and a brown roll. "It's not much, but maybe it'll help still your nerves. I can offer you something stronger to drink, if you prefer."

Aletha waved her hand as she sipped the water. "This is fine, thank you."

As she drank, she was aware of the regent's curious gaze. He had a way of observing that reminded Aletha of a bird, with a slight tilt of his head and a patient expression. When she finished her water and roll, he spoke.

"Are you here in the city by yourself? And what brought you up here, to the armory—if you don't mind my asking?"

"My brother is here. I think he arrived some days ago and I need to find him. He is all the family I now have. I thought perhaps I would come up here and see the layout of this city, and now I realize what an impossible task it will be to search for him with so many people everywhere." Aletha did not want to get emotional, but all the events of the day came crashing down on her, and her eyes filled with tears.

The regent waited for her to catch her breath and compose herself. He ran a hand through his short, curly hair, staring out the door at nothing in particular. "I try hard to keep my men in line. Most of them are dedicated to this cause; many are farmers and laborers—never wielded a weapon in their lives. They come from all over and some have not been raised with proper manners." He paused. "As the conflicts increase and more are injured, tensions are growing. I find it harder to keep the men from volatile eruptions; there are more fights and arguments, more recklessness. It is like keeping all ten fingers plugging a dam about to burst."

Aletha found the regent's strange accent soothing. His voice had a softness to it, but it did not make him sound weak. His speech revealed an inner wisdom and a resignation to the way of the world.

"Where are you staying?" he asked. When Aletha shook her head, he reached under his cot and pulled out a box. He opened it and procured a pen and bottle of ink and a sheet of parchment. Aletha watched as he dipped the pen in ink and sketched a map.

"It is getting late, but if you hurry, you should be able to find this place before dark." Kah'yil drew her route. "My sister, Brynn, has a tavern in the heart of the city, with *mow'lone*—a room to let. If you follow this road, then turn here." He marked an intersection with a bell shape. "At this corner is a chapel—with a small bell tower. Here you will see the cobbles begin and the street narrow. We call this area the *ma'ar'ab*, the marketplace. Go two blocks and look for a sign with a drawing of a sheep. That is the Sheepshead Tavern, and Brynn may have some room to put you up. If not, she can at least direct you somewhere safe." The regent looked Aletha over as he handed her the map, but he was not leering.

"Better put your hair back up in the hat. And keep your cloak wrapped around you. Even though many walk the streets, the city has become unsafe as of late." Kah'yil sighed. "It is a sorry state of affairs when a land becomes unsafe for its citizens." He smiled as he stood. "I am sorry—I did not even ask your name."

"Aletha—and my brother is Adin. If you see him, would you please get word to your sister? He is not easy to miss, as he has a hunched back, and walks with a pronounced limp. He is my twin and, apart from the obvious differences, we look much alike."

The regent extended his hand to Aletha and led her out the door. "Then he must be a very *ya'feh* young man. I am pleased to meet you, Aletha, and now I must tend to two fools who need severe discipline, although the proverb often proves true: 'A scoffer who is rebuked will only hate you.'" Kah'yil frowned. "It seems I make as many enemies as friends these days. Well, I trust the next time we meet it will be under much happier circumstances."

"I look forward to that time." Aletha bowed her head and began walking down the hill, aware of the regent's watchful eyes. She stuffed her hair under her cap and drew her cloak closed. As she navigated her steps down the muddied lane, she wondered at her encounter. Kah'yil—the first regent of Sherbourne. She remembered the glass pane in the Council chamber, depicting a dark, tall man with an air of wisdom about him. The painting did not do him justice, capturing only some of his qualities. Possibly he was her ancestor, a great-great-grandfather, perhaps. How strange to stand there, speaking with him, and to think his blood might be in her veins. Being here, having this encounter, was nothing like reading about Sherbourne's history in dusty old parchments. When she returned to her own time, she would write true accounts of her history—that is, if she could ever find Adin and return with him.

Dusk painted the smoky skies and Aletha, watchful, wended her way through the streets, looking for the bell tower. After nearly an hour of jostling through the crowded lanes, she spotted the chapel and turned onto the cobbles. She passed dozens of small shops with goods displayed in the windows; some items she assumed were beyond the monetary reach of most in the city. But perhaps there were those who had lived here for a while, even before the walls had been formed, and who had enjoyed a thriving business and a comfortable existence.

Finally she spotted the sign of the tavern and, just before she reached the door, a crack of thunder and flash of lightning bolted across the sky. Rain pelted the street, and people pulled cloaks over their heads and hastened their steps. Aletha opened the heavy door and let out an inviting smell of simmering stew and baking bread. Her stomach growled in response. Collapsing on a bench at the far table, she looked around at the patrons tucking in to huge bowls of food and passing large mugs of ale. A hefty woman with an apron hurried to refill pitchers from a wooden cask behind the polished counter. The tavern hummed with noisy, lively discussion; it seemed an ale or two did wonders to soothe the anxious concerns of those faced with impending war.

In the warmth of the room, Aletha shed her cloak and finally caught the harried woman's attention, signaling her to her side. The barkeep pulled out a rag from the pocket of her apron and briskly cleaned away the crumbs and spills on the table in front of Aletha.

"What'll it be, lass? Two brass for supper and a pitcher of ale."

"Are you Brynn, the regent's sister?"

Brynn stopped wiping and gave her a tired smile. "In the flesh. And you are?"

"Aletha. Your brother said you may be able to help me find some lodging."

Brynn whistled through her teeth and wiped sweat from her forehead. "Ah, miss, I do have a room upstairs, but it's being used at present. Not many places will take in folk, and the city's so crowded."

"Is there an inn—or even perhaps a house to let?"

Brynn shook her head, glancing across the room at her patrons. "Times are tough these days. So many just pitchin' camp along the side of the road." She took in Aletha's crestfallen expression. "But, seeing as my brother sent you here, I'll see what I can find out. Maybe someone's heard of a room. You can pay?"

Aletha nodded. "I don't have coin for your city; is there a place I can exchange gold or silver?"

Brynn's eyes widened as she composed herself. "You'll find most folk agreeable to those forms of payment. But," she whispered, "I wouldn't announce to the world what you carry, miss. Now—how 'bout I bring you supper and ale and see what I can do to get you tucked away, at least for tonight?"

"Thank you, Brynn. I am grateful."

Looking around, Aletha noticed the tavern was not unlike the ones in her day. She even knew a few that dated back at least two centuries, having survived fire and flood and the occasional remodel. For all she knew, she could be sitting in her own Swan's Tavern. The plaster walls were supported by huge carved beams of dark wood, and in the far end of the room a fire blazed brightly. A tide of discouragement and worry lapped at her heart, but she was determined not to let despondency get the better of her. For now, she would eat and get warm. She hoped Brynn could find her a room somewhere, and then tomorrow she would continue her search for Adin.

Brynn delivered her bowl of stew and loaf of bread with a smile, hurrying off to greet a group of old men coming through the door and shaking rain from their cloaks. Aletha devoured every morsel of the meal but drank only a small glass of ale. It would not serve her well to end up asleep on the bench under a haze of alcohol. When she was able to catch Brynn's eyes, she asked for a pot of tea with a splash of milk.

As evening wore on, Aletha's eyes drooped closed. She rested her head on the table, keeping her bag on the floor by her feet. The tavern's clientele dwindled and, in time, only Aletha and a young couple remained. Aletha hadn't realized she'd dozed off until a gentle hand touched her shoulder. She looked up at Brynn, who carried a tray of dirty dishes.

"You're in luck, miss. There's a *ra'pha* who's been asking around for a helper. Now, he's an old fellow, harmless, and from what I hear, has a spare room."

"What is a *ra'pha*?"

"A person who makes cures, fixes people up. He helps with the wounded; Kah'yil knows him. Been here forever, long before the town was settled."

A healer. Maybe not so different from Reya.

Brynn continued, "I don't think he's interested in a roomer, but if you're willing to work, maybe he'd let you stay."

Aletha stood and stretched the kinks from her back. The hard wooden bench had put her legs to sleep. "Where can I find this man?"

Brynn nodded over at the boy washing dishes behind the counter. "Hadar lives right near him. He'll take you when he's finished up his chores." Aletha watched the young boy scrubbing the inside of a heavy iron pot. He glanced over at her and grinned.

The front door swung open and caught Brynn's attention. A man wrapped in a dripping cloak threw off his hood and shook himself like a dog. He carried a large bundle wrapped with twine. His black hair hung wet into his eyes, and he brushed the sodden mass aside and squeezed the water from his short beard and mustache.

Brynn laughed. "I've a better idea." She waved over to the man, who set the package down on a nearby table, threw his cloak onto a peg, and hurried to the fire, rubbing his hands. Luxuriating in the warmth, the man stood before the crackling flames, steam rising from his toes to his head. He turned and caught sight of Aletha, who found herself staring at a piercing set of blue eyes. She turned politely away.

"Ah, now *you've* found a stray, Brynn." He gave Aletha a big smile, raising his eyebrows as if waiting for her response. He gestured to Brynn. "This bundle is for your guest upstairs. I promised him some clothes."

Brynn walked over and took the package wrapped in coarse, damp paper. "You didn't need to go to the trouble tonight. He's not going anywheres soon."

"I'm heading back to the barracks; I was over at the east patrol. Anyway, can't a man get a pint without having to come up with an excuse? I'm stalling out the weather, hoping this deluge will let up some before I drown like a rat and get swept into the river."

Aletha chuckled as the man leaned his head near the hearth and shook his thick hair, delighting in the simple joy of a warm fire. To her surprise, he ran over to her table and scooted in along the bench next to her.

"I hope you don't mind my company, my lady. But I spend nearly every waking moment with dirty, smelly men. You would do me an honor to share an ale with me." His laughing eyes met her own, and taking her expression as consent, he stripped off his heavy vest and set it on the bench.

Brynn called over from the kitchen, poking her head out the door. "This here is Jered, captain of the *tsa'ba*. Don't worry, he's harmless." She returned with two large mugs of ale and placed them on the table in front of Jered.

He gave Brynn a sour look. "Well, here's mine, but aren't you going to bring the lady a drink?"

Brynn cuffed him on the side of his head. "Since when do you indulge in more'n a glass when duty calls?"

"Ah, bless the heavens, I have a day off tomorrow—the first in fifty, I think. So keep those glasses coming. Better yet, bring me a pitcher." He moved over to get a better look at Aletha. "And you are a quiet one. Tell me, what is your name, and how did you end up in this lonely place?" He slid one of the glasses over to her.

"My name's Aletha. I just arrived in town and Brynn is trying to help me find a place to stay."

Jered's eyebrows lifted. "Another with a strange *la'shone*—an odd accent. Every day we get more and more people here from strange lands. Soon there will be so many new ways of talking that our own language will disappear."

Aletha smirked. *If only this man knew how prophetic his words are.* This close, she could tell the captain was not much older than she. How young to be in command of an army! Either he was very brave or very foolhardy. Or the regent found in him a man he could trust.

Brynn called over again, her voice gravelly and tired. "Jered, how 'bout you taking this *ab'ay'da* to O'lam's place? 'Tis on yer way."

Aletha turned to Jered and asked, "What does that mean—*ab'ay'da*?"

The captain took a long pull on his ale and wiped the foam off his mustache. "A lost thing, an orphan." He called over to Brynn, "How could I turn down such a pleasant assignment? The easiest one I've had in days." He spoke to Aletha. "You will like the old *ya'ale*." When he saw her puzzled expression, he leaned over and whispered as if in conspiracy. "You know—the little animals we milk—with the horns." He put two fingers alongside his forehead and made a baaing sound. Aletha laughed.

"Oh, we call them goats."

"*Goats.* Now *that* is a strange word. Goats." He let the word roll around on his tongue, and Aletha laughed at his funny expression.

"Just where are you from?" he asked.

Aletha lowered her head and considered what to say. "My home is far from here, a great city not unlike this place. But, I am afraid it is impossible to get there easily from here. I endured something of a perilous journey to arrive at these walls." Aletha closed her mouth, worried the ale was loosening her tongue more than was safe. The room grew quiet, and Aletha stared at the flames crackling on the hearth. Out of the corner of her eye she could tell the captain stared, too, lost in thought. She could only imagine what kind of life he led each day, in charge of so many men and gearing up for war.

Aletha broke the thick silence. "Do you work for the regent, Captain?"

He turned to her and gave a tired smile. "Have you met our marvelous *tsa'va*?"

Aletha nodded. "He is the one who sent me here."

"Well, our regent is a great man—a *ghib'bore*—and it is a *ha'dar* to serve with him." He tipped his glass and drained the ale down his throat. "But the hour has grown late." He leapt from the bench with the agility of a deer, despite his tall, muscular frame. "As much as I'd like to stay and drink myself under the table, I don't believe O'lam keeps such late hours. Shall we be off, then?" He offered a hand to Aletha, and she let him lead her out from behind the table. He called over to Brynn, who was drying glasses and stacking them on a counter against the back wall. "What about Hadar; is he ready to go? I'll see him safely home."

The boy looked questioningly at Brynn, who nodded. He wiped his wet hands on a rag and mumbled his thanks, then ran to the back room and returned with an old oversized coat. Aletha went up to the bar and thanked Brynn, leaving a few pieces of silver on the counter. From Brynn's expression, Aletha was sure she had paid enough.

Bundled in her cloak, she pulled open the front door to the tavern and looked out on a night full of stars. She walked into the street, staring up at the familiar constellations of the autumn sky as she had done countless times at home. A wave of homesickness hit her and she felt oddly displaced. She *was* home; these were *her* stars. She looked to where she thought the knoll rose above the city, but there were no palace lights to illuminate the hill.

Even this late, groups of people walked through the narrow, winding streets, speaking quietly among themselves and venturing a glance at her as they passed by. She could feel the tension of the city coating the restless and worried inhabitants—a tension strangely similar to the trepidation she had left behind on the streets of Sherbourne in her own future time.

The captain came out of the tavern with the boy clinging to his arm. Aletha sensed a camaraderie between the two as Hadar playfully punched at the captain and he reciprocated with a feigned hard blow to the gut. The captain had a confident and easy stride and, pulling Hadar along, he came and entwined his other arm through Aletha's. She couldn't help but laugh. It felt good to release the worry she had been keeping clenched in her stomach. Maybe, she allowed, things were not as hopeless as they seemed. Maybe tomorrow she would find Adin, and between the two of them they would solve this mystery. It was possible.

As she walked arm-in-arm with the captain and Hadar, she listened, amused, as the two sang a goofy song about a snake, a rope, and a pig. A huge sickle moon broke through clouds over the rooftops of the city, and the air, washed of its smoke, smelled fresh as a morning when riding across the vale.

Yes, she tried to convince herself, anything was possible.

Aletha apologized for the late disturbance, but the old, gray-haired man cheerfully puttered around the small entry room in his long, white nightshirt, clearing clothes off an upholstered bench so he could offer his guest a seat. Seeing that Aletha was in good hands, Jered said his farewells, the old man assuring the captain that Aletha would enjoy a pleasant sleep once he cleared away the clutter in the back room. Surely, he promised, there was a bed in there somewhere. It would just take a bit of searching was all.

Jered took Aletha's hand, and before she could say good-bye, he kissed it lightly and gave her a wink. From any other man she would have thought the gesture presumptuous—even overly forward—but she sensed only a polite respect in his eyes as he nodded and backed out the front door.

Aletha offered to help the old healer, but he waved his arms in protest. "Now, now, lass, you just caught me off guard a bit.

What do you think about brewing us a cup of tea while I set things right?" Mumbling something, he disappeared in search of a bed.

Glad to be busy, Aletha went into the kitchen and found a pot of water sitting on a counter that ran under a row of mullioned windows. She set the pot on the hot stove and searched around for some mugs. The healer's kitchen reminded her of Reya's, but with a bit more mess. Odors of cooked food and boiled herbs lingered in the air. Stacks of parchment and a pot of ink sat on a small table against the wall next to a wooden stool.

What caught her interest, though, was the room off the kitchen that, in the dark recesses, looked like a huge storage and treatment room, with a raised platform bed in the center. She could make out shelves from floor to ceiling on all the walls— shelves crammed with thick books with strange bindings. Many of the held large ceramic jars marked with unusual writing in black ink. On the floor were baskets filled with odd instruments—perhaps to use in surgery—and rolls of cloth gauze.

As the water heated, Aletha peeked her head through the doorway and resisted the urge to pull down books and open them. Where could all these tomes have come from, and in what language would they be written? She imagined few people in this time were able to read and write, so this discovery intrigued her. Could this healer have some of the ancient herbal guides that Reya had learned from?

Aletha turned her attention to the task at hand, opening jars and sniffing their contents. She finally settled on one blend that smelled like lemon verbena and wintergreen. She shook the herbs into the boiling water and stirred. After wiping out two clay mugs, she waited for the leaves to steep, listening to her host tossing things to the floor in what she supposed was to be her bedroom. After a minute more of thumping and banging, the noise stopped, and she heard the healer's cheerful voice calling out to her.

"Now, that's a good choice, my lass. Just what's needed after the long day you must've had." Padding into the kitchen in his large bare feet, he leaned over the pot and smelled the steam, closing his eyes in pleasant appreciation. "Here's one who knows her herbs. Your name again, lass? I'm afraid names fly out of my head these days faster than a mudswift after a June bug in a dung heap."

"Aletha, sir."

"Oh, my, my. You must call me O'lam. That's how I'm known around here. Now." He poured two cups of tea through a linen cloth, that strained out bits of leaves and flowers, and brought them to the entry area, a tiny den with a giant stone hearth. Aletha sat on the bench and the healer sank back into an oversized stuffed chair close to the fire.

Aletha found him oddly different from most of the people she had seen around the town. His skin was pasty, almost white, but he had rosy pink cheeks and a bulbous nose that dwarfed the gray eyes that sank back into his face like small marbles. A bushy gray mustache fell over the sides of his mouth, perhaps making up for the thinning hair on the top of his head, which left a bald circle on the crown. His teeth were large for his mouth, and when he smiled, that smile took up a good part of his face. He was not fat, but meaty, with thick fingers and nicely trimmed nails, and he was barely as tall as Aletha. She could not guess his age, but despite his energetic demeanor, she figured him to be at least eighty years old, gauging from the mass of wrinkles etching his face.

He studied Aletha as if he were contemplating the medicinal uses of a plant. And Aletha did feel under scrutiny when he asked her a barrage of questions: Where was she from? How much learning did she have? Could she read? How much did she know about plants? He grew excited when Aletha related her years with Reya, gathering herbs, making poultices and potions, tinctures and liniment oils. He clapped his hands as excitedly as a child being handed a plate of cookies.

"My lass, you are heaven-sent! We have few healers in this city, and I find I cannot keep up with preparing what is needed—not just for the apothecary shops, but for the regent and his injured. If you would grace me with your help, I will put you up and feed you for as long as your precious heart desires."

Aletha drank her tea and the lateness of the night hit her with an intense need to sleep. "O'lam, I would be overjoyed to assist you, although I fear I may not know as much as you hope. Your plants and practices are no doubt different from mine, but I'm eager to learn, if you're willing to teach me. But—you must know the reason I'm here is to find my brother, so I need to spend time searching for him."

O'lam pulled on the ends of his mustache and smiled from ear to ear. "You, my lass, need sleep. So, to bed with you, and we'll work out a schedule in the morning. No doubt we can come to a mutual arrangement. Oh, it's been so long since I've had a house guest—or an assistant." He bounded out of his chair and led her to the door to the back room. "Now, I sleep in there," he said, gesturing to the entry room. "I've grown quite fond of my old chair, and I tend to snore, so you'll want to keep the door closed tight-like. You'll find a wash basin and washing cloth in there, and extra blankets. And just off your room is a place for other necessities. Good night."

Entering the little room, Aletha startled. Instead of the mess she expected to see, the room was neat and tidy, with everything in place. A small dresser stood against the wall, with a comb and mirror laid out on top of a hand-stitched coverlet. A single bed with a carved wooden headboard was perfectly made up, with two plump pillows on top of a blue quilt. An oil lamp, lit and glowing, shone from one nightstand, and a pitcher and glass of water sat upon the other stand. Another thick quilt lay neatly folded on a trunk at the foot of the bed. Wide wood planks covered the floor, oiled and gleaming. Aletha had never seen a wooden floor before, and she knelt down to feel its smooth surface. Her head spun from the abundance of surprises that day.

After washing and changing into her sleeping gown, she slipped under the thick quilt and relaxed as the warmth spread from her toes to her neck. Every muscle in her body ached. She turned down the wick in the lamp, and in the dark she noticed the silence settling over the room, almost like another blanket, smothering her tired, restless thoughts. Slowly her worries settled down like an old dog, and as Aletha drifted off, she could hear the rhythmic rumble of the healer's snoring charming her to sleep.

SEVENTEEN

ADIN LOST track of how many days he had spent in the upstairs room at the tavern. Twice Jered had come by and checked his wounds and was encouraged by signs of healing. He gave Adin a salve to rub into his skin and scalp, a warming lotion that gave off the fragrance of spring flowers and mint. The clothes Jered brought fit him fairly well; Adin needed only to roll up the sleeves of the shirt, and the trousers hung loose but comfortably. He expressed his gratitude again to the captain, who merely waved his hand in dismissal, as if saying, "Don't even mention it."

With Jered's encouragement, Adin got up from his bed and walked around the room, then up and down the stairs. The wound in his side throbbed with a dull ache, but he found it tolerable. Finally, his headaches were gone, although the smoky haze infecting the city hurt his eyes and tended to make him cough. Jered told him that in time he would get used to the pollution and had Brynn bring him up pots of Mouse Ear tea. Adin was horrified when he heard the name of his drink, but Jered, chuckling, assured him the tea was brewed from a small dandelion-type weed that grew along the roads. Many in the city drank it to dispel the discomfort brought on by the foul air. And no mice had been injured in the process.

The boy, Hadar, had faithfully come to his room each morning and afternoon, between busy times at the tavern, to help Adin with his lessons. Adin appreciated the task of setting his mind to learning something new; sitting hour upon hour in a lonely room depressed him. As he learned dozens of words from the strange language, he realized many of them were familiar. Not exactly the same pronunciation as the bits of the *law'az* he knew, but after a while he began to see a pattern in the way these words varied in sound and content.

For example, in his tongue, *a'mon* meant "faithful." In this time, the word was *ay'moon*, and it meant not simply faithful, but someone you could trust with a secret, or a regular repetition, like the sun rising each morning. Hearing long, lilting sentences of the *law'az* was like listening to the murmur of the wind through trees. Somehow over the centuries those words had grown sharp and harsh, but in this time they were soft, falling off his tongue like a flow of honey. Adin quietly practiced one of the proverbs Hadar had taught him yesterday, something he said his uncle, the regent, came up with. The regent was fond of sayings, according to Hadar, and always had a new one to spring on the boy when he saw him.

Adin spoke, trying to recall the way the words were strung together. "*Ber'aw'ka yashar k'reth room. Harak peh rasha.* 'By the blessing of the upright—or righteous—a city is exalted—or raised up, lifted high. But overthrown by the mouth of the wicked.'" It was not lost on Adin that the word for *wicked* was the same as the name of his father's councillor. He wondered if the creepy old man had deliberately given himself that fitting appellation.

Adin rubbed his sore back and went over to the window. This particular morning, after a night's hard rain, the air was fresh and the sky a radiant blue. Adin breathed deeply as he stood looking down into the lane. People jostled along the puddled cobbles below, pushing carts and carrying baskets, leading animals on tethers and carrying tools. Down the next block, peddlers sold fruit, vegetables, and flowers from their wooden stands, their customers haggling with them over prices. The heart of the city was a busy place, and Adin had grown restless from his inactivity and was anxious to search for the Keeper. He wanted to believe there was a chance the captain would find his stolen map, but he didn't dare hope.

As he had lain in bed hour after hour these last few days, he wondered if he should try to accept fate's hand in abandoning him here in this time. He nursed a glimmer of hope that the Keeper would know of another way to return Adin back to his Sherbourne, since he had heard rumors from the time he was small that the Keepers were some kind of wizards who held great magical powers. Maybe that was just another tale, a stretch of the truth, but then again, would he ever have believed in the existence of a magical map—or an enchanted labyrinth? For all his years of scoffing at Reya's stories, those tales had proved more truth than fancy. He should have taken her more seriously, asked more questions. But how could he have known that he'd end up here—centuries in Sherbourne's past?

As he watched out the window, he was surprised to see the captain riding up to the tavern on a horse, with another saddled mount trailing on a lead rope. Jered threw the reins over the post and came inside, and Adin heard him greet Brynn and come bounding up the stairs. Adin opened the door as the captain's hand hung in midair, preparing to knock.

"Adin, you are dressed! You look ready to go out and take on the world." Jered's infectious joy still baffled Adin. How could this man, weighed down with preparations for war, always rise above his burdens to face each day with such enthusiastic passion? In some ways, the soldier's tireless optimism reminded Adin of Aletha. There was always another way of viewing each situation, always a silver lining somewhere—you just had to look for it. Even in her moments of indignation, she would often laugh—unless her ire was in defense of her brother, or her kingdom.

Then heaven help anyone who dared challenge her stance! Before the thought of Aletha engulfed Adin with sadness, Jered interrupted him.

"Hey, my perky friend, why the sad face? I'm here to spring you from this prison and whisk you away." Jered wore his uniform, and his boots shone from polish. He had a brown-and-gray-striped cloak draped across his shoulders, and in his arms he carried another dark brown one. He handed it to Adin.

"I thought you might be ready for a tour of the city. I have to go to the southern wall and confer with the commander. Because of circumstances, it appears I'll be staying there awhile, making sure we have the necessary defenses in place. If you are well enough for work, there are many things I can find for you to do, to help me. Tomorrow I ride south, to meet up with the *tsa'ba* trying to hold back the *ghed'ood*." The captain's face grew grim. "Things are not going well in the skirmishes." He shook off his mood. "Come, I will set up another cot in my quarters there, and I have brought you a horse. Do you ride?"

Adin noticed the captain made no mention of his glaring deformities. Jered looked past them as if they didn't exist, and except for the concern over his stab wound, uttered no word of worry over Adin's abilities. Never once had Jered's eyes betrayed pity or scorn; he only saw a man in need of a job. And for that unusually rare kindness, Adin's heart warmed ever more to the captain. He would help this man as best as he could, wholeheartedly and without complaint. And in his spare time he would search for the Keeper and any other clues he could pick up along the way that would help him in his *ma'gur*.

"Captain, I've been riding from infancy. It has always been easier for me than walking." His mind fumbled for words of gratitude to express to Jered for all he had done—and was doing—for him. But Jered was one step ahead of him and saved him the effort.

"Reserve your thanks for later—until after you see how hard I work you. But I can pay you twenty brass a week—and when you are at the post, you'll be fed as well, although you may get tired of potatoes and pole beans. Fortunately, many in the city are not only grateful for the protection we are attempting to provide, but have the means to keep us in food and uniforms and weapons. How long until that support runs out, time will tell." Jered bounded down the stairs, and Adin followed after in his hobbling gait. "Hopefully, this *la'kham* will end soon, and soon is not soon enough for me."

Adin found Brynn and thanked her for all her hospitality. She complimented Adin for being such an easy guest and hoped he would return often. After he assured her and Hadar he would be back soon for more fine stew and language lessons, he put on the cloak and opened the front door to the tavern. Outside, the captain untied the extra bridle from his saddle and fitted it on Adin's horse. "You'll like this fine fellow. His name is O'kel—"

"Food?" asked Adin as he adjusted the stirrups hanging off the side of the chestnut-colored horse.

The captain looked at Adin curiously. "You are learning fast. Your teacher is doing a good job—teaching you the important words, I see." He chuckled and mounted his fidgety black mare. "You will see the reason for the name. Your gelding has a one-track mind, so keep him on a tight rein around the fruit stalls in the marketplace. Or you may have to spend your brass on items O'kel has decided to buy—without your consent."

The captain waited as Adin managed to get a foot in the stirrup and swing up into the saddle. Adin was glad Jered didn't offer his help, even when he saw Adin wince from the lingering pain in his side. With a nod of readiness, the captain untied his helmet from the back of the saddle and put it on his head. He adjusted the sword slung across his hip, then shook the reins and eased his horse into the busy street, creating an impressive presence that caused people to murmur and step aside. Adin's horse took up behind Jered's, and for the first time since Adin had arrived inside the walls, he had a chance to sit back and look at Sherbourne in its infancy, the city that would one day be ruled by his family.

As they walked their horses briskly through the heart of the city, Jered rambled on to Adin about the days before the wall was built. Adin learned that many centuries earlier, nomadic tribes had traversed the land, hunting the herds of *yak'moor*, a small reddish deer that used to graze in huge numbers. Eventually, enticed by the fertile soil and mild seasons, some settled and began farming. Most of the early people were from an ancient and magnificent kingdom far to the southeast, a fertile valley surrounded by leagues of unforgiving desert. It was said a giant, slow-moving river—so wide a man could not see the other side—meandered through the heart of that great empire into a nameless sea of radiant green water. As the desert encroached more and more upon that kingdom, eating up land through cycles of drought, groups of families left, seeking an easier way to subsist. They were the ones who brought the original language, said by some to be the pure language given to man at the dawn of creation. Whether that was so, Jered did not know; these were stories his father had told him.

Jered knew little of his own background. Those from the ancient kingdom were darker-skinned, with thick, curly, black hair and large, dark eyes. The beauty of their race could be seen intermingled with the blood of many who now lived here in this city. Jered assumed he shared some of that ancestry, though those attributes were not readily apparent in his features. His sapphire blue eyes were uncommon among the city-dwellers, although he and his brothers had inherited them from two blue-eyed parents.

For generations, Jered's family had farmed only three leagues from here, and as a boy Jered would ride his horse to the small open market—the same one he and Adin were now passing through—to buy the necessities his family did not themselves grow or build. The recent booming expansion of the city imposed a hard new reality that overshadowed the fond memories Jered had of the quiet and peaceful village he'd enjoyed visiting as a child.

After nearly an hour of riding through congested streets, they entered the flatter land along the river that Adin knew as the Heresh. Adin noted the that finely crafted bridge of his day had not yet been constructed; instead, two large flat barges capable of ferrying people and animals across the slow-moving water were tied to docks at the shore. Jered and Adin went to the river's edge and let the horses drink. A heavy fog settled in the valley, and Adin, now that he had stopped moving, felt the dampness soak through his clothes. He pulled his cloak tighter and reached for the water jug Jered had strapped to his saddle.

"Jered, do you have a name for this river?"

The captain looked south along the bank, trying to see through the fog. "The *na'har*? It is called the *Ka'shah*. The word means 'to be restful or still.' He smiled. "We catch some very tasty bottom fish here—I will see if we can find some at market for you. But, as you can tell, the water here is clouded; too much waste and runoff. We used to be able to drink from this river at any location, but now people get ill. And the wise fishermen go way upstream, near the northern wall, where even the fish escape to get away from the filth. There are enough small clean springs tapped throughout the city that, at least for now, good water is plentiful. But there is nothing like the taste of the water from the *mowt'sa* at the top of the hill."

Adin followed the captain's gaze west to where he could make out edges of the bluestone rocks peeking out from the skirt of white cloud ringing the knoll. The sight was breathtaking, catching Adin off guard with its unexpected radiance. Sunlight shone down upon the rocks in shimmering bands, streaming from a crack in the heavens. No wonder the place was revered as sacred.

"Jered," Adin asked, "when you were small, did you ever go up to the top of the knoll, to the spring?"

"Of course. My family would sometimes picnic there to enjoy the wildflowers growing on the hill. That was the view that filled my heart with a longing to explore the world, for on clear days I could see for leagues upon leagues and I wondered just what lay beyond all those mountains I could barely make out far, far away." Adin looked at Jered's downcast face and sensed the captain's restlessness and frustration. Like Adin, he belonged to another time— one of peace and simplicity.

Jered continued. "That was before men began pulling down the stone ring. For centuries that hill was considered *mik'dash*, a holy place. People treated it with a certain respect. But with the influx of people came a fervor for building; strangers new to this city saw how the large rocks could serve useful purposes. So, with giant ropes, they pulled them down and broke them into smaller blocks for their foundation stones and fire pits. Only when Kah'yil—the regent—formed and organized the *tsa'ba* were there enough men to stop the ravaging and stand guard to prevent further desecration. I'm afraid it was too little too late, at least for me. I will never understand those who destroy with such disregard for history. All for a few building blocks."

Adin tried to imagine sitting on the knoll and gazing at the complete ring of rocks. Reya had called it one of the gates of heaven—the *sha'har*—places the Keepers were meant to protect from evil. Could this vandalism be the cause of the desecration and the beginning of the evil curse? The hermit had said the map would take him to a time where he would be able to witness the onset of the *qa'lal*. So, it hadn't happened—not yet. But somehow, intuitively, Adin sensed that pulling down "the gate of heaven" was the first pebble in the avalanche that tumbled the city toward ruin. Why hadn't the Keeper stepped in and stopped the violation of the site? Was the Keeper even here, or alive? Or was he—or she—powerless to restrain men from their madness? Adin hoped he would learn the answers to those riddles, for his own future was intrinsically woven into them.

As the captain led Adin south along the road beside the river, Adin asked about his new duties. How many hours was he needed, and what would his tasks entail? He worried that time could run out, and the event he needed to witness would catch him unprepared. He breathed relief when Jered revealed his plans to send Adin out by horse throughout the city to secure contracts with vendors—those who provided food, metals, even wagons used to bring back the injured from battle. While out on his rounds, Adin could use every opportunity to locate the whereabouts of the mysterious symbol he sought. Adin was overjoyed; he could not think of a better assignment. To the captain's mind, it served both their purposes well.

By the time they arrived at the tower perched above the south wall, Adin was tired, clammy, and ravenous. Jered shared his list of complaints, so after he introduced Adin to the fighters stationed at the post, he made sure the cook scrounged up two hot meals for himself and his new assistant. Adin felt welcomed, his status elevated by the respect shown him by Jered. Some of the men exhibited wounds; some had lost a limb. Many had scars that made Adin cringe thinking about the pain inflicted to create such marks. Among this group of walking wounded, Adin felt comfortable. No one paid any attention to his twisted leg or hunched back. No one had any inclination to judge him by his appearance. Already Adin felt his spirits lift; he was at ease with a table of men joking in camaraderie with their captain.

As he wolfed down a giant bowl of potato soup, he thanked the heavens that, of all people, Jered had rescued him. He could almost believe deep in his heart that what had happened to him in that alley, being attacked by those men, was part of heaven's plan—although he couldn't see how anything but his own stupidity could be responsible for losing the map. Yet now, sitting in the tower and watching the fog lift from his kingdom, he felt that familiar, subtle touch of destiny pulling him along, although he was blind to its leadings.

"It is the glory of God to conceal things, but the glory of kings to search things out," the hermit had told him. Adin sighed. Who was he to question the way heaven guided the steps of mere men? His task was to search these mysteries out, whether he understood them or not. And, after he'd washed and changed his clothes, that was just what he intended to do.

EIGHTEEN

ALETHA STOOD and stretched. Her back ached from bending over the worktable for countless hours. Fog swirled against the large window in the workroom, and Aletha took a moment to drink a tall glass of water while she leaned on the sill, looking out into a small, secluded yard—one of the few she had seen in the city. She could tell the healer's home had been here for many years, much longer than any other cottages on this road. A tall, rickety fence enclosed a garden entangled with the detritus resulting from neglect. One of Aletha's jobs would be to clean, prune, and winter over the plants, and collect any last remaining fall roots. But first, O'lam was in need of ten dozen jars of a liniment made from St. John's wort—fuzzy yellow blossoms the healer had gathered last month, now dried and crumbling in the woven straw basket at her feet.

At the first sign of morning light, Aletha had heard O'lam banging around in the kitchen, and upon dressing she had come out and found a bowl of cooked oats waiting for her on the tiny table. Somehow the healer had made room for two place settings, and Aletha shared tea and breakfast with her vivacious host. His voice bursting with excitement, he rattled off a list of all the wonderful things they would accomplish today, but he encouraged her to first spend a few hours getting her bearings and looking for her brother. There was a small town hall, he told her, where men volunteered for the *tsa'ba*—the militia—and where others sought work. Perhaps her brother had been directed there when he arrived in the city. Aletha did not think Adin would have had any reason to stop at such a place, but any lead was worth a try. At the very least she could leave his description, and directions to find her at the healer's.

So immediately after breakfast she washed dishes—an activity that simply tickled her host—and headed out the door. Only after walking a few blocks did she realize how close the cottage sat to the road leading up to the knoll. Yesterday she had nearly passed the healer's home on her way to the tavern, as his small lane veered off from the main thoroughfare. She retraced some of her steps to the older section of the city, where she found the town hall. After leaving information with the recruiter sitting behind the desk, she spent two hours walking up and down streets, occasionally asking a merchant or old man on a bench if he had seen anyone resembling Adin, but learned nothing. At least his hunched back would make him memorable to many he encountered. Someone, somewhere, would recall him. It was only a matter of time. This was her first day of searching, she reminded herself. No reason to allow discouragement to set in.

When she returned to the cottage at midday, she could tell O'lam had been busy. With a big-toothed grin, he remarked that his order of jars had just arrived. A stack of wooden crates sat in the entry, the tops pried open. What looked like a long list scribbled on a parchment rested on the kitchen table. O'lam ushered Aletha into the back room and lit a bright lantern and set her to working—once he was doubly assured she had eaten lunch and, no, was truly not hungry.

Making this potent ointment for muscle pain was a messy job. First, she crushed the flower blossoms with a pestle in a large ceramic crock, adding drops of oil to moisten them. The yellow flowers turned to a red paste, and, once it was thoroughly mashed, she put the paste into the bottom of the jars, filling the jars to the top with more oil. Despite her care, her fingers were already stained a deep, stubborn crimson. O'lam had instructed her to place all the jars unopened on the shelf under the window, where they would ferment for five days. Then she had to seal them with liquid paraffin, topped with a linen cap, and put them out in the sun—if they had any sunny days coming. The jars had to be shaken daily until the contents turned flaming red. At that point the liniment would possess the greatest healing properties.

Most of the remedies O'lam made treated one of three types of ailments. First were the bruises and injuries resulting from battle, or from building the wall—suffered by men either unaccustomed to hard labor, or, as O'lam put it, too foolish to know when to get out of the path of a falling stone. His herb of choice was meadowsweet— a plant Aletha knew from the woods around Reya's cottage—which put out a flush of butter-colored blooms on a long, slender stalk. The flowers and leaves served as an anti-inflammatory, and aso calmed digestion. This plant dispelled aches and pains, complementing the liniment she was preparing.

Then there were the numerous complaints of headaches and coughing from the soot and smoke in the air. Lady's Slipper root, elder flower, catsfoot, mullein—these were boiled to make teas and syrups, sold bottled in the shops.

For more serious wounds, O'lam prepared poultices of arnica, yarrow, and marigold—plants he grew in his yard but which were now past season, and had been picked, dried, and stored in the many jars on the shelves in the workroom. One of Aletha's jobs would be to make the poultices, mixing the flowers with flaxseed and boiling the mixture for hours until it thickened. Aletha could easily see why O'lam had expressed such enthusiasm over her willingness to help—he had regrettably fallen behind in meeting the demands pressed upon him.

She returned to the worktable and set about her task of crushing flowers, adding oil, and making a paste. From time to time she switched hands, as the grinding cramped her fingers. O'lam came in from something he'd been doing outside, and she noticed his fingers were stained dark blue.

"Ah, lass, look what we have here." He opened his apron to reveal a small pile of dark berries, a kind she was unfamiliar with.

"What do you use those for?"

He reached down and popped a handful into his mouth. "Eating is what. Here!" The old man walked in a funny swaying manner, something that at first had made Aletha giggle. He poured the berries out of his apron into a bowl and pushed them toward her. "'Fraid these are the last we'll see of them until next year. Bogberries we call 'em; heaven knows why—no bogs to be found anywheres near. Make a fine pie, those. If you have a hankering to bake." Aletha could tell from the twinkle in the healer's eyes his statement was more of a hint.

She smiled. "I make a mean tart, if that will suit your fancy."

"Lass, mean or no, tarts are one of my favorites. Been many years since I've had someone to bake for me." The healer got busy searching his shelves and pulling out jars to set on the table. Aletha had the feeling that O'lam had touched upon some memory that saddened him. Perhaps he'd had a wife, or a family he'd lost. She didn't want to be nosy, so she quietly went about her work, occasionally reaching for a handful of the plump, sweet berries.

"Do you know this plant?" O'lam held up a small piece of woody branch with glossy, dark leaves.

"It looks like something we call prickly ash. Does it have fuzzy berries, like peas clumped together?" The healer nodded, looking pleased that his assistant recognized the plant. Aletha continued, "We collect strips of bark in the spring and make a strong infusion from it. My nursemaid used to make this for my brother, who suffered terribly from leg cramps."

"As do I, my dear lass. Not getting any younger, it seems. The berries, as well, carry a potent oil that I make into an astringent. Helps on cold nights." He gestured to the jars on the worktable. "So, what do you think of my thriving business, eh? Can make a bit of brass and live quite comfortably, if that's what you're after." The healer blinked at Aletha with his smoky gray eyes, waiting for her response.

"Oh, wealth holds little appeal for me, sir. I just find it satisfying to learn how I can help others." As Aletha spooned her paste into the jars in front of her, the healer's gaze changed in the harsh glare of the lantern, summoning her attention. Aletha stopped and set down the spoon. She met his stare and O'lam's eyes widened in surprise. He, too, set down the branch from which he was picking leaves and tilted his head. His voice lowered.

"What are you seeing, lass? Tell me."

She didn't want to be rude, but suddenly she could not turn away from the healer's eyes. She found nothing sinister or frightening in them, but as Aletha was pulled into their depths, a strange sensation came over her. A feeling of falling, slowly, calmly, into a sea of water. Then the sense of being in a warm womb, of hushed quiet and safety. A wave of comfort cradled her—so strong her throat choked, and before she realized it, tears streamed down her face. A flood of emotions overwhelmed her—sadness, loneliness, but also a tingling of peace and joy. Nothing in her life had ever provoked such feeling, and by the time she found her way back from those depths and returned to herself, she was unable to speak a word.

O'lam reached over and took her hands in his. She glanced down and saw her hands were shaking. "Aletha, I didn't realize you had the sight. But, well, hello, there's a surprise."

She finally found her voice. "I was taught little about this sight. Sometimes—I see something in people's faces; other times there is a layer underneath that belies what appears on the surface."

"Yes," O'lam said, speaking in a tone of voice different than usual. "That is one of the ways of sight."

"But . . . what just happened now, when I looked in your eyes?"

"What did you see there?"

Aletha told him, then asked, "What does it mean?"

O'lam took a deep breath, his expression now a puzzle. Finally, he chose words and offered them to her. "Aletha, you did not land on my doorstep like some magpie who lost her way on an overcast night. Now I know you were *sha'lach*—sent to me. I have lived many, many years in this place, and never have I come upon one like you." His face clouded over with memory. "Would I be wrong if I guessed there is more to your presence here than flushing out a lost brother?"

Aletha hesitated, then nodded. O'lam searched her face as if trying to decipher a cryptic language. ". . . that you seek something else, answers to a mystery, answers . . ." Now his eyes widened even more and his cheeks flushed a hot pink. ". . . to your—past?"

Aletha gasped. "Who *are* you?"

He patted her hand, and a smile pushed against his bright red cheeks, easing Aletha's agitation. "My dear lass, we have much to talk about. You are just as much an enigma to me as I am to you. Tell me . . . where you come from, is there a prophecy concerning a deliverer, a . . . *pa'lat?*"

Aletha felt her face flush, remembering Reya's words. "The Deliverer . . ."

"Yes!" O'lam said, excitement spilling out in his voice.

Aletha shook her head emphatically. "But that is not me!"

"Oh my, oh no, sweet girl. You are not the *pa'lat*. But you are connected somehow to the prophecy—that I can see."

"I came here—to uncover the mystery of what we call the *qa'lal*."

"*Qa'lal*? What is this curse you speak of?"

"You don't know it?" Aletha furrowed her brows. "The *pa'lat* is the one who undoes the curse."

The healer chewed on Aletha's words. "You have one piece, I have another. All I know of the *pa'lat* is that the Deliverer is sent to save a kingdom—this kingdom."

"Yes, exactly."

The healer held his head as if her very words spun around inside it. "My, my dear lass, you are indeed an unexpected surprise—in more ways than one. But, this is not something to be carelessly chatted about. Have you spoken to anyone at all about this since you've arrived?" Aletha shook her head, and O'lam let out a relieved sigh. "Some things are not safe to speak of—some people are not to be trusted. Please believe me when I tell you that what we discuss must not leave this cottage."

Once more Aletha nodded. The healer pulled a cloth from his pocket and dabbed his glistening head. Shivers ran up Aletha's spine. O'lam squeezed her hands and spoke, his words barely audible. "One more question . . . but I don't know if I want to hear your answer."

Aletha watched the healer swallow. Her heart pounded in anticipation. When he spoke, she had to strain to hear him. "Lass, how did you get here, to this place? From where did you travel?"

"Not where." Aletha paused, then her voice trembled as she uttered the next word: "*When*."

The healer's face turned even whiter than Aletha thought possible. She added with hesitation, "I followed my brother's footprints. He used a magical map that led him here—from centuries in the future." She loosed a breath and slumped her shoulders. "I know you will find it impossible to believe."

There—she'd said it.

"No, my dear lass, no," the healer replied, his voice a whisper. "I believe it with all my heart." He squinted, and added in a burst of clarity, "For I have seen it!"

NINETEEN

WHEN CAPTAIN TEBRON entered his room in the south tower, he could tell Adin was taken aback by his appearance. He did look like something that had been dragged behind a horse in the mud for a dozen leagues—and that was how he felt. But his appearance was nothing a hot bath and stiff scrub brush couldn't remedy. He had only planned to stay with the *tsa'ba* for a day, but when he arrived and found them embroiled in a fight that showed doubt of success, Jered kept with them three days until their enemies had been sufficiently routed—for the time being. Just his presence there had given the men a boost of confidence, and the captain knew confidence was half the battle.

However, when he and a scout crawled for half a league to a rocky ledge and looked out over the enemy camp, Jered found his own confidence rattled. Below him, in the dim moonlight, he saw well-organized groups of mighty warriors equipped with sturdy armor and thick leather leggings. Swords, bows, spears, and axes lay piled alongside the cook fires as far as his gaze could reach in the night, their metal ornamentation glinting in the flickering light. Jered took a mental count, and the numbers were disheartening. As they turned to head back to their encampment, the scout gave Jered a questioning look. Jered tried to assure the man, with a forced smile, that things weren't as hopeless as they seemed. He knew recent losses weighed heavily on the fighters' hearts, but every day that they held back the *o'yab*, they bought another day of peace for the city.

Jered had spent most of last winter and spring at those front lines, coordinating raids into enemy camps, ambushing supply wagons. He would still be there if he hadn't met with a finely sharpened arrow in his thigh. Without the means to be evacuated quickly, his leg had badly festered. Fortunately, a break in the fighting allowed him to be carted back to the healer, just in time to save his leg. With a fracture threatening to break the bone, the healer told him to apply himself to less physical duties—at least for a while. Kah'yil silenced Jered's protests and, in the end, ordered him to stay in the city to take care of matters just as important as mowing down the *ghed'ood*. Still, his work far from the front lines felt like a betrayal of his men, and caused him daily agitation.

After washing up and trimming his beard, he sat in the dining hall with Adin, catching up on three days of missed meals. The *tsa'ba* hiding in the southern forests lived mostly on dried fruit, bread, and hard cheeses. What food they ate had to be carried in on foot, as there were no roads near their encampment. So Jered suffered his usual twinge of guilt, indulging in such a hearty, hot meal while he knew that his men, cold and uncomplaining, ate what was available. And that knowledge lent a bitterness to each swallow.

He was pleased to hear how adept Adin had been in procuring and negotiating for the items the fighters needed. Between bites, he rattled off other supplies he needed Adin to seek. When his assistant reached into a sack and pulled out parchment, pen, and ink, he stopped chewing.

"What do you have there, Adin?"

"Your lists grow to be so long, I have a hard time remembering them. I am still learning my way around the city, and can't keep all those names straight." Adin dipped the pen into the ink jar and began writing.

The captain watched in amazement, and leaned closer to see Adin's scratching. "You know how to write! But what strange letters. I have never known anyone who can put words to parchment—other than O'lam and the regent—and it took the regent countless hours of study and poring through indecipherable books to be able to write even the most basic words. Tell me—how did you learn to do this?"

Adin shrugged and withdrew other sheets from his sack, covered in writing. "See—these are the words Hadar taught me, so I can read and practice saying them. Where I come from, most people learn to write and read when they are young. Without that, how can anyone send a message or formulate laws to govern a kingdom? You would have to pass these things from mouth to mouth—and we all know how messages get jumbled with such retelling." Adin paused. "Instructions get confused, and misunderstandings result."

"I have always thought that myself! With such a large population, there can be little order if no one agrees on what has been said. Tell me, Adin—is your writing difficult to learn? Can you teach me?"

Adin laughed. "Really, it is very simple. All you need is a primer . . ."

"What is that?" inquired Jered.

"I will make you one. A chart—to show you each letter and the sound that goes with it. If I draw you pictures of things that have that sound, you will know how to connect the shape of the letter with it. Then, to write any word, just sound it out slowly, putting letters to it. A child can do it."

Jered's head swam with ideas. "Just think—if we could post these charts throughout the city, eventually everyone would be able to read and write."

"Well, there are always some who will not want to make the effort. You would have to come up with a good incentive to encourage them to learn."

"How 'bout the threat of a hot oil dipping?" Jered chuckled. "No, but I see your point. I will think hard on this and come up with something. In the meantime, work on that chart—in your spare hours. Let me see you make a list."

Jered watched, fascinated, as he told Adin the places he needed to go, and Adin responded with a trail of ink neatly covering the page. He finished his meal, his eyes glued to the shapes coming out of Adin's pen.

"Well, this is a lot to do," Adin said. "I'd better get ready and saddle up."

"How has O'kel been behaving? If you would rather have a faster mount, I'm sure I can round one up."

Adin stood, list in hand and a smile on his face. "He suits me fine. We have come to an understanding; as long as we have our regular snack breaks, he is content to follow my prompting without argument."

Jered lowered his voice. "Have you had any leads to point you to your star?"

Adin shook his head. "Nothing so far. I even went to a jeweler's shop, and they had never seen anything like it."

Jered got up from the table and gathered his dishes. "I will check again with my contacts about your . . . missing items. I should hear something by late today, when you return."

"What are your plans now, Captain?"

"I need to report back to the regent; he is anxious to hear how the men are faring." A smile crept up his face. "And there is a young lady I hope to drop in on and visit along the way."

Adin's eyebrows raised. "How does such a busy, important man like yourself have time for romance?"

He chuckled. "I don't."

Since arriving in the city and joining in the regent's cause, Jered'd had no time to even think about women. Five years back, he'd almost married—a girl he had grown up with. She was more like the sister he'd never had, and they'd hoped to settle down after Jered finished his charting of the western ranges. But the attack on his village had destroyed those plans.

Jered felt the bile rising in his throat, and the fury he kept restrained raised a noisy complaint. He never did find Sa'rah—in any of the resettlement camps. He hoped in his heart she had fled to a safe haven, but it was a fool's hope. Her family home suffered such a thorough burning that he found nothing identifiable in the cinders. No one had seen her sister or parents since that loathsome day. Jered sighed and unclenched his fists while Adin watched his face.

He shook off his mood with a flip of his head. "Well, my friend, what about you? Do you have someone special waiting for you back home?"

Jered saw deep pain harbored in Adin's eyes. "No one. All my family is . . . lost to me. My father, mother, sister—all gone. I will have to learn to live with that, I suppose."

Jered set down his plates and placed a hand on Adin's shoulder. "In these hard times, Adin, we make what family we can. I am happy to have you as a brother, if you'll have me."

Adin nodded, and tears pooled in his eyes. Not wanting to distress him any longer, Jered said a warm farewell and took his dishes to the kitchen. In under an hour he had met with the outpost commander and taken his muddy clothes to be washed. He allowed himself to linger on the memory of Aletha's sweet face, and smiled when he thought of her dancing eyes and infectious laugh. He would pay a friendly visit, make sure she was comfortable. That wouldn't be too pushy of him. There was something unique about her, an elegance of demeanor that intrigued him—not to mention, she was undeniably beautiful.

But one thing he knew about beautiful women—they were usually plenty aware of it. Yet he hadn't sensed any arrogance in her manner, unlike the pretty girls from his village. She seemed concerned with more important things than her own looks, and he had a hunch that that pretty face hid some secrets.

Jered mounted his horse and rode north along the river. Fat clouds threatened to turn the mild afternoon into a wet, miserable ride. Surely, he told himself, *that* was the reason he spurred his horse to a gallop, not allowing that an intriguing young woman could have anything to do with his desire for haste.

After knocking at the front door to the healer's cottage, Jered waited, enjoying the unseasonably warm afternoon. His horse, loosely tied, snuffled as she grazed the few tufts of grass lining the road. A few people passed along the sparsely traveled lane, and Jered nodded at the polite greetings he received. Impulsively, he peeked through the window into the dark entry room, but saw no one. With a frown, he untied his horse, ignoring the fluttering in his stomach. Disappointment settled over him, and he silently kicked himself for getting worked up over nothing. The last half a league he had found himself rehearsing strings of words, trying them aloud, then discarding them. He never worried what to say to a hundred men in his charge, and no one would ever describe the captain of the militia as shy or self-conscious. So what in heaven's name was wrong with him?

Just as he unclipped the halter, he heard a noise from behind the cottage. He stopped and listened to an irate voice grousing in a foreign tongue. Jered had no doubt whom the voice belonged to, and his curiosity overcame any residual nervousness.

Peering over the dilapidated fence boards, Jered found Aletha sitting on the dirt in a heap of weeds, her head hung over something in her lap. He called out, "I heard a cry. Are you all right?"

Aletha's eyes found Jered's. He watched as a flush of emotions crossed her face: surprise, embarrassment, delight—but the foremost was frustration. He reached his hand over the top of the gate and found the latch. After some wiggling of the rusty hardware, he managed to unhook the catch and made his way over to Aletha, who had turned her attention back to the hand she was holding elevated. A steady trickle of blood seeped into the old tunic she wore, and she hastily stood.

"I'll survive," she said. "I am such an idiot. I need to wrap this."

Jered couldn't help smiling at this woman standing before him: filthy, with mud streaked across her face, her messy hair braided down her back, blood dripping down her arm. Jered found her absolutely enchanting. "Wait here—I'll find something inside. No sense tracking mud into the house." Jered ran in through the back door and gathered supplies he found in the back room. When he returned to the yard with his arms full, Aletha laughed.

"What?" he asked.

Aletha shook her head in amusement and gestured at his armload. "Captain, it's just a little cut. One small bandage will surely do."

"Here, let me," he said.

Aletha stood still, her eyes following Jered as he wiped dirt off the wound with a damp cloth, and then deftly wrapped gauze around her palm, neatly tucking in the loose end. "There. Good as new." He relinquished her hand with reluctance.

"I'm impressed. You've done a lot of this kind of patching, I can tell."

"You have no idea."

As Jered set down his supplies, Aletha brushed off her clothes. She wore what looked like an old pair of the healer's trousers, rolled up at the cuffs. Her feet were bare and covered in mud, and under the tunic she wore a green long-sleeved shirt that made her hazel eyes shine. If she was embarrassed by her appearance, she didn't show it, and that warmed Jered to her even more.

"You look as happy as a rumphog that's been playing in the dirt."

She smiled while she used a corner of the wet rag to clean her face. "I was—until I lost my grip on that knife." She pointed to a small paring blade on the ground.

"I'm not sure what you're doing back here, but it looks like a massive undertaking. What are these piles?"

Aletha pointed. "Weeds, over there. Roots, here. The ones with the wilted stalks are valerian. They'll make a strong pain reliever. Those with the purple lily-type blooms are Lady's Slipper—for headaches. And rhubarb—the one I cut myself trying to loosen—helps digestion."

"Is that the same rhubarb as in 'pie'?"

Aletha nodded. "But you make pie from the stalks, not the roots." She picked up a gnarly dirt-encrusted root. "This would make one ugly pie."

Jered laughed. Aletha looked at him curiously. "Why are you here? You certainly didn't come dressed in all your finery to have a gardening lesson."

"On my way to the armory. To report to the regent. I thought I would see how well you've settled in."

Jered could almost detect a blush on her cheeks, but she busied herself gathering up the roots and putting them into a wooden barrel.

"I'm enjoying O'lam's company. And he is teaching me much."

Her look of frustration was not lost on Jered. "But?"

She sighed and quickened her pace. Once the barrel was full, she walked over and lifted a board away from a cistern set into the ground. As she lowered a bucket, she looked over at him. "I'm sorry, Captain. I don't mean to be impolite, but there are pressures weighing on my heart. Things I need to do but cannot see my way to doing."

He came over to help, lifting out the bucket which was spilling over with water. She pointed to the barrel, and Jered emptied the water over the roots. Aletha reached her hands in and grabbed a root, then rubbed away the encrusted mud. "One more?"

After replacing the cistern's cover, he dumped the second bucket of water into the barrel. He watched Aletha pick at the roots, her face lined with worry.

"Let me help you, then. It's not good to keep your concerns all bottled up. Maybe I will have some ideas." Jered could tell his voice sounded overeager.

Aletha stopped and placed a wet hand on Jered's wrist. The touch sent another flutter to his stomach. "Jered, I sense you are a lot like me. You want to get things done, feel useful. Make sure everyone is well cared for. Fix everyone else's problems." Her tone was kind and thoughtful, and he was surprised how perfectly she assessed him. She smiled sadly. "But as much as I wish I could confide in you, I cannot. I cannot risk involving anyone in what I have to do."

Jered walked around the yard while Aletha placed the cleaned roots on a towel spread at her feet. He tried to push past the dejection he felt. How did he expect her to trust him?—they'd only just met. Maybe, in time, she would open up to him. He only needed to earn her trust.

"I grew up on a small family farm—not far from here," he said. "I always liked digging in the dirt, planting seeds and watching them grow."

"So did I. I never had my own plot, but when I was young, my brother and mother and I would help out at the abbey. The monks had a huge garden and would feed families for leagues around." She wiped her hands and came over to Jered. "Those were some of my happiest days. Funny, this is the first time I've worked in a garden since . . . the year my mother died." Her voice trailed off. "After that, I guess I found it too painful. Too many memories."

Jered watched Aletha pick up a rake and begin working the weed pile toward the corner of the fence. He found another rake and helped her. "I lost my mother too. When I was eleven. That year the fever took many. I almost lost my youngest brother as well, but he pulled through."

Aletha stopped raking and looked into Jered's face. "So, we share this loss as well." Her words carried so much pain Jered wanted to gather her in his arms. But she set down her rake and put a hand on his shoulder. "Come, let's have some tea and you can have a bogberry tart."

As Jered sat at the small kitchen table, Aletha retreated into the back room to change clothes. He sipped tea and calmed his heart. There was something about this woman that pierced him, like a sharp arrow through faulty armor. Was it her sensitivity, her intuitiveness? Maybe it was just the way she exuded a simple honesty about her—no pretense. But, troubled times tended to strip away superficialities, leaving the hardness of reality exposed. And yet Aletha, while carrying some heavy pain, seemed anything but hardened herself.

She came back into the room in a beige gown trimmed in lace. The design was simple, but to Jered she looked like a princess. He quickly stood and pulled out her tiny chair. Maybe just washing up and putting on clean clothes had brightened her mood, for she gave him a big smile and took her seat gracefully. She poured herself a cup of tea and watched him eat a plate of tarts. At her urging, Jered told her about his childhood, and she asked about his dreams. He noticed her interest heighten when he spoke of his years exploring the mountains.

"Tell me, Jered, what are the Sawtooths like? I have often looked on them from a distance with a longing to see them for myself. I just never have found the time."

"Oh, there is nothing like climbing up through all the sharp granite crags and looking down. There is this beautiful valley, ringed by the tallest trees you can imagine. Thick trees, wider than this cottage." Aletha's eyes grew wide as Jered continued his description. "And a forest hugs the ring of mountains, with a huge meadow to one side, and a creek that winds and twists out to another land."

"Are there any villages there?"

"None. I have never seen another soul in that valley. But I plan to live there someday. There is something magical about that place, and it calls to my heart, as if I am destined to go."

A knowing look came over Aletha. "Yes, I know that feeling well. It is something you can't ignore. You may be able to put it off for a while, but it always comes back to haunt you."

Jered nodded and leaned on his elbows, getting closer to Aletha. "Tell me—do you feel that way sometimes . . . that you are pulled by the hand of destiny? That there is something important you are being called to do, but you're not sure what it is?"

Aletha almost dropped her cup. In a soft voice she said, "You have no idea . . ."

Jered studied her face, and when Aletha saw the look in his eyes she laughed heartily. "Now, my dear Captain. You've had your tea and tarts." She laughed, this time at something private.

"What?" he asked, wondering if he had berries on his face. He wiped his beard with his napkin.

"Nothing. You just remind me of my brother—the way you wolfed down your food."

"I've always had a good appetite. And I'm hopeless around anything sweet." After the words came out, he realized Aletha took them to have a different meaning. He felt his cheeks blush. He stood and put on his cloak, and wiped crumbs from his uniform.

"But I wouldn't want to overstay my welcome. Then you may not invite me back."

"An extra hand in the yard is always welcome, Captain." Her eyes shone. "And such pleasant company would never be turned away." She walked him to the front door and opened it for him. "Go and discover your destiny, Captain Jered, and I'll try to tackle mine."

Jered used every ounce of control he could muster. He wanted nothing more at that moment than to take her in his arms and kiss her. But she saved him the agony of taking that initiative, for, before he realized it, she placed a hand alongside his head, and her soft lips brushed his. It was not the kiss he longed to share, but it held promise. And that was more than enough for now.

TWENTY

FINISHED EARLY with his list of stops, Adin decided on a whim to pay a visit to Brynn at the tavern, and see if Hadar was available for another lesson. He was happy he had a pouch of brass; now he could pay the lad as promised. After he tied his horse to the post, he wiped sweat from his forehead. He couldn't recall such warm fall days in his time, and he could nearly taste a pint of ale soothing his dry, dusty throat. He ran his hand over the short beard now covering his chin; all the men at his barracks had beards and that prompted Adin to grow one too. He actually liked the way it felt, and how it gave his face more maturity. Yet now, with such warm weather, his skin itched under all that hair.

As he entered the cool room, Brynn recognized him and came out from behind the counter. She gave him a big hug and remarked on his wonderful recovery.

"Heavens, I almost didn't recognize you—so dashing and healthy. I hear the captain's recruited you. And from all accounts, looks like you're being fed well enough. Like Kah'yil always says, 'A cheerful heart is good medicine.' Has done you some good, can tell."

As Adin sat at a table, Brynn fetched him a pitcher of ale and a large glass. Adin was disappointed to hear Hadar was at home, busy with chores for his father. Brynn promised to give him the three brass Adin owed him. When she heard how Adin's search for his belongings had come up dry, she clicked her teeth. "Just the nerve of some people. Preying on the weak and helpless. But how were you to know to watch for such trouble, being new to the city and all? 'Like fish in a cruel net, birds caught in a snare, so men are snared at a time of calamity when it suddenly falls upon 'em.' That's what the regent says."

"Your brother sounds like a wise man. I hope I will meet him sometime."

"Oh, no doubt you will."

Adin asked Brynn how things fared at the tavern, and she scooted in next to him with a heavy sigh. "Times are getting worse. Harder these days to get enough food for the customers. Merchants from outside the city fear for their lives; fewer risk the trip. And prices are getting beyond the means of most. Soon, no one will be able to eat." She spoke in a hushed whisper, looking at the few patrons eating at the tables. "You know, Jered's Pa and brothers farm up in the northern part of the city—on the farm collective. And I hear the demand's just been too high. With cold coming and planting starts hard to come by, I can tell you it'll be a rough winter. And when food runs out and people are shiverin' and miserable, that's a recipe for *sha'mad*."

Adin pondered Brynn's words. Maybe the captain was right to hope for war to come sooner rather than later. What use was it to hide behind protective walls when inside those barricades you either starved to death or died in a riot? Well, Jered might just get his wish. Just in the last few days, reports had come in of the steady, driving movement of fighters heading toward the city. Jered's men had retreated again and again; now they were holding lines only a few leagues away. Adin had watched in horror as wagons rolled through the southern gate filled with the injured and dead, and the men in the barracks had grown uncharacteristically somber.

The captain had left to see the regent three days earlier and had yet to return. Adin wondered what delayed him. Were final war preparations locking into place? He shuddered to think of droves of men attacking the walls and the terror it would induce. Now that he was getting to know some of the *tsa'ba*, he wanted more than ever to help them, even though he'd be useless as a fighter. Adin sighed and drank down his ale. And in the midst of all this, Adin needed to keep searching for the Keeper. Somehow he had to find a clue to lead him to the curse. Was he just not seeing it? What if the *Sha'kath*—the Destroyer—was right under his nose? How in heaven would he know?

Adin finished his ale; although it cooled his throat, it did little to cheer him up. Noticing Brynn busy with a customer, he left two coins on the table and slipped back outside into the warm, muggy afternoon. He patted his horse and pulled a small sheet of parchment out of his saddlebag, a drawing he had made back at the barracks—of the pentacle. He had already shown it to at least a hundred people without garnering a glimmer of recognition. Perhaps some of the older residents might be of more help, those who had been here longer than the rest. And many of those people had shops in this district. So he started at a dry-goods store adjacent to the tavern, showing his drawing to those inside. From there, he went from shop to shop, knocking on doors and hoping for someone to recognize this symbol.

After an hour, he had covered six blocks, and with the day growing late, he decided to finish with the side of the street opposite the tavern. The corner shop was a musty, cluttered store filled with herbs and lotions, and an old woman with white hair and no teeth yelled to him from a rocking chair. She held long sticks in her hands that moved quickly in a pile of yarn. Without raising her eyes from her task, she asked Adin what he wanted. By the loudness of her speech Adin guessed she had trouble hearing. He came close to her and held out his drawing. She stopped rocking and set down her sticks.

She took a good look at Adin and scrunched up her face. "What is this?"

"I'm looking for someone who has this star. Do you recognize it?"

"Heavens, child, I'm not deaf. No need to shout."

Adin backed up as the woman took the drawing from his hand and turned it in different directions. He could tell from her bewildered expression that he was wasting his time. He was tired and the ale had made him sleepy. And he still had an hour's ride ahead of him back to the barracks.

Adin reached for the drawing. "I'm sorry I bothered you."

The old woman slapped his hand away. "So impatient, all you young ones. Always in a hurry, want everything now."

Adin resisted tapping his feet and let his eyes wander the room. Finally, she handed the parchment back to him.

She smiled with her toothless mouth. "I have seen that star. I am certain of it."

Adin checked his excitement. "Do you recall where?"

"Give a person time to think, child!" She mumbled to herself and then spoke. "Someone who comes to the shop. Yes, he wore this around his neck. This big." She held her fingers a coin's width apart. "On a silver chain. But the face . . ."

Adin held his breath while the woman rummaged through her mind. She licked her lips and shook her head. "Gone right out of my thoughts. Can't picture the face." She raised her voice. "But, I've seen it, I have. Will just have to think on it awhile." She waved Adin away. "You come back another day. Maybe then I'll have a name for you."

As Adin mounted and walked his horse along the cobbles, he wondered how much stock to put in the old woman's words. Very likely she was mistaken—or if she actually had seen the pentacle, what were the chances she'd remember who wore it? Adin was not encouraged by the prospects of this new lead. If only he knew more about the Keeper.

Reya's words came to him—the *ra'wah ten'uah*. Keepers of the Promise. Chosen to watch over the sacred sites. Adin unconsciously pulled the reins and stopped his horse. Wouldn't it make sense that a Keeper would be found near the stones, in order to watch over them? Perhaps. That gave him the idea to focus his efforts closer to the knoll, for that is where the curse was destined to arise, where evil would get a stronghold over men. If the site was to become desecrated, then Adin should be *there*, not leagues away at the south wall.

He clucked at O'kel, weaving through the mass of pedestrians until the flatlands opened up before him. Giving rein to his horse, Adin galloped back to the tower, the westering sun tinting the sky pink. He hoped the captain had returned so he could speak with him. He hoped tomorrow he could visit the spring and search the surrounding area for the Keeper. He hoped with all his heart he was not too late to uncover the source of the curse. Now that he was all alone in this strange and tumultuous time, having lost the map and everything familiar to him, hope was all he had.

"How many days?" the regent asked. He stood with the captain of his militia on top of the knoll, looking down at the distant lights of cookfires and lanterns sprinkled across the dark city below.

"Four. Maybe five." Jered stared at the starless sky; he could feel more than see the gathering of thunderclouds. Soon rain would pour down, heavy and unrelenting. He thought about the hundreds of *tsa'ba*, crouched under the cover of branches, shivering and miserable, waiting out cold nights. He walked back and forth next to the spring, knowing the regent's eyes rested upon him.

"Then it is time to go over the plan. And tomorrow, at first light, we meet with all the *tsa'va* of their regiments, make sure they understand their assignments. And I want to be sure I am not over-looking anything."

"You've been over every possibility a thousand times, Kah'yil."

"Still, 'where there is no guidance an army falls, but in the abundance of counselors there is safety.'"

Jered managed a smile. Even with war at his doorstep, the regent recited his sayings. He looked in his friend's face and could see the telltale signs of fatigue and worry. To most, the regent presented a calm, unflustered demeanor. Quiet, private, a man of few words: that was how he was known among his men. Only on rare occasion had the regent shared his personal thoughts with Jered, who even then could tell Kah'yil held much back. But tonight Jered could sense Kah'yil wanted to talk, knowing he held the fate of a thousand men in his hands. Every decision, even a small one, could cost someone his life. And Jered knew the regent considered every life precious.

"Come, Jered, share a drink with me—I need your *ayt'saw,* your counsel." Kah'yil's tone was somber, but he tried to lighten it with a grin. Jered followed him back to the small hut and sat on one of the stools while the regent filled two glasses with an amber liquid. Kah'yil handed one to Jered. "I am wondering what to tell those living in the city. Do we warn them the *o'yab* is coming? I fear panic will ensue, and yet, how can I keep them in ignorance when their very lives are at risk?"

Jered sipped his drink, and a warmth spread down his throat. "They should be warned—and encouraged not to panic. You cannot control their behavior, but at least if they know war is upon them, they can make necessary preparations. Kah'yil, if it goes badly, even the common folk may have to arm themselves and join in the fray. We have community leaders—why don't we have them call their neighbors to meet and organize? We will not be able to help them once the *mil'ka'ma* reaches these walls. They will be on their own."

The regent nodded while he paced the room. "You are right. After tomorrow's meeting I will send some of the guards out to inform the districts of what is to come. And to urge them all to remain calm and develop practical plans. Food, water, and weapons will need to be collected and centrally accessible if the walls are breached. A safe place, a *mik'dash*, needs to be chosen for women and children and the elderly. If there can be any such place." With a heavy sigh, he sat on the stool next to Jered. "And there is something else worrying me, my dear friend."

Jered waited while the regent gathered his thoughts. "There is some kind of treachery—here, within our ranks. Stores have been stolen from the armory. Food, knives, swords. Too many men have access, and some are untrustworthy. I cannot watch them every minute of the day, and it disturbs me to think of it."

"Can you not take them aside and question them?"

"I am too busy to deal with this. And it is more a matter of disappointment than danger. How can any man be so dishonorable? He who steals from his brother is hurting himself. If you cannot be *aymoon* when entrusted with the small things, how can you be relied upon to protect your brother in battle?" Kah'yil's eyes flared in anger. "I will never understand those who abuse such trust, seeing it as an opportunity for selfish gain."

Jered let the regent fume for a moment, then spoke. "Is there no one you can use to be your eyes? Your thief could be working alone, but perhaps his actions are not a secret to the other men."

"For all I know, it could be any one of them. Appearances are deceiving, and I cannot read hearts." Kah'yil put his head in his hands and rubbed his eyes.

"Perhaps I can bring over my new assistant," Jered said. "He is an honest man, and is faithful to me. Since he doesn't know your men, he would hold no loyalties to them."

The regent raised his head. "Jered, I will need you posted here from now on. Bring your man, and we will see if he can uncover this *ga'nab*. Within two days we must have every fighter at his post along the wall, and all the weapons and supplies at the ready. Each *tsa'va* will need to be sure his regiment is equipped, and that his supporters and runners are there to back them up." He narrowed his eyes, and Jered could see the weight of worry lining his brow. A huge crack of thunder rattled the wooden hut, followed by the patter of heavy rain on the roof.

Kah'yil got to his feet. "We have been preparing for this eventuality for many months now, my friend. The people in this city chose me to defend them, and I gave my *aw'law* that I would do everything in my power to end this battle. I vowed I would restore peace to this place, remove the threat of fear, and bring back the simpler, kinder days. I have done everything possible toward that end, and now the day of reckoning is upon us—and heaven help us."

Jered huddled in the long ditch hastily dug by the handful of *tsa'ba*. Explosions rocked the ground and shook the pool of water around his ankles. He was soaked from head to toe, his helmet and cloak giving him no comfort. The moonless night, though providing the fighters with obscurity, made it difficult for them to find their targets: the *o'yab* crawling through the mass of thick underbrush not a half-league south. Glancing to his left and right, he could identify the men flanking him by their postures. Shouts volleyed, voices of the regiment advancing ahead of them. Maybe a hundred yards, Jered estimated, by the clamor and clanking of swords, and the heartrending cries of men pierced and drawing their last breath.

Jered listened with seasoned hearing, then, when a lull settled over the field, nodded to those watching for his signal. As one body, the dozen cold and wet men scrambled from their hiding place like scurrying beetles and ran headlong into the night.

Shapes emerged from the brush. Jered swung his sword wide and fast at men he could barely see. Around him, swords whirled and men fell, their screams slicing through the darkness. The fighter on his right grunted and collapsed as a spear lodged in his chest. One quick look told Jered the man was beyond help, and he retuned his attention to the huge bulk of a warrior bearing down on him, sword raised and swinging.

Jered's blood raced with fury and determination as he hacked left, then right, severing the *o'yab's* arms from his shoulders. With a quick swipe of his sleeve, he cleaned the splattered blood from his face, then spit blood from his mouth. Another hasty wipe of his sword against the fallen man's pants cleaned the blade—clean enough for his next target.

In the dark, Jered could see the shapes of men lunging and falling, yet he could not assess his losses. Noise cascaded from all directions, as if the very night air groaned with the weight of death. He had no idea if the leading regiment had reached its mark or had been decimated in the attempt. Then he paused, hearing something odd, something that did not harmonize with the battle's vicious ballad. It sounded like the heavy beating of wings.

Suddenly he was attacked from all sides. At first he thought he had been impaled by a half-dozen spears. Things slammed into him—not the bodies of men, but heavy dark shapes, shapes impossible to decipher in the inky night. Over and over they pounded him, and with each thrust Jered felt knives sink deep into his flesh. Fresh fear, unlike any he had ever experienced in battle, swept over him and swallowed him whole, shocking him with its potency. Even his voice fled in that fear, leaving his eyes wide and his throat open to scream, but no sound able to break free from the clutches of horror.

Seconds stretched to hours as Jered felt himself fall to the ground, sensing his life seep out of him and soak the mud. Tiny darts of rain struck him in the face as he lay in agony, watching almost detachedly as the world melted away. Through half-closed eyes he noticed the dark night soften to gray. Now the only sounds he could hear were the shallow rise and fall of his breath and the weak thump of his heart against the wall of his chest.

Through the blurry haze Jered became aware of hair brushing against his face. Dark bronze tresses caressed his forehead and tickled his nose. He almost laughed. And then a gentle finger ran along his lips, then hands cradled his head. Whatever shred of fear lingered now drifted away as warmth emanated from the fingers buried in his hair. How long he drifted this way, he could not tell. But he knew he never wanted to leave this haven enclosing him in such safe comfort.

Without warning, Jered's body shook violently, and the hands, once caressing, now jerked his shoulders forcefully. Piercing green eyes, exhibiting alarm, peered into his, jarring him from his lethargic mood. He saw Aletha's leaning over him in the coolness of a quiet starry night, with a full moon rising over her shoulder. Despite her terrified expression, Jered could not miss the love radiating from her gaze. He found himself mesmerized by the texture of her skin and the fullness of her mouth as she bit her lip.

Somehow Aletha had saved him—but from what, he was unsure. In some strange way he understood that she had not only saved him from death, and from the ugliness of the battle, but also from a larger ugliness, some evil infecting the world around him, an evil that even poisoned his own vulnerable heart. He felt oddly changed, but before he could ask her what had happened, and how she had found him in the midst of the fighting, he awoke.

Jered sat up in the cot with a start, taking a moment to orient himself. The smell and the soft snores around him brought him back from his dream and into the barracks next to the armory. He recalled his evening with the regent and his finding an empty bunk in the late hours. From the quality of the light, Jered could tell dawn neared. Soon, the commanders from all posts would arrive.

Jered's dream came rushing back, and he wondered at the meaning. He thought of Aletha's concerned face and sensed that there was more to those images than just a fancy of sleep. That strange feeling he and Aletha had discussed—that nudge of destiny—lay over the dream, heavy and ominous. Now, more than ever, Jered felt linked to Aletha, believing it more than a mere attraction. But what could it portend?

Jered quietly eased his body off his cot and pulled on his uniform. Questions consumed his thoughts, but he had no time for them. Today, he had a war to plan for, and as much as he wished otherwise, thoughts of Aletha would have to wait their turn.

TWENTY-ONE

ALETHA WAS glad the old wagon had an overhang. Rain still blew in, smacking her face, but at least she wasn't drenched—yet. O'lam sat beside her on the bench, humming distractedly. Aletha felt sorry for the two black mules pulling the cart with their heads bowed against the wind. When they finished their deliveries, she would rub them down and give them a treat. O'lam kept the rig and animals in a stable near his cottage, and they proved useful for transporting heavy loads of medicines or even those ill or injured. For hours they had faithfully trudged across the city and now, finally, they were coming to the last stop. Three empty crates lay behind her on the flatbed, leaving only a half crate of the pain ointment she had recently prepared.

O'lam reined in the mules as they turned into the heart of the business district and stopped at a tiny shop on the corner.

When Aletha saw the tavern sign, she was tempted to suggest to O'lam that an ale by a warming fire would be a nice reprieve from the rain. But she couldn't see indulging in that pleasure while the two poor mules stuck it out in the downpour. What she really wanted was a long, hot bath. She smiled, reminded of Reya. Somehow her nursemaid would have found room in the warm cottage for even those mules. What Aletha wouldn't give to be there right now, wrapped in a blanket next to Adin, listening to one of Reya's stories. Aletha had only been back in this time a little more than a week, but her heart longed for home as if months had passed. She had never been separated from Adin this long, and it stirred a strange loneliness in her heart.

O'lam set down the reins, and the mules shook water off their heads. Pulling the hood down over his face, the healer squeezed drops from the ends of his mustache and reached a hand to Aletha, helping her down from the seat. While gripping her cloak, she leaned over the low side of the wagon and grabbed the crate. As he did at every stop, O'lam took the load from her, and once more Aletha marveled at his strength. She was young and strong, yet the stacks of jars were too cumbersome for her. Earlier, when they had loaded the wagon, she had tried to lift a crate and could barely budge it. O'lam had come into the workroom and hefted each one without even a grunt, and nearly ran to stack them in the wagon. He attributed his youthfulness to all the many herbs he ingested, but Aletha suspected there was more to the old man's vitality than just a healthy diet.

She held the door open and followed him into the stuffy shop. An overpowering smell of dust, rain, and mold made Aletha sneeze, and O'lam turned. "Ah, lass, I've kept you out in the weather too long. But, after this, home it is, and a pot of elder flower and yarrow tea." He looked around and raised his voice. "Now, where's our lovely shopkeep?"

Those weren't the words Aletha would have used to describe the tiny old woman who hobbled in from a back room. Her gnarled hands reached out and clasped the healer's and shook them. A big smile revealed a mouth without teeth, but O'lam feasted his eyes upon the woman as if she were a goddess. Aletha shook her head, amused; the woman actually blushed. One thing she would say about O'lam—he constantly surprised her.

"O'er here, lass." He motioned to Aletha. Carefully, Aletha stacked two dozen jars of ointment on the counter while the woman procured a cloth pouch and counted out coins. The shopkeeper set the brass on the counter, and then her eyes lit on the healer. Suddenly she gasped and pointed at him. O'lam jumped back.

"What is it?" he asked, nearly knocking over a bin of something grainy.

"You!"

O'lam exchanged looks with Aletha, his eyebrows raised. "Me? What did I do?"

"I knew I had seen it before. Just couldn't remember for the life of me. The memory isn't what it used to be." The woman gave a chuckle and put her pouch away.

O'lam placed a hand on the woman's arm, and she halted and blushed again. "My dear lady, what did you see?"

She pointed again, this time at his neck. "Your chain. With the star. Now I can tell the young man the next time he comes back."

To Aletha's surprise, O'lam gripped the woman's arm tighter. She came alongside him to see what the shopkeeper was referring to.

O'lam fingered his neck, and Aletha saw his hand shake. He pulled on the silver chain and brought it out from beneath his tunic. It was a small silver charm, shaped like a star, with a gold star inside it, and a blue gemstone inset in the center. Aletha guessed it was very old, and although pretty to look at, it wasn't especially ornate. But to O'lam it obviously held a special meaning, for Aletha had never seen the healer so agitated.

"Tell me," he demanded gently of the woman, "what young man? Who came asking about the star?"

"Heavens, man! You don't need to shout—I'm not *ka'rash*! The poor child was in here—just yesterday, it was."

"Poor?"

"A cripple, he was, with a hunch in his back." She looked over at Aletha, as if noticing her for the first time. She pointed. "With hair and beard—your color."

Aletha went pale. *Adin.* Adin had been here—yesterday.

"My brother . . ."

O'lam turned to Aletha. "Your . . ." He whistled and dabbed his brow with his sleeve. "Madam, do you have a chair? I'm sorry, but I think I'm about to faint."

Aletha shook herself out of her stupor and found a stool behind the counter. The old woman watched curiously as the healer sat and Aletha ran out to the wagon for the jug of water. Aletha's mind raced with questions as she hurried back in and gave O'lam small sips from the jug. Seeing O'lam cared for, the old woman went about carrying the jars of ointment into the back room, glancing back at the healer as if he had lost a few pebbles.

Aletha knelt next to the healer and searched his face. "What does this mean? My brother has been looking for you. Why? How?" She lowered her voice and leaned in close. "What is this star you wear?" She looked at it as it rested against the healer's tunic. There was something oddly familiar about it. *Very familiar.*

"The brother you mentioned. This is the one you followed . . . here?"

Aletha nodded, her heart racing. Adin was here, in the city, somewhere. She had just missed him!

"Then someone sent him to look for me. That is why he seeks the star. Someone who knew—" He turned and noticed the old woman listening at the doorway, pretending to be counting something. "We should leave. These walls have *o'zen.*" He gave the shopkeeper a reproving look, and she retreated into the back room. O'lam raised himself from the stool and, for the first time, looked as old as his wrinkles implied. Aletha held her questions in check, despite her urge to blurt them out. She helped O'lam into the cart and untied the mules. Then she took the reins and turned the cart around, heading back west, toward the healer's home.

The rain had lightened to a soft drizzle. "How are you feeling?" she asked.

The healer slumped in the seat next to her. "Ah, lass, I'll be perky in a moment. Thank you for your kindness."

Aletha gave O'lam a stern look. "There is something you are not telling me."

"Correct you are, lass. But you've a right to know, then." He took a deep breath. "I came to this place a very long time ago. Long before there was a city, when these hills were forests, filled with deer and few men. A peaceful time, long lost. Before men filled this world, times were different. I was chosen to come here, given a task to do, and did it to the best of my power. Do you know about the *mowt'sa*, there, on the hill? It is *ko'desh*, holy . . ."

Pieces began to click into place in Aletha's mind. Thoughts tumbled over one another as she tried to sort through them. The sacred sites. The Gates of Heaven. Above all, Reya's clear voice rang out. The *ra'wah ten'uah* . . . She looked at O'lam in disbelief and sucked in her breath.

"You. You are a Keeper! A Keeper of the Promise."

He reflected back the same look of amazement. "Ah, yes, lass. And . . . ah, there is more." He exhaled deeply and shook his head in wonderment. "Your brother—he is the one. The *pa'lat*."

"The regent does not seem to be here," Jered commented after checking the hut near the armory.

Adin could tell Jered was anxious, but certainly not as distressed as he himself at this moment. He could still feel the crush of the mobs, grabbing at his horse and yanking on his boots as he and the captain literally pushed back the hordes of panicked people in the streets. Word had gotten out of the approaching *ghed'ood*, and as they rode toward the knoll, Jered, sitting on his mount like a beacon of hope and safety, drew hysterical crowds to him at every block. Adin had watched frustration well up in the captain's face as he yelled to them, giving instructions and trying to pacify them.

As they climbed the hill, a deafening explosion shook the ground. Adin knew his eyes reflected the same terror as the eyes of those crowding their horses. At that moment Jered stopped and his face paled. Adin feared to ask him what the noise signified.

Not until they had reached the last cottage on the hill were they disentangled from the mass of frightened residents. Seeing guards run down from the armory with swords raised was enough incentive for the crowd to disperse. Jered, dismounting, gave hurried instructions to four of the men to remain there and bar entrance. Waving Adin along, the captain had rushed to the top of the knoll, and through the gray and drizzle scrutinized the area and assessed its security.

Jered signaled two guards to tend to the horses, and then pointed to a large wooden building situated behind the hut. "Adin, put your things in the barracks over there. We'll have to get you settled later. Right now, I need to find Kah'yil. When you're done, come back here, to the regent's hut. And keep an eye on the comings and goings at the armory entrance." He tipped his head toward the stone building.

Adin had been told about the thefts and his new assignment. He well knew how to appear invisible, go unnoticed. Jered would tell the guards that the young crippled man in the brown cloak was a guest of the regent's; he was to be left alone and allowed access anywhere he liked. The guards would show little interest in one inconsequential man, especially at this time, when a tide of darkness moved against the city, visible from the knoll even through the wispy fog.

Adin took his bag over to the barracks, a large messy space cluttered with cots and clothing, presently vacant this late morning.

Unsure where to put his things, he finally decided on a low bench in the corner, then hurried back to the hut. Cold chilled him to the bone. Riding at that insane pace through the city, sweat soaking his clothes, had left Adin damp and shivering. By standing a foot inside the shelter he avoided the nipping breeze coming up from the lowland. What he would give for a warm fire!

Adin watched men hurry into the armory and bring out swords, shields, and spears. In less than an hour, more than two dozen fighters had been handed weapons and sent away. Another explosion shook the ground, and Adin saw the guards turn and look south. If they felt any fear, they masked it well, for their expressions told Adin nothing. Only one guard took notice of him, staring from time to time with a scowl stretched across his broad face. Adin was sure he and another dark man discussed him as they conferred at the entrance to the armory. Adin buried himself in his cloak and stamped his feet, trying to keep his toes from going numb.

He heard a yell, and recognizing Jered's voice, stepped out of the hut just as two large horse-drawn wagons came barreling up the hill. Jered ran ahead of them, signaling them to stop in front of Adin. Men in uniform came running from behind the wagon and lifted bodies from the back. Adin moved away and watched the mayhem as the captain directed toward the barracks those carrying the injured. A crack of thunder was followed by a downpour of rain, but Jered ignored the stream of water running down his face. Miserable and feeling useless, Adin pulled his hood tighter against the elements.

"Find room for them in there—just clear whatever space you need," he ordered the guards. He spotted Adin and ushered him inside the hut. "I should not have brought you here. The *ghed'ood* are breaking the walls with giant logs, and they have strange contraptions that hurl boulders through the air. Already they have breached the south wall in two places. Our *tsa'ba* are holding them back—for now."

The captain held the curtain aside and scanned the grounds. He shook his head. "No one seems to know where the regent is, but I must get to the *tsa'va* of the south regiment. Stay here, and try not to get hurt. More injured are on their way. Help the medics if you can. There are stores of medicines in the armory—the guards will show you where." He grasped Adin's hands and held them tightly. "Be brave, my friend. Heaven favors the true of heart. I will return quickly—the men all have their orders."

Adin watched Jered run down the hill and fetch his horse. As the captain disappeared into fog and rain, Adin's heart thumped hard in his chest. He wished he had Jered's bravery. But, bravery or no, at least he could make himself useful in some small way. He hurried over to the barracks, and the sight of the men bleeding and moaning gripped his heart. Guards came in with buckets of water and armloads of linens, scurrying under the medics' directions. What moments ago had been a messy dormitory was now a hospital. Adin stepped over puddles of blood and made his way to a medic struggling to hold a compress against a fighter's chest. The man told Adin what he needed.

Adin rushed to the armory, slipping in mud, and reached for the door handle. A hand grabbed his, forcing him to stop. Adin turned and saw the dark, broad-faced guard sneer at him.

"What do we have here? Some little sneak?"

"I'm here at the captain's orders. I need supplies—let me pass."

The other guard snickered. "What do you think, Ka'zab? Maybe he's looking for free food."

Adin fumed. "Men are dying. The medics sent me. For heaven's sake, let me in. And show me where the medicines are kept."

Ka'zab sighed and motioned to the other guard. "Bat'sa, take him inside. But watch him good." He removed his hand and backed away a step.

Adin followed the guard through the door, aware of Ka'zab's glare. For a quick instant, Adin met the guard's eyes, and a chill shot up his spine. The guard's face grew vague and blank, and his eyes misted over, turning vacant and cold. A surge of malevolence exuded from him. Adin turned away, saturated with utter fear.

As Adin collected what he needed from the shelves, putting jars and boxes into a sack, a wave of sickness came over him. Never before had he encountered such an immediate, concentrated touch of evil. That was the only word he could think of to describe the sensation. Not even his father's councillor Rasha caused him such agitation.

Adin tried to bring his shaken attention back to his task. Under the watchful gaze of Bat'sa, he finished filling the sack and hefted it over his shoulder. On the way out, he kept his eyes down and his thoughts fixed on the bleeding men in the barracks. As he passed Ka'zab standing defiantly with his arms crossed against his chest, Adin felt the pain of hatred pelt him as surely as if he were struck in the back with a dozen rocks. Catching his breath, he hobbled across the path to the barracks and set the sack down with shaky hands. Adin was certain his distress came not from the encroaching battle or from the scent of fear given off by those injured, but from one powerful source alone.

That tingling nudge of destiny called to Adin—the same sense of destiny that had washed over him when he entered the labyrinth, and when he looked out over the future desolation of his kingdom. It was as if a hand of heaven reached down and grabbed him by the collar, shaking loose a veil that covered his eyes.

Something was about to happen.

He did not know what or where or how. All he knew was that all his choices and mistakes had led him here, to this place, in this time. He no longer worried he might fail, or make a wrong decision. He saw destiny rush at him like a flood of water, sweeping away everything in its path as it rushed toward an inevitable end. How could he—one small, insignificant man—stand in the way of such a flood? Surely, he could not.

Each time the cottage shook, Aletha cringed. Jars rattled precariously on the shelves, but fortunately nothing had been broken yet. All morning she and O'lam had packed crates. The shouting had begun at dawn, and for hours now, without letup, Aletha listened to the fighting, screaming, and crying as people ran down the roads. O'lam had busied himself in the workroom, searching labels and pulling out jars. He warned Aletha not to leave the cottage alone for any reason. People gripped by fear were dangerous—to themselves and others. And he and Aletha had an urgent job— to get medicine to the barracks as quickly as possible. So, Aletha packed while O'lam left to rig up the mules and load the wagon, but still she fretted. O'lam had assured her no one would harm them, but how could he be certain? A wagon filled with supplies would be a tempting target.

Even with a battle at her doorstep, her thoughts dwelt only on Adin. He was out there, in the city, somewhere. Was he safe? How in heaven could she find him? That desperate need made her want to jump out of her skin. She knew she could do nothing but wait. Yet here she was—with the Keeper! She had no doubt Adin had followed the map back in time to find O'lam, for he had to be the key to the *qa'lal*. The Keeper was the link between the sacred site and the start of the curse. Why hadn't O'lam known about the curse? It didn't make sense.

The front door opened and O'lam came inside, breathing hard. He wiped his bald spot and sighed. "Ah, lass, things are bad, bad. The city's in an uproar and the wall's attacked. So many men, like flies on a dead rat, coming against us. Some are saying we stand no chance against these *o'yab*." He slumped down in his chair by the hearth as Aletha kept packing. "But I have to trust you when you say all will be well in the end. You came from the future, where this city still stands."

"And thrives. History is sparse on details, but the battle will be won, the *o'yab* defeated, and Sherbourne will one day be called the 'Crown of the East.'"

O'lam cocked his head. "Sherbourne?"

"That is the name given to this kingdom."

O'lam smirked. "Kah'yil must win a great victory for us, then, for the people to name the city after him."

Aletha gave the healer a puzzled look.

"That is his name," he said. "Kah'yil Sherbourne."

Of course! Aletha recalled her history and the lesson of the first regent of Sherbourne. Not the regent *of* Sherbourne—she corrected herself—but the "Regent Sherbourne." She thought of the kind, soft-spoken man responsible for bringing people into the safety of a walled city. And here she was, helping in some small way to ensure he succeeded. But that success would come at a high price—she remembered this from her lessons as well. Before this battle ended, many would die. Again, her fears returned to Adin.

"O'lam, I need you to tell me more about the sacred sites. I was told the Keepers were appointed to protect them."

O'lam leaned toward her and spoke. "As I told you, lass, I was directed here long ago, in a different age, before men harbored wickedness in their hearts. Evil has always sought to take control, in every world, every chance it gets. Since men are so vulnerable and easily corrupted that without some protection from heaven, they would succumb utterly to evil, and this world would be destroyed. That is the intent of the *Sha'kath*, the Destroyer. To corrupt and poison the hearts of men, to make them turn against each other, as he did the very first brothers. Do you know that story, lass?"

Aletha shook her head.

"Well, the elder was jealous of the younger, for heaven favored the kind, gentle child over the impatient, haughty one. So this brother's jealousy grew daily. Finally, he decided in his heart to kill his innocent sibling. Heaven questioned him and asked, 'Why are you so jealous? If you do good, will you not be accepted? But now, evil is crouching at the gates and its desire is for you. Will you not get the mastery over it?'

"What happened?"

"The elder brother chose to give in to the evil urgings and killed the younger. *Qowl d'am tsa'aq adamah.* 'The voice of blood cries out from the ground.' Innocent blood was shed, and for that reason the elder brother was cursed, and his life ruined."

Aletha let the healer's words sink in. "So, how do the sacred sites fit in?"

O'lam stroked his mustache thoughtfully. "Seeing how easily men fell to evil, heaven chose seven places of purity and empowered them to be resistant to the schemings of the *Sha'kath.* These places were sanctified, and they emanated such a power for so many leagues around that people, unwittingly, were drawn to these sites—like a moth to a *shal'he'beth.* They stopped wandering and settled down to farm, using the untainted, life-giving water from the *mowt'sa,* and for a time, blessed by its power, their crops and livestock flourished, and people lived long, peaceful lives.

"As you've seen, lass, huge stones were erected to mark the sites, and the magic protecting these places was intertwined into the *sha'har sha'ma'yim*—the Gates of Heaven. These were set up because of the promise made to never let evil destroy the world of men. The role of the Keepers was to keep this promise by guarding these sites, making sure these places did not get contaminated by evil. But over time, humans desecrated these places, pulled down the stones, and broke apart the careful web of magic that held them together.

"There is an old saying among the Keepers: 'Do not remove the ancient landmarks that your ancestors set up.' I tried, lass, to stop those who defiled the *mowt'sa*, but I am only one lowly wizard, and although I have longevity and the few powers granted to those of my race, the Keepers can only do so much when the heart of man is bent toward wrongdoing. We may have special sight, and the ability to read hearts, but, dear lass, we are powerless to change men, to make them noble and honorable. That is the choice of each individual—their gift and their curse."

Aletha placed the last jar in the crate, then covered the crate with the lid. "I don't understand. When the stones were pulled down, is that when evil took over? I was taught something sets a curse in motion, fixes it to the site. A curse that has a direction attached. Until Sherbourne 'lies waste' and 'desolate' forever."

"No, lass, that has not occurred. And that is no doubt why the *pa'lat* is foretold. There is another cause, but I cannot see it. Removing the magical web could not result in a curse that specific and that final. But tearing down the protection around the site has now made an opening for the *Sha'kath* to act. All the magic I can gather cannot hold back such a *khay'fes*, a wicked plot. So, we shall have to be patient and wait. *'Eth khay'fets sha'ma'yim.* 'There's a time to every purpose under the heaven.' As I said, lass, you were sent to me, and your brother was given the map leading him here, to save his kingdom. Heaven has a plan."

Seeing the worry etched on Aletha's face, the healer got up from his chair and patted her shoulder. "Trust heaven, Aletha, for no evil in the world can ever thwart heaven's hand. *Pe'ree tsa'diyk.* 'Truly there is a reward for the righteous.' Righteousness will prevail in the end—you will see."

• PART THREE •

SHA'KATH

(THE DESTROYER)

TWENTY-TWO

PARTIALLY SHELTERED by the eave of the barracks roof, Adin dunked his arms into the bucket of icy water as rain steadily turned the ground into a mud pit. The water turned red while Adin scrubbed his hands and tried to push the visions of suffering out of his mind. After a few hours, he had stopped reacting to the horrors pouring into the now-crowded room. He just followed directions, handed things to the medics, wiped up blood from the planked floor, fetched supplies. Exhaustion hit him full force, and he collapsed on the ground and slowed his breath. He would have stayed inside, but now that the tide of injured had momentarily slacked, he had been ushered out, with heartfelt gratitude. He should rest while he could, the medics told him. Before they would need him again.

As Adin sat, his body and mind numb, he stared at the rain and the muddy rivulets streaming down the hill. Over at the armory, three guards argued. Adin could make out the large, bulky shape of Ka'zab pushing another guard against the building. He shifted his attention as the men suddenly stopped their personal conflict and turned toward someone coming up the hill.

A group of uniformed fighters stopped in front of the armory. One man removed his helmet and spoke to the guards. By his gestures, Adin guessed he held rank over them, and the men stood still at attention as they listened. The leader turned toward those accompanying him, and they dispersed. When Adin saw him go into the hut, he realized the graying, dark-skinned man had to be the regent. He wondered if Jered had ever located him.

Adin got up and went over to the hut, aware of his own scruffy appearance. Even though he'd worn coverings, some blood from the barracks had splattered his clothing. He knew his hair and face were unruly, and he wished he could present himself in a neater package. But, given the affairs of the day, he was sure the regent would understand.

Upon knocking on the side of the hut, he heard a tired voice. "Come."

The regent, hanging his cloak on a nail, tilted his head and looked Adin over as he motioned him to sit. Adin saw the regent was neatly dressed, and although his boots were muddied, the rest of his uniform was clean and of simple fashion. A scar was visible just above his beard, on his right cheek, and as he walked across the room, Adin detected a subtle limp.

"Sir, I am Captain Tebron's assistant. I am sorry to disturb you, but he seemed anxious to find you this morning."

"Ah, Jered has nothing but praise for you. And he did get word to me. He should be here shortly." Kah'yil went over to a small cupboard and opened the door. "From your appearance, I think you could use a drink. Tell me," he said, pouring two glasses of something dark, "how are the men faring?"

"The barracks have been turned into a hospital. The medics are working hard and many lives have been saved. Although others . . ." Adin sighed deeply. The regent handed him a glass and sat on the stool beside him.

"You are not used to seeing this—although I don't suppose one ever gets used to facing violence of this sort. We've been fighting these marauders for nearly two years now. They just keep coming." The regent grew quiet, lost in thought. Adin appreciated the warm flush brought on by the drink. He could hear the rain lessen; its steady pattering on the roof lulled him into a sleepy stupor. He shook his head to stay awake.

"You have a strange accent—yet, I'm sure I have heard it before." Kah'yil reminded Adin of a curious bird, his dark, thoughtful eyes watching him without judgment. "Jered never said where you were from."

"Not far, sir, but sometimes I feel as though I am a thousand leagues from home."

"Call me Kah'yil, please. I am sorry, I have been rude. Your name is?"

"Adin."

The regent extended his hand, and as Adin shook it, he stopped suddenly. "Your name is familiar." His eyes lit up. "I would ask if you had a sister, for I am sure she said her brother's name was Adin. But Jered told me you are all alone, that you'd lost your family."

Adin nodded. "The captain is right." His voice filled with emotion. "I had a sister once. We were very close—twins."

"Yes!" the regent responded with excitement. "She mentioned she was looking for her twin, who looked much like her, but—" He hesitated, a confused look in his eyes. "With a hunched back and pronounced limp. Surely there cannot be two such sets of twins?"

Adin's hand shook as he set down the glass. This was too strange and inscrutable. There was no possible way Aletha could be here, was there? There was no other map, no other way to the past. It was impossible! The idea of his sister here, in this time, in the middle of this chaos, brought a wave of panic to Adin's heart. But he had to ask, although his throat was so choked he could barely speak.

"Did . . . she give you her name?"

The regent concentrated and tipped his head in frustration. "Something like Alia, Athea . . ."

"Aletha," Adin said. The name hung on the air, potent and stark.

As the word left his lips, he didn't even have to look at the regent's face. He knew. He knew Aletha was here, in this city, just as strongly as he knew he was alive. She had been in this very place—he could feel it. But how? His mind fought the desire to believe the truth. Maybe the hermit had known of a way, and had sent her to him. What folly was this—for her to leave Sherbourne and chase after him? Adin's thoughts spun like a whirlwind. Aletha—here! Where?

The regent offered what information he could. "She arrived well over a week ago. I sent her to my sister's tavern, hoping Brynn could help her find a place to stay."

Adin stood abruptly. "That's where I was! Upstairs, in the spare room." Adin frowned. "Would Brynn know where to find her?"

"Perhaps. But, Adin . . ." Kah'yil put a gentle hand out to calm him. "Today is not the day to search for her. It is too dangerous, and you would never even make it to the tavern with all the rioting and panic in the streets. It would be madness."

Adin was infused with worry, but Kah'yil was right. Who knew how many days this battle would drag on? Hopefully, Aletha was sequestered somewhere safe, out of harm's way. And once the fighting ended, Jered would surely help him find her. He shook his head in disbelief. This was too strange to comprehend.

A violent argument erupted outside the hut. The regent jumped up and hurried outside. Adin followed him out into the fog. A cold wind had kicked up, and wisps of cloud broke apart, revealing patches of blue sky. Over at the side of the armory stood Jered, with his hands clenched around Ka'zab's collar, and three other guards stood steps away. The captain had clearly just arrived, for his horse wandered nearby, the reins still draped across her neck. Adin walked over and slipped his fingers under the horse's mane and gathered up the reins.

Adin could tell Jered was restraining his fury, with his face flushed red and anger brewing in his eyes. Jered planted his feet firmly as the regent approached, careful not to loosen his grip on the man who grumbled something at the captain.

"Here is your thief," Jered announced loudly, making sure all could hear. "And traitor!" The regent stood beside Jered as a crowd of men gathered. Another explosion rocked the building, and the rumble traveled along the ground like an earthquake.

"Explain," said Kah'yil, listening intently.

"This man has been stealing from the armory—and supplying the *o'yab* with more than just weapons." He shook Ka'zab, who only reacted with a look of disgust and amusement. "He has been feeding the enemy information, and that is why they know the places in the wall that are weakest."

Ka'zab laughed. "You have caught me, but there are others, many others, who know your pathetic *tsa'ba* don't stand a chance. Before this week is over, the walls will be rubble, and those who resist capture will be killed. You—" He pointed with disgust at the regent—"will no doubt be tortured and your head paraded on a stick for all to jeer at. Your laughable walls won't save you, you poor, weak excuse for a *na'gheed*. You, with your soft words and stupid sayings."

Jered lifted a hand, about to slap Ka'zab across the face, when another giant blast unsteadied his feet. His prisoner took the opportunity to reach under his tunic, and with a quick flick of the wrist, slashed his short dagger across the captain's arm. As Jered yelped in pain, Ka'zab used the opportunity to wriggle free from his grip and run across the knoll toward the spring.

Adin's jaw dropped as the regent grabbed the hilt of Jered's sword and pulled it from the scabbard hanging at the captain's side. Seeing Jered safely tended to by two of his guards, the regent chased after Ka'zab, followed by at least a dozen other men, pulling knives and swords from their scabbards as they raced after their leader.

Adin hurried to catch up, and Jered, shaking off the men trying to wrap his arm, followed closely behind. By the time Adin arrived at the spring, Jered had run past him, and Adin could only stand and stare as the events he would later replay over and over in his mind unfolded before him.

Almost as if time slowed, Adin saw the regent circle the spring, the sword glinting in his hand as the sun peeked through a break in the clouds. The grass, slick and wet, glistened in the light, and as Kah'yil parried Ka'zab's knife thrust, he slipped.

Adin gasped as the regent caught himself and righted his footing. Jered watched anxiously, positioning himself on the west side of the pool of water with a knife in his own hand. The guards with their swords drawn—and Jered—allowed the regent this fight. But they had no intention of letting him lose it. Now Ka'zab was sandwiched between the two men, and had to either fight or run down the hill.

But the traitor had no intention of fleeing. Adin saw on his face a look of contempt so potent that Adin feared for the regent. Kah'yil drew closer and lunged at the man, who only laughed and jumped aside. He teased Kah'yil, trying to fuel his anger, but the regent kept calm.

The regent thrust again with his sword, and this time Ka'zab ducked and sliced at the regent's thigh, opening up a wound that dripped blood down his leg. Jered held back a guard anxious to join in the fight. Adin could tell the captain was barely holding himself in check.

Just then, an eerie hum grew on the air, like the buzzing of insects, and a strange chill started creeping up Adin's neck.

Something menacing came near him, and he quickly looked around to see if anyone else was reacting to this unsettling phenomenon. But all eyes were on the regent and his attacker. Adin shook from the cold seeping into every pore of his body, as if a frost covered him from head to toe.

Slowly, time unwound, and Adin could not lift even a finger. The regent moved as in a dream, taking—what seemed to Adin—minutes just to lift his arm and prod Ka'zab with the sword, forcing him ever closer to the edge of the spring. Water gurgled so slowly that Adin could see each bubble rise and spill out from the black rock. Sounds were muffled, and soon all Adin heard was the water percolating and the swoosh of the breeze through his hair. Everything else around him in the world—the guards, the noises of the city below, the warmth of the sun as it chased away the clouds—was muted and faded. Only the regent and his target stood in sharp focus.

Adin's head burned while his limbs froze. He felt feverish and faint but unable to move; he could only watch as Ka'zab leaped on the regent like a ferocious beast and jammed the knife into Kah'yil's gut. Kah'yil doubled over, but found the strength for one last swipe with his sword, and swinging his right arm around, he slashed at Ka'zab's throat, nearly severing the head. Blood gushed everywhere, soaking the regent's vest, spraying the ground, and dripping from the traitor's neck into the pool.

Suddenly, all Adin could see was blood, dark red blood, filling his vision. He heard nothing but the shrill buzzing in his mind, although he could tell by the men's mouths that they were shouting, and the regent was groaning. Jered held the regent—who doubled over and clutched his gut—and as the traitor Ka'zab dropped, all eyes turned in shock and stared.

Adin did not know if the men heard the loud cackle and screech, but finding his hands free to move, he covered his ears to block out the piercing noise. With a strong shudder, Ka'zab's falling body transformed, and in a matter of seconds, what had been human changed to a large black bird resembling a raven. With a triumphant cry, it took wing and wheeled off into the air.

No one moved. Terrified faces followed the path of the bird as it disappeared into a deep blue sky. But Adin's eyes were drawn to the spring. For what he saw there shook him to the core of his being.

Where the blood had dripped into the water, Adin could see a fizzle and sputter. He stumbled to the pool's edge and studied it. Men hurried around him, and he sensed rather than heard Jered helping the regent to his feet, ordering men to his aid. Out of the corner of his eye he saw Jered and two other guards carefully carry Kah'yil back toward the armory.

Adin could not take his eyes from the water.

A sticky black substance gathered at the spot where Ka'zab's blood had dripped from his throat. Like an acid eating at metal, the black goo festered and slowly spread outward until, long moments later, the entire pool was an ugly, poisonous brew. Then, even the pure water coming up from the basement of the world gurgled out of the rock dark and ominous.

Adin clutched at his chest and stumbled. He leaned over the water, and the acrid smell made him gag. Fighting nausea, he fell back, tears flooding his eyes, then he felt a gentle hand on his back.

"Adin," Jered said softly, "are you all right?"

Adin pointed, tears running down his face. "The spring—look!"

Jered leaned closer and scanned the pool, then, to Adin's horror, dipped his hand in and let the water spill from his palm. Adin watched as the sticky black liquid ate away Jered's fingers, bubbling and hissing until his hand was gone.

Adin screamed.

"What!" Jered cried. "What has happened? Are you hurt?"

Adin grabbed Jered's hands and turned them both over, front to back. They looked fine and unchanged. Adin gasped.

Jered helped Adin get to his feet.

"Don't you see it? The black water?"

Jered shook his head. "I see nothing out of place." He coaxed Adin away from the spring, but Adin stopped and turned back to look once more.

Slowly, the water cleared and the fizzing stopped. Sounds of fighting returned to fill the air, and Adin could hear the uproar of the guards by the armory, frantic over the regent and mystified by what had just happened at the spring. Now pure, clean water bubbled quietly from the rock.

Adin turned to look at Jered. "You *did* see the bird."

Jered nodded briskly, searching Adin's face. "What *la'at* was that? You seem to know something you are not saying." He stopped far from the crowd at the building, but lowered his voice anyway. "Adin, does this have something to do with your mystery, why you came to the city?"

"Yes, but Jered," Adin whispered, "I can say no more. Something has happened that I do not understand. It is just as much a *yo'shana* to me as to you. And now I must use every moment to find my sister . . ."

"Your sister? I thought you had no family."

"I cannot explain right now. But I know I have little time; this truth I feel in every bit of my bones. Please let me leave and search for her."

Jered nodded his assent. "I would help you myself, but I have a battle to win. Can I press upon you one more urgent favor?"

"Of course. I would do anything to help you in your fight. But, believe me, what I have to do will have even greater consequences than the outcome of this war."

Jered paused and took in the import of that statement. "Then go with haste, but first—the regent needs to get to a healer, and there is one close by, at the bottom of the road. Will you take him there, quickly? I have sent a rider ahead, to let the *ra'pha* know you are coming. Guards will ride with you and show you the way." He held Adin's hands and squeezed them. "I trust no one more than you to safeguard the regent's life. Once you see to his care, then, with heaven's blessing, find your sister."

By the time Adin retrieved his bag from the barracks, Jered had the regent's wound wrapped and had placed him on his own mare, tying him securely to the horse. The regent was still conscious, but his face paled from more than just the loss of blood. Men stood off to the side speaking in hushed tones, the fear and shock still evident in their expressions. Jered spoke privately to the regent, who weakly nodded. Adin mounted up and took the mare's lead rope from Jered's hand. Four guards flanked the two horses, walking two on each side with their swords drawn. Adin didn't expect much obstruction to their passage; he only hoped this healer knew how to treat more than knife wounds. For he feared the regent had been struck by more than just steel, and whatever evil had been wielding that blade may have given the regent more than he'd bargained for.

With the wagon loaded and the mules rigged, Aletha clasped her cloak around her and went to look for her scarf in the workroom. She heard a frantic pounding at the door and came into the entry to find O'lam listening to a uniformed man who gestured emphatically.

O'lam closed the door as the man rushed off and then turned to Aletha.

"Dear lass, the regent's been badly hurt, and he's heading here." He pulled off his coat and hung it on the hook by the door. Aletha started to remove her cloak, but the healer stopped her with his hand.

"You must take the wagon to the barracks, at the top of the knoll. The injured need our supplies." He put his finger to his lips. "Never fear, it won't take long, lass, and you'll be safe. You'll find your captain there; he'll be sure to get you unloaded and back in a flash."

The thought of venturing out alone rattled her, but mentally summoning Jered's face, with his deep, reassuring eyes, she found her courage. She thought of the kind and thoughtful regent. Although she knew he would survive, she hated to think of him in pain. "Don't you need me here, to help?"

O'lam pressed her gently toward the door. "I can manage just fine, lass, until you return. But make haste!"

Aletha ran to the wagon and clambered up onto the seat. She shook the reins and clucked at the mules. Shouts and screams carried on the air, and explosions rocked the lane as she encouraged the nervous animals to move forward. Upon entering the main road, Aletha gripped the leather straps even tighter. People ran mindlessly in all directions, pushing and shoving, falling down. Overturned carts lay alongside the road, and a small child stood crying, obviously separated from his mother. Aletha wanted to stop and gather up the babe, but knew she had to get to the barracks. Someone, she hoped, would tend to him.

When Aletha saw the crowds part before her as she urged the mules up the hill, she knew O'lam had cast a spell of protection over the wagon. Not one person saw her or her rig; she was as good as invisible. Pushing the animals hard, she worked her way up the muddy road, surprised to see the sun breaking through the mat of clouds. On any other day that would be a cheering sight, but not today, with the war on their doorstep casting a dark pall over everything.

Suddenly, a large contingent of guards and peasants came hurrying down toward her. In the center of the crowd, a man wrapped in a brown cloak rode a dark horse. Aletha noticed he held the lead to a horse trailing behind him, and, with a start, she recognized the slumped body of the regent lying across the neck of his mount. She pulled her wagon far to the side of the road to let them pass, her eyes searching to see if the captain was among them. Not finding him, she shook the reins and continued up the hill, anxious to unload her medicines and get back to assist O'lam.

Upon reaching the crest, she stopped in front of the armory, where she read the faces of the many guards milling about. But what she saw were not the expressions of men who had encountered the horrors and pains of battle. Something else filled their eyes, a look of terror that set her hands trembling. The fear was so palpable Aletha's throat clenched. Stepping down from the wagon, she hesitated, wondering what had occurred to cause such a dread to come upon these men.

"Aletha!"

She turned her head to find Jered walking toward her from behind the regent's hut. His clothes were rumpled and dirty, but her gaze was drawn immediately to the bandage wrapped around his arm. Blood stained the cloth, and as Jered reached out to take her arm she frowned.

"Captain, what happened? Let me see your arm."

Jered smiled and placed a hand on the side of her head. "The medics have already stitched me up. I'll live." Aletha became aware of the stares of the guards as they watched their captain speak. Jered noticed her reaction and called over to his men.

"Quickly—unload the wagon. Take these supplies to the barracks, and carefully." To Aletha he said, "Come, this day is not even half gone and I am spent." He ushered her into Kah'yil's hut and went right to the cupboard to pour them drinks.

As Aletha sat on the stool, Jered came to her side and handed her a glass. "But seeing you brings a joy to my heart. Did you pass the regent?"

"Yes. How bad is he? O'lam knows he is coming."

Jered sat facing her, his eyes taking her in. "He has a deep gash in his gut. And he'll need stitches in his leg." Jered smirked. "His good leg. Now he will have a double limp for a while."

"But I don't understand. How did this happen—here, away from the battle?"

As Jered recounted the attack at the spring, Aletha felt her face drain of blood. To have to fight an army of vicious attackers was hard enough—but to have a traitor like that in his own ranks! When Jered mentioned Ka'zab's name, she shuddered.

"That was the guard who grabbed me the first day I came here. If the regent hadn't stepped in . . ." She shook off the thought. "That man is evil."

"Aletha . . ." Jered took her hands in his, and she felt another shudder. The warmth of his fingers and the kindness in his eyes set her heart pounding. "Something bizarre happened at the spring. The regent fought with that traitor and finally bested him with his sword. But as the man fell, he changed—"

"Changed?"

Jered nodded. "You will think I am mad, but we all saw it. One minute he was human, the next, he became a huge, black bird, and just . . . flew away." Jered gestured with his hand in the air. "Just like that!"

As Jered's words settled around her, a strange feeling came over Aletha. Images of black ravens entered her mind. Big, bothersome birds lighting on the ledge alongside the spring, gathering in the branches of the orchard. Tipping their heads and listening.

She spoke softly. "Jered, there is some *yo'shana* at work here. Will you take me over there—to the spring?"

He eyed her curiously, then nodded. Jered took her hand and led her out across the knoll. Guards were unloading the last of the crates and carrying them into the barracks. Even the sun, now shining brightly, could not take the chill from the air, and Aletha wrapped her cloak tighter. As she walked, she looked down the hill and could see the shapes of men moving along the wall, and a mass of bodies engaged in fighting outside the city. In contrast, a quiet lay over the knoll. Up here, away from the insanity below, Aletha could almost pretend the city was not under siege. As they walked, Jered squeezed her hand and looked at her.

"Aletha, I know I have a battle to fight, and this is not the best time, but I worry I may not get another chance."

Aletha stopped in front of the pool, where the water bubbled quietly, the agitated noises drifting up from the city barely audible. "A chance for what?"

Jered tried to hide his nervousness, but Aletha could see it all over his face. Her heart warmed to this complicated man. Tough, strong, courageous, loyal—but such a dreamer with a big, tender heart. Yet how could she encourage the feelings she read in his eyes—and the ones crying out to her in her own heart? As soon as she could find Adin and finish what they came to do, she and her brother would use the map and return home—centuries into the future, where a captain named Jered would have died long ago.

Sadness tugged at her like a heavy weight. She wanted to let go, lose herself in those penetrating eyes, learn all about him, and spend days laughing and exploring mountains with him. But that was a life that could never be. She had a kingdom to save, and per-haps one day rule. She was born to these privileges—and responsi-bilities. They could not be shirked for such a personal indulgence, however tempting. And the painfulness of this understanding ate at her heart. Tears started falling down her cheeks, despite her resolve not to cry.

Jered lifted her chin and wiped a cheek with his fingers. Without another word, he pulled her close and kissed her tenderly, and Aletha could do nothing to stop the love from bursting the dam in her heart. Why, oh why, did this have to happen to her—and now?

Jered pulled back and saw the sadness on Aletha's face. "I know what you are going to say. There is no room in your life for this, for me. But Aletha—" He stroked her hair and drank in every bit of her. "Just for today, this moment. Let me believe. Let me hold on to a shred of hope."

Aletha laughed, tears streaming. "Captain, are you always this melodramatic?" She touched his face and ran a hand along his soft, trim beard. "Perhaps when this battle is over, we will have time to talk. And I will explain everything to you then. But believe me, what I have to do will have even greater consequences than the outcome of this war."

Jered's face suddenly froze. He studied her face with agitation. "What did you just say?"

Aletha cocked her head. "I said, what I have to do will have great consequences, and I need to attend . . ."

Jered shook his head and spoke more to himself than to Aletha. "Those are the exact words Adin used—"

"Adin?!"

"Yes, my assistant. He was here with me—"

"Jered!" Aletha grabbed his shoulders forcefully. "Adin is the brother I have been searching for. Do you mean to tell me all this time he has been by your side?"

"He never mentioned a sister—until just a little while ago. He said he urgently needed to find you."

"And I him!" Aletha was flustered. "Tell me—where has he gone?"

"Why, you passed him on your way up here—taking the regent down to the healer's."

Her eyes grew wide. "The man on the horse . . ."

"Aletha, I didn't know. But you will find him there now. Come." He took her arm, shaking his head in amazement. "You do look like Adin, and you are just as secretive and confusing." He pulled her close, delighting in her. "But that's what I love most about you—your mystery." He kissed her again, and Aletha let herself melt into the comfort of his arms.

Aletha pulled away. "I must go. O'lam needs me, and if Adin is there—" She had so much to talk to Adin about! And to know he was safe brought more tears to her eyes. She would give him the biggest, longest hug imaginable!

"Then, let's get you on the wagon. There are some things I need to take care of. But, promise me," he said with a stern face, "you will stay at the healer's *bay'ith* and wait for me. I will come later to check on the regent. I am worried his wound may be fatal." He turned and looked back at the spring. "What kind of creature could change from man to bird, and what kind of poison might that dagger bear? And another thing . . ."

Aletha waited for Jered to continue, as he watched the water spill down the rock into the pool.

"Adin saw something in the water. Something that terrified him. When I put my hand into the spring, he screamed in fear."

Aletha drew closer to the pool and looked in. She let her eyes soften and her gaze wander. Nothing stirred. But then—there! On the far side of the pool a dark shadow floated. She walked around for a better look and stopped.

Jered watched her curiously. "That is precisely where the regent was wounded—where you stand. And where Ka'zab fell."

Aletha dipped her hand in the water and watched, mesmerized, as her fingers turned black and started to burn. The water in the pool hissed and sparked, and a blackness spread out from her hand until the entire pool was dark and putrid. Aletha quickly withdrew her arm and shook the water from her fingers and the vision from her mind. Slowly, the blackness faded and the water returned to its former purity. Now some things were beginning to make sense. She hoped O'lam would be able to explain those other things that didn't.

She came back over to Jered and took his arm. "There is a great evil at work here, but I don't have all the answers."

"Is the water safe to drink?"

Aletha nodded. "It is not the water that has been tainted."

She said no more. They walked, deep in thought, back to the wagon where Jered helped her up onto the seat. She read the concern and fatigue in Jered's face. She reached a hand to caress his cheek.

"Don't worry, Captain. Everything will turn out all right. You and your *tsa'ba* will win this battle. And the regent will fully recover."

Jered handed her the reins, a puzzled look on his face. His voice came out hushed and trembling. "But, Aletha, you speak with such confidence. How . . . do you know?"

She took his hands in her own and squeezed them. "I believe this with all my heart, Jered," she answered softly. "For I have seen it."

TWENTY-THREE

ADIN DISMOUNTED in front of the small cottage and
backed out of the way as the guards carefully lowered
the regent off his horse. The front door opened, and
an old, wrinkled man waved his arms wildly, ushering the men in.
Adin followed them into a back room, where the guards gently set
Kah'yil down on an elevated table covered with a thin mattress. By
the bright lantern light, the healer worked quickly, ripping cloth and
unwrapping the makeshift bandages Jered had hastily put in place.
Guards fetched him rolls of gauze and jars from the shelves as the
healer pointed. Catching a glimpse of Adin, he called out to him.

"You, lad, fetch the water heating in the kitchen. There's a
bucket on the floor in there."

Adin quickly poured the water from the pot into the bucket
and carried it to the back room. The healer pointed to a spot on
the floor for Adin to place the bucket and then turned to the two
guards.

"I've no more need of your help, then. Go about your duties
and I'll see to it your regent gets properly tended. You'll just be in
the way." Without taking his eyes from the regent's gut wound, he
waved them away. They left the cottage, but Adin remained.

"I'll stay and help. What can I do?"

The healer gave Adin a cursory glance and handed him a folded
cloth. "Here, clean the wound, but be gentle about it, lad." The old

man wobbled over to the far set of shelves and ran a finger along the jars while Adin washed the wound. Blood seeped slowly from the short gash below the regent's navel. Adin looked at Kah'yil, who moaned and tried to open his eyes.

The healer returned with two jars. He opened one and stuck in his finger, removing a glob of green paste, which he then pushed under the regent's tongue. The other contained a fine orange powder, and this the healer sprinkled on the wound Adin had cleaned. In silence, they both watched as the powder soaked in and the flow of blood stopped.

"Good. Let's tackle this leg wound, then." As before, Adin cleaned the long gash in Kah'yil's thigh, and the healer repeated his applications until he was satisfied he had done all that was needed. With a long sigh, the old man wiped his forehead and stepped back. The regent's breathing deepened as he settled into a heavy sleep. "That's all we can do for now, lad. Until he starts to wake."

The healer raised his eyes in relief. Wiping his hands on a cloth, he said, "Name's O'lam. And I am grateful for your tending, lad. But my helper should be here soon. No need for you to stay."

"The captain wants me to watch over the regent until he arrives."

"Ah then, lad, let's have a pot of tea while we wait." As O'lam leaned over to pick up a blanket from the floor, Adin noticed a chain with some sort of pendant dangling from the healer's neck. The bright lantern's light caught the silver, and as O'lam spread the blanket over the regent, Adin's eyes locked on the hanging charm. They widened in recognition, and he sucked in a breath.

The healer, suddenly aware of Adin's sharp attention, stopped abruptly. He looked into Adin's face and turned pale.

"You . . ." Both O'lam and Adin spoke the word in unison.

Adin reached over and grasped the silver star in his hand, turning it over in utter shock. He met O'lam's eyes with disbelief.

"You are the Keeper!" The room spun, and a loud roar rushed through Adin's ears. He felt as if the roof would crash down upon him. "I have been looking for you for days!" As Adin began to swoon, the healer grabbed him under the arms.

"Here, sit." O'lam led him to his chair in the entry and lowered Adin onto the cushion. As he wiped his bald head with his sleeve, he whistled. "Well, will surprises never cease? You—showing up on my very doorstep." He brought a glass of water from the kitchen and handed it to Adin.

Adin gulped the water and looked up at O'lam. "How do you know me? We have never met."

"Ah, lad, I would know you in a crowd of a thousand." He sat on the floor next to Adin and took his hands in his own. "You are the one foretold—the *pa'lat*."

"The—what?" Adin shook his head in denial. The *pa'lat*! That was crazy. Hadn't he been sent back in time to discover the start of the curse? The hermit said he was sent to search things out, not act as some kind of deliverer. His head spun in confusion. What was going on? "I don't understand," he muttered weakly.

"What is there to understand, lad? You followed yer map back in time, and you're here to learn of the curse. And you came to find the Keeper—that's me. You're meant to fetch a cure, so you can save yer kingdom, deliver it from evil. And between us, dear fellow, we will unravel this mystery together—of that you can be sure."

Adin gasped. "You must be a powerful wizard—to know all these things about me."

O'lam laughed and patted Adin's shoulder. "A wizard I may be, but my powers had nothing to do with it. 'Twas your sister who told me all about you."

Adin jumped out of the chair. "My sister?"

Suddenly, the door blew open and a voice spoke from outside. "Yes, your sister!"

Aletha rushed in with her arms outspread. Adin froze in astonishment. Every thought fled from his mind as Aletha wrapped her arms tightly around him. A flood of tears filled his eyes and ran down his face. Aletha squeezed him so tightly he could barely breathe, and a deep and soothing comfort flooded his heart. He buried himself in her embrace, never wanting to let go, but Aletha pulled back.

"Look at you—a beard! Adin, you seem so much older!" She hugged him hard again.

"I feel years older. Aletha, you wouldn't believe all the things I have been through." He ran his hand through her hair, still unable to grasp that she stood right in front of him. O'lam chuckled at their reunion.

Aletha laughed with abandon and wiped the tears off Adin's cheeks. "Oh, I can't tell you how happy I am to find you—at last!"

"And I am utterly dumbfounded you are here. How did you get here without a map—to this time?"

"The pig told me to look for your footprints . . ."

"The pig? Winston?"

"And the abbot showed me where he had dropped you off, at the crossroads. I searched around until I found the outline of your footstep. All I had to do was follow the trail you left."

Adin's mouth dropped open and O'lam chuckled again. "Well, young ones, I'll make us all some tea. You both have much to catch up on, but the day is still an evil one. We must tend to the regent and be ready to help the captain when the need arises."

Aletha looked toward the back room. "O'lam, how is he? Jered is worried about his wound."

"He is resting and stable. Out of danger, from what I can tell. I don't doubt he'll be up and leading his men before long."

Aletha turned to Adin. "Have you told him what happened at the spring?"

"How do you know about that?" he asked.

Aletha waved her hand impatiently. "I just came from there. Jered told me." She went into the kitchen and helped O'lam pour tea.

Adin struggled to piece the day together. "But how do you know Jered?"

Aletha brought him a mug, laughing heartily. "Adin, stop asking so many questions. I will enlighten you with my whole lengthy tale soon enough. But please, you must tell O'lam what happened at the spring, because I think it has something to do with the *qa'lal* we are attempting to uncover."

O'lam sat back down on the floor at Adin's feet, sipping from a steaming mug. "Yes, lad, tell me."

Aletha knelt next to Adin and entwined her arm through his. The healer listened intently as Adin related the whole story—from the time he felt Ka'zab's evil presence at the armory, to his experience with the black acidic water at the spring. Aletha tightened her grip on Adin, nodding her head in agreement.

"O'lam, I saw it too. Where the blood had dripped into the pool, the water turned putrid and dark."

Adin interjected. "And what's odd is I had a similar thing happen before. In the future, as I was leaving the palace to search for the firebird. I filled my water jug, and for an instant saw the black liquid in the spring."

The healer stood and stroked his mustache. "So, that's it, then. The *Sha'kath* has bound the curse to the spring, using this creature Ka'zab."

"He couldn't have been human," Aletha said.

"No, the Destroyer has many minions, in many forms." O'lam scrunched up his face. "Aletha, remember the story I told you? *Qowl d'am tsa'aq adamah*. 'The voice of blood cries out from the ground.' Blood is a symbol of life, of purity, and of health. It feeds the heart. It is no accident that the *qa'lal* is linked to the blood that fell into the spring. For all it takes is one drop of evil to contaminate all that is good."

"Do you mean that Ka'zab's blood—or whatever it is that gushed from his throat—is a kind of poison?" Adin asked.

"Yes and no. The poison is not something tangible, something you can touch. Evil, once it enters the heart and is nurtured there, defiles and poisons a man. Hate, greed, lust, jealousy, murder, betrayal. These are the things that fester and come out of the heart. Men have always been susceptible to these dark things, but the *qa'lal* guarantees their inevitable succumbing. And as you told me, lass, left unchecked, this curse will lead to Sherbourne's ultimate destruction. Unless the poison can be halted and its effects reversed."

Adin strained to concentrate amid the shouting and bustle filtering into the cottage from outside. "So, how do we do that? What is the cure?"

"Well, it's simple, lad. Quite simple, really." He chuckled to himself. "And that's the paradox of God, isn't it? One simple drop of evil requires one pure drop of innocence." He looked at the twins' faces and frowned. "It's not confusing. That one act of betrayal contained the essence of every evil act—hate, murder, disloyalty, cruelty. Ka'zab shed innocent blood—the regent's— and merged it with his own, creating a sort of potion. Because the *mowt'sa* was sacred and uncontaminated, this new poisonous mixture tainted the spring that symbolizes the essence of all that is good—unselfishness, purity, kindness, love, hope. Now it will spread outward, like an invasion over the land and over time, and slowly it will annihilate all that is holy and innocent."

Aletha scrunched her face. "How can a thing as small as a drop of blood do so much damage?"

"That is the mystery of heaven, lass. Small things are big; big things are insignificant. One small spark can set an entire

woodland on fire. One small lie can destroy a marriage—or a kingdom. Say the word, one word, and you can kill or heal. That is why
we say, 'He who is faithful in little is faithful in much.' It's not the
amount of the betrayal or the size of the lie that matters. What
matters is the choosing—to do it or not. So even one small drop of
evil can contaminate the whole of humanity." He paused to let his
words sink in. "And then the cure, also, is simple."

Adin and Aletha exchanged confused looks as the healer got
up and went into the workroom. He returned with a small glass
vial that he handed to Adin. "Here, lad. All you have to do is put
a drop of innocent blood in the bottle. From one who has never
harbored any hatred or ill will toward another."

"Can't we stop the curse here, in this time?" Aletha said. "Stop
this thing before it has a chance to spread?"

"No, lass. You see, what has taken place has already created
your future. All these centuries, the course of the curse has led to
the formation of your kingdom, and your very lives. There is nothing you can do here in this time to stop the spread of the *qa'lal*.
But take the remedy back to your own time and pour it into the
spring, and you should be able to stop its further spread, and perhaps counteract some of the wicked magic it will have fomented.
Destroy the curse in your time, lad, before Sherbourne falls to
ruin."

Adin held back the panic starting to grow. "But whose blood?
How will I choose?"

"Trust heaven. You will know at the right time."

"But, O'lam," he added, "I no longer have the map. It was stolen the day I arrived here. How can we return to our time?"

Aletha's eyes widened. "The map was stolen?"

O'lam narrowed his eyes in thought. "Well, lad, why not do as
your sister did—and follow your steps back?"

"But, Adin," Aletha blurted, "the pig said the steps will fade, and that I would have to hurry before they would forever disappear."

Adin jumped up. "Then it may already be too late." He took hold of the healer's loose sleeve. "Is there no other way to get back, O'lam? Any magic you can use, a spell or something?"

O'lam shook his head. "I have no way to link this world to yours, or this *time* to yours."

"Then we must hurry, Aletha. I have to see if the footprints remain. Or everything we have done and seen will be for naught."

Aletha grew quiet, then went into the back bedroom to gather her things. O'lam placed his arms on Adin's shoulders and gave him a kind smile. "I told this to your sister, and I will tell you as well. As willful and destructive as evil is, it is no match for heaven. Love is stronger and always conquers." His face turned wistful. "The Keepers have an old song, written long ago to give us hope."

Adin listened to the beautiful lilting words of the ancient language as O'lam sang them to a haunting melody. Although he caught the meaning of only some of the words, the soothing sound stilled his anxious heart and filled him with an unexpected joy and peace. Aletha came out to listen, with a calm, softened look on her face.

O'lam let the notes die out, and then spoke quietly, giving the twins a nod of reassurance. "Set me as a seal upon your heart, as a seal upon your arm. For love is as strong as death; its flames are the flames of fire. Many waters cannot quench love, nor can the floods drown it."

Adin looked at Aletha and saw her touch the locket around her neck. Adin knew that she, too, was remembering their mother, and that last day by her bedside. Slowly, a strange look came over Aletha's face, and she removed her fingers from the chain and held them in front of her as if they had touched something. "*Now* I know where I've seen that star." She turned to O'lam and looked closely at the pentacle around his neck.

"Where?" Adin asked.

The color fled from Aletha's face. "Adin, do you remember the velvet choker Reya always wore—the black ribbon tied around her neck?" She paused in astonishment. "With the silver star . . . holding a blue gemstone?"

As soon as Aletha mentioned it, Adin could see it in his mind's eye. Reya! Who watched over the twins from the day they were born. Who had a gift of sight, and knew the prophecies of the *qa'lal* and the *pa'lat*. Who stayed close to the palace, in order to protect them, to do all she could to prevent evil from infecting him and Aletha. Adin thought back to Reya's words, that rainy day in the cottage before he left on his journey. How she knew the Deliverer would come. That she had *seen* it.

Adin was at a loss for words. His own nursemaid. One of the Keepers. How much had she kept secret from him? What else did she know? He scowled. If he ever made it back, she would get an earful from him!

"Who is Reya?" O'lam asked.

"Our nursemaid. Now I understand why she told us all those stories about the sacred sites."

O'lam nodded. "Since the founding of the sites, there have always been Keepers. And, lad, there always will be, as long as evil is in the world."

Adin stood at the door, his hand on the latch. "Aletha, we must go. We have to get outside the walls, and it won't be easy."

O'lam spoke. "Adin, are you sure you want to leave right now? It can hardly be safe. I can put a protective spell around you, but I am not sure it will be enough, what with all the fighting and panic.

Can it not wait another day? Perhaps tomorrow the siege will be over."

"I can't take that chance." Adin saw Aletha hesitate. The stricken look on her face caused his heart to clench. "What's wrong, Aletha?"

Whatever distressed her, Adin sensed it stemmed from more than a fear of danger. He knew her too well. He watched as she tried to speak, but instead of answering, she shook her head and tears squeezed from her eyes. The emotion in the room grew so thick that the hard knocking at the door startled them both.

Adin opened the door and the captain flew in. Jered took one look at Aletha's face and ran to her, grabbing her arms. "Aletha, what is it? The regent?"

She shook her head, unable to speak. Jered reached out a hand and wiped the tears from her face. She lowered her head, and more tears came. Confused, Jered looked over at the healer.

O'lam sighed. "Your regent is recovering. He is resting in the back room and responding well to the medicine." He studied Aletha sobbing in Jered's arms. "But, for what ails this lass, I'm afraid I have no cure."

All it took for Adin was to read the expression in his captain's face. Would the surprises of this day never end?

So. He watched Aletha raise her eyes and gaze at Jered. *This is the young woman Jered went to visit.* In all his years, Adin had never seen Aletha look at any man the way she looked at the captain. And now he knew why she cried. *Oh, my poor, heartsick sister.* His heart felt her pain. Why, of all times, did she have to go and fall in love now? How could she have let this happen?

But, just looking at her forlorn expression, Adin understood. Aletha well knew she would have to leave this man. That she must return home, where she belonged. Could this cruelty be from heaven, that Aletha should find such a perfect match—for the captain was truly her match in every way—only to have to part from him forever?

Aletha pleaded with Adin with her eyes. She needed time to tell him. To say good-bye. O'lam had already disappeared into the workroom, checking on the regent. Adin turned and opened the front door, then sat on the stoop, letting the flood of emotions and the excitement of the day numb his mind.

The city was still in uproar, although the ground no longer shook. Over on the main road, people ran and yelled as before, but Adin didn't hear them. Visions of the spring, with black water spreading, flitted through his mind. Reya, O'lam, the pig, the hermit—all their warnings and words of advice cluttered his thoughts, overlaid with the image of Aletha in Jered's arms. Blood spilling from the bodies in the barracks, the regent slashed with the dagger, and Ka'zab turning into a bird.

All these floated before his eyes and overwhelmed him. Now he feared to think how this day would end, how his life would end. How much of the future was fixed, and how much could he alter? The pig said wisdom would hold him in good stead. That it helps you make decisions, keeps you out of trouble. Well, if that was the case, then the pig must have been unable to grant Adin's wish. For Adin knew he was anything but wise; he did not know how to determine his next steps, and he certainly had not kept out of trouble's path. But if the saying proved true—that 'in wisdom is much grief, and he who increases knowledge increases sorrow'—then perhaps at this moment, Adin was the wisest man in the world.

Aletha didn't expect Jered to believe even half of what she told him. How fantastic this all must sound! A magical map, a talking pig, and an evil curse meant to vanquish a kingdom. But, surprisingly, Jered showed no hint of cynicism or scoffing. For once, he set aside

his usual joviality and listened respectfully as Aletha told of her life
as a princess in a Sherbourne that would not exist for hundreds
of years. She fought with her heart as she spilled out the story, for
who knew what effect Jered's knowledge of his future would have?
Knowing the outcome of the battle and the existence of the curse
might change the choices he'd make in his life. But, then again,
maybe he was meant to know. Heaven had brought Jered into her
life, and her heart would forevermore be intertwined with his.

When she finished speaking, she dropped her head and sighed.
She resolved that nothing Jered could say would weaken her deter-
mination. Sherbourne needed her. Adin needed her. She worried
Jered would beg her to stay, and that thought brought more tears.
How would she have the strength to turn and walk away from him?

Jered sat quietly beside her on the bench. He stroked her hands
and looked off into space, deep in thought. Finally, he spoke, his
words breaking a silence as brittle as a thin sheet of ice.

"Aletha, Adin is right. You must go, and quickly." He lifted
her chin with his hand and smiled. "Remember that day when we
talked about that sense of destiny? That feeling you get, knowing
there is something you must do, something calling you?" Aletha
nodded, wiping her face.

"Aletha, you cannot outsmart that calling. It is as you said:
What you have to do has much greater consequence than the outcome of the battle. If this is true—this *qa'lal* of which you speak—
then you must stop it."

"But why? Why should I really care if my kingdom ends in
ruin? Someday, far off in the future? If men want to be evil, isn't
that their choice?" Aletha realized she was sounding like Adin,
echoing his disbelief in his ability to stop the inevitable.

"Because, Aletha, you *do* care. And you *can* prevent it from
happening. Look, didn't you say even your father, the King, was
under evil's curse? Don't you want to help him come back to his

senses, be freed from the blindness of his greed?" Jered tried to encourage Aletha with his eyes, but she didn't want to hear his words. She wanted to be stubborn and selfish. But Jered was right. And, sadly, he knew he was right too.

He stood and reached for her hand. "Come, let's gather your things. I will take you and Adin to the forest outside the north wall. It is much too dangerous for you to attempt the trip yourselves."

Reluctantly, Aletha stood and went to the door to lift her cloak from the peg. Jered walked up behind her and turned her toward him. He took her in his arms. "My sweet Aletha, letting you go is the hardest thing I have ever done. I would fight a thousand men to rescue you, climb a thousand treacherous mountains. And yet, how can I fight destiny if it is tearing you away from me? How?" Jered's eyes filled with tears and he made no move to stop them from pouring down his face and into his beard.

Aletha caressed his cheek and leaned her forehead against his. "You cannot, Captain Tebron. We cannot." Her words all spent, she found his lips with her lips and kissed him, her love gushing out of her, a bittersweet kiss. She let go of Jered and opened the front door. Adin jumped to his feet and searched her face.

"Adin," she said quietly, "it's time to go."

Adin came in and picked up his sack from the floor. He reached in and removed a bundle of parchment. "Here, Captain," he said, handing it to Jered.

"What is this?"

"Your primer. So you can teach yourself to write."

Aletha saw Jered's face light up and she smiled. It would be just like Jered to set his mind to such a task. She went into the back room and found O'lam leaning over the regent's face.

"How is he?"

O'lam nodded, pleased. "He's a strong one, this regent. When he awakens, lass, I imagine I will need guards here to keep him from charging out the door. But he'll be needing a few days of rest, battle or no. And I intend to make him get it."

He raised himself up and ran a hand along his plush mustache. "So, you're off then? Have all your things?"

Aletha read the sadness in O'lam's face. "I'm sorry to be leaving you at such a time. I know you could use my help." She took his hands. "Thank you for your kindness, and for teaching me so much. I would like nothing more than to stay and learn all about healing."

"Yes, it's been a blessed time, lass. And heaven be with you on your journey." He walked with her back into the entry, where Adin and Jered stood ready, next to the door. "Don't forget, you dear twins. Let your love give you strength and courage to do what needs be done. Love is as strong as death—*ahabah 'az ma'veth*—and it conquers all.*"*

Aletha hugged the healer, and O'lam's cheeks turned pink. "You should look for another assistant," she said as she followed Jered out the door. "Someone who can bake a mean tart."

"I'll try, lass, I'll try."

Adin shook hands with O'lam. "Thank you for caring for my sister."

"No, lad, she cared for me. She's a precious treasure. Watch over her." The healer looked deeply into Adin's eyes and cocked his head.

"Something tells me, lad, this will not be the last time we meet."

Adin shrugged. "I don't know how that could be possible, unless you find a way to travel through time too."

O'lam patted his shoulder brusquely. "Well, we'll just have to see what heaven has in store, won't we, lad?"

Adin nodded and took Aletha's arm. With a sigh, Aletha closed the door behind her and Jered wrapped an arm around her shoulder. Already the day waned, and the soft evening light lay across the sky. In silence, they rushed down the lane to the main road, and turning north, paid no heed to anything other than the ground in front of them. Aletha noticed a strange quiet, with only a few fighters marching south, passing them without recognition. People who would normally be returning home from work were sequestered in their hiding places, and from time to time Aletha saw a face peeking from behind a curtain or shutter of a cottage as they passed. An eerie calm hung over the city.

When they reached the north gate, blocked by the lowered portcullis, Jered motioned her and Adin to stay where they were. He left and spoke to the guards at the gate, and after what looked like a heated debate, returned to Aletha's side.

Aletha sensed Jered's tension; he was like a cat ready to pounce. As they walked up to the tower, Jered nodded at one of the guards who then pulled on the ropes and raised the gate. With a hand on the hilt of his sword, he walked out of the walled city and looked in all directions.

"Come quickly!"

Aletha could hear the sounds of fighting: men shouting, an occasional scream, rumbles that rolled across the dirt road as they walked quickly, hunched over. The fighting seemed far away; she could see no one anywhere outside the walls. She watched Jered's face for any signs of fear or concern, but his serious look of concentration never wavered. Finally, after an interminable time, they reached the edge of the field. Aletha grabbed Adin's hand, helping him wade through the thick, knee-high grass as they ran silently through the meadow. When they arrived at the border of the woods, Jered stopped and knelt down. He looked questioningly at Aletha.

Adin dropped down beside him, his head darting from side to side in nervousness. Aletha knelt next to the captain and caught her breath. "Here. This is the place." She pointed into the trees and Adin nodded in agreement. Adin seemed anxious and restless, wanting to see if the footprint was still discernible. "Adin, go check. We'll wait here."

As Aletha watched Adin wend his way into the dense wood, she turned back to Jered. He gave her a quick, sad smile, then returned his attention to scanning the fields. She then saw his hand tighten on the hilt of his sword.

"What is it?" she whispered, searching across the meadow to see what had caught his awareness. But Jered's eyes were lifted up to the sky, where a dark shadow blotted out the glare of the setting sun.

In the flash of a moment, the dark cloud descended upon them, a flock of large, black ravens, squawking ferociously. With strong wing beats they focused their gaze upon Jered, who pulled out his sword and pointed it toward the sky. The birds dove at full speed, as if ripping the air with their beaks.

Jered swung wildly. Not having a weapon, Aletha ducked behind the captain and covered her head with her arms. Blocking her with his body, Jered hacked away as more than a dozen birds, their faces brimming with hate, rained down on the two. Aletha screamed, and out of the corner of her eye saw Adin running back, pushing branches away from his face.

As he stumbled out of the wood, Adin pulled out his dagger and came alongside Jered. The birds kept whirling and circling, diving again and again. With each attack they struck Jered on his arms and back, and in return he slashed wings from bodies and severed heads from necks.

Adin thrust upward, and a bird cried in pain and tumbled to the ground. Adin crouched, waiting for another bird to come at him, but the entire flock seemed bent on attacking the captain. Aletha watched in horror as the giant black creatures came barreling at Jered from every direction.

Adin waved his arms and yelled, trying to scare them off, but they did not relent. Aletha heard the sickening sound of their beaks ripping skin. Jered's sword kept swinging and birds kept dropping until, finally, the last few withdrew, circling angrily and screeching. Aletha stared into the sky as the birds vanished into the approaching night. Beside her, Jered collapsed to the ground, and Adin ran to stand over him, his dagger poised.

Aletha, shaking with fear, turned and crawled to Jered. She gasped as she scanned his bloody face and torn clothes. His eyes were swollen, and Aletha realized he'd been pecked at so fiercely that he could not open his lids. She removed his cloak and lifted off his tunic, which hung in tatters. Pulling up his shirt, Aletha cried out, for Jered's chest and stomach were a pulpy mass of flesh and blood.

Adin, after scanning the sky one last time, dropped to his knees beside Jered and put his dagger back in its sheath. He locked eyes with Aletha, sharing her shock and horror.

"Adin," she said. "You know we have to get him to O'lam. He is losing too much blood, and I have nothing with which to bind him."

"Here." Adin pulled off his tunic and shirt. He handed the shirt to Aletha. "Use this."

Adin helped Aletha rip strips of fabric and tie them around Jered's head and waist. Aletha shook her head. "This won't help."

"Aletha," Adin said quietly, his eyes intense. "I found the footprint. It's nearly gone. Just a tiny glow that I could barely find by using my sight. We've run out of time."

Aletha's breath caught. "Adin, I can't just leave him here. He will die!"

Adin stood unmoving. "I know."

"Well, what do you want me to do?" Her voice grew hysterical. "What *can* I do?"

Adin shook his head, and Aletha read a look of resignation on his face. "Aletha, I must go back. You know that." He looked over at Jered, who lay unconscious on the bloody grass. A full moon peeked out from behind the eastern ridge of hills into a pale pink sky. Aletha felt her heart pound in her chest loud as a drum. She began to cry.

"Adin, tell me what to do. I can't think." She stared at Jered, watching blood darken the makeshift bandages. She turned to Adin and pleaded with him with her eyes.

"Aletha, you can't let Jered die. You must hurry and get help, get him to O'lam. I will go back to Sherbourne, to the future, and do what I can." He stopped and smacked his hand against his head. "How can I return? The vial is empty. I have no way to stop the curse."

Without a pause, Aletha reached over and pulled Adin's dagger from its sheath. She held out her palm, and before Adin could protest, ran the edge of the blade across her hand. Blood pooled in her palm.

"Here, this will have to do. I do not know how innocent I am, but the regent's royal blood was used to make the curse. I have no doubt his blood flows in our veins as well. Maybe because we share the same blood that will make a difference."

Adin stared at Aletha's hand. "You are willing to forfeit everything and everyone you love—even me—to save this man's life. I don't know how much more heaven can ask for. There is no greater love than that." Adin took the vial from his pocket and scooped up some of Aletha's blood. He corked the bottle and put his hand on her shoulder as she clenched her hand into a fist.

"Adin, I can't bear for you to go. How can I live without you? You are more precious to me than life itself."

"And you to me." He mumbled the words he had heard from O'lam, and a strange calmness came over his face. "'Set me as a seal upon your heart, as a seal upon your arm. For love is as strong as death; its flames are the flames of fire. Many waters cannot quench love, nor can the floods drown it.' "

His eyes joined Aletha's and she stood and embraced him, her heart breaking in two. She pulled back and looked at him. "Adin, go. Pour the blood into the fountain and stop the *qa'lal*. You can do this. Find Reya. Perhaps she will know of a way to bring me home—or for you to return to me. Don't lose hope, and don't stop trying."

Adin rested his hand on Aletha's head, then stroked her hair. "Someone once told me, 'It is the glory of God to conceal things, but the glory of kings to search them out.' Aletha, O'lam is right. Heaven is guiding us, and we cannot see the way. We just have to trust the words of that man in the orchard. Remember? *Yesh 'achar'ith tiq'vah k'rath.* 'Surely there is a future, and your hope will not be cut off.'"

Aletha nodded. Adin handed her the sheath for his dagger, then unstrapped Jered's sword and hung the scabbard around Aletha's shoulder. "You may need these. Be cautious, and hurry. Tell the guards at the gate to come and retrieve the captain. Threaten them with the regent's wrath if they show any hesitation." Aletha nodded, steeling her face with courage. Adin smiled and kissed her on the forehead. "And once the captain is patched up and this *mil'ka'ma* is over, marry him before he knows what has hit him."

Aletha forced a smile, pain wrenching her heart. "Believe me, I will."

She embraced Adin again, fearing in her heart it would be the last time. She couldn't bear to think of it. Quickly, she disengaged herself, straightened her clothes, and backed away. So many words flooded into her thoughts, things she wanted to say to Adin, memories she wanted to share, but she had run out of time. Unable to say even good-bye, she turned and ran across the thick grass, leaving Adin and her future behind.

With tears blurring his sight, Adin stumbled through the thick coppice of trees, uncaring that branches scratched his cheeks and caught in his hair. Leaving Aletha was unimaginable, unthinkable. But what other path could he take besides the one that would begin with a fading footprint? Falling to his knees, Adin crawled along the mat of crimson leaves and panic grew in his heart. Nowhere could he see the glow of his boot's outline. In the dim moonlight he searched the forest floor, running his hands over the ground, trying to get his bearings.

There! A thread of light, dull and throbbing, lay between two saplings. He crawled over and looked closer. He could barely tell where to step.

Taking a deep breath and wiping his eyes, Adin stood next to the remains of his magical print. Reaching into his sack, he pulled out a clean shirt and put it on. He wrapped his cloak, torn by the attacking birds, around his shoulders. Above him, the bulging body of the moon climbed the sky, and Adin could hear the quiet rustlings of the forest animals settling down for the night.

Far away, although he could not detect the sounds of war, he knew men were fighting for their lives along the magnificent wall Kah'yil had built. Frightened women and children huddled together in hidden places in their homes and shops. The regent of what would shortly be called the kingdom of Sherbourne lay half-conscious in the back room of a healer's cottage. And Captain Jered Tebron, leader of the *tsa'ba*, lay fighting for his life, buried in thick grass, unaware that the woman he loved had just given up everything she held precious in order to save him.

Adin felt the weight of his *ma'gur* heavy upon his heart. How could he just walk away, leaving this place and his sister behind?

Guilty feelings of his betrayal and abandonment washed over him, making him hesitate. Yet, he told himself, if he didn't leave, didn't try to stop the spread of the curse, then all those people—the fighters, the regent, the captain, and even Aletha—were toiling for nothing. He would be letting them all down if he failed in his task.

Although this realization did nothing to ease the pain in his heart, at least Adin could see his way forward. With a deep breath, he lifted his foot and set it upon the imprint left in the leaves. And in seconds the world vanished in a loud whoosh.

Again Adin was swept up in a maelstrom that battered him with wind and flickering light. He bent far over, his eyes glued to the ground, searching for one elusive footprint after another as his head swam with vertigo. Only tiny shreds of white light dangled over the black chasm below, indicating to Adin where to step. Time moved agonizingly slowly, and Adin walked for an eternity.

With shaky legs and his neck screaming in pain, Adin pressed forward. Seasons roiled around him—heat, cold, rain, snow—and he paid attention to nothing but the faint lines below him and the incessant ache in his heart. He said Aletha's name over and over, mindlessly, like a mantra.

A shape approaching out of the gloom shook him from his concentration. Just as before, he could make out a man, draped in shadow, emerging from the whirl of color and tunnel of chaotic noise. Only when the man was upon him did Adin see a parchment gripped in his hands and a look of terror upon a face he knew better than any. With a heavy thud, Adin collided, then merged, with himself. Now he understood why he had seen the bearded man with a tattered cloak as he had traveled back in time.

Each step forward hurled him years from Aletha, and as much as he wanted to believe he would one day see her again, he knew he was foolish to hope. Step after step, the world dissolved and reformed around him, but with each step he left a small piece of his heart behind. By the time he came to the last thread of light fastened to the dark void whirling beneath him, Adin's chest felt empty, drained.

The hermit's warning came into his mind—to take care that he didn't misstep by even a hair's breadth, or he could arrive weeks earlier—or later—than the day he had left. But how could he tell? There was not enough of an outline to show him exactly where to step. And he knew this had to be the last print, for ahead of him were his tracks that led into his distant future, hazy tracks that stepped back over themselves. He would just have to guess.

Carefully, he set down his boot and stopped. The rushing noise retreated, like water rushing down a precipice, settling Adin into a quiet fall day. The flickering lights assaulting his eyes faded, and a few spindly trees came into focus around him, their bare branches clinging to autumn's last leaves. Adin reached out a trembling hand and touched the slab of bluestone rock, partially buried in the ground, looking just the same as when he'd left it only a few weeks earlier. Crisp, cool air blew gently against his face, and off in the distance Adin could make out the guards pacing in front of the north gate. Every muscle in his body shook from exhaustion.

With a quiet groan, Adin dropped to his knees, and, holding his face in his hands, wept until his tears ran dry.

• PART FOUR •

PA'LAT

(THE DELMERER)

TWENTY-FOUR

PULLING HIS hood down over his head, Adin marched toward the north gate, knowing no other way to get to the palace. Two guards stood idly at the entrance, engaged in discussion. All Adin could hope was that he had made it back to the right time. How bizarre it would be to show up at the palace only to find himself there, weeks before he left on his journey.

The thought befuddled him. Traveling through time posed endless complications. What if Aletha was still there—he could stop her from leaving! But, then, if she never ventured after Adin, he would never have known to follow his prints to return. For that matter, he could stop himself from ever starting his *ma'gur*. Then where would he be? He would never take the map through time, and then could never be standing here—at the gate—with the vial in his pocket.

Adin sighed, his head spinning. O'lam was right. Once events had happened, they were destined to play out, for the future was built upon those events. It was too hard to understand. All he knew was that he must not interfere with the course of time. He— the other Adin—must be allowed to leave, and Aletha to follow. If need be, he could hide, wait until the right time for his return. That was why it was vital he learn what day it was—and he hoped the guards would not find his appearance suspect.

As he neared the gate, the two guards noticed him and approached cautiously. Adin drew back his hood, and they halted suddenly, exchanging serious glances.

"Prince Adin!" one declared as both guards lurched for him.

Before Adin could reply, one of the men grabbed his arm and spoke to the other. "Alert the King! I will hold him here until you return."

Adin pulled against the guard's rough handling. "What are you doing? Release me!"

The man steeled his face, and Adin could see conflicting emotions in his eyes. This guard had known him since he was a boy; what could possibly cause the man to grip him so tightly? Adin fought the urge to struggle, remembering he'd given Aletha his dagger. He sighed. He had seen enough violence this week, and the last thing he wanted was to stain his hands with the blood of one of his own subjects. Besides, this burly guard would easily best him—and there was the man's sword to consider.

So, without resisting, Adin let the sentry bind his hands and lead him to the steps of the tower.

"Sit here. And don't try anything you'll regret." He backed away a few steps and assumed a stance of authority, turning to avoid Adin's gaze.

"Tell me, please, what is going on. I have been . . . away. What day is it?"

The guard sneered. "You finally show up, weeks after your disappearance, and put on this innocent act? You know plenty well it is the full moon before winter solstice. What have you been up to? Plotting with your coconspirators?" The man snorted in disgust.

Adin was taken aback. *Winter solstice?* He quickly made a mental count and gasped. He was not early, but twenty-three days late! What treachery had gone on in his absence? Clearly, his father had misunderstood his leaving to seek the firebird. Well, why should that surprise him? Of course his father would. The King forever accused him of plotting against the throne. But now, with the vial in his pocket, Adin had a chance—a chance to make everything better. Gladly would he be taken to the King. And even if his father refused to listen to his words, Adin needed only to pour the blood into the spring and wait.

A stirring of hope rose in his chest as he sat quietly on the stone stair. As an hour passed, Adin huddled, arms wrapped around knees, ducking his face against the cold wind whipping through the gate. Only when he heard agitated voices approaching did he raise his head. A squad of uniformed guards, marching in double file, followed the tall, hooded man who led the brigade. Rasha's words, laced with acid and contempt, instructed those with him to grab the prince and take him to the dungeon.

The councillor approached Adin, stopping only inches from his face, and looked him over in disgust. Adin flinched as spittle hit his cheek, but he reined in the anger aching to lash out. The black beady eyes pinned him with accusation, but Adin met that stare with unruffled calm. Then, Adin caught a tiny flash of surprise in Rasha's baleful gaze, and suddenly the old advisor's face changed.

Over the deep wrinkles in Rasha's cheeks grew a slick layer of black feathers. The hooked nose changed to a bone-hard beak. The councillor cocked his birdlike head, and at that moment Adin knew he was in unimaginable danger. For clearly, Rasha now detected more than just a foolish prince standing in defiance of him. Adin was the promised Deliverer—the *pa'lat*—someone a servant of the Destroyer would be alerted to. And now, to his horror, Adin understood that Rasha was no ordinary man.

For the first time in his eighteen years, Adin saw the councillor flinch. Rasha signaled to the guards, then backed away as his prisoner was marched toward the palace. Adin's legs trembled as he stumbled under the quick stride of the men flanking him, their arms under his, dragging him along. This stark realization of Rasha's true nature shook him with dread. In his mind's eye he replayed the regent swiping the edge of his sword across Ka'zab's throat and the blood spraying out over the regent's clothing and face. Then the evil guard falling, his head lolling off his neck, and the shimmer of dark enchantment engulfing him as human changed to raven.

Adin's abrupt insight that evil held the monarchy in such an intimate grip, and was so entrenched in the King's inner circle, came ringing as a death knoll. As his view of the palace grew ever clearer, Adin knew absolutely and undeniably that he was doomed.

Drenched in the sweat of fear, Adin tripped down the flight of stone stairs that led from the outer palace door into the dark, dank hold. The two guards released their grip on him as they unbolted the thick wooden door and threw Adin to the cold floor with unnecessary force. Wordlessly, one of the men yanked the pack off Adin's back and turned to leave. Only after the bolt was thrown and the echo of the guards' footsteps died out did Adin catch his breath. Ominous silence fell around him in the confines of the dungeon, where only a trickle of light seeped through the cracks in the wooden door slats.

Amid the stench of the cell, Adin shivered with more than cold. With Rasha in control of both the King and the kingdom, Adin could not bear to think what fate awaited him. He wasn't a bit surprised, then, when he reached a trembling hand into his shirt pocket and, with a heart already drained of hope, found a small handful of broken glass coated in a smear of blood.

He stared blankly at the pieces of broken vial resting in the palm of his hand, and then slowly let the shards drop to the ground, a gesture that sealed the complete failure of his *ma'gur*.

Reya lost herself in thought as she poked at the smoldering embers glowing on the hearth. She was cold—through and through.

Nothing these days seemed able to draw the chill from her old bones—or the alarm that rested on her heart like a block of ice. Ever since the cook's son had come to the cottage three weeks ago, Reya had feared the worst. Her efforts to gather information while lingering around the palace proved unfruitful. Both Adin and Aletha had left the kingdom, and the note Aletha sent her did little to dispel Reya's trepidation. Aletha, so spontaneous and hard-headed—off to find her brother, who had rushed headlong toward disaster in order to win the King's love.

Reya picked up a thick shawl and draped it across her shoulders. The night was so black she could not even see the outline of the woods from her windows. She felt as if a great darkness had descended upon the world and she was right in the thick of it. Yet, in the midst of all her worry, ancient words drifted into her heart, calming her.

How easy it was to let the appearances of the world cast a shadow over the true nature of things! How easy to let the evil infecting the land eat away at her faith, one bite at a time! In the end, all things worked for the good of those whom heaven favored, and this was something Reya had needed to remind herself each agonizing day that the twins were gone. Heaven had a plan, and some things could not be seen clearly, only inferred. Like the magic surrounding the mysterious firebird.

Reya leaned closer to the hearth and fingered the choker around her neck and waited. She did not need to wait long, for within the hour a desperate pounding fell upon her door. Reya opened it to find the young man Merin, breathless and frightened, standing on her stoop. She ushered him in and set his lantern down on the kitchen table. Reading the young man's eyes, Reya understood her that presentiment of disaster was well-founded. She sat him down in the chair by the fire, and once he had caught his breath, he spoke in a frantic whisper.

"Prince Adin, ma'am! Oh, it's bad, it is."

Merin buried his head in his chubby hands and heaved great sobs.

"Tell me, Merin." Reya stroked his mop of sweaty hair, trying to calm herself in the process.

With a great gulp of air, Merin raised his woeful eyes. "They're sayin' the King has been murdered—stabbed in his own bed! And by the prince's hand!" His voice pleaded. "Prince Adin would never do such a thing—you must know't to be the honest truth!"

Reya held her breath. "And the prince—what have they done with him?"

"Tossed into the dungeon—like some worthless criminal." Merin heaved again, and fat tears rolled down his bulging cheeks. "Ma'am, isn't there something you can do? They plan to . . . chop off 'is head." He grabbed Reya's hands and kneaded them like pastry dough. "You just can't let it happen!"

Reya pried her fingers from Merin's desperate grip and stood. "No, I can't." She found her heavy coat and put it on, then picked up the lantern. Merin's eyes shone with hope. "Hurry, we've a prince to rescue, and I will need your help," she urged him.

The cook's bulky son nearly leaped into Reya's arms, and Reya steeled herself against his embrace. She smiled warmly as Merin resolutely wiped the remaining tears from his cheeks. "Prince Adin is blessed to have a friend such as you."

She reached for a muffin sitting on a plate on the table and handed it to Merin. "Be brave, Merin."

As he followed Reya out the front door with the muffin stuffed into his mouth, all he could do was nod. Reya tightened her coat against the foreboding night. *You be brave too, Reya*, she ordered herself. For she knew it would take all the courage she could muster to rescue Adin, knowing as she did what evil held him.

O'lam stamped the dusting of snow off his soft boots and tossed his heavy coat onto the hook by the door.

"You're letting in the weather, O'lam," Aletha playfully chided.

"Oh, right you are, lass." With a deft kick, O'lam slammed the door shut and then wiped the clinging snowflakes from his drooping mustache. "Smells good. What are we cooking?"

Aletha shared a smile with Jered as they leaned against each other on the bench by the blazing hearth. She gave his hand a squeeze and made for the kitchen, aware of Jered's eyes following her like a hawk. Returning with a large wooden bowl, Aletha lifted the top to the iron pot simmering over the hearth and ladled out three large scoopfuls. "Winter squash stew."

Jered motioned the healer over to his padded chair. "Having Aletha here has added some inches to both our girths, O'lam."

The healer plopped down with a grunt and stretched his hands close to the fire. He patted his generous belly. "Well, you'd better be taking her away from here soon, Captain, before I burst my trouser buttons."

Jered chuckled. "Soon enough." He shook his head in thought. "I'm plenty restless, now that this *mil'kama* is truly over. All the men have returned to their wives—and their lives—and I'm glad for it. And the regent has his hands full with those grand plans for the city. A library, a bridge across the *Ka'rash*—even a university."

O'lam slurped his stew appreciatively. "Well, lad, don't you want to be a part of it all?"

Aletha sat back down next to Jered and entwined her arm in his. It warmed her heart to see the color returned to Jered's cheeks and his enthusiasm restored. For two weeks she had nursed him here, as he lay in her own bed. And O'lam had almost never left the captain's side once the regent was healed and back at the barracks, coordinating the war effort once more.

The old healer had battled Jered's festering wounds in his own personal war, and had finally conquered them about the same time the *tsa'ba* routed their enemies. Now the scabs itched, and although Jered walked like an arthritic man, Aletha knew that in time all his aches would fade. She shuddered as she recalled the attack of those vile creatures and the sound of Jered's flesh ripping under the strength of their beaks. Even his bones had been bruised.

Jered looked over at Aletha, and she could almost see the longing stir within him. "What the regent is doing has inspired the town," he said. "And, no doubt, will help toward healing all those who suffered during this foul time. Many who would have returned to their former villages have decided to stay and make this place their home. But I am not a man comfortable with city life." He squeezed Aletha's hands with his own bandaged ones and gave her a knowing wink. "Once winter is over and the roads are dry, it's off to the mountains for us. Open spaces, open sky." He took a deep breath, as if he could already smell the fresh air drifting down from the Sawtooth Mountains. "But, until then—" Jered stood and stretched, carefully reaching his arms upward and wincing with the effort.

Aletha winced along with him. She thought of a saying from her past: "Take away the wicked from the presence of the king and his throne will be firmly established." Surely Regent Sherbourne had done just that. Aletha chuckled. She could picture Kah'yil adding that little homily to his collection of sayings, upon seeing the fruition of all his dreams. How blessed was this new and hopeful city to have such a wise and considerate ruler! And yet, with the curse in place, she knew heartache and violence would follow. It was inevitable.

She gathered up Jered's cloak and handed it to him. "When you see Kah'yil today, tell him I'll be up soon to help him with his writing."

Jered put on his cloak and fastened it. He looked at Aletha with a love radiating so warmly that Aletha could almost feel its heat. "I won't be long. He wants my advice on his design for the new gathering hall. I hear he plans to build a circular Council room with towering painted windows. I can just see it now."

Aletha chuckled and exchanged a smile with O'lam. "Oh, so can I."

The gathering hall Kah'yil was planning would one day grow into the ornate palace of her time. Already, the battle had reduced much of the great and impressive wall to the sections of rubble that would litter the ground for centuries to come. She sighed. She would have to stop thinking in those terms: my time, this time. She had made her choice—and here she would stay. Like most everything she knew about the future, she kept this vision to herself, not wanting to influence matters more than was necessary. Jered would sometimes catch her about to say something and put a finger to her lips. "The only future I want to hear about, my love," he would tell her, "is the one that involves just you and me." She knew his was the wise course, making her focus on the new life she and Jered were inventing.

She leaned over to her captain and gave him a warm kiss. She ran her fingers through his hair and gently touched the scars healing on his face. He frowned, but Aletha could see his eyes laugh.

"What a fine, strapping wench like you wants with a beat-up, broken-down soldier like me, I'll never know." He playfully swung her around. "Oh, excuse me—*princess.*" He corrected himself with an exaggerated bow.

She wrapped her arms around Jered and pressed herself hard against his chest. She felt so absolutely right, ensconced in those strong arms. Only the company of one other man made her feel this safe and warm. A tear ran down her cheek as she thought of Adin. She gripped Jered even tighter.

"Hey," he said, stroking her hair, "I'll only be gone a few hours. But I'm glad to know I'll be so missed."

Aletha raised her head, and Jered searched her eyes. An understanding came over his face and he spoke softly. "Have faith, Aletha. Someday Adin will show up on our doorstep, and he'll have lots of stories to tell our children about his exciting adventures. You'll see."

Aletha nodded, her throat too choked for her to speak. She kissed Jered briefly and stood motionless as the door closed behind him. A few flakes of snow whirled and settled at her feet, melting quickly in the warmth of the room.

She turned to O'lam, who scooped up the last spoonful of stew from the bottom of his bowl. "O'lam, do you really believe Adin will return?"

He patted the bench and Aletha came and sat near him. "Lass, I know not when, but he will. There's business he needs to finish here, but I cannot see what. Time will reveal, as it always does, lass." He set the empty bowl on the floor. "Now, that was a fine stew, and I'll rue the day when you and your captain abandon me for the wilds."

"Well, there are still many months of winter left."

O'lam chuckled. "And that means a good many tarts. I was just thinking, lass, by the time spring arrives, with your help, the regent'll have his book of sayings printed up, and everyone in the city will have learned to read." O'lam reached back into his thoughts. "Once upon a time many knew how to fashion words in the ancient language. Perhaps there's still a place in this world where they do. But that age is passing, and it's sad in a way, lass. For the writing is a beautiful one, and even the spoken words fade over time, losing their richness and power." O'lam's eyes grew misty.

"Will you teach me, then?" Aletha asked him. "I would love to learn those letters, although I may find little use for them other than to enjoy their beauty."

"'Twould be my pleasure. And you would find use, if you want to bury yourself in those books back there." O'lam gestured to the shelves in the workroom. "All the ancient formulas, passed down by the first healers, are written in that script. 'Twould be a shame to lose those treasures of antiquity."

Aletha's face lit up with the challenge. "Then let's start now. I think I'm just as restless as the captain, and I tire of watching the snow pile up outside the window."

O'lam rose from his chair and slapped his belly. "Well then, lass, follow me, and we'll get you set up with brush and ink."

Aletha picked up the bowl from the floor and took it to the kitchen. Outside the small window, snow whipped in the wind. Aletha was glad for the comfort of the healer's cottage. The heaviness in her heart never completely abated, and as she thought of Adin, she let the worry rise once more. It did no good berating herself for her decision. In her heart of hearts, she knew she had chosen rightly, for if she had let Jered die, she would never have forgiven herself—and neither would Adin. It hadn't been a selfish decision, abandoning Adin to complete his quest alone. Yet each moment she indulged in her joy with Jered, she felt a twinge of guilt.

Enough already, she chastised herself. For all she knew, Adin had saved Sherbourne and one day would rule as king. And yet, none of this would happen for hundreds of years. Oh, it was too confusing to fret over. She had to stop worrying over the distant future. For now, she had her own immediate one to participate in. And she owed it to Jered—and to Adin's memory—to live it wisely and fully.

TWENTY-FIVE

WHEN THE bolt snapped open, Adin didn't even bother to look up. Someone, probably his jailer, held high a lantern that cast streaks of light across the gray stone floor. His misery held him in such a numb state that it took moments to register Reya's face, alongside his old friend Merin's. He gave them a cursory glance and then buried his head in his arms. A hand shook his shoulder forcefully.

"Adin, come, we must hurry."

Adin looked up and saw the strain on Reya's face amplified by the harsh lamp light. "Why? It's over. There is nothing more to be done."

Merin fidgeted as Reya grabbed Adin's arm. "We've still got to get you out of here. And a little cooperation would be appreciated."

Reya tugged with all her strength until Adin let himself be pulled upright. Pain shot through his back and leg, and his head throbbed where he had smacked it on the wall. He smiled grimly at the irony of it—the same spot on his head that met with the last wall he'd been thrown against. At least that time he'd been mercifully knocked unconscious. He didn't even get the luxury of oblivion this time.

He squinted at Reya. "You shouldn't have come, taken this risk. You should leave."

Adin knew Reya so well he wasn't surprised when she punched him hard in the arm. "Up with you, now!" she barked. "You can wallow later." She waved a hand at Merin, who came alongside the prince and supported his weight.

Between the two of them, they managed to haul Adin up the flight of steep stairs and out into the night. Adin was startled to see a guard slumped on the ground beside the staircase, snoring heavily. Adin stared at Reya, and she shrugged.

"Sleeping spells I can manage. Getting you safely away from the palace is another matter altogether. Hurry!" Reya snuffed out the flame in the lantern and left it beside the guard.

Seeing how hard Reya and Merin grunted and panted made Adin feel worse. Why were they bothering? Didn't Reya understand? Adin had no place to run from the consequences of his failure. The King—his father—would be murdered tonight, and tomorrow Rasha would eliminate the "culprit" quickly and efficiently—with a swift, sharp blade. Adin wanted to cry, but his tears refused to cooperate. If only he could make things better in his death—but even that honor was to be denied him.

At least he could try to save these friends, for if they were caught he knew they would share his fate. Conspiring with a traitor was punishable by death. He put his effort into hobbling along as quickly as he could bear. Only when they had arrived at the north gate did they stop to catch their breath. Seeing no one around, Reya turned to Merin, who had collapsed onto the dirt road, one hand clutching his chest.

"I'll be fine," he gasped. "Give me . . . a few moments."

Reya placed a hand on Merin's head and Adin noticed Merin's breathing slow noticeably. "Go, Merin," she said quietly. "And not a word."

Merin wobbled to his feet and nodded in understanding. Fearfully, he looked around and then turned to leave.

"Don't worry, Merin, just go back to your room. No one will see you." Reya waved him off with her hand. Adin could tell Merin wanted to speak but could not find the words.

"You've always been a true friend," Adin said. "Thank you, Merin."

The young cook wiped his face with the back of his hand and nodded again. Adin had seen Merin cry that way from time to time when they were boys. How much simpler life was back then, when all they had to cry about were simple insults and skinned knees! The pain of lost innocence struck him as hard as a physical blow.

Reya watched alongside Adin as Merin blended into the blackness of night. The full moon had set long ago, and to Adin's eyes the world was already desolate and ruined. The hush of night stood in judgment of him, giving him a glimpse of the future he had wrought. His *ma'gur* was over. Sherbourne's curse fixed forever. And now the fate of the city rested in Rasha's control. He should stop feeling pity for himself and mourn for the poor citizens of his kingdom—for what lay ahead of them was too horrific to imagine. And all because of his own carelessness. If only he could go back and make it come out differently!

Adin let Reya lead him through the gate and north toward the crossroads. Reya finally stopped behind one of the pieces of bluestone slab and lowered Adin down out of view from any possible passersby, although the road would probably remain empty until dawn. She reached out her hand to Adin's chin and felt his beard. Adin tried not to look into Reya's eyes, for he knew it would break his heart. Instead, he stared out at nothing, feeling pain course through his body and welcoming it.

"Adin, you must tell me everything that has happened since you left."

Adin's cynical expression made Reya jerk back. He reached over and put his fingers around her black choker. Even in the dark he could feel the outline of the pentacle and the swell of the inset gem.

"Were you ever going to tell me?" he asked. "Or did you just plan to toy with me my whole life?" He let his hand drop.

"Adin, I told you as much as was safe. Any more and you may have made other decisions, chosen other paths."

Adin's voice shook with anger. "And well I should have. For the choices I *did* make will lead to Sherbourne's ruin. Everything is now lost—because of my stupidity." Adin's breath caught in his throat and an even greater pain shot through his heart. "And, I had to leave Aletha behind. I have lost her as well. And that is too high a price to pay, even if I had succeeded."

Reya waited patiently while Adin cried in great racking sobs. He felt like a small boy again, lost and alone. Why, oh why, had he listened to that hermit? If he had just gone after the firebird instead, he might have been back at the palace with Aletha, and between the two of them they could have found a way to counteract the evil curse. Maybe, in the end, Sherbourne would fall, but what of it? Cities rose and fell over the centuries, and men continued to do evil. Was it worth losing all he loved in an effort to prevent an inevitable future?

And now—what could he do? Where could he go? One thing he knew for certain was he could not stay in Sherbourne. If he did not have the courage to end his own life, then he would take his shameful cowardice and disappear to some place where he could cause no more harm.

"Adin, do you remember your mother's illness?"

Adin looked back at Reya, wondering why she brought that up. "Of course I do."

"You were young then, and did not know what you know now. What we both know now. For, after the Queen died, I pondered the mystery of her illness for many seasons. And although I shun invoking the dark arts, I had to delve into that realm to learn its source. What bound your mother was a deeply evil spell, and heaven forbid I would allow a thing of that cruelty to show its ugly face again! What if you were its next victim—or Aletha? I was not about to let that happen."

Adin studied Reya's shadowed face as the memory of his mother's death weighed heavily upon her. Had Reya known all along that he would undertake that quest? Had all her hopes of deliverance rested upon him all those years? Had she clung foolishly to the expectation that the deformed and weak prince of Sherbourne would save the day? No doubt she had, and Adin could only imagine her great disappointment.

Having Reya disappointed in him was the final blow. If only he were near a cliff, or a fast-moving river, surely he could find enough resolve to throw himself to his death.

Reya spoke again, and the firmness of her voice drew him out of his thoughts. "Adin, you must pay attention."

"Why?" he snapped.

"Because you need to understand this. From my research I learned that no cure exists capable of halting the *ro'osh* of that spell. It is so entrenched with magic that only magic can oppose it. And my greatest fear proved true—that the magic of that enchantment was interwoven with the castings of the *qa'lal*. The Queen's illness was fed by the evil of the curse. How that was possible is beyond my comprehension. How could a curse set hundreds of years ago be woven into a spell newly formed?"

"It can if those setting the curse and forming the spell are one and the same creature."

Reya's eyes widened. "What are you saying, Adin?"

"Let me tell you my story, and then you will understand." With a sigh, Adin recounted to Reya all that had occurred since he left the palace, explaining how the *Sha'kath* used Ka'zab at the spring. The telling took a long hour, and left Adin's throat parched.

Reya had been so engrossed that she hadn't noticed the raspiness of Adin's voice until he finished his account. She reached into a pocket and produced a flask. "Here, drink this."

Adin pulled out the cork and poured a thick, soothing liquid down his throat. Instantly, some of his aches subsided and his head stopped throbbing. He handed the flask to Reya, who had tears in her eyes.

"You have suffered much in these last weeks, my sweet boy. If only I could have spared you these things. I now see what you mean. The evil used to set the *qa'lal* in the past is the same as that used on the Queen. That the agents are different is no matter. This only confirms my assessment—that the only way I could have saved your mother was by suspending the enchantment. And that would have called for magic more powerful than I have ever wielded. Dangerous and risky, it would have been. But, perhaps by altering the Queen's nature, I could have confounded the spell." Reya sighed again. "Well, knowledge too little, too late, as some say."

Reya caught Adin's eye and stared with such an intense gaze that Adin froze. A shiver ran up his spine, reminding him of the emotion he had felt when he looked in O'lam's eyes at the discovery that he was the Keeper. It was as if Reya was trying to explain something in a foreign language, but he failed to understand. One thing was certain: Reya was holding back, and he knew better than to press her. But the moment passed, and along with it the strange presentiment.

"Adin, I know you feel things are hopeless. But heaven uses all circumstances to its advantage. Do you really think our small failures can stop the intentions of heaven? Believe me, Adin, they cannot." Adin could tell Reya longed to hold and comfort him but kept her distance because of his mood. Surely she could see that coddling him was not going to make everything all right.

"You don't understand," he protested. "I don't doubt heaven has its plans. I just doubt they can be accomplished with my help. Reya, I have tried and failed. Maybe heaven will find someone else to stop the curse over Sherbourne, if that is heaven's will. At the very least, whatever confidence heaven had in me, it was misplaced." Tears once more poured down Adin's face. "And it cost me my sister. Oh, Aletha . . ."

Adin no longer cared that Reya watched him weep, no doubt judging him. Bitterly, he recalled a saying Reya used to recite when trying to help heal those who had lost a loved child or mate. "The human spirit will endure sickness, but a broken spirit—who can bear it?" *No one—that's who.* All the power of medicine and magic in the world paled next to the cruel permanence of fate. And a broken spirit—what could ever remedy it?

Adin stood and looked Reya sharply in the eye. "Go home, Reya. You shouldn't have bothered to rescue me."

Reya did not even ask Adin where he planned to go or what he would do next. It was best she didn't, for Adin had no idea himself. Without another word, or embrace, or smile, Reya squeezed Adin's hands one last time, then turned and walked slowly toward the north gate. Adin watched her go, seeing her age weigh heavily upon her as each step took great effort. Once she vanished inside the walls, Adin began walking in the opposite direction.

He lifted his face to the sky and stopped. A great emptiness engulfed him, whisking away all his emotion and leaving him barren. He felt no hunger, thirst, or weariness. His life snapped closed like the covers of a book. The story was over, and it had ended badly. A story no one would want to read.

Please, he pleaded to heaven in silent anguish. *Don't let it end like this. Don't let mine be a tale of a wasted, useless life. Give me something worthy to do, some little thing. Anything. Just not this!*

All he desired at this moment was to sit beside Aletha. Not so she could comfort him with soothing reassurances, for she would know better. He only wanted to feel her near, to know she was happy and had made a life for herself in the past. Then he could die satisfied. Was that too much to ask?

Without realizing it, Adin had retraced his path back across the meadow and into the small patch of trees just north of the road. He found the place where his last print would have been, and sighed. An invisible thread now linked him to Aletha, and somehow, standing there made him feel a little closer to her. If only . . .

He squatted, his attention caught by a tiny shimmer of flame. Was it possible? Could he try to go back, back to Aletha? No, he had barely made it to this time. Yet what did he have to lose? His life here was over. What better way for him to disappear than to stumble back into some strange era? Unless heaven showed him kindness and let him, just this last time, make his way back to his sister.

Clutching that wish with every ounce of faith he had, he turned his face once more to the heavens and mumbled a silent prayer. The fiery outline briefly flared and caught Adin's attention. He looked down at the ground and for the tiniest instant saw the complete trace of his boot burn a thin line into the leaves—and then vanish. Before he could lose the image in his mind, he set his foot down in the direction of his beckoning past and was sucked away into darkness.

Adin hovered in the air, with dark colors whirling and wind whipping his face. Time slowed to a creep, and after an interminable wait, Adin caught a brief flash of spark in front of him. As he set down his boot, another spark flared before him in the black nothingness spinning around him. All was eerily quiet except for the whoosh of the wind. And then, even the wind faltered, and Adin was left in total, silent blackness.

The air warmed. Adin futilely searched the void in front of him as light seeped into the world. There were no more prints, no more flares of light or sparks to show him the way. The last bit of magic drained into the void and left him standing under boughs sprouting new green leaves. Birds chattered and flitted from tree to tree, and Adin recognized the loamy smell of spring thick in the air.

By the look of his surroundings, Adin knew he had not gone far. Months, years maybe. But not centuries. He had known better than to hope heaven would send him back to Aletha. Why would he think he deserved such happiness? It was enough to be taken this far, to a place where perhaps he could start a new life, one where he didn't cause any more harm.

Fatigue hit him hard. Was it just a few hours ago he had stood over the bleeding body of Captain Tebron, then said farewell to Aletha? And then been captured and thrown into his own dungeon, then rescued by Reya, only to end up in yet a third age of time? His body felt battered, for he hadn't even recovered from the trauma he had experienced at the barracks, tending to the wounded and witnessing the regent's fight against evil. How long had it been since he slept? Too long.

The drone of insects hovering in the balmy air lulled Adin into a stupor. Tinglings of thirst and hunger reawakened in him, but he shoved them away. He tried to keep from collapsing as his knees buckled under him. As he dropped onto the soft grass, a warm morning sun splashed beams of light onto his face and limbs, and as he drifted off to sleep, the face of Ta'man came to him.

The hermit's gentle voice soothed him like a lullaby: *"Shemesh tsa'daq zar'ach marpé ka'naph. 'The sun of righteousness will rise with healing in its wings.'"*

TWENTY-SIX

ADIN AWOKE with the midday sun burning on his face. It took him a few moments to realize he hadn't been dreaming—he really was in the woods north of the palace, in some unknown time. The short sleep refreshed him but left him with a dry mouth. Well, he knew one place where water was plentiful, but he would not be so stupid this time. No more marching blindly into the palace.

He recalled a creek, not too far into the King's wood; he would go there first and clean up and drink his fill. Since he had only the clothes on his back—and ratty ones at that—he would need to find food somehow. Everything depended on discovering in what time he had landed. Had he yet been born? Who ruled as king? The more he pondered his predicament, the more anxious he grew.

Stiff and bruised, he trekked into the woods and immediately noticed that no posted warning or locked gate barred the entrance to the forest. He tried to think back to when his father had instituted the ban. Sometime during Adin's young teen years, if his memory served him well. So he was in Sherbourne at least five years back—but five or fifty?

As he walked to the creek, he mentally redrew the forest as he knew it in his time. Hours of tromping through these trees told him little had changed. He would just have to venture out into the world of men and learn more. At least it was safe to assume no one would recognize him. With a ratty beard and his cloak covering clothes from a distant land, he would be judged a stranger. He hoped that would gain him some sympathy, and maybe a hot meal or two.

He would be a beggar, then, and contrive a story of how he had been beset by robbers. At least that was true.

As he walked slowly through the north gate, he glanced around but found no guards at the walls. As he neared the palace, the lack of activity set off alarms in his head. No servants out in the gardens, no visitors on horseback, no one milling around the entrance? This seemed odd. A beautiful spring day—and the doors closed and windows shut? Even the drapes had been drawn over the banks of windows on both levels of the palace. Was anyone even there?

His curiosity led him to the servant's entrance to the kitchen, near the herb garden. Here, he huddled by an open window, where he heard voices speaking in hushed tones. Smells of roasting meat and baking bread set his mouth watering, causing his hunger to squelch his caution. Without hesitation, Adin lifted a hand to the door and knocked. A young kitchen maid opened the door, and a face that seemed vaguely familiar stared at him curiously.

He explained his need, and the girl did not doubt his story. His appearance would probably arouse pity in even the hardest of hearts. She returned shortly with a large chunk of bread, a flask of wine, and a block of cheese. Adin thanked her, using all his self-control to resist devouring the food as she watched. And then he noticed tears running down her cheeks.

"Pray tell me, miss. What are you sad about? What has happened here?"

The servant wiped her face and snuffled. "Don't you know? It's the Queen; she's dying, sir. They say she won't last the night."

Adin's breath caught like a sharp wedge of steel in his throat. He bowed politely, hiding his shaking legs, and offered a mumbled condolence. When the door clicked shut, he hurried around the corner to the edge of courtyard and fell weakly onto the grass. His mother—still alive! Well, he now knew not only the year but the day he had arrived!

All at once, images flooded his mind. His mother, lying deathly pale in her bed; the King grieving in his chamber; and Aletha and her distraught brother following Reya up the stairs to see their mother for the last time. He raised his eyes to the second level of the palace, to the large windows with curtains drawn.

His mother lived! At least at this moment.

Adin frowned. This was too strange—to have landed back in time on this very momentous day, a day so deeply etched in his memory! He reached for his throat, remembering that this was the day his mother would give him and Aletha the lockets. A locket with the key to the map. A map hidden in a labyrinth in the abbey—a map he would one day go in search of.

Adin's head spun as the threads of his life were woven together into a pattern. But what strange tapestry would form? As he rummaged through his recollections, he tried to think of all that had happened that day, eight years ago. He stood and walked along the courtyard wall, lost in thought. As he turned the corner and faced east, the city of Sherbourne—his city—spread out like a jewel before him. He leaned back against the warm stone of the courtyard wall and stared absently at the view.

Eight years.

Seeing no one around, he quickly wolfed down the food and drink, and his stomach grumbled in response. He knew, without knowing how, that arriving on this day had been no mere chance. Was it possible heaven had truly heard him, and had brought him to this particular day for a reason? But why? *Why?*

Adin's thoughts were interrupted by voices talking in the courtyard. And they were heading toward him.

As he scrambled under a bush outside one of the archways, Adin's blood chilled, for he knew those voices well. And knew he must not be seen or heard. For he only needed to see the shoulder and arm leaning against the archway to recognize Rasha and know that if the councillor spotted him, he would be nabbed and questioned.

Adin stilled his breathing as fear pounded in his veins. Now that he knew Rasha's true nature, Adin doubted his beggar's ruse would fool one who served the *Sha'kath*. Adin's only hope was to quiet his thoughts and imagine himself invisible. And not move a muscle.

"The King is distracted."

Adin heard Rasha speak as if he were only inches away.

"The Queen will be dead by morning."

Adin heard one of the other councillors speak—the small one. "You were wise to slow the *ro'osh*. Dragging out the illness has proved beneficial. Look how the King has steadily fallen apart."

Rasha replied. "The King is a fool. Humans are such weaklings. They are obsessed with love; it blinds them to everything else. He does not know what he is fighting. There is no cure, no *ga'haw*, for this *keh'ber*. No potion in this world has the power to undo it."

Adin listened through a long, silent pause.

"See. The King is tumbling toward ruin. His queen will die and he will be consumed by it. Little by little his precious city will suffer from neglect. Heavy taxes will be levied; there will be more revolts. Famine, disease, and unrest will plague Sherbourne. This 'Crown of the East' will tarnish and decay. And, true to prophecy, will one day only exist in memory. If it exists at all. The *ne'buah* cannot fail."

"M'lord, what about the prince?" Adin recognized the voice of the tall councillor.

Rasha laughed. "That *na'baal*? In time the King will grow to believe his son plots against his life."

"But the prince is but a child."

"We will bide our time. You see how the King detests his son. And that . . . unfortunate incident with the stillborn child . . ."

The small man chuckled. "A work of genius, m'lord. There is no greater bitterness than losing what could have been."

Adin muffled a gasp of horror.

"Yes," Rasha muttered. "Yes." Another pause, and Adin fought the need to stand and stretch his cramped legs.

"And in time, slowly, the King will suspect his son, and the son's anger and humiliation will fester. It is . . . inevitable."

"Then you need not do more than put the knife in his hand."

Adin looked at his trembling hands and shook his head in amazement. Reya had been right; her potions had never stood a chance against the evil perpetrated against his mother.

Relieved, Adin heard the rustle of cloaks and soft footfalls walking away. He loosed a long-held breath.

Quietly, he came out from behind the bush and stood against the wall, leaning his face into the radiating warmth of stone. A great surge of anger welled up in him, anger that had no outlet— for what could he do? Confront Rasha and demand he stop this evil? Find some way to kill him? Adin laughed weakly. He was no match for such a creature, one fed and nourished by the Destroyer himself! Then what in heaven's name could he do? The longing to see his mother grew into a horrible need, and the thought of letting her die—again—was unthinkable!

Maybe he was not meant to interfere with history, but then, why had he been sent back to this point in time? Adin now knew these were no mere coincidences, and heaven had to have its reasons. There must *something* he was supposed to do, some way to save his mother before the night's iniquity took her away.

His thoughts drifted back to the day he and Aletha had sat in the orchard, mourning their mother's passing in the chilling rain.

That would be tomorrow! And the strange man who had beckoned them over to the far corner of the courtyard, who told them with confidence that the Queen lived . . . The man in the dark brown cloak, with a beard and shining eyes . . .

NO!

Adin clutched his chest as if he had been rammed with a spear. How could it be? But, Adin could see no way around the truth that glared like harsh daylight. No wonder that man had seemed so strangely familiar to him and Aletha.

He was that man!

Tomorrow—he knew where he would be: sitting in the corner of the courtyard, away from curious eyes, consoling two children stricken with grief. Telling them their mother lived.

But why? How? He thought back to the stranger's confident face, his reassuring words. He had spoken with such absolute certainty that Adin had been carrying that hope with him in his heart all these long years. Absolute certainty!

Now what Reya had just told him only hours ago, under a dark night sky at the edge of the woods, made perfect sense. He shook his head, stunned once more, realizing Reya had known.

Known *everything*.

She knew he would be thrown into the dungeon. She knew he would fail at his quest. She knew he would return here—Adin gasped. To find her and tell her how to counteract the evil spell killing the Queen!

Adin search his mind frantically. What was it she had told him to listen to carefully?

He replayed her words as if hearing them for the first time: *"The only way I could have saved your mother was by suspending the enchantment. And that would have called for magic more powerful than I have ever wielded. Dangerous and risky, it would have been. But perhaps by altering the Queen's nature I could have confounded the spell."*

So, Adin thought, *Reya is the key, and the solution.* By this time tomorrow, Reya will have found a way to confound the spell, for that is the only way he could tell the twins so assuredly their mother lived. He pursed his lips.

Think, think! All this time travel was making him insane. If his figuring was correct, the Reya of his future had already saved the Queen eight years earlier. And that meant that all this time she knew what had been done this night and had never told him, never a hint of it.

Peeking into the courtyard, Adin saw no sign of Rasha, or of anyone at all. He knew clearly what to do and this knowledge flooded him with great relief and joy. Finally—to have a plan, and to see heaven's hand in all his choices! Reya was right; heaven uses all circumstances to its advantage. She had told him, "Do you really think our small failures can stop the intentions of heaven? Believe me, Adin, they cannot." Adin now knew with every fiber of his being that those words were true.

Adin walked as quickly as he could back toward the northern wall. *This* Reya was still at the palace, but she would return home before supper. Adin thought back to the hopeless look of failure on her face as she had left the palace that same afternoon, and the soft kiss she had planted on his young forehead. Well, she would have a surprise waiting for her at the cottage this evening—if anything surprised that woman. Oh, how he hoped he would startle her! For once, Adin knew something she didn't—what needed to be done to save his mother.

He just couldn't wait to see the look on her face!

Before her hand touched the latch on her cottage door, Reya knew she had company. But who, on this ominous night? She let a sigh escape her, aware her emotions were all a-jumble. The Queen was not only her ruler and her patient, but a long-trusted friend. Reya had been there the day the King had arrived in his carriage with the young, fragile-seeming bride. Yet this woman, the oldest of six daughters from a noble, established family, handily learned her way around both the palace and her demanding husband. Reya found the Queen's knack for mollifying the King's temper inspiring, for often all she would do was whisper a few words in his ear, and the King's countenance would brighten like the sky after a hard rain. And her gentleness with the children was heaven to look upon. How sorely she would be missed!

Reya pushed open the door, tears filling her eyes. So many would mourn this sweet woman, most especially Adin. Oh, the agony exposed in his eyes as he had gazed upon his mother. No child should have to experience such despair.

Reya set her bag of medicines on the kitchen table and thought about how she could comfort him. If only the King had let her bring the children home with her tonight. At the very least she could have given them both something to help them sleep, and stroked their hair. Anything.

"Who visits me this mournful night?" she asked into the dark.

"Reya," a voice spoke from the den.

She spun around, confused. Surely she must know this man who came toward her from the shadows of the room. The one word alone revealed a voice as familiar as her own, a voice that plucked at her heartstrings.

She quickly took in every feature: his stature, his ragged clothes, his face. Reya froze as she searched the stranger's secretive eyes.

"Who are you?" she barely whispered.

The stranger approached, and Reya let him take her hands. "Take a closer look, Reya." Her wolf, Yo'fi, flanked the young man in a way she rarely did with strangers.

Reya jerked back as she saw who looked out from those deep-green eyes. Was this some devilry? "Adin . . .?"

But it couldn't be him! Yet, if Adin were a man, he would have this form, this face. No one else carried the same deformities with the same compensation of posture. Reya raised her eyes to the roof of her cottage and pleaded.

"A'zar sha'ma'yim kheh'sed!"

When Reya lowered her eyes, she wondered at the stranger's amused smile.

"Your prayer is answered, Reya. For heaven has come to help you, according to its mercies. Just as you asked."

"The *law'az*—how do you know the ancient language? Please," she begged, her knees giving out beneath her, "tell me who you are, and who sent you."

The man helped her to the chair in the den, letting her down gently. Yo'fi plodded to his side and pushed her muzzle against his hand.

"A few weeks ago I would have expected a surprised reaction from you, Reya. But now I know better. Are you truly that shocked to see me?"

She lifted a trembling hand and pointed at him. "It *is* you. Adin, how is this possible? And the young prince—"

Adin kneeled on the floor and studied her face. "Back in the palace, sleeping beside Aletha." His face saddened. "And he will have terrible nightmares, tonight and for many nights to come."

Reya couldn't stop staring as Adin continued.

"Reya," he said kindly, taking her hands and squeezing them. "We have little time, so I will relate my whole tale as we hurry back to the palace. Here is what you need to understand about the Queen's illness, and what you will need to do."

Reya's eyes widened during Adin's telling, as she wondered how he knew about the evil at work. Her heart longed to question him, for she could think of no explanation for his appearance. Magic was the answer, and heaven was the source—of this she was now certain. But when he told her she would have to harness magic to confound the spell, to alter the Queen's nature, she shook her head defiantly.

"No, this must not be done, Adin. It is too dangerous. Magic of that power has an intent all its own. I can wield it, yes. But I cannot direct it." She let out a huge sigh and caught Adin's piercing look.

"Reya, trust me. You have to do it." He paused to let the words sink in. "You have *already* done it."

Her heart nearly stopped beating. A sense of understanding came over her, breaking her resistance. Now it all became clear. Not the mysteries behind Adin's presence in her cottage, but heaven's need to prod Reya into acting. For it would take something this outrageous to convince her to attempt such madness. With such power unleashed, the whole palace could dissolve in an instant. Or, even worse, the entire kingdom could ignite. She once more met Adin's eyes with her own frightened ones.

"Tell me what happens. When the magic is unleashed."

Adin, still kneeling, reached over and stroked the wolf. He chuckled and gave Yo'fi a kiss on the nose. "I have no idea. I wish I could tell you, but the Reya I know"—he scrunched up his face in frustration—"didn't see fit to tell me. And, no doubt, for good reason. Although I must tell you that your secrecy is driving me batty. You could have told me you were a Keeper. It would have helped."

Reya shrugged. "You never know, my dear prince, whether one small word will destroy a kingdom. Sometimes it's better to hold things back."

Adin stood abruptly, offering Reya his hand. "O'lam said the very same thing to me. Funny, it must be a Keeper saying." He shook the thought from his head. "Come, Reya, the Queen needs you."

Reya hesitated. Only rarely had she evoked magic for such a purpose. Magic was not like the easy wishfulness portrayed in fairy

tales. One did not just wave a wand and mutter a few words and—
poof! One with skill could pull threads of magic from the deep
recesses of the earth, and with skill could braid those threads into
shapes using feelings and imaginings.

Magic was not clay to be molded; it was more like hot lava
restrained by a thin crust of earth, that when it finds a crack bursts
through with terrific force. Reya would need every ounce of concentration and mental strength to constrain that force and channel
it—somehow, in some direction. She had no way to know where
her own intent would direct it. For magic drew its path from hidden motives and inclinations of the heart. The Queen would not
be harmed; yet, if changed profoundly, how could she survive? And
would she ever return to her natural form?

She was second-guessing herself, as well as the power of
heaven—and that only wasted time. "You are right, Adin. Let's go.
But I want to hear your tale—every detail—before we arrive at the
palace. And if what you say is true, we had better take great care
not to be caught."

She walked over and opened the door. "Just because destiny
has led us to this place, doesn't mean we can be cavalier about the
whole thing. Heaven expects us to keep our wits about us and not
put its mercies to the test."

Under a shroud of obscurity, Adin and Reya hurried through the
courtyard and snuck into the library. With a careful finger, Adin
pressed the latch and pushed the doors open to the long corridor,
glowing from a thousand lit tapers. Behind him, Reya whispered
ancient words, releasing them into the air. Adin watched her
mold the heavy despair saturating the palace into fatigue, then
stupor. As they crept down the hallway toward the Queen's chamber, servants slumped on benches, snoring. Reya had assured
Adin that the King, sedated with one of her sleeping tinctures,

would be in his own deathlike trance in the bedroom down the hall from his wife.

As Adin stooped to look upon the face of a sleeping servant girl who still held a broom while she leaned against the wall, he shook his head in astonishment. He wondered just how much magic Reya had wielded over his family throughout the years. Just a meek little nursemaid, with a few potions up her sleeve. Ha! He wouldn't be surprised if he learned she had even made the map.

When they arrived at the Queen's door, Adin took a deep breath. He looked over at Reya, whose face paled in nervousness. On the walk over to the palace, Adin had related everything that had happened in the last few weeks. She asked few questions. Only when Adin told of the birds wounding Jered, and Aletha's anguished choice to stay behind, did Reya sob quietly and mutter words of grief. Aletha would not leave Sherbourne for eight more years, but she grieved the loss as a painfully fresh wound.

Reya nodded and Adin led the way in. The candles flickered and cast shadows on the walls, the once cheerful room now a shrine to death. Just seeing his mother again after so many years— sunk down in the mound of blankets, her matted copper hair tangled around her porcelain face—wrenched Adin's heart so violently he stumbled and dropped to the floor. Reya rested a hand on his shoulder, a light, knowing touch.

Adin couldn't take his eyes off his mother. This vision of her, like this, with death claiming her, had been seared into his memory and haunted him these many years. Like the fairy tale princess cursed with a sleeping spell, his mother lay there just as she had the last time he saw her. Unchanged. Unreachable. Incurable, except by magic.

He forced his gaze away from the enormous bed and toward Reya, whose eyes closed in concentration. Adin retreated to the far wall, Reya's earlier warnings sounding in his ear. She would call magic and it would come. She would beckon it, not to fight the evil that drained the Queen's life away, but to deceive it. Magic would be summoned, but once released, it would do as it wished. She would pray to heaven for mercy and kindness, and then step back and watch helplessly. Magic was the snarling beast straining at the leash, the hawk swooping from the sky with talons extended toward its prey. Once it was unchained, there was no turning it back.

Reya's mouth formed silent words; her hands hovered before her in midair. Adin's shirt stuck to his skin. The air, thick with candle smoke, hurt his lungs. He tried to soften his thoughts, rest them on his mother as Reya had urged him, for even his musings could catch magic's attention, and with dangerous consequences. So, he stared at the Queen, letting love well up in his heart, and found it easy to intend only good for her. Deep he went, deep inside his love, to a hidden place he cherished. There, his mother lived, in all her beauty and strength, protected and immortal, forever young, forever safe. His secret treasure, the center of his heart.

Reya's words reached his ears, first softly, then louder as the strange syllables flitted around the room. Words heavy with power careened off walls and picked up speed. Adin felt their blast of wind and ducked as they came at him from all directions. Reya kept chanting, standing motionless with her eyes closed, oblivious to the force whipping her hair and clothing.

Adin pressed harder against the wall as the words from Reya's mouth gathered into a whirlwind of light. Shapes formed and dispersed, reminding Adin of the madness of time travel. Soon, the glare grew too bright to watch, and he shielded his eyes. Reya's words reverberated off the ceiling and floor, crisscrossing each other and multiplying. The room became choked with magic, unformed and reckless, aching for direction. The stone wall shook—first in shudders, then violent temblors. Adin spread his feet apart, searching for balance as the floor teetered first one way, then another.

Grit and chunks of stone shook loose from the ceiling, only to be sucked up into the fury of enchantment.

Reya yelled. A string of phrases punctured the air, freeing the beast from its leash, the hawk from its tether. Her eyes sprang open and she dropped to the floor, shaking. Adin ran to her side and cradled her in his arms. She barely breathed. Around them, magic collided into furniture, overturned chairs. A dazzling funnel, so brilliant Adin could only watch its wake, spun around the bed where the Queen lay asleep and undisturbed. The candles on the sideboard blew out and fell to the floor.

Then, magic found its target.

The tapestry on the wall next to the bed shimmered and stretched. Adin watched agape as the golden threads of the firebird unraveled, dozens at a time, like fiery worms wiggling in the air. Reya languidly raised her eyes as she lay in Adin's lap. He heard her gasp as the threads, spun by a magical hand, gathered up the Queen and wove her into their pattern.

The tapestry on the wall dulled as the Queen became enwrapped. Golden sparks coursed through her locks of fiery copper hair, sank into her cheeks. Her dressing gown dissolved and something brilliant and blinding sprouted from her body.

Feathers.

Soft, sparkling, gold feathers flowed out from the bed. Where the Queen's head had rested, a smaller sleek head rose from the pillows, its creamy beak protruding where a nose once sat. In a sea of flames, the firebird coalesced. Arms thickened and grew into two massive wings that stretched, testing their strength. Tail feathers sprouted like vines, trailing over the blankets and spilling onto the floor.

A calm returned to the room as the graceful bird rose from the covers and hovered in the air before them, so blindingly breathtaking that Adin nearly fainted.

Adin held his breath. Reya clutched his arms. They uttered not a sound as they watched the firebird flap toward the windows. Drapes yanked open and a windowpane melted. With a rustle of feathers, the firebird flew out the opening into the dead of night, leaving behind an empty bed and tangled covers.

TWENTY-SEVEN

ALETHA STOOD in the center of the stone ring on the night of the spring solstice. O'lam rested a hand against one of the huge slabs that rose high above him. The creamy moon, round and bright, moved through a sky splattered with stars. A sense of peace flooded Aletha's heart as she took in the beauty of the knoll for the last time. Oh, she would surely return; she had friends here: O'lam, Kah'yil, Brynn. Yet she knew this place would change. Already the Council chambers stood completed a hundred yards away. Stoneworkers had nearly finished carving out the Council seats from the gray stone. Someday, colored panes would replace the clear beveled glass ones ringing the chamber, panes depicting Sherbourne's history, a history now in the making.

O'lam looked up at the night sky. "There's the *sho're* there, lass." He pointed low on the horizon. Aletha came to his side and looked up. "The Mighty Bull. And the *kar*, the Ram." He chuckled and smoothed his mustache. "The bull chases the ram across the sky but never catches that wily ol' sheep."

Aletha sat on one of the flat rocks and ran her hand across the surface. The stone felt cool and the soft green moss spongy to the touch. She searched the dome of night until her eyes rested on a constellation rising in the east. "Do you have a name for that one, over there?" She pointed.

O'lam sat next to her and let his gaze follow her arm. He pinched his lips together and looked at Aletha. Sadness laced his voice. "The *taw'ome*. The Twins." He let the words die out on the still night air. "As I remember it, lass, one twin there faces the moon; the other holds a sword high, protecting her brother." He raised his arm above him, as if wielding a sword. "The *kef'eer*, the Lion, charges." O'lam feinted with his sword, then jabbed playfully at Aletha. "But the twin with the sword keeps the fierce beast at bay, always keeping her brother safe as they journey across the sky."

O'lam lowered his "sword" and sighed. Aletha nodded.

"Yes, I was shown that constellation when I was very young. Reya would tell us stories, not unlike yours." Her voice grew wistful and tears filled her eyes. "She said our lives are written in the stars, and they are just as fixed and constant. But, what did she mean? That we are so bound by our destiny, we have no choices?"

O'lam shook his head. "No, lass, heaven always gives you choices. But we cannot deny our nature. Our nature determines those choices, lass. Given the same chance over and over again, we would always make the same choice. We can learn from our mistakes and grow wiser, make better decisions. But we cannot change our true nature."

"Then a bad person will always be bad?"

O'lam smiled. "Ah, there's the catch, lass. For deep within us all, goodness can be found. Even in those who succumb to the greatest evil. Even they can be redeemed. Another paradox of heaven, you could say."

Aletha shrugged. "Why so many mysteries and paradoxes? I wish life were simple."

"Ah, lass, that would take away the surprise." O'lam's eyes brightened. "Look!"

O'lam stood and wobbled to the center of the ring. Aletha came to his side and stared curiously at the pattern on the grass.

Moonlight, streaming through the cracks in the slabs, bounced off rock and etched a design at their feet: a pentacle, missing one arm and half a leg. The star, outlined in moonlight, was just a bit larger than Aletha. She looked at the gaps in the circle, guessing the stones had once formed a perfect star.

She turned slowly, looking at the rocks erected around her. Two vertical slabs topped by one flat rock, then three verticals, then one with a small cap.

"Wait . . ." she said.

Pointing at the slabs, she drew with her finger in the air. Two verticals, one cap. The ancient letter *he*. Three verticals. *Shin*. And there was a *resh*. Aletha's eyes widened. "O'lam, they are letters!"

The healer took her arm and led her outside the stone circle. He chuckled. "Of course they are, lass. See?" They walked back from the circle a dozen yards and stopped. "Some of it's missing, of course. But you can make out the words now, can't you, lass? Start with this one." He pointed to the three vertical stones.

Aletha mouthed silently, shaking her head in wonder. She turned to O'lam excitedly. "*Sha'har*. These say *sha'har!*" The next rocks made another *shin*, but there followed a large gap, and then something that looked like a box. *Mem*.

Aletha hurried around the circle and O'lam followed, chuckling behind her. "There's nothing mysterious about the stones, lass. The *sha'har sha'ma'yim*. The Gates of Heaven. Just a sign marking the place, is all."

"Well, I never . . ." Aletha gave O'lam a big hug, and the old healer smiled, his big teeth shining in the moonlight. He pulled back and studied her face.

"Before you leave tomorrow, lass, with that handsome captain of yours, there's one more bit o' business we need to discuss." O'lam patted a stone, and Aletha sat beside him.

"What is it, O'lam?"

"Well, lass, it's a matter of a project that needs seeing to. And you're just the one to do it."

Aletha looked deep into O'lam's eyes and, like the first time, she lost herself in their inky depths. A powerful feeling swept her along, that huge pull of destiny calling her. Behind O'lam's eyes, a vision materialized. Snippets of her life appeared in flashes before her: sitting with Adin next to Reya's hearth, riding her horse through the city, the King stroking her hair, Rasha sneering at her.

Dozens of images assaulted her, roiling her emotions. Her life unrolled like a carpet, and as it unrolled she traveled forward upon it. Following Adin's bright footprints; now meeting Jered at the tavern. Digging roots in O'lam's garden. War encroaching upon the city. The regent stabbed. She and Adin hurrying to escape. Black birds attacking Jered, leaving him bleeding on the ground. And holding Adin one last time, then turning away.

Tears poured down Aletha's face, but she did not wrest her gaze from the healer's eyes. There was more.

She watched herself riding in a carriage, Jered by her side. A team of horses heading west, and the Sawtooth Mountains rising before them in splendor. Trunks full of clothing, and gifts from the regent, piled behind the seat. A cottage nestled at the foot of giant trees, with smoke rising from the chimney. A baby in her arms, and Jered cooing over him.

Aletha gasped in joy.

And then: O'lam visiting, snowflakes on his cloak and moustache, as he stood at her door. Two small children clinging to her legs. A weaving loom in the corner with a shuttle wedged between threads of gold.

Aletha narrowed her eyes to see.

Drawings spread across the large kitchen table. O'lam bent over, sketching. Aletha pointing to the parchment and nodding. Jered sipping tea while sitting in his chair, smiling.

Aletha honed her focus and looked closer at the drawing. She froze as understanding filled every cell in her body. Before her, outlined in detail on the parchment, was the layout of the abbey. Sketches of the peaked walls, the rooms, the dining hall. The labyrinth.

The labyrinth. In the abbey.

Centuries before she was born, someone had built the abbey. Someone, desiring anonymity, donated a parcel of land. Someone designed the labyrinth and cloaked it in magic. And someone placed the map inside, knowing that one day Adin would arrive to retrieve the map.

Aletha wrenched her eyes from O'lam and caught her breath. The healer smiled at her and patted her hand.

"See, lass. Heaven had a reason for keeping you here."

Aletha held out her hands in protest. "O'lam, I have no experience in building things! And certainly not in magic."

"Leave that part to me, lass. And others will build it. Remember, you of all people know what the abbey will look like. You can see it as clearly as if it stood right in front of you."

"Yes," Aletha muttered, "I can."

"Well, lass, it will take many years to complete—a lifetime at that—but I know you're up to the task. Besides, who are we to resist heaven's plans? Once you've settled in your new home, I'll be by. In the meantime, start that new life with your dashing captain. That's part of heaven's plan too."

O'lam extended his hand toward Aletha. Her body trembled with overwhelming astonishment. Heaven would use her to build the abbey. And . . . would bless her with children!

She let the healer gather her up in his old everlasting arms as she luxuriated in a bottomless joy. Together they walked down the hill toward the Keeper's cottage, the moon behind them, shining its light of promise over the new city of Sherbourne.

Late into the night Adin and Reya stared at the fire, speaking little. Adin rocked in his chair, causing the old floorboards to squeak. Yo'fi snored contentedly on the rug next to him. As tired as Adin was, sleep eluded him. Images of his mother transforming into the firebird festered in his thoughts.

Reya got up and fetched the kettle. She came back to the den and refilled Adin's cup. Adin nodded thanks, his eyes mesmerized by the flames dancing in the hearth.

"She's safe, like this," Reya said. "Nothing can harm her. Not even the *Sha'kath*."

Adin turned to look at her. "For how long? What kind of life is that—wandering the world, seeking rest but finding none?"

Reya exhaled deeply and sat by the fire, warming her hands. "Until the threat of evil is gone, she will remain as she is. Adin, the magic formed her in response to the evil binding her. They are two sides of the same coin. Once the curse is countered, she should be restored."

"Should. But you are not sure." His brows furrowed. "And what about Rasha and the other councillors? If they learn what you have done—"

Reya snorted. "You need not worry about them, Adin. The Queen has died. That is what they will believe, what they want to believe. Those who lie easily to others lie to themselves quite handily. That is their weakness, and one I can exploit."

Adin turned and looked out the window at the shifting light. "Morning has come. I must leave."

Reya stood and faced him. "But, Adin, where will you go?"

"Far away. East. Some remote village where I can live out my years in obscurity with a new name. The young prince must be allowed to grow up unhindered." Adin shot Reya a warning look. "Eight years from now he will start his journey, and Aletha will follow after him." Confusion filled his face.

"Reya, I just don't understand. If everything has already happened and the future cannot be changed, then how can the young prince succeed where I have failed? Won't he make the very same choices—and mistakes—I already made? It doesn't make sense."

Reya squeezed Adin's hands. "Adin, I don't know; I wish I had an answer for you. You will just have to trust heaven."

Adin scrunched up his face. "I knew you would say that." He retrieved his ratty cloak from the wall hook next to the fire and put it on. He ran his hand across his thick red beard. Reya walked him to the door, her face sad.

Adin bent a knee and hugged the plush black wolf who sat patiently at his feet, thumping her tail. He stood and embraced Reya. "I will miss you so much," he said, his words laced with sorrow. "More than you can imagine."

Reya rested a hand on his cheek. "And I will miss you too. I hope you will find a way to let me know you are well, wherever you end up."

Adin opened the door and the coolness of the spring day greeted him. He could smell rain coming, although few clouds gathered overhead. His thoughts drifted to the palace, where the twins would soon awaken to find their mother gone. Eight years since that day, and he could still feel the pain like a knife in his gut. Now he would go to the palace and sneak into the courtyard from the eastern hill. The ten-year-old twins would be sitting by the fountain, buried in grief, wet to the bone. He would wave them over from the back of the orchard, and they would come to him.

He remembered that day as if it were yesterday. He knew exactly what he would say to the twins, as every word spoken that morning had been burned into his memory. He would tell them their mother lived, even if they found it hard to believe. For it was true, he would tell them. "Keep this *mik'vah* hidden in your heart and let it give you strength."

Adin shook his head, baffled by heaven's will. All these years he had wondered if the man in the garden had spoken the truth. Now, finally, he knew he had.

Adin wrapped his cloak around him, eyeing the two huge ravens huddled on the tree branch near him. He took one last look at the young twins; he searched their eyes for a spark of hope. How unsettling it was to speak to the young Adin—his younger self! His was an anguished face, so innocent, so vulnerable. How could such a countenance not inspire sympathy—or pity?

And to feel Aletha so close, to see how much she loved her brother. He physically ached to wrap her in his arms. He had to summon every ounce of constraint to bottle the emotions aching to burst forth. Their suffering was his suffering, and he knew the words he had just spoken to them would not just give hope, but would also cause arguments, doubt, and anxiety for the twins in the years to come. Yet these things had to occur.

He took Aletha's hand once more, squeezing it tightly in urgency. He whispered in her ear.

"There is a proverb: *yesh 'achar'ith tiq'vah k'rath.* 'Surely there is a future, and your hope will not be cut off.' I must go. Never forget!"

He jumped down from the bench and hurried out the closest archway without looking back. He could almost feel the twins' gaze boring through his back, almost hear Aletha's words to her brother: "We will never speak of this."

Adin willed his heart to stop pounding. As he stumbled down the hill toward the city, his legs shook. His hands shook. A chapter of his life had now ended; he felt finished, empty. There was nothing left for him to do but wait. And watch. Sadness welled up in his heart. Was this all?

At the bottom of the knoll, he turned and looked back up to the palace, the stately, sprawling palace he had called home for eighteen years. He knew beyond a doubt he would never step inside its walls again. Never visit Aletha in her room, eat in the dining hall, dip his hand in the fountain. Perhaps the younger Adin would find a way to stop the curse, to do what he himself had failed to do. He hoped with all his heart for that outcome. That the curse would be lifted. That the King would be unchained from his mad greed, and that his mother would be restored.

And yet, if that happened, he would be far away. He would rejoice in Sherbourne's future—a future that was not to be cut off, not to end in desolation and ruin. But he was no longer part of the story; he was now an outsider, a distant observer.

Loneliness numbed his limbs as he aimlessly wandered through the city, rain soaking him to the bone. More than ever, he felt invisible. He passed people who saw through him, never meeting his eyes. Others crossed the street when they encountered the hunched, ragged man with tears on his face. Hours passed; the occluded sun arced across the entire sky without Adin's notice. At dusk, Adin drank two pints of ale he never tasted, ate a bowl of soup that failed to satisfy his hunger. When he couldn't walk any farther, he curled up on a bench near the river Heresh, content to let the lull of the slow-moving water ease him into sleep.

Morning greeted Adin with a chorus of bird song and a stabbing headache. Bright sunlight bouncing off the water hurt his eyes. He gathered up his meager belongings and walked across the bridge, so stiff he could barely move his legs. His right hip pained him with each step; his back throbbed from hours pressed against the hard wooden bench. He stopped and drank water from a jug Reya had given him.

As he replaced the jug in his pack, he noticed bread and fruit stuffed at the bottom. He reached in and pulled out a pouch that contained gold coins. Reya. Always one step ahead of him. She must have put these in his pack before they left her cottage last night. He shook his head at her foresight. Here she was, preparing to unleash magic that could annihilate Sherbourne, and she stopped to make sure Adin had food and coin for his journey.

As he walked under the tower at the east gate, a sense of finality hit him. His life in Sherbourne was now behind him; a new life loomed ahead. Surprised, he noticed his spirits had lifted a little. Perhaps there was some relief in knowing heaven had finished with him. That the burden of saving Sherbourne had been removed from his shoulders. That he faced no more agonizing decisions and would make no more mistakes of huge consequence. That, at least, was a blessing.

The day warmed. Insects buzzed in Adin's face as he traveled down the dirt road leaving the city. He stripped off his cloak and tunic and enjoyed the wildflowers dotting the fields on either side. The aroma of warm grass and lilacs filled his nostrils. Not long ago he had walked down this same road—confused, angry, and hurt. Seeking the firebird, seeking to win his father's love, seeking redemption. Instead, he had found a muddy pig and a mysterious hermit.

The hermit!

Adin stopped and frowned. If anyone had the answers Adin sought, it would be the hermit. Just who was that strange man named Ta'man? If he remembered correctly, the word in the *law'az* meant "secret." How appropriate! Adin pictured him, poised and graceful, with his long beard and bizarre clothing. Was he a Keeper? Someone from the past, from Kah'yil's time? How had he known about the map?

Suddenly, Adin's feet were running. Excitement stirred in his gut; questions piled up, one on top of another. His need to understand spurred him down the road in a frenzy. A man coaxing an ox yanked the reins and moved out of Adin's way. A family carrying baskets laden with potatoes halted abruptly as Adin squeezed around them. He shoved aside his body's cries of discomfort in the face of a greater need. What if the hermit knew of another way back through time, or could lead him to the one who made the map? Surely another map could be made. The ache to see Aletha overtook him like a sudden fever.

There! Through a small wood, down a shaded path, stood the hermit's cottage. And sitting on the small front porch was a huge white pig.

Winston.

The pig looked up curiously as Adin arrived at the door, panting hard.

"My, my. Right on schedule, dear boy." The pig rose on his haunches and wagged his corkscrew tail. "Could use a spot of tea, if you have a hankering to make us some, lad."

"You." Adin scowled. "You and your promise of wisdom." Adin bent over and eyed the pig, who took a hasty step back.

"What are you carrying on about, lad? Have we ever met?"

"Yeah, eight years from now in a mud puddle. I should have known you were pulling my leg with all that talk about wisdom. 'Wisdom helps you make proper decisions, keeps you out of trouble.' As you would say, 'A lot of stuff and nonsense.'"

Winston edged up to Adin and sniffed him over. "Well, you're here, aren't you? Finished some task and now, off to see the world, is it? Imagine that."

Winston trotted past Adin's legs and pushed the door with his snout. Without turning back he grunted and spoke. "I could use a wee bit o' help with the kettle, lad. If you've a heart to help."

Adin sighed and rolled his eyes. He followed the pig into the cottage.

The appearance of the cottage gave Adin pause. Aside from the furniture, the living room was bare. No parchments or drawings. No mice running across the floor. No curtains on the kitchen window.

The place did not look lived in, other than the worn rug by the hearth and Winston's food and water bowls sitting on the floor.

"Got all that ol' junk cleared out, years ago I did, lad. Every last piece, down to the silver lockets."

Adin glared at the pig. "What on earth are you carrying on about? Where are all the paintings?"

"What paintings, lad? Never had any. Just that big tapestry— the one with the bird. Sold it for a few silvers at market, oh, three, four years ago. Are you feeling up to snuff, lad? Need something to eat? I think there may be some food in the kitchen. Why not take a look-see, tha's a boy."

Adin followed the pig into the kitchen and found a bowl of fruit on the counter. A loaf of bread, still warm from some oven, sat beside the bowl. Adin's mouth watered.

"Help yourself, lad. There's an ice box yonder with some meat and cheese. Don' think you've had a proper meal in a while, have you, lad?"

As Adin bit into a ripe strawberry, he turned to the pig, who had plopped onto the planked floor and closed his eyes. "Hey," Adin asked, "where's the hermit?"

"The hermit?" One pig eye opened. "What hermit?"

Adin stuffed another strawberry into his mouth. "You know— Ta'man. The man who lives here. Who takes care of you."

"Been living by me-self these many years, lad. No man's lived here for ages, and only one is expected."

"The man with the long beard. Who is he? And when will he get here?" Adin's voice grew anxious.

The pig raised his chin off the floor and gave Adin a look that made him feel stupid. "Why, what a silly question, lad! That man's just arrived. As I said, right on schedule."

"I don't understand . . ." Adin's voice trailed off. A look of disbelief spread across his face.

"You, lad. It's you who's meant to move in, who I've been fixin' up the place for. Done a nice job of cleanin', if I do say so me-self. Why, even carried a basket to market in my—"

Adin had his hands around the pig's neck, which forced a high-pitched squeal out of the animal's throat, before Winston could finish his sentence. "What in heaven's name are you talking about? I'm tired of your games."

The pig's eyes rolled up into his head, and he let out a pathetic gurgle. Adin reluctantly released his grip on the pig's neck. Winston collapsed to the floor in a pant.

"Wha's gotten into you, lad? Where's your appreciation? You've done a jolly good job; things are moving along swimmingly. I need a drink."

Winston trotted back to the living room and slurped water from his bowl. Adin turned slowly, looking at the cottage, thinking hard. The pig was confused—or was deliberately confusing him. Or maybe the animal was just loony. One thing was certain—the hermit did not live here—yet. Winston was mixing him up with the hermit, but why? Why was he expecting Adin? How was Adin "right on schedule"? Or was the pig just babbling nonsense? And how did the pig live there all alone, with no one to feed and care for him? Nothing made sense.

Winston came back into the kitchen. Adin sat in the chair and ate an apple. Why should he ask any more questions? He would not get any sane answers. Maybe he would just wait here awhile. A few days, maybe a week. See if the hermit showed up.

He set his pack on the floor and ate in silence. Winston stared up at him, waiting.

"Well, lad," he said. "You know the tale of the three choices, eh? Small acts of kindness do not go unrewarded. *Pe'ree tsa'diyk* and all that."

" 'Truly there is a reward for the righteous.' I remember." *You'll tell me that in eight years.*

"Yes, tha's how it works, lad. You get three choices, always three. Riches and gold. Tha's thrown in there as a test, you see. Most choose that one. Then, in your case, a new body, one without the twists and slumps. But you even turned that down, now, di'nt you?"

Adin tipped his head and studied the pig. Winston's tone of voice set off an alarm in his head. How did the pig know what he would choose eight years from now? Adin stopped chewing and listened more closely.

"Now," the pig continued, "you chose wisdom. And tha's why you're here, dear boy." Winston leaned closer to Adin, his feral smell strong in Adin's nose. "When you choose wisdom, you get everything else!" The pig laughed in happy snorts. When he caught his breath, he added, "Tha's how it works, lad!"

Suddenly, the room spun. A flash of light made Adin cover his eyes. The air thrummed with a low rumble. A strange sensation came over him and hit himself with a wave of nausea. His body began to tingle; his back grew hot and itchy. His leg trembled and ached. Pins and needles attacked his cheeks and lips.

The room blurred and Adin fumbled blindly, reaching for the table, a wall, anything to stop him from falling. He found the edge of the table and hung on. Through all the confusion, he heard the pig chuckling as if he were enjoying Adin's distress. Whatever Winston was doing to him, Adin swore to himself he would make that pig pay. He would lift that fat hog and toss him in the creek. He should have never stepped foot in this cottage. He had let his need for answers lead him here, to the one place he should have avoided. It wasn't wisdom that had brought him here—just stupidity.

Adin gripped the table so hard his knuckles turned white. He thought his leg would break off. The pain in his back spiked, then subsided to a dull twinge. He rubbed his face to help the muscles relax. Then he straightened up.

Straighter than he ever had.

Adin lifted his head, and his back followed. Another inch straighter. And another. The cramp in his leg eased, and Adin took a step. A perfect, unfaltering step.

He looked down at his trousers and saw two perfectly aligned legs. Was he hallucinating? Had the pig put him under a spell?

Adin ran his hands down his legs, felt through the woolen fabric to the evenly matched limbs underneath. His mouth dropped open. The pig chuckled and snorted.

"See, lad? Wha's with all your fuss?"

Adin probed his own face with his fingers. An unfamiliar face.

"Come," the pig said.

Adin followed Winston into the back bedroom, and the pig motioned with his snout. A mirror hung on the wall, one tall enough to show Adin a reflection he had often longed for but never dreamed he would see.

Adin heard Winston trot out of the room and drop down on his rug by the hearth. Adin stared at his reflection for a long time, so astonished that words failed him. Tears welled up in his eyes as eighteen years of pain, humiliation, anguish, and shame drained out of him, as if captured in the water flowing down his cheeks, flowing out of his heart, out of his life.

Adin saw in the mirror a handsome, strong man, without a blemish or deformity. A man who looked just like his sister. He ran his hand over his beard, picturing what he would look like in eight years if he let his hair grow long. He grinned. He could envision it easily.

He would be the hermit.

After a long time, with shaky legs, Adin went back into the living room, where he found Winston snoring loudly on the rug. Quietly, he sat in the chair next to the pig and thought.

He thought until the sun turned the sky a soft orange and the birds began to settle into their nests. He thought until stars splattered the night sky with countless pricks of light. He thought until the rested pig lifted his head, his jowls bulging, and smiled at him.

"Like I said, lad. He's just arrived." The pig snorted knowingly and added, "Right on schedule."

TWENTY-EIGHT

ADIN STOOD back and studied the painting. He chewed the end of his bristle brush thoughtfully and then added another swipe of paint to the canvas. Satisfied, he dunked the paintbrush into a jar of murky water and picked up the iron poker to rearrange the burning logs. Water boiled softly in the large cauldron hung over the flames. He leaned over carefully and looked into the pot, moving his long beard aside. The swath of red hair had already fallen into the steaming water once today, and he'd had to wring it out, making a wet mess all over the floor. He attributed his carelessness to his nerves.

Eight years spent waiting. He had used the time wisely, of course. Made the time pass more quickly. At first he thought the months would drag by in agonizing slowness, but once he set his mind to painting, the days sped by. He had even taken trips—east as far as Wentwater and west to the Sawtooth Mountains. Beautiful lands that stirred his heart with melancholy and an intolerable desire to share these sights with Aletha.

He'd cut his last trip short; he had almost grown ill from the weight of his loneliness. When he found Winston waiting for him at the cottage door, his goofy tail wagging happily, Adin had actually rejoiced at the pig's greeting. Throughout the years, a few friends helped ease the loneliness—neighbors he shared pleasantries with. Yet he mostly kept to himself and kept his life private, and that self-imposed privacy had cost him much.

Now, the day he had anticipated was upon him. He glanced outside the window facing the creek. A few leaves still dangled from thin branches; one more brisk wind like last week's would scatter them on the ground. As he lowered the bucket into the hot water, he thought of Aletha crying in her room after Adin's hasty departure. He imagined that by now the young prince had left the city and would soon come across a pig stuck in a mud puddle. He chuckled at the memory of being covered in mud from head to toe, and Winston exasperating him with his annoying patter.

Winston. Eight years living with this pig, and Adin had no better understanding of the creature than on the day they first met. He had his suspicions; Winston had to be some kind of powerful wizard. But the pig never let on, always laughed at Adin's inquiries—even at his threats to turn him into rashers of bacon. Some days Winston drove him mad, but he had to admit the pig was an entertaining companion who was now quite dear to his heart.

Adin hefted the bucket of water and headed for the bathing room. He reflected on his diligent patience. On a few occasions he had found ways to send cryptic messages to Reya, letting her know he fared well, but never telling her where he lived. He remembered Reya's warning not to be cavalier and test heaven's mercies. Perhaps it didn't matter what he did, with whom he spoke. Perhaps he could even waltz right into the palace and tell the King all he knew. Maybe nothing would affect the outcome of this day. Whatever he did had already been done. Still, he had been discreet.

For years, Adin had wrestled with the bizarre situation in which he found himself. But after today, he would be free to leave. He had thought long and hard about where he would go. The Logan Valley enticed him, with its mild weather and rolling hills. He longed to ride a horse under the mighty oaks and sleep under their boughs. He had saved enough silver from the sale of his paintings to provide him with a comfortable life.

He looked up at the wall filled with depictions of Sherbourne—memories of his time with Jered brushed onto canvas. He had thought that by pouring those memories out onto a surface that he could stare at, he would somehow exorcise them. He had been wrong. The images only made the past more palpable. He often found himself staring for untold hours at the portrait of Aletha, wallowing in the sweet misery of his loss. No, the only way for him to leave the past behind would be to leave all his paintings behind as well. The first thing he planned to do, once he sent the young Adin on his way, was sell all his artwork and buy a horse. A chestnut gelding he would name O'kel—for old times' sake.

As he smiled at the memory, he heard the door swing open. Winston had returned. And, no doubt, was caked in mud. Adin poured the bucket of water into the nearly full wooden tub. He startled at the sound of his own younger voice in the next room.

Adin calmed his heart. The last time he had seen his younger self was eight years ago in the orchard. This Adin would now be a young man. It had rattled him to look in his own eyes back then; he knew this time would be even more disturbing. He listened at the door as Winston's cheery voice rang out.

"Come on inside," the pig said.

He was Ta'man, he told himself. An eccentric hermit. He waited a few moments, listening to his visitor's hesitant footsteps enter the living room. He found his voice.

"Right on schedule. Adin, your bath will be ready momentarily."

Taking a deep breath, he walked out of the bathing room and caught up with his destiny.

He set the bucket down next to the hearth. "Oh my," he

said, filled with a giddy, light feeling. "You really do need a bath! Come." As the young prince followed his host into the warm bathing room, the "hermit" noticed his visitor was too speechless to utter a sound.

Later that night, as his guest slept restlessly in his own bed, Ta'man sat on the front porch and stared at the stars. Tomorrow, he would send the prince off to fetch the map. He sighed deeply. Winston lay at his side, snout resting in the dirt, and taking up most of the porch with his substantial girth. The pig looked up at Adin and smiled.

"You're worried, lad. I c'n tell."

Adin scratched the top of Winston's head absentmindedly. "I can't help thinking I am sending him off to make all the same mistakes I made. I want to warn him, so he won't get caught as I did. But, if he doesn't get caught, he won't run away and follow his steps back to this time. Then I wouldn't be here—to send him on his *ma'gur*."

Adin sighed even more deeply and hung his head. "So he will have to fail. Just as I did," he added.

"Tha's human thinking, lad." The pig snorted. "You're all a-tangle because you don' understand heaven's ways. Heaven's thoughts are not your thoughts, nor heaven's ways your ways. Show me, lad, where the stars end—or where they begin. Count to the last possible number and tell me what it is. Point to the storehouse of snow or the place time begins. You can't, can you?"

Adin stopped scratching and met Winston's eyes. He looked deep into the small pupils and detected an unfathomable wisdom. The pig raised his fuzzy, dirt-caked snout into the air and sniffed.

"Smell that, lad?"

Adin shook his head. "Smell what?"

"That, my dear boy, is the scent of destiny. Sit back and enjoy the roses, I always say. So there you have it."

Adin snorted. Would he ever understand that pig? Unlikely. And Winston was right—he would never understand heaven's workings. He was just a small-minded human, one actor in an epic story that transcended time and place. One little cog in a big wheel, one tiny pebble in the stream. Maybe someday all his questions would be answered; all the mysteries would become clear. Maybe. If that day ever arrived, he would rejoice in it.

Adin got up and quietly entered the house, the pig trotting at his feet. With a thud, Winston slumped and was instantly fast asleep on the rug, seemingly unconcerned with heaven's mysteries. Adin wrapped a heavy blanket around his own shoulders and nestled into his big padded chair. As his eyes drooped closed, words in the ancient *law'az* drifted through his mind, their lilting syllables unmooring his cares. He saw Aletha's mouth move, heard soft words meant to reassure.

"Set me as a seal upon your heart. For love is as strong as death; its flames are the flames of fire. Many waters cannot quench love."

Adin stood on the stoop, the clear morning air stinging his cheeks. Ta'man took his hands and shook them tenderly. "Good-bye, Adin, and safe journey. May heaven guide you wisely on your *ma'gur*." The door gently closed with a click.

Adin stood on the porch, lost in thought. He wanted to believe the hermit—but a magical map? There was only one way to determine the truth of Ta'man's words, and that was to go to the abbey and see for himself. What did he have to lose?

He turned at the sound of a snort. "Well, lad, you're off then?" The pig trotted briskly alongside Adin as he approached the road. "By the way, you made the right choice, you see. Wisdom and all. Will serve you in good stead, my boy. Cheerio!"

With that, the pig returned to his snuffling and turning up dirt with his snout. Adin adjusted the satchel on his back, and, taking one limping step after another, set his face to the road turning north.

"Oh, one more thing, lad." The pig trotted over to Adin's side, panting hard from the exertion. Adin bent down to listen.

"Do yerself a favor, lad. When you make it back with the cure, bide yer time. For heaven's sake, stay hidden until night. Then, sneak into the palace quiet-like and do the deed."

"What deed?"

Winston snorted. "Just heed the warning, lad. Otherwise it'll all be for naught."

Adin nodded and straightened up. As he started back down the road, he heard the pig grunt and call after him. "Don't forget, lad!"

He looked back to see Winston waddle into the woods. The cottage wavered and blurred until Adin could barely make out the roofline and chimney. He rubbed his eyes, wondering if the last two days had been a dream. Well, he would soon find out, wouldn't he? At the next intersection he veered west toward the abbey where, maybe, a magical map awaited him.

• PART FIVE •

RE'SHEETH

(THE BEGINNING)

TWENTY-NINE

ADIN AWOKE with a start. Disoriented, he peered through the darkness. As his eyes adjusted, he made out the shapes of small trees enclosing him against a backdrop of stars. Now he remembered, and his heart filled with pain. Hours ago he had stood on the edge of the wood, back in Sherbourne's past, saying good-bye to Aletha. Jered had lain bleeding on the ground. The black birds had screeched off into the evening as the *mil'ka'ma* descended upon the terrified inhabitants of Sherbourne. With a heavy heart, Adin had stepped into the lingering outline of his footprint and had been whisked away like a leaf in a windstorm. The images rushed at him with agonizing force.

Adin touched his clothes—the clean shirt he had put on, the ratty cloak torn by the beaks of vicious birds. After a tumultuous journey through time he had landed here, exhausted and heartbroken. He patted his pocket and fingered the small glass vial wrapped in a cloth. He breathed a sigh of relief and searched the ground around him, finding no trace of his print. Earlier, he had peeked out from behind the slab of rock and seen guards posted at the north gate. With the sun still climbing in the sky, he knew he had many hours to wait.

The pig's warning rang in his ears. *"Stay hidden until night. Then sneak into the palace."* Adin didn't know why the pig had told him to wait, but he would not be foolhardy. He had already made enough careless mistakes on this *ma'gur*. He certainly could not afford to be hasty and ruin everything, since the cure to this curse came at such a high price. With nothing else to do, and feeling the full measure of his exhaustion, he had curled up and fallen asleep in a tangle of moldy leaves.

He ached for Aletha. If only he could have stayed behind with her. He could have watched Sherbourne become a great city. He could have given Aletha in marriage to Captain Tebron. Many among the *tsa'ba* had become his friends. He could have made himself a life there, and he knew he would have been happy. He did not think he would ever find happiness here, even if he did succeed in removing the curse.

He wondered how many of the fighters had survived the siege against the city. As badly as Jered had been injured, he knew Aletha wouldn't have let him die. O'lam would see to his recovery. And he knew the regent would become a great ruler. That was something he would have loved to witness.

Adin sulked as he reached for his jug. He swished the water in his mouth and eased his dry throat with a few swallows, emptying the bottle. He pushed aside his dismay; he had made the only wise choice possible, and his kingdom needed him. If the cure truly worked, Sherbourne would have a future, and a hope that would not be cut off. Was that worth giving up the life he had abandoned in the Sherbourne of the past? Adin searched deep in his heart for a true answer. Yes, his heart told him. For the first time in his life, Adin felt kingly, and that feeling invigorated him.

Under a moonlit sky, Adin made his way to the palace, slowly and determinedly. Hunched low to the ground, he snuck under the Council chamber windows and entered the orchard through one of the stone archways. The fountain bubbled softly. There was no one is sight. He had to trust that heaven had sent him back at the right time. There was no way to know if he was too early or too late without asking someone, and that couldn't be risked. The pig had told him to wait until nightfall. Not three days or three weeks.

Adin hurried to the spring where the water spilled over the black obsidian rock. A damp mist hung over the knoll, but he did not feel cold or wet. Visions of the regent rushed at him. Kah'yil swinging his broadsword and Ka'zab falling to the ground. Blood dripping into the water. Fighters looking on, aghast. Jered grabbing the regent to keep him from falling.

Adin shook the scene from his mind. He reached into his pocket and pulled out the small vial. He looked up to heaven and voiced a silent, urgent prayer. And then he uncorked the bottle.

As he emptied the drops of blood into the pool, the water darkened. Adin's breath caught in his throat as he watched the water sizzle and steam. Black paste oozed from the opening in the rock. Soon, the inky liquid spread across the entire fountain, thickening like blood. Adin watched, greatly agitated. Minutes passed and nothing happened. Adin's spirit sunk into despair.

And then he looked more closely.

The black goo pouring from the rock began to thin and lighten. Soon, clear, pure water pushed its way out, and as it flowed into the pool, the black liquid dissipated, first turning gray, then vanishing altogether. Adin touched the water and, instead of a stinging acid, a cool refreshing tingle met his skin. Reflecting the night sky, the water sparkled like a million stars.

He dipped in his hand again, bringing water to his mouth. More than water trickled down his throat. A surge of hope and joy overflowed in Adin's heart. Satisfaction and relief bubbled up in the center of his body and spilled out in uncontainable joy, releasing a clarity of understanding. He leaped onto the fountain ledge and danced around the spring, bounding like a deer and laughing heartily. He had done it!

He spun and skipped until he fell to the grass, tears of happiness forming another spring that ran down his face. He leaned over the edge of the fountain and scooped up more water in his cupped hands. The water traveled down his throat, washing away the last traces of sadness, leaving Adin unburdened. A veil lifted from his eyes. Adin saw the palace grounds as if for the first time. His love for his home welled up inside him. His love for the people of Sherbourne. Even a rekindled love for his father.

He glanced up to the King's darkened chamber windows. He needed to see his father! He needed to tell him how much he loved him. His father would think him mad, but Adin didn't care.

Adin pulled the empty jug from his pack and filled it with the pure, healing water. He corked the jug and cradled it in his arms as he pushed open the library doors and entered the hall. His footsteps echoed as he traversed the banquet hall and headed up the stairs. The entire palace rested under a blanket of sleep; even the guard outside the King's chamber didn't awaken when Adin quietly pushed the door open and approached the huge bed.

Adin picked up a chalice from the sideboard and filled it with the water from the jug. He looked over at the King, who slept with furrowed brows. Adin studied him, never having had the opportunity to look at his father's features so closely. Lines etched his father's harrowed face. The King's graying hair receded from his forehead, lying in a thin mat across his pillow. Candles, pooling in their trays, cast an orange glow on his leathery skin. Strange. The last time he had seen his mother, eight years ago, she had lain in a similar fashion in her own bed.

Adin set the chalice on the nightstand next to his father's bed. He felt something he had never before felt in his father's presence.

Happiness.

Adin left the room, passing the sleeping guard, and found the door to his own bedroom unlocked. He peeked in, just to be sure he didn't find "himself" already asleep under the covers. But the bed was empty and the room clean. Adin sighed in relief.

He stripped off his clothes and picked up his nightshirt, still hanging on the hook beside his bed. After he shed his filthy clothes and donned the nightshirt, he slipped between silky cool sheets and sighed. The evening's excitement drained from him in a rush. In a matter of moments, Adin sank his head into his pillow and fell into a hard, welcome sleep.

Adin woke abruptly as arms grabbed him and yanked him from the bed. He squinted at the bright morning light streaming in through the window.

"What . . . who?"

The uniformed guard threw him with a thud to the stone floor. Adin rubbed his bruised hip and looked up at the scowling man.

"Take him to the King!"

The commanding voice came from the doorway. Rasha stood proudly, a victorious smile on his face. The councillor walked with his head held high over to where Adin lay. As the guard forced Adin to his feet, Rasha sneered.

"Thought you could sneak into the palace? Disappear for three weeks and think we would be none the wiser?" Rasha spit in Adin's face. "The King knows of your conspiracy. Your treason has cost you your life." He turned to the guard and waved him on his way with his prisoner.

Adin, still in his long nightshirt and bare feet, wiped the spittle from his cheek. He did not resist as the guard tied his hands. He met Rasha's eyes and a smile crept up the sides of his mouth. Rasha could do what he willed; Adin no longer cared for his own fate. The joy that had infused him last night still pumped vigorously through his veins, spurring a giddy sense of freedom. Even if his life was forfeit, no one could take that joy away from him.

The councillor glared at Adin in disgust. Then, as he searched deeper into Adin's calm face, his own eyes widened, first in surprise and then in fear.

Adin did not know what Rasha saw, but as the guard pushed Adin from behind, urging him toward the door, Adin kept his eyes locked on Rasha in challenge. For the first time in memory, he saw the councillor's hands shake.

With Adin in tow, the guard marched down the hall to the King's chamber. Out of the corner of his eye, Adin noticed two other councillors join Rasha. As the door was thrown open, Adin stopped and turned to the three conspirators, who spoke in hushed, frantic whispers.

"Well, aren't you coming—to accuse me to the King?" Adin's words came out strong and confident. He surprised himself with his lack of fear. He knew he should be trembling, but an aura of confidence and serenity seemed to envelop him.

He turned his attention to his father, who, awakened by the disturbance, struggled to sit up in his bed. The King brushed hair from his face and reached for the chalice on the nightstand. Adin's gaze locked onto the cup. He watched breathlessly as the King drank the water, then set the silver chalice back on the nightstand. His father huffed and cleared his throat.

"What is the meaning of this intrusion?"

The guard pushed Adin forward, knocking the prince to his knees. Adin winced as his kneecaps hit the hard stone.

"Here is your traitor!" Rasha sauntered into the room appearing confident, but Adin saw through his ruse. The councillor's face was stricken with fear. And then, Adin saw more.

As Rasha came alongside the King's bed with his two cohorts behind him, a shadow passed across the councillor's face. Adin stared harder, and Rasha's nose and mouth blurred, and his eyes turned black and empty. Black feathers sprouted from the old man's cheeks. The two men flanking Rasha crossed arms over their chests, arms that became black wings. Adin's breath snagged.

The King got up from his bed and wrapped a thick robe around his shoulders. He pulled open the drapes and pale morning light spilled across the floor.

Rasha squinted at the harsh light and spoke, his voice hurried and emotional. "Your Majesty, the penalty for treason is death. I have caught the prince in acts of treason, and he must be punished! Guards!"

Rasha motioned to a group of men standing by the door. The King held up his hand. "Stop!" he commanded, rubbing a tired eye.

The King turned and stared at his councillor. Rasha cocked his head, puzzled.

"Since when do you give the orders around here?" the King asked.

Rasha raised an eyebrow, then politely lowered his head. "Pardon me, Your Majesty. I just thought . . ."

"Silence!" the King ordered. Rasha closed his mouth.

Adin's heart pounded so hard he thought his chest would burst. Now that he "saw" Rasha's true nature, he understood everything. The evil behind the curse. The *Sha'kath* and his accomplices. Rasha's determination to bring Sherbourne to ruin at all costs, to ensure the fulfillment of the *qa'lal*. He always knew Rasha had a secret agenda, but he had never anticipated this.

Adin held his breath, anxious to know for sure what effect, if any, the water had had on his father. He didn't have to wait long.

The King's eyes widened. "Look at me, Rasha."

Slowly, the councillor lifted his bowed head and reluctantly met the King's curious gaze.

The King circled the group of hooded advisers, now huddling together like cornered beasts.

And then he noticed Adin.

He stopped and looked at his son. Adin, still on his knees, searched his father's eyes. What he saw made his heart beat wildly in the cool chamber.

Years of anxiety fell from the King's face. His gray, worried countenance transformed into a soft, compassionate expression. He looked upon Adin as if seeing him for the first time.

"Adin?" The King took a few steps and hesitated. He proffered a trembling hand to the prince, who dared not breathe.

The shroud of disgust and disappointment that had blinded the King for years now lifted, and a long-buried love surfaced in its place. Adin watched and remembered.

This was the look Adin had buried deep, locked in a secret cache of memory. The face of a father who could see past the infirmities and failures of a deformed, awkward child. The love of a father for an only son, a son who desperately longed for that love. The tears streaming down Adin's cheeks were matched by those on the King's face.

"Adin . . ." His voice trembled. He put a tentative hand on Adin's shoulder.

Adin got to his feet, encouraged by the warmth of his father's hand.

"Oh, Adin, what have I done?"

Arms wrapped around Adin—large, powerful arms. Adin was a child once more, small and vulnerable, but now comforted and safe. Not even in his wildest imaginings had he anticipated this moment. He rested his cheek against his father's warm chest, listening to the rhythmic pounding as love coursed through his father's heart. Then, as he opened an eye, he caught a glint of metal.

Adin spun around and clamped his hand onto Rasha's wrist. A curved, sharp blade hovered in the air, inches from the King's neck. The King gasped and backed into the bed. Rasha struggled, his arm trembling as he pushed against Adin with all his might, revealing a strength uncanny for his old, bony stature.

Words burst from Adin's mouth. *"Ya'lak meh'lek!* 'Depart from the King!'"

The phrase he voiced came from a recess deep in his soul, an untapped well of power and authority. He had not asked for this mantle, but heaven had appointed him *pa'lat*—Deliverer. It was not borne of *his* power, but heaven's force, which slammed against its enemies, the ancient words unraveling an evil web.

Adin heard the blade clatter to the floor. From the periphery of his vision, he saw guards leapt forward, lunging for the councillors. A raucous laughter, forced and chilling, sliced the air.

Robes shimmered and darkened. Shapes wavered. Adin covered his ears. Three huge black ravens screeched as they winged around the room. Guards ducked and the King yelled.

"Get them!"

Adin picked up the knife from the floor, his head spinning. Just yesterday he had stood at the edge of the wood, alongside Aletha, his blade outstretched against another horde of black birds. Images of Jered bleeding on the ground infused Adin with anger. He, of all those in the room, knew what evil these creatures were capable of.

Adin slashed as a bird dove toward the King. Black blood spurted in his face as something fell at his feet. Around him, swords swung. A guard screamed, and Adin turned to see the man covering his eyes with his hands. Another guard squatted as a raven came at him with claws outstretched. Adin lunged, pushing past the groaning guard on the floor. A quick swipe of the knife severed a wing from the bird's body; it fell to the ground with a heavy thud. The rest of the bird careened into the window, shattering glass across the floor.

Adin positioned himself in front of the King, who cowered on the bed in shock. Adin locked eyes with the last bird. In the corner of the room, near the ceiling, it waited, wings flapping steadily, panting in loud spurts. Then, the creature he had known for eighteen years as Rasha, his father's devoted councillor, screeched with one final piercing shriek, then wheeled with all speed out the broken window.

Adin set the bloody knife down on the nightstand and watched as the black speck in the sky grew smaller and smaller until it vanished from sight. With a sigh, Adin knelt at his father's bedside and took the King's hands in his own.

The King tore his gaze from the window and looked around the room. The two dead birds lay in puddles of dark blood on the floor. One guard wrapped an arm around another and quietly escorted his companion from the room. Other guards stood speechless, terror written across their faces.

Quiet filled the chamber. After many minutes, Adin heard the guards cross the room, then the door close softly behind them. The King looked at his son, questions flickering in his eyes.

"Adin, what is happening? Why are you here, in my chamber, in your nightshirt?" He smoothed back his hair from his face with a shaky hand. "I feel so weak."

Adin helped his father to his feet. "Let's get you dressed, and round up some breakfast. Then I will do my best to answer your questions."

Once Adin knew the King had found his balance, he went out into the hall and summoned two servants. As the two young men busied themselves, laying garments out on the bed and fetching hot water, another set of servants came with mops and buckets and began scouring the blood-stained floor. Adin reentered the room and watched as one of the servants picked up a dead bird between two hesitant fingers. Instantly, the body of the raven sizzled and hissed, and the servant dropped it with a yelp to the floor. The web of magic disintegrated, leaving nothing but a small dark splotch on the cold stone.

Adin walked to the door and turned to look back at his father. The King raised his arms as a servant pulled a deep green tunic over his head. Another servant smoothed out the King's clothes and ran a comb through his ruler's tangled hair.

Already his father looked years younger. Adin marveled at the rosy glow lighting up his cheeks. He tried hard to recall the last time he had seen the King so relaxed and unburdened. He couldn't. No doubt the *qa'lal* had infected his father from the moment the crown was placed on his head. With such evil permeating the palace, his kingdom, and the King's life, Adin guessed his father had never truly enjoyed even one day of his reign.

It was as Reya had explained: evil prevented men from keeping their sinful desires in check, allowing those desires to get mastery over them. His father had been powerless to fight the growing greed and obsession that consumed him. Now, with the *qa'lal* removed, the King's madness ebbed away.

If only Aletha were here to see this! What relief and joy it would bring to her heart. She would wrap her father in her arms, tears running down her face. And she would be so proud of her brother for having saved Sherbourne from the Destroyer.

The wonder and joy of the victory faded, leaving Adin with a heavy lump of loss in his gut. He had done this—all of this—for Aletha. He had set out to follow the map across time to save their family and their kingdom . . . for her. Hers was the only happiness that mattered, and she—now long dead—would never know he had succeeded.

With a heavy heart, Adin walked back to his room and rummaged through the closet. He dressed and went downstairs to the dining room, where his father awaited him. Servants hurried to bring food to the table, smiles illuminating their faces. Instead of barking orders, his father spoke with kindness and gratitude to those around him. The transformation of Adin's home came like a cleansing spring breeze, bringing the newness of a clear morning after a night of pounding rain.

Adin sat beside his father, the King of Sherbourne, and for the first time in untold years shared breakfast with him. The King ate heartily, stuffing a forkful of eggs into his mouth. While he chewed, he waved an arm around the room, gesturing at the dozens of animal heads mounted on the walls.

"Where did all this clutter come from?" His eyes rested on the cabinets stuffed with treasures from all over the world. "What is all this for?"

Adin chuckled as he bit into a walnut scone. "I have no idea. But if you'd like to do a bit of winter cleaning, we can auction off some of these items at the Giving Festival next week. The proceeds could feed a lot of needy families this winter."

"Splendid idea. Something you and your sister could start on." The King's brows knitted in thought. "Where is your sister? Where is Aletha?"

Adin set down his scone. "She's gone on a journey. Far away."

"A journey? Where? When?"

Adin had never heard his father ask so many questions; he didn't know how to answer them. Adin felt the King's eyes boring into him.

"I can tell you have much weighing on your heart, Adin." The King wiped his forehead with his napkin. "And I feel as if I have awakened from some horrible nightmare. Please, Adin, help me understand."

Adin nodded, wondering where to start. "I will tell you everything. But you might not believe my story."

A breathless voice came from the hallway. "He will, young prince."

Adin looked over to see Reya running toward him. She threw her arms around him, pinning him to the chair. She released him from her hug, her eyes wild with happiness. Adin sensed something else simmering beneath her joy, something unexpected.

"Oh, he will believe every word, Adin, for look!"

Reya pointed out the huge beveled windows to the fountain bubbling in the courtyard. The King rose hastily to his feet, knocking his chair out from under him. A servant dropped a tray of dishes; plates and cups smashed against the floor. The old cook rushed from the kitchen, gasping and pointing at the orchard through the glass, words failing her.

Adin's mouth dropped open in surprise. As if in a dream, he walked to the window and placed a hand on the cool pane. His fingers traced an outline on the glass. Drawing the most beautiful creature he had ever seen in his life, perched on the edge of the fountain.

The firebird.

THIRTY

THE KING came alongside Adin. Was he dreaming? He had seen this creature, but where? He hacked away at the cobwebs cluttering his mind. Memories of recent years lay obscured and elusive. He searched hard and found the image of a blind man lost in the forest. A blindingly bright feather set in a golden block on his desk. An intricately woven tapestry hanging beside the Queen's bed. His queen, lying in death's grasp under mounds of blankets.

The King choked and doubled over.

Adin wrapped an arm around his shoulders. "Father, what is it? Are you ill?"

The King shook his head. He dared another look through the dining room window as images avalanched through his mind. He steadied himself against the wall, his face pressed against the glass. Gathered around him were a throng of servants. No one uttered a word.

The firebird walked on graceful legs along the fountain's edge. Behind her trailed a sweep of feathers that fell to the grass in a soft array. She lifted her elegant head to the sky, and a headdress of smaller feathers spilled down her back. The King marveled at her size, for he had never seen a bird as large as a man. A thousand golden feathers glowed under the morning's crisp light, sparkling brighter than any gems. Yet the light soothed rather than blinded—a healing light that seemed to penetrate right to his aching heart.

The King felt an inexplicable sense of peace. He turned to Adin, who watched him with concern.

"Adin." The King looked deep into his son's eyes.

Suddenly, a dam burst in his mind, releasing years of memories. The King saw himself yell at Adin, accusing him of treason. He saw his hand run through Aletha's hair and cringed. He saw an arrow leave his bow, time and again, and strange, noble beasts fall in pain to the ground. He heard Rasha whisper poison in his ear.

His mouth fell open in shock as he remembered. The images filled him with such pain he could barely breathe. Memories of emotions barraged him. Hate. Jealousy. Greed. Why had he felt these things? From where had they sprung?

Adin quickly supported him, to keep him from falling, but the King held out his palm to stop him.

There was so much he wanted to say, but the words would not come. He finally managed to speak.

"Can you forgive me, Adin?"

"There's nothing to forgive, Father. You were under a spell, a curse."

"A spell . . ." The King grew aware of another at his side. He turned to see Reya's wrinkled face smiling at him.

"Your Majesty, Adin has saved your kingdom." She took his arm and drew him away from the window. "Come. Follow me."

The King watched curiously as Reya stopped before Adin and studied his face. She started to say something to the prince, then her eyes widened as if she was surprised by what she saw. She entwined her other arm through Adin's.

"Come, young prince. It seems you have a surprise waiting as well."

Reya led the King and his son out of the dining room and into the library. She threw open the doors to the courtyard, letting in a cool stream of winter air. The firebird turned, cocking her head in a quizzical manner. Behind her, the wind kicked up a whirl of fallen leaves. Reya motioned for Adin and the King to remain by the doors while she cautiously approached the firebird.

The King held his breath. His heart pounded in anticipation, and his breath came out in frosty steam. Time crawled to a stop.

Reya edged up next to the firebird, resting a hand on the creature's lowered head. She closed her eyes and lifted her chin. Her lips mouthed words as the firebird stood motionless on the ledge. Reya stepped back. The bird ruffled her feathers, then dipped her pointed beak into the fountain.

The King watched as the bird tipped back her slender neck and swallowed. And then he gripped Adin's sleeve as the firebird vanished.

Now he knew he was dreaming.

Sitting on the fountain's ledge was a striking woman with long copper hair, a golden robe wrapped around her and trailing on the grass. She wiped her mouth with the back of her hand and then froze. She turned and looked at Reya, who stood beside her, laughing in joy.

Then the woman glanced over at him.

The King began to weep. He told his legs to move but they refused to listen. He heard Adin gasp beside him and incoherent voices around him grew loud and boisterous. In a daze, he found a way to put one foot ahead of another until he arrived at the spring.

In this dream he had dreamed a thousand times, he lifted his queen into his arms and embraced her with tenderness and passion. He smelled her freshness and health, a sweet incense that set his soul to rest. In his arms, he held his dream tightly, determined never to let go, never again to lose what he had once lost. He raised his face to the heavens in promise.

Never again.

Adin's head reeled from hours of celebration. Even this late into the night the banquet hall still overflowed with guests. Platters piled with food covered every inch of the massive table. Servants hurried to whisk away the dirty dishes and discarded goblets. Flowers spilled out of silver vases placed against the walls of the room, their scent mingling with the aromas of roasted meat and apple tarts. Wine flowed steadily, like the river Heresh, filling hearts with cheer and goodwill.

Adin sat on the bottom stair and reveled in the sight. The King danced with his queen, spinning her across a floor strewn with flower petals. A band of elegantly attired musicians strummed instruments, accompanying a bard who sang with a sweet voice. Guests dressed in glamorous costumes clapped in glee as the King careened into chairs and his wife laughed heartily.

Before the party, Adin had sat with his mother and father in the library, telling them the whole of his story. During the telling, he couldn't take his eyes off his mother. He drank in her every movement, her every expression. His heart had soared in her presence. But how in heaven had she been transformed into the firebird? She had died that night, eight years ago. It didn't make any sense. He had suspected there was one person who could explain this mystery, but when he searched out Reya later that day and questioned her, she only shrugged.

As Adin recounted his adventures, his parents listened with wide-eyed attention. His mother had no recollection of her years under enchantment, and Adin could tell she was astounded at how grown up her young son was. Her last memory was of the small grieving boy who cried at her bedside, clenching her hands. Now, a man sat before her, older and much wiser. Her face gleamed with pride and love.

When Adin told how he had had to leave Aletha behind, both the King and Queen began crying. His parents would never see their daughter again, and Adin shared their terrible pain. In the Queen's mind, Aletha would always remain a strong, feisty ten-year-old. Adin knew the loss of Aletha would hang over their happiness for years to come. Yet he comforted them with the knowledge that Aletha had made the best choice. Not only had she assured Adin's success at stopping the curse by urging him to return home, and by giving her blood, but she had found love.

The Queen's face grew peaceful as Adin described the brave Captain Tebron and how he had doted on Aletha. They had to trust that heaven had cared for Aletha and had granted her a happy, fulfilling life. That hope gave them all a bit of joy.

When his tale had ended, his parents embraced him, spilling over with thankfulness and appreciation. Ta'man's words had really proved true: that the sun of righteousness would rise with healing in its wings. He thought back to the stranger in the orchard who had promised him a hope and a future that would not be cut off. How had the man known? Just who was he?

His head spun with the rumblings of destiny and all the strange people he had encountered. He still had so many questions: Who made the map? Who were the strange hermit and the cloaked man in the orchard? Where did that crazy pig come from? And why had heaven chosen *him* to be the one—out of millions who lived across centuries—to be the *pa'lat*? A most unlikely choice.

Now, as he sat and drank his wine, listening to the minstrels play a jig, he chastised himself. He was always questioning. Why couldn't he just accept that he would probably never find the answers to those plaguing questions? He had tried to second-guess heaven all along the way. And despite all his mistakes and foolishness, heaven still accomplished its will.

Adin chuckled. He thought of O'lam and his paradoxes. How heaven counted small things as great, and powerful things as inconsequential. One small act of betrayal had nearly destroyed a kingdom. And one small act of sacrifice had saved it. No doubt heaven chose the weak and foolish to achieve great things for a reason. Maybe, Adin mused, it was to keep men humble. To make them rely on powers greater than their own. To show them a better way to live in a world saturated with evil. Heaven's ways were not man's ways—of that Adin was certain. And grateful.

Adin emptied his cup and tried to stand. He had lost count of all the glasses of wine he had drunk. Tomorrow, a new day would dawn over Sherbourne, and Adin would rejoice to see it.

"—Tebron."

Adin spun around at the name. Tebron? His heart pounded as he searched the room. Nearby, a tall man with a trim white beard spoke to a younger woman in a sequined gown. Adin walked over to them, his head woozy.

The pair bowed respectfully. The gentleman spoke. "Good evening, m'lord. We share in your joy." He tipped his head again.

"Forgive my intrusion, but did you mention Tebron?"

"I did, m'lord. 'Tis one of the stops on my route. I collect the annual tax, you see."

Adin frowned. "So this is a place of which you speak."

"Yes, m'lord. A small village. Way west of here, at the foot of the Sawtooth Mountains. Few have heard of the place, but it's a charming little town."

Tebron. A village. Adin smiled. He shook the man's hand and bowed to the lady. "Thank you for coming. A safe journey home."

Adin rushed up the stairs to his room, as fast as his wobbling, twisted legs could carry him. Why had he never heard of the village? He pictured Captain Jered, off exploring on his horse, mapping uncharted lands. He remembered him telling tales of his journeys with longing in his voice. Had he married Aletha and taken her to live there? Adin thought of the many times he and his sister had talked about traveling to the Sawtooths, and the dreamy look that had welled up in her eyes. He had little doubt.

Maybe he would never see Aletha again, but what if he could glean information about her? Maybe someone there would know the history of the village, how it was founded. If only he could be sure she had lived a long, happy life. Then, perhaps, he could live out his days in peace.

Adin undressed and put on his nightshirt. His heart raced with excitement. He pulled out a satchel from under his bed and stuffed it with shirts and trousers.

Tomorrow, he would take a journey.

THIRTY-ONE

TA'MAN, THE hermit, stood looking at his reflection in the mirror as he set down his razor. He had grown his beard for eight years, and now his face looked funny without all the hair. Winston trotted in and snorted.

"Well, lad. There's your face. I knew you'd find it."

Adin dunked the shaving blade in the cup of water and wiped his hands on a towel. He ran his fingers across his bare chin. "I look so young."

He felt where his lip used to pull up at the side of his mouth, an ugly feature he had been eager to hide. Now a wholly unfamiliar face stared back at him with squinting eyes.

"And a handsome chap at that. No doubt will have the ladies chasin' after you." Winston huffed. "Still planning on a long journey, lad?"

Adin gathered his things and went into the entry room. He looked around at the bare walls. Now that he had sold the last of his paintings, the place he had called home for eight years no longer held him.

"The kingdom is in good hands, Winston. I don't know what you did, but I am glad of it."

The pig snorted again. "'Twasn't my doings, lad."

Adin sighed. "I saw my mother, in the procession through town. She looked . . . beautiful."

Adin's voice trailed off wistfully, then he pasted on a smile. "Everything's as it should be. Without the *qa'lal*, the King can rule in righteousness. He can pick a handful of new councillors, ones with the city's best interests in mind. Someday, the King will retire and his son will rule in his place. And a fine ruler he will make."

"There's an old proverb, lad: 'Take away the wicked from the presence of the King and his throne will become firmly established.' Tha's the way 'twill be, then."

Adin pulled on his boots. "In the meantime, there's a world to explore. I've given up trying to understand the ways of heaven, Winston. I am just content to know that Sherbourne will have a future. *Yesh 'achar'ith tiq'vah k'rath*." He chuckled. "The first time I heard that was in the orchard, from the 'mysterious' man in the torn clothing. But it was Captain Jered who showed me the hope of those words, and I will never forget them."

Adin draped a heavy cloak around his shoulders. Winston trotted alongside him to the door.

"Will you still be here when I return?" he asked the pig.

"Of course, dear lad. I'll just be biding me time on this ol' stoop, eager to hear of your travelings—so there you have it."

Adin patted the pig on the head. "Try to stay out of deep mud puddles."

"Oh, will do, me boy, will do."

The pig followed him out the door and down the stepstone path to the road. Adin took one last look at the cottage set back in the woods. For a moment it wavered and faded, then reappeared. The man who had once been the hermit shook his head and chuckled, then set his face east.

The King and Queen stood at the north gate, waving as Adin spurred his horse down the road. He urged his mount into a canter, lingering on the image of his mother and father, leaning into each other, hand in hand. Would he ever stop gaping in amazement at the sight? To see his parents mooning over each other like newlyweds was more than startling. Try as he might, he could not recall a time when he had seen them happy together. All during Adin's childhood, his father had ranted and his mother had cowered. The last year before she grew ill, Adin had rarely seen her in the King's presence. They had even taken to sleeping in separate rooms after the death of her baby.

A light snow fell from the ballooning clouds overhead. He passed no one on the road until he made his way down the hill to the vale. At the creek, he watered his horse and rubbed his gloved hands. A few travelers hurried by with their heads tucked into scarves, mumbling greetings, heading up the road to the abbey. But Adin had no plans to stop.

He had chosen the strongest, fastest horse in the stable, a ten-year-old gelding he had ridden since he was young. Na'thar. Adin now knew the ancient meaning of the horse's name: "to set loose, to set free." *How appropriate.* For the first time in his life, Adin reveled in freedom: freedom from worry, from expectations, from doubt. A curse no longer hung over his house and his kingdom. The future he had seen—with Sherbourne in ruins—was no longer fixed and unavoidable. He could plan a new future, one that embraced hope. He had so many ideas to implement—ideas that would make Sherbourne live up to its name: "Crown of the East." Aletha would expect that from him. He would honor her memory with every great project.

By nightfall, he made it to a lonely outpost—a small, one-room building at a crossroads in the middle of a barren land. Grateful for shelter from the biting wind, he slept inside on his bedroll on the floor and awoke to a foot of snow on the ground outside.

After a cold breakfast of dried fruit and cheese, Adin galloped his horse through a steady snowfall that lasted until noon, following the cart road that hugged a winding creek. Finally, the clouds parted and a weak winter sun shone through. He slowed Na'thar to a walk as he entered the town, a pristine village with a cobbled lane running through its center.

The moment his horse clip-clopped onto the stones, Adin noticed the limp. He stopped and dismounted as a chill wind whipped his face and neck. Adin hunkered down in his cloak and lifted the gelding's foot. The iron shoe hung tenuously from two nails.

Pulling the reins over Na'thar's head, Adin led the horse down through the town. A few people ventured out of the shops as the snow stopped falling. Drifts of white powder piled up next to doorways. Warm lamplight glowed from shop windows that displayed their wares. Soon, a few shopkeepers emerged from their stores with brooms and shovels in hand and went to work clearing paths to their doors. Adin passed a row of empty stalls, signs of a marketplace. But on this wintry day, the only person he saw working outside was just the man he'd hoped to find: a blacksmith, stoking the fire in his forge with a bellows.

Adin walked over to the stall and ducked his head under the thatched overhang. The blacksmith, a young, fair-haired man, looked up and drew off his large, heavy gloves. Adin removed his hat and wiped snow from his face and beard. He offered his hand.

"Name's Adin. My horse could use a new shoe."

The blacksmith shook his hand. "Joran. Pleased to meet you." Adin watched curiously as the blacksmith looked over the horse. Na'thar whinnied, and Adin could almost swear his horse had smiled. Joran chuckled and pulled a net bag from behind a row of tools. He hung the bag stuffed with hay next to the horse and tied the reins to the rail. The horse pulled greedily at the treat. Adin's eyes were drawn to a strange mark on the blacksmith's forehead: a crescent moon that seemed etched into his skin.

"Been traveling far?" Joran asked, reaching for an iron shoe from a barrel at his feet.

"From Sherbourne."

Joran whistled and raised his eyes. "That's quite a trip, this time of year." Adin nodded and stood quietly, watching as the blacksmith heated the shoe and fitted it to his horse's foot. Pounding the nails, the blacksmith had the new shoe fastened against Na'thar's hoof in a matter of minutes.

Joran walked around the horse and checked the other shoes. "The rest look fine." He ran a hand through his curly hair. "Adin." A look of recognition crossed his face. "The King's son."

Adin nodded. The blacksmith tipped his head respectfully. "We don't hear much about Sherbourne out this far. Just stories—and they are greatly exaggerated. Would you honor my wife and me by staying the night? Our place is small, just outside town. But we do have a stall for your horse and an extra bed. Unless Your Majesty would prefer nicer accommodations . . ."

"Please." Adin waved his hand in dismissal. "Just call me Adin. And I would be grateful for your hospitality, as long as your wife doesn't mind."

Joran smiled. "She would be thrilled to hear the news of the city. You'll earn a fine meal for your tale."

"And I am eager to hear your stories too. Tell me, have you lived here long?"

"All my life."

"Then perhaps you can help me. I am interested in learning about the beginnings of this town. Where it got the name Tebron, and who first settled here."

The blacksmith pointed down the street to the only large, two-story building around. "That's the woolen mill. See the place next to it? That's where the first house was built in Tebron. It burned down many years ago and has been rebuilt since. Some say it is hundreds of years old, and I don't doubt it."

Joran gestured to the giant trees bordering the town, trees that towered into the sky. Adin hadn't even noticed them as he entered the town, so huddled into his coat he had been to stave off the cold. He had never seen trees that magnificent! He thought of the beautifully oiled desk in the Council chambers, with its concentric rings.

"The wood from these trees takes centuries to rot. That's why our lumber is so valuable, and our forests protected. I imagine some of these newer houses will last centuries as well."

Joran untied the reins and handed them to Adin. "Come back here at the end of the day and I'll take you to my house." Joran paused. "Funny, your name, Adin, is uncommon. Yet the woman who lives in that house has a son by that name."

Adin thanked the blacksmith and mounted his horse. He passed a bakery with racks of scones in the windows. His stomach growled in response. He pulled a roll from his saddlebag and ate it as he traversed the town. At the end of the long street, he tied his horse to a lamppost and walked to the front door of the dark wooden house.

Someone pulled aside the window curtain and looked out. The door opened and a woman his mother's age greeted him.

Her dark red hair was pulled back from her face, showing green eyes that bore some resemblance to Aletha. But when she spoke, he saw Aletha's smile, passed down through a dozen generations.

Adin introduced himself but didn't know how to explain his visit. He hadn't planned what to say ahead of time, and his awkwardness took him by surprise. When he told her his name, her eyebrows rose.

She ushered him into the warm den where a fire blazed heartily. She motioned him to a sofa, and he sat and removed his hat.

She sat across from him in a rocking chair. "My son's name is Adin. It's a family name, that."

Adin hesitated. "I know this may sound strange, but have you ever heard of a woman named Aletha? She would have lived here long ago, when the town was first settled."

The woman scrunched up her face. "Let me show you something."

She left the room through a rear door and then came back with two books; one she offered to Adin. The binding was old, made of some kind of dark leather, and when Adin opened the pages, the parchment nearly crumbled at the touch of his fingers. He held the book with care, turning each page without comment. The woman waited by his side, looking at the strange scribblings along with him.

"Odd writing, that. Do you know what to make of it?"

Adin turned page after page of neatly penned letters. "This is the *law'az*, the ancient script." Had Aletha learned to write this, or had it come from O'lam?

The woman handed him another small book, similarly aged, but this one was in writing Adin understood. The title was worn but still readable: *The Book of Kingly Sayings*. This was the oldest copy Adin had ever seen outside the library in Sherbourne.

Adin jerked in his seat. It hadn't occurred to him until now that the reason the people of his kingdom knew how to read and write was because he—Adin—had given Jered a primer. And Jered had taught the regent. How strange!

"There's one more thing," the woman added. "And you tell me if it means naught to you. Something that's been handed down in my family, passed on from my mother to me and so on. My mother told me what her mother told her. To give this to the one who asks for it."

She reached into her pocket and pulled out a chain. Dangling from the chain was an old tarnished locket of simple design. Adin repressed a cry. He took it from the woman's hand, under her watchful gaze, and looked at the back of the locket. He knew what the words spelled in their odd shapes. The abbot had told him.

Set me as a seal upon your heart, for love is as strong as death. He didn't want to cry, but the tears came anyway. The woman sat quietly and handed him a cloth.

Adin gathered his breath, then reached under his shirt and pulled out the locket he wore around his neck.

The woman bent over to examine it and muttered, "Well, I'll be . . ."

With soft, worn fingers she closed Adin's other hand around the old locket, making his hand into a fist. "I can see this belongs to you. And the books. I wish I could tell you more. All I know is my ancestors built this house and started a town. Someone who liked to stitch began making linens and pillow cases and tapestries. That's what started the woolen mill. Others came and logged the trees. It's a quiet town of hard-working people; a good place to live out your days and raise a family."

Adin stood, wiping a last tear from his cheek. He thanked the woman for her kindness, the books, and the locket in his hand. He said good-bye to someone who was his great-great-great-niece or some distant relation, and walked away from the house.

Adin stopped at the street and looked back. In his mind's eye he pictured Aletha, stitching by the fire, her children playing on the floor. There would be a cat curled up somewhere, perhaps a wolf and a hedgehog or two enjoying the heat from the hearth. And there would be her captain, with his dark hair and striking blue eyes, making her laugh and rubbing her feet.

Adin smiled at the image and his heart trembled with joy. Aletha had raised a family. She had made a home in Tebron with Jered, the handsome captain of the *tsa'ba*. Adin could now bring honor to her life by living his. He was now *na'thar.*

Free.

THIRTY-TWO

"WINSTON, I never thought I would say this, but I am thrilled to see you." Adin stooped down and threw his arms around the fat pig.

Winston squealed. "Easy on the ol' bones, lad. A bit tender under all that meat, you see."

Adin pulled a soft cap from his head and wiped away the sweat that dripped down his forehead. He had worn his soft muslin shirt and pants, clothing embroidered by the desert seamstresses, and he was grateful for their cool feel against his skin. His horse, tied to a young sapling near the cottage door, snuffed and pulled on his tether, his lips inching toward a tuft of grass. Adin released the pig and went over to his mount. Behind the leather saddle hung canvas bags that flanked both sides of the horse.

"I need to get O'kel some water and hobble him to graze." Adin deftly loosened the girth and unstrapped the bags, pulling them down with a thud to the ground. Soon, saddle, bags, and headstall lay in a heap. Adin found a brush and worked the sweat off the horse. "This must be the hottest day of summer yet."

"'Tis, lad, to be sure." Winston lowered himself onto the porch and watched Adin with a smile. "Wha's all that stuff, lad? New decorations for the cottage? And look at you—in all those fancy trimmings! Gold baubles and such. Fit to be a king."

"Well, I suppose I am. But these were given to me."

Adin untied the halter and led the horse down to the creek. Winston trotted at his heels. "And all this 'stuff' is just gifts for friends. And art supplies from a place called Ethryn." He played out the lead so the horse could drink. "You would be amazed at that city. Round clay houses baking in the desert. There's a breathtaking oasis with frond trees. And camels! And they make these honey cakes that melt in your mouth. I thought I would stop for a short visit but ended up staying there six years."

When the horse had his fill of water, Adin led him back behind the cottage to the open field. After hobbling two of O'kel's legs, he removed the halter and patted the horse on his rump. O'kel went to work mowing the tall grass with fervor.

"Let's go inside. I even brought *you* a gift."

"Me, lad? What could I possibly need?"

Adin walked happily to the house; he was glad to be home. He carried his heavy bags inside and set them by the door. But as he entered the small room, still quite empty and unadorned, his heart sank. Winston ambled over to him and sat, waiting.

"What is it, lad?" he asked.

Adin sighed and fell back in his padded chair, one of the few pieces of furniture left in the house. A slight breeze cooled the room, and Adin heard insects buzz in the woods around the cottage. He had ridden for six days straight, camping along the way. He needed a bath and some clean clothes. Then he would prepare dinner with the grains and spices he had brought with him from the south. But then what?

He thought awhile and then turned to Winston. "I've been traveling for ten years now, Winston. And I've seen things more wonderful than you can imagine. I thought I would travel to every part of the known world, but there is so much out there. I only scratched the surface. There are fantastic kingdoms hidden away in mountains and ice. Bears as large as this house." Adin's eyes grew sad.

"I saw wars and struggles. Famine and drought. Suffering beyond hope. But I also met wonderful people who taught me much about the world—and about myself."

Adin pursed his lips and exhaled deeply. "I even fell in love, Winston, with a wonderful Ethryn woman, but I just couldn't settle down. My heart is restless, always restless. I thought if I came back here . . ."

The pig interjected, ". . . you'd feel at home. But your heart's not here, lad, is it?"

Adin looked hard at the pig. "No, it's not. I left it behind, with Aletha, all those centuries back."

Adin paused, his eyes filling with tears. "I don't belong here, Winston. Not in this place or this time. This Sherbourne has its prince." He fiddled with the fabric on the armchair, worrying at some loose threads. "I hear the King plans to crown him next spring. And as I rode around the city today, I saw prosperity and happiness. Sherbourne is thriving, and that at least makes my heart sing."

Adin got up from his chair and went over to his bags. He searched inside one until he found a large sack made of white gauze. He untied the strings and went over to Winston's bowl, filling it with golden clumps. Winston came over and sniffed curiously.

"What's this, lad? Smells divine."

"The Ethrynians call it 'caramel corn.' It's corn, Winston—your favorite. Just puffed up and topped with some gooey, sweet coating."

Winston had his mouth stuffed before Adin finished his sentence. "Excellent, lad," he mumbled, corn spilling out the sides of his mouth.

Adin laughed. "Mind the mess, Winston."

"Oh, will do," he said, happily snuffing up the crumbs. "Delicious. Imagine, turning corn into this."

Adin patted the pig's head affectionately. "I thought you'd enjoy it."

He went into the kitchen and found a pitcher of water next to the wash sink. He had stopped wondering long ago how Winston managed on his own. The pig surely had no way of filling the pitcher—or putting it up on the counter. It would have to remain one of life's mysteries.

Adin drank a glass of water and filled it back up. He returned to the entry to find Winston licking the sides of the bowl. The pig smacked his lips.

"Right decent of you, lad, to cart this treat all the way home." As Adin sat back down in his chair, Winston came and stood attentively at his feet.

"Did you have time to paint, lad? Practice your art?"

"I did. That's how I earned my keep most years. I was even commissioned to paint huge murals on many of the walls in Ethryn. The people there are very artistic—they even decorate their pottery with images of animals and people. They grind roots and berries and plants to make the richest pigments."

"Excellent, lad. All that training pays off, you see." Winston gave Adin such a strange look that Adin stopped and felt his flushed forehead with the palm of his hand.

"I feel a bit odd," he said.

Winston chuckled. "Tha's the magic stirring, lad."

Adin remembered. He had felt the same wave of dizziness ten years before when the pig had altered his deformities. Panic set in.

"Oh, no, what now? What are you doing, Winston?"

The room wiggled. Adin's vision blurred. He stood and tried to find his balance as the floor swayed and rocked.

"It's time, lad. Still a few loose ends need to be tied up, you see? And you've been preparing for them—so, there you have it."

Adin tried to focus on the pig, but he started to disappear. "Wait!" Adin shouted.

His words were sucked up into a vortex of harsh light.

Winston was gone. So were the cottage and the woods and the creek.

Wind spun Adin around, and for a timeless age he saw nothing but shadows flickering like ghosts. Heat beat down on him, followed by icy blasts. Adin shivered, racked with nausea. He wrapped his arms around his chest to keep warm. His teeth chattered so hard his jaws began to ache. Although he knew better than to mouth curses at Winston, he still hoped he would see the pig again so he could throttle him. Why didn't he give him even a little warning? Or at least ask permission before he pulled Adin into his magic spells? *Someone ought to teach that creature some manners!*

Minutes, hours, days—Adin had no way to tell how long the magic held him in its grasp. Finally, the wind abated, and Adin fell exhausted to hard dirt. His face stung from the constant battering of air, and his knees shook from the strain of bracing himself against the endless barrage of the elements. He raised his weary head and looked around. For a moment he thought he was still home, for the cottage appeared before him, coalescing into wood planking and windows. A hot sun glared down on his shoulders and the air was balmy.

Adin studied his surroundings, confused. He stared at the plain wooden door. This was not his cottage, but he had seen it before. He had been here. He looked down the road and noticed people walking, riding horses, and goading oxen that pulled wooden carts. People wearing odd clothing, glancing at him curiously. The boughs of the overhanging trees soughed gently as Adin stood, stiff and alert. As the recognition of the shaded lane sank in, Adin clutched his chest and his breath grew shallow.

He turned back to the door, afraid to touch it for fear he would awaken from a dream. Fear that he was imagining all this. A deep breath heaved in his chest. He lifted his hand, but before he made contact with the weathered wood, the door opened. Adin looked into two friendly eyes and started to faint. His knees gave way and he dropped, only to be caught by strong, supportive arms.

"Ah, right on schedule, Adin. I've been expecting you."

Through a haze of dizziness, Adin looked up at the smiling face. The Keeper grinned, his big teeth sparkling in the summer light. His gray mustache flopped along the sides of his mouth as he chuckled. "Oh, my," O'lam said. "We need to make you a strong tonic. Get some life back in you, dear boy."

"What am I doing here?" Adin managed to whisper. "How . . ."

O'lam helped his visitor to his feet. "Ah, you should know better than to ask that, lad. Didn't I tell you we'd meet again?" He brought Adin into the kitchen and set him down at the tiny table. Adin, still shaky, watched him pour a cup of steaming tea, from a pot O'lam had been steeping before his arrival. He *had* been expected.

Adin sipped the bitter tea and his head cleared. Strength returned to his limbs, and the chill finally left his bones. He looked around the familiar room, sensing Aletha there. She had stood only paces away—crying in Jered's arms. And had sat there, by the hearth at O'lam's feet, her face animated and excited.

Aletha!

"Is she here? O'lam, where is my sister?" Adin jumped up from his chair. The Keeper laid a hand on his shoulder.

"I'll take you to her soon enough, Adin."

The reality of sitting in O'lam's cottage, hundreds of years in the past, hit Adin like a cartload of bricks. He was really here—back in time! All these many years, he had dreamed and wished and hoped without hope. He had fallen on his knees more times than he could count and pleaded with heaven, and thought his cries had fallen on deaf ears. But heaven had heard him! He was truly here. Never in his life had this much joy coursed through his soul. Winston had done it—he had sent him back to Aletha. But, why now? Why not ten years ago when he suffered so?

"There's a time for every season, Adin. A time to mourn and a time to laugh. Heaven has perfect timing, lad, and it's very seldom when we think it should be."

"What year is it, then?" Adin assumed he had returned to the same season he had left, but that might not be the case. Was Aletha still eighteen—or eighty?

"Relax, Adin. Time's passed the same for you as for the lass. To the day."

Ten years. Adin grew quiet. A lot could have happened for Aletha in ten years—it *had* for him. He knew the years showed on his own face. Would Aletha even recognize him, changed as he was? And Aletha! He knew she would still be beautiful, even more so.

Adin searched O'lam's face, almost afraid to ask. "Tell me, O'lam. How is my sister?"

"Happy as a badger in a chicken coop, Adin. Married to her captain and living in the west, in a forest. And she has a son—and a daughter."

Adin gasped and tears spilled down his cheeks. "A son . . . and a daughter . . ."

O'lam smiled and sat next to Adin. He drank his tea quietly as the images formed in Adin's mind. Adin could just picture Aletha with children gathered in her arms, their smiling faces beaming up at their mother. He let the tears fall freely down his cheeks. Oh, how kind heaven had been! And how wrong he had been to doubt.

"Doubts are what create our trust, Adin," O'lam said. "Can't have one without the other."

He added, "By the way, she named the lad after you. And a bright-eyed little chap he is."

Adin shook his head in wonder. He was so anxious to see Aletha he could barely stay in his chair. All traces of exhaustion fled, replaced by a surge of anticipation.

"I know you're excited, lad. We can leave tomorrow, at first light." O'lam got up and went over to a small wooden chest in the corner. "But, dear boy, before we go, there's a matter we need to attend to." He rummaged through the contents and pulled out a rolled parchment.

"I've set up some paints and brushes on the work table in the back. If you're feeling up to it, lad, then we'd best get started."

Adin set down his empty cup, feeling better than he had in years. A new strength invigorated him as excitement pumped through his veins. He would see Aletha soon! He stood and followed O'lam into the back room.

"Get started on what, O'lam?"

Adin looked at the table where Kah'yil had lain, bleeding from the wounds Ka'zab had inflicted. There the healer had leaned over the regent, treating his gashes. It seemed only yesterday he himself had stood on this very spot, cleaning Kah'yil's injuries.

And now, O'lam bent over something altogether different—a large parchment unrolled across the high table. Adin looked at the blank sheet before him. His eyes questioned O'lam.

"Just start in the center, lad."

The ageless Keeper handed Adin a slender bristle brush. "With the pentacle. First, the outline, then the colors. Just the way you remember it."

Adin held the brush over the unmarked ivory parchment. "I don't understand, O'lam. What am I painting?"

O'lam laughed heartily and slapped Adin affectionately on his back.

"Why, the map, Adin. The map! Where do you think it came from—thin air? You need to take it to Aletha so she can put it in the abbey. So you can retrieve it three hundred years from now."

The map! Adin had forgotten about it. This was impossible! His mind looped in circles trying to think about it. In the future he would get the map out of the abbey, a map he had made in the past. But he could not get to the past to make the map until he fetched it from the abbey. In the past, the map would be lost forever, probably under a pile of refuse in a cluttered alleyway. Yet, it had to have a beginning. Someone had to make it. And he was that someone! He was really beginning to hate these time paradoxes.

And what did Aletha have to do with the abbey? Was it even built yet? Adin looked over at O'lam, who stood grinning.

"It's just heaven's plan, lad. Just trust."

Adin saw the map in his mind, remembering the way the images had painted themselves. The brushstrokes and detail reminiscent of his own technique. The invisible hand that put ink to page, then filled in with color and shadow, was his. His unique style, no one else's. Adin was flabbergasted. Now he understood what the pig meant when he said Adin had been preparing for this. This day, this moment. This task.

O'lam looked on as Adin dipped his brush into a glass of water. Open pots of paints lined the table's edge. Adin closed his eyes and envisioned the pentacle—silver, with a smaller gold star inside. Then a round blue gemstone in the center. He opened his eyes to see O'lam setting his neck chain down next to the paints, the pentacle staring back at him in the soft light streaming through the window.

"To help nudge your memory, lad."

Adin's memory needed no nudging.

Adin dabbed silver paint with his brush, then touched the bristles to the parchment. On the edge of his field of vision he saw O'lam lapse deep into concentration. The Keeper's eyes closed tightly and his lips muttered, weaving a spell that blanketed the room. Adin felt a tremor travel down his head, through his fingers, and onto the blank sheet on the table. Color flowed from the brush as magic moved his hand. Time slowed to a stop as he watched the star form before him on the parchment, bathed in a shimmer of light.

If he had had to describe to someone what he felt as he stood there—creating his destiny, his future—words would have failed him. For he stood, not at the completion of his *ma'gur*, but at the *re'sheeth*—the very beginning.

"Mama, look how many berries I got!"

"'Look how many berries I *have*,' Ra'nan. Not *got*." Aletha peered into the wicker basket her five-year-old daughter held out to her. "Why, sweetie, you almost have enough for a pie!" The small, black-haired child nodded excitedly, shaking curls about her face.

"*Bogberry* pie!" she added, running back to the row of trellised brambles growing along the fence.

Aletha removed her straw hat and basked in the unusually sunny day. The first few years they had lived among these towering trees the constant fog had dampened her mood. How could a place be so gray every day? And so much rain! But Aletha grew to love the rain—the way it pattered gently on the roof, the profusion of plants it nurtured. So much green all around her. And quiet.

When Jered had told his former villagers his plans to move to the Sawtooths, a whole entourage of people had come along with them. Most of Jered's childhood friends considered two years in a settlement camp and nearly a year behind stone walls punishment enough. In the first three years after arriving in this hidden glen, the small band of families had built a thriving village, with more settlers arriving weekly. Jered and a dozen other men had just completed the new sawmill, ensuring even more newcomers would join their community in the months ahead.

Jered, kneeling in a patch of snow peas, popped his head up.

"Where's the little guy? Why isn't he out here helping?" He plucked a handful of peas and put them in his basket.

"You know him, love," Aletha said. "Always painting."

"There's lots to paint outside too. Ra'nan, go fetch your brother. Tell him it's too pretty a day to be indoors."

"'Kay, Papa." Aletha watched her daughter run to the back door.

Aletha yelped. "Hey!"

Two strong arms grabbed her from behind. Aletha looked at the soiled hands clasped around her waist.

"Captain Tebron, you're getting my smock all dirty." Aletha giggled as Jered kissed her neck, then squeezed her ribs.

Aletha yelped again. "Why you . . .!" She lunged for Jered, but he sidestepped her quickly with his battle-trained reflexes. Before she fell, he caught her in his arms and swung her around. Jered drew her close and kissed her tenderly. Aletha wondered if she could be any happier.

When the *mil'ka'ma* had ended and spring had come to Sherbourne, the regent had seen her and Jered off with a trunk full of treasures in gratitude for their devotion and assistance. The defeated kingdom to the south had paid tribute to Sherbourne's new king, promising to stay outside marked borders. The regent hoped to pursue peace, as far as it was possible, with the routed *o'yab*. Aletha had little doubt he would succeed.

At Aletha's request, the regent had granted her a plot of land in the vale northwest of the city. The lands for leagues in all directions now came under the jurisdiction of the newly established kingdom. He had wondered at Aletha's request for land to build an abbey. Why not closer to the city, he had asked? And why an abbey? Aletha had told him her vision of a place to raise food for a growing community, as well as to tend to the spiritual needs of those seeking heaven's will. He applauded her plan. And sent her and the captain off west, to settle a new land.

The moment she had arrived in this forest of red-barked trees, she had known just the place to build their cottage. Jered had agreed wholeheartedly. On the south edge of the forest, the woods gave way to a huge meadow, and across the meadow stretched a slow, meandering creek. Jutting up behind the creek stood craggy mountains with their peaks scraping the sky. The sight was breathtaking.

Jered set to work felling trees and trimming them into logs for the cottage. At the same time, with the gold and gems given them, Aletha financed families who had settled in the northern vale to work on constructing the foundation for the abbey. The pale yellow stone of the surrounding hills was easy to quarry and much more abundant than lumber for building. Once their cottage was built, O'lam had visited Aletha many times; they even kept a spare room ready for him.

Aletha sighed. O'lam was right when he said building the abbey would require a lifetime. The project was slow-going, but in her mind's eye she could picture it completed in all its glory. Every few months, she and O'lam rode by carriage to the site, to check on the progress and give further instructions to the builders. And back home, when she wasn't working on designs for the abbey, she wove on her loom.

Her dream was to start a weavers guild and eventually build a place where artisans could work together and make beautiful things for the people of the village. Already, she and her best friend, Hirah, had almost a dozen orders for shawls. Quantities of yarn made from washed wool came by cart from Sherbourne; all they had to do was separate the skeins into bundles and dye them.

O'lam had procured pigments for her, beautiful rich colors for her yarn, unlike any seen in the kingdom. She hoped that someday her small town would be known for their woven works.

Aletha knelt next to Jered, who was now thinning the onion patch.

"I'm glad you've taken a day off to help around the house," she said.

"I can think of nothing I enjoy more than crawling in the dirt with my family." He stole a quick kiss as he pulled plants from the ground. He held up his trowel. "I'd rather wield this than a sword any day. I hope those times are far behind us."

"Now all you have to combat are weeds and potato bugs. Do you think you are up to the challenge, brave captain of the *tsa'ba*?"

Jered raised his tool in mock attack. "Bring them on. They don't stand a chance!" He stabbed the air a few times and laughed.

"I thought all the peace and quiet here would bore you," Aletha said. "But I was wrong. You're not one of those restless types, are you?"

"I have plenty of challenges here—helping this town get on its feet and getting the mill built. Once we get the steam engine running, you will be amazed. The saws will spin so fast your eyes will pop out of your head. And then we can mill boards and build furniture much more easily. Things will change greatly."

Aletha smiled at Jered's enthusiasm. She loved that about him, more than any other quality. He spoke of change as if it was a good thing, but Aletha wasn't too sure. She thought back to the sprawl and filth of the city. She hoped her little hamlet was far enough off the beaten track to avoid that kind of change.

Aletha lifted her head at the sound of her son's voice.

"Mama, look who's here!"

Her son, Adin, came around the corner dragging along an old man in a soft white shirt and green trousers.

"Easy on the old fella, son," Jered chided. "O'lam can't run as fast as you."

Aletha and Jered straightened up as O'lam waddled toward them. Aletha smiled at her son. He was only nine, but was almost as tall as his father, and had the same strong face and black hair. Both her children favored Jered but they had her green eyes. In many ways this boy was like her twin—gentle, kind, introspective. Every time he tipped his head and smirked, a little arrow pierced her heart, for that was just how her brother used to look at her.

"O'lam's brought you a present, Mama. A man!"

Aletha laughed and raised her eyebrows at the healer. "I already have one man, O'lam. And he's a handful enough." Jered punched her playfully. "Although, I can think of a few useful things another set of strong arms could do around here . . ."

". . . like what?"

A stranger came around the side of the house. Aletha studied him curiously. His auburn hair was pulled back behind his neck in a ponytail, revealing a tan, sincere face. He stood straight, with poise and a calm demeanor, but his eyes danced with happiness. There was nothing unusual about his simple clothing and appearance, but something about him sent a shudder through her entire body.

Jered went up to the stranger and greeted him. The children stood and watched, eager to learn who their visitor was.

The stranger spoke in a cheerful voice. "Jered! You've grown older. Do I detect a bit of gray in that head of thick black hair?"

Jered looked him over as Aletha watched the odd exchange. "Excuse me, do I know you? Were you one of the *tsa'ba* camped outside the city?"

Aletha came alongside Jered. She turned and eyed O'lam, who wandered around the yard, pretending to study the plants.

Now her curiosity heightened. Just what did O'lam have up his sleeve?

"See," the man called over to the healer. "I told you they wouldn't recognize me." The stranger turned directly to Aletha and gazed into her face.

"Come now, Aletha, you must look a little harder. I haven't changed all *that* much."

Aletha searched his face. She knew this man; she did! Her gaze finally rested on his eyes, and the way he stared at her greatly unsettled her.

"I'm sorry . . ." she began.

"Aletha," he whispered, his voice trembling. She startled at the touch of his hands, warm and gentle as he took hers. Tears pooled in his eyes. He looked at her with such anguish, yet with such joy. Now she knew. She had seen this exact look countless times, and it belonged to only one person.

She touched his smooth, even cheek. "Adin. How . . .?" She backed away from him and looked at his legs, his back. "It is you?" she asked, afraid to believe what her heart insisted was true. The man before her was handsome and—perfect. Not a blemish or deformity or stoop. She quickly looked back at O'lam, who tipped his head in a simple nod.

Behind her astonishment, she did recognize him, and understanding washed over her. For she had always seen her brother in just this fashion, through eyes of love. To her, he had never been deformed or crippled. The man who stood before her was the Adin she had truly known. Beautiful, poised, perfect. The young, troubled child who had suffered humiliation and shame was just an illusion.

"Oh, Adin!" She fell against him and squeezed him with all her might.

Adin lifted her off the ground in a strong embrace. "Nothing that a bit of magic couldn't remedy," he said, laughing heartily.

Jered threw an arm around Adin and joined in the hug. "You made it back—after all these years! I am so glad to see you again, my friend!"

"Mama, who is he?" Ra'nan asked. "And why are you crying?"

Aletha found her voice buried under a blanket of joy. "This is your Uncle Adin."

"Adin?" she asked. "But that's *his* name," she said, pointing to her brother, who watched the goings-on with amusement.

"Well, now there are two of them. Big Adin and little Adin," O'lam said, his smile as wide as his face.

"Hey, I'm not that little," the boy interjected.

The healer came over to him and patted his head. "No, you're not, lad. Soon you'll be towering over me, I imagine."

Aletha couldn't get enough of her twin. Her eyes drank in every inch of him, and he seemed to be doing the same with her. "I just can't believe it. You're here! How did you get back here? Did you stop the curse? What about Father?"

"Easy," Adin said, wiping tears from his cheeks. "There's no hurry; I'm here to stay. And what I have to tell you will take days. So, let me start at the beginning . . ."

Aletha took Adin's arm and turned to her son. "Adin, go pour some glasses of iced nettle tea. And help O'lam with the carriage and horses. Ra'nan, come inside and let's show your uncle the beautiful pictures you've made."

Her brother shook his head. "I can't believe you named him after me. I'm honored."

"What else would I name my firstborn?" Aletha squeezed his arm. "I feel like I'm dreaming. If I am, please don't wake me. This is the happiest day of my life!"

They walked through the back door into the kitchen where the young Adin filled glasses with tea. Aletha led her brother into the den. She waited as he surveyed the room, his eyes coming to rest on the large loom in the corner. He turned in surprise, and a question spread over his face.

She watched as he ran his hand over the golden threads woven between the loom's warp strings. The tapestry was near completion. The shuttle rested at the base of the design, surrounded by stitching that implied trailing feathers.

"You. This is *your* work." Adin's mouth fell open and Aletha could see his mind turning.

"I always loved the tapestry that hung in Mother's chamber. I thought I would try to copy it."

Adin narrowed his eyes. "Aletha . . ." He shook his head, trying to loosen the words that seemed trapped in his throat. "I found out that the firebird tapestry was centuries old. It had hung in the abbey before it was sold. And you will be dumbfounded when you hear what happened with your tapestry."

Aletha put her hand to her mouth. "Are you saying . . .?"

"O'lam told me you're building the abbey." He gestured to her loom. "I imagine you'll have that done long before the abbey's complete."

Now it was Aletha's turn to gape. Adin studied the tapestry and added, "You're not finished. There were words, ancient letters."

Aletha nodded, speechless. She had never considered putting the writing across the bottom, but now she supposed she would. She thought back to that day in the library, when the monk had come in looking for a book on ancient writing to help the King translate the phrase stitched in the tapestry. In her mind's eye she saw the embroidered letters in the ancient script, letters she now easily understood. Who but she would know how to fashion those words?

O'lam spoke from the kitchen as he sipped his tea and munched on a cookie. "The lass had been learning the ancient writing. She's become quite the scholar."

Ra'nan climbed down from her stool in the kitchen and brought a book over to her uncle. "Here, Uncle Adin, see what Mama wrote."

Adin opened the leather-bound book and turned the pages, admiring the neatly inked letters of the ancient *law'az*. He smiled and handed the book back to Ra'nan, who hurried to the kitchen for another cookie. His face turned wistful.

"Funny, now that I'm here, I feel as if I'd never left. It feels like . . ."

Adin searched for words that wouldn't come.

"I know," Aletha said, resting a gentle hand on his cheek. "It feels like home."

After a hearty dinner of steamed vegetables from the garden and lamb from a neighbor's farm, Adin helped Ra'nan serve bogberry pie to everyone relaxing in the living room. Aletha had lit candles, and their glow matched the glow in Adin's soul—warm, comforting, peaceful. Aletha was right; he finally felt at home. All those years—wandering, searching for a place to live out his days—had left him empty and unsettled. He had told Winston he'd left his heart behind with Aletha, and here it was—waiting for him all this time in a cottage sequestered in a remote forest.

Ra'nan dropped down beside her uncle with a fork in her mouth and a plate in her hand. A large ginger cat rubbed up against her, then settled on the rug by her feet.

"That's Brynn. Our kitty."

Adin smiled, wondering if the regent's sister knew a cat had been named for her. O'lam came over and sat on the rug next to

Ra'nan, a huge slice of pie on his plate. The healer always seemed to prefer sitting on the floor.

"What does *ra'nan* mean?" Adin asked. Aletha sidled up next to Jered on a small brown sofa. She fed a forkful of pie into Jered's open mouth. Adin couldn't stop looking at his sister. She was thirty-six years old and still looked so youthful. *Happiness becomes her.*

"To rejoice, to laugh joyfully," Aletha answered.

Adin ruffled his niece's hair. "Then it's the perfect name for you."

Ra'nan giggled and attacked her pie in earnest. Adin laughed. "She has your appetite, Aletha."

"No, yours!" his twin retorted.

Aletha's son came in from a back room, carrying a stack of papers. "Here are my drawings, Uncle Adin." He handed them over with a shy smile.

Adin worried that he would have to take care to be polite, for he could see the apprehension on the youth's face. But Adin was impressed. Clearly, his nephew had spent many long hours with pen and brush; his sketches were imaginative and detailed.

Adin looked at the boy with pride. "You have a great talent, Adin. These are truly beautiful."

O'lam looked over at Aletha and Jered. "And, lass, your brother is also quite an artist. In fact, before we came, he did a little paint-ing for me."

Aletha's eyes narrowed at the tone of O'lam's voice. Adin laughed silently. Aletha knew the old Keeper well enough to guess he was hinting at something of interest. Adin waited as O'lam fetched the map from the carriage and brought it into the house. Adin excused himself and went into the kitchen to get a glass of water, listening to Aletha's astonishment and Jered's confusion. He heard the captain ask, "Did you find the lost map, O'lam? Where was it?" As O'lam explained the paradox of the map, Adin stood and watched from the doorway.

Earlier, while preparing dinner, Adin had told Aletha and Jered his tale—how he had gone back to his future only to be captured, then rescued by Reya. When he told her how he had traveled back eight years earlier, to the day their mother was about to die, Aletha grew pale. He then told her who the man in the orchard was, and how he helped Reya turn the Queen into the firebird as magic ravaged the palace. And then Aletha fainted.

Jered revived her with a cool rag as O'lam concocted a tonic. Adin went into a fret; he had never seen Aletha faint.

"She only faints when she's like this." Jered gestured to her belly. O'lam gave Aletha a cup to drink from as Jered patted her forehead.

"Please." She waved her hand at all those fussing over her. "I'm fine. Just pregnant."

"With another son," O'lam added.

Adin couldn't help gawking. No wonder she glowed so beautifully!

Now, with the whole story filled in like the last dab of paint on a canvas, Adin let out a big sigh. Recounting all his adventures had exhausted him, as if he relived each moment in the telling. He found a comfortable chair and sank into it, happily closing his eyes and listening to the wonderful cacophony of a joyful family. Jered told him the regent had remarried, and already had three sons in his old age. Adin was glad for him. Jered teased Adin, reminding him he still had enough years left to settle down and raise a family. Now, as Adin sat with a heavy cat on his lap, he wondered if that joy would ever be his. If not, he knew he would be content, here with this family who loved him.

Jered had already thought of a perfect place for Adin, up the road just outside town. A sunny hillside with a large pasture—perfect for grazing a horse, and with a stunning view of the mountains. Adin could set up his easel right outside his back door and paint to his heart's content—and his nephew could work alongside him. With the help of their friends, they could build him a house before winter set in. Jered's kindness moved him to more tears. He couldn't think of the right words to express his gratitude, but Jered repeated the phrase Adin had heard him say years earlier: "Reserve your thanks for later—until after you see how hard I work you." He added, "Maybe we'll make a builder or a millwright out of you in time."

A rap at the door startled them. Aletha answered it. Through the open doorway, Adin saw the moon rising in a deep blue sky behind the silhouette of a woman.

"Hirah! I'm glad you came. Ra'nan's made us a pie." The woman came in and removed a shawl from her shoulders.

Aletha took the shawl and held it up to the lamplight. "Oh, Hirah, you've finished it—how beautiful!" She showed it to Jered. "Look, my love, isn't she just the most amazing weaver!"

As Jered complimented Hirah, Adin saw her blush. She looked a bit like Jered—with long black hair trailing over her shoulders, and a strong, happy face. Adin could tell she was close to his own age, but she moved like Aletha—with a carefree and youthful spirit.

Aletha took her by the hand and presented her excitedly to Adin.

"Hirah, you will not believe this, but this is Adin, my brother!"

Adin was suddenly drawn into a pair of piercing blue eyes; he found it difficult to tear his gaze away. Hirah leaned closer to him, and her smile caused a shiver to dance across his neck.

"Aletha, how can this be? After everything you've told me . . ." her friend said.

Aletha laughed, and then noticed Adin's expression. Her mouth dropped open just enough for Adin to guess her thoughts. He blushed.

"Come, Hirah, I'll tell you everything while we get some pie."

Hirah smiled at Adin, and his heart fluttered. He quickly looked over at O'lam. The old Keeper watched Adin with an amused smile. Adin looked back at Hirah.

"I'm so glad you're here," Hirah said to Adin. She lowered her voice and the words fell on Adin's ears like flower petals. "You have no idea how much she's missed you." He watched a tear run down her face, and it took all his self-control not to reach out and wipe it from her cheek. "You have no idea," she repeated, and her hand rested briefly on his.

As the two women walked to the kitchen in animated discussion, Adin took a deep breath. He thought of the word *smitten*. He'd heard people use the word before, but never known what it meant. Until now. He furrowed his brow and glared at O'lam, but the healer, if he was up to any mischief, did not let on. He just sat at the kitchen table, sipping a mug of tea, throwing in a comment or two Adin could not hear. But he knew what they were talking about—or rather, *whom*.

Ra'nan and Little Adin sat on the floor playing a board game with dice. Brynn, the cat, swished her tail over the board, eliciting irritated cries from the children. Jered lay back on the sofa, his feet propped up on a stool, reading a small book. Adin could make out the title, penned in a writing style similar to his own: *The Book of Kingly Sayings*. A cool evening breeze wafted through the partly open living room window.

Adin felt full, not just from a hearty dinner and two pieces of bogberry pie. He was full with life, with joy, and with hope.

When he had returned from his long travels and walked into the old cottage where Winston awaited him, he had thought his life was wrapping up, that all the surprises were over and he had seen all there was to see. He was glad he had been wrong. Another wholly unexpected life stretched ahead of him. What it held, he had no idea.

It is the glory of God to conceal things, but the glory of kings to search things out. He finally understood the joy underlying that saying. Before, he had viewed those words as a challenge and a frustration, for who wanted things to be mysterious and unknown? Now he embraced them for the comfort and excitement they meant to impart. What was life but one big, mysterious journey? Humans were meant to enjoy the mystery, and find happiness in the searching, not just the finding.

THIRTY-THREE

ALETHA, ARE you certain you don't want us to come with you?" Jered asked, leaning on his staff.

Adin stood next to the carriage, patting one of the draft horses. He watched Aletha push her long gray hair behind her and adjust her cloak. "You know how riding in the carriage causes your legs pain," she reminded Jered. "Besides, your grandson has never been to the abbey, and I promised to take him along. So there's no more room in the carriage."

Adin saw a look of hurt come over Jered's face, but he knew his friend was pretending. Adin knew full well Jered would rather spend the weekend coloring with his granddaughters and wrestling with them on the bed.

After a splattering of early rain, the crisp spring day cleared to reveal a bright blue sky. Adin glanced up at the ridge of the Sawtooth Mountains, frosted with snow and glistening like diamonds. He ran a hand through what was left of his white hair. It seemed every day that there was less of it, but Hirah never failed to tell him how distinguished he looked. *Distinguished? How?* Adin had no idea, but his wife still looked upon him each day as if he were still the dashing young prince come from the future. She always made him sound so mysterious, but Adin knew better. He was really just a simple man who loved a simple life. And, thank heaven, that was what the last thirty years had been—simple and undisturbed.

Adin watched Aletha say good-bye to her sons and daughter. How had they grown up so quickly? Where had the time gone? Now they were adults with families of their own.

And Adin thought about his own children—his twins—now strong, capable adults. His son, Jacob, had his own thriving business in town, crafting beautiful furniture from wood. He had yet to marry, but had his eyes on the mayor's daughter. Adin's daughter, Ka'nan, had married a fine horse breeder, and loved to ride for hours in the mountains with her father. Already, Ka'nan's eight-year-old daughter could handle a horse better than Adin ever could. And her quiet, young son wanted only to paint—and be a famous artist like Grandpa Adin.

Adin felt heaven's blessings pour down on him like a torrent of rain, drenching him to the bone with deep-seated joy. He had left Hirah at the cottage, minding the grandchildren. She knew what an important day it was and wanted to let Adin have his time with Aletha. She and Aletha had grown even closer over the years, raising their children together and turning the weaver's guild into a viable business. More than twenty women now worked at looms in the impressive two-story building next to Aletha and Jered's home. It was the pride of the town—everything Aletha had dreamed it would be.

O'lam hefted a heavy trunk and tossed it behind the buckboard. Adin shook his head. The old healer never aged a day, never lost any more hair off the top of his balding head. His thick gray mustache still hung along the sides of his mouth, and his eyes sparkled with youth and vigor. Adin had once asked O'lam how old he was, but the healer had just laughed and waved him away.

O'lam reached down and lifted a package from the ground. Adin knew what the long leather case contained. He had finished painting the map years ago and had watched in awe as O'lam had enchanted it. He thought about the day he had stumbled through the maze in confusion and fear—how it seemed the twisting paths went on for miles. Years ago he visited the abbey, when the labyrinth had been completed. He walked through the corridors and found there were only a half-dozen hallways, and the same number of doors leading to small rooms. He easily navigated the labyrinth in a puzzling few minutes. But that was before O'lam had worked his magic. Once the healer placed the hidden chamber under enchantment, the door to the stairs leading down to the maze had been locked, and Adin never ventured down those stairs again.

Aletha's grandson tugged on a rolled-up cloth sticking out the back of the horse-drawn cart.

"Careful with that, lad," O'lam warned. He hurried to the boy's side and helped him lug the bulky load to the carriage. Adin had watched Aletha finish the firebird tapestry all those years ago. Seeing the ancient letters appear strand by strand had been a magic of its own. Now, woven below the image of the golden firebird, were the words in the ancient *law'az*: "Set me as a seal upon your heart, as a seal upon your arm. For love is as strong as death; its flames are the flames of fire. Many waters cannot quench love, nor can the floods drown it."

Aletha had thrown a dinner party to celebrate the completion of the tapestry, and O'lam had sung the ancient song before all the hushed guests, bringing tears to the eyes of many who had no idea what his strange words signified. They only sensed he sang of a time long past and long forgotten. It was a song that stirred up visions of a rolling countryside, and a spring of fresh water bubbling up from the ground. A time of peace and tranquility that stirred restless longing in his listeners' hearts. The tapestry had hung on Aletha's living room wall for nearly thirty years, and every time Adin had looked at it, he thought of his mother and how much he missed her.

Adin approached the carriage, and Aletha held out her hand. He opened the small door and helped her into her seat. Her grandson clambered in and sat across from her.

Aletha smiled at Adin. He could see the excitement in her eyes. She took his weathered hands in her own and caressed them.

He said, "You'll have a wonderful time at the dedication. No doubt the King will be there, and all the important people from Sherbourne's Council."

Aletha's face grew sad. "If only Kah'yil had lived to see it completed. He would have been pleased."

Adin squeezed Aletha's hand. Both the regent and his sweet wife had died a few years back. Adin was glad Kah'yil had not lived long enough to see the treachery of his oldest son. As soon as the regent had died at a fine old age, his oldest—a mean-spirited man—had murdered his younger brothers, fearing a challenge for the throne. The grief had killed Kah'yil's wife. The news had likewise sent a shock through the kingdom as far west as Adin's small town. Ra'mah had quickly set himself up as king and ruled the land with an iron fist, garnering reluctant obedience and feigned respect. Adin knew Aletha would be uncomfortable with the new king's presence at the abbey, as she always was, but she would tolerate it in restrained silence.

Adin thought of the story Aletha had recounted to him—one of O'lam's tales from ancient times. It told of the first brothers, and how evil welled up in the heart of the elder brother, causing him to murder his sibling. Now the story had found its match in the sons of the first regent of Sherbourne. What a bitter and tragic start to a kingdom that held the potential to become a shining light in the east!

Strange—Adin could not recall having learned of this horrific tragedy in his history lessons. Perhaps the affair would be covered up in years to come. One thing was certain—the evil of the *qa'lal* had taken root and would now play out for the next three hundred years, wreaking havoc and mayhem in the palace and causing grief to all Sherbourne's subjects. But as O'lam had assured Adin on that day he had fled the battle, "As willful and destructive as evil is, it is no match for heaven. Love is stronger and always conquers." Heaven may take a longer time to conquer evil than humans want or expect, but in the end all things work to serve heaven's plan. Adin had learned this lesson well.

Adin pictured the stone circle, the *sha'har sha'ma'yim*, at the top of the knoll. He envisioned the first people settling by the spring, erecting the stones, using levers and animals to heft the huge slabs into place. He pictured heaven's blessing pouring down through the "gates," infusing the land with peace and prosperity. Then he watched as evil invaded the land, and the city walls were built. The slabs came down and the *ghed'ood* attacked. He saw Ka'zab thrust with his knife and the regent's sword flash. Drops of blood turned black as they spilled into the pristine pool.

Aletha searched Adin's face with a look of concern, and he brushed away his memories and looked at her. He was still holding the carriage door open. "I suppose my mind was wandering again. It does that more and more," he said by way of apology.

Her voice was tender. "There's still one thing I need, Adin." She lifted her hand and pointed to his neck.

Adin reached for his throat and found the chain. "My locket?"

Aletha nodded. "I'm to give it to the head abbot."

As Adin handed the chain to his sister, he remembered. She opened the locket, now empty, and placed a small piece of parchment inside. She explained why, but Adin already knew.

"I wrote down the translation of the writing on the back of the locket and put it inside. So they would know what it means." Adin looked at her own bare throat. She had already given her locket to her granddaughter with implicit instructions to pass it on to her own children as a family heirloom. He had forgotten about the head abbot with the empty locket. But then, he had forgotten so many things over the long years.

Adin felt a hand rest on his back. He moved aside to let Jered lean in and kiss his wife. Adin walked over to Aletha's sons, Adin and Onan. Her daughter, Ra'nan, took his arm and leaned affectionately into him. Adin watched as Jered and Aletha shared a few words. O'lam neatly hopped up onto the carriage and picked up the reins. The two draft horses snuffled and pawed, eager to start their journey.

As Adin, alongside his niece and nephews, waved good-bye, the carriage started down the cart road leading out of town. Jered hobbled over to him, walking erect and trying not to depend on his staff. Tears welled up in his eyes.

Ra'nan chided him. "Papa, she's only going to be gone a few days."

Jered's voice cracked. "Well, I miss her already."

Ra'nan punched him playfully in the arm as her brothers chuckled. "Come on, Papa. And you too, Uncle Adin. We have a busy day planned. There're strawberries to plant and onions to thin!"

Jered let his daughter take his arm. Adin followed behind Jered's sons, sending a silent prayer along with Aletha. She had done it—she had built the abbey, with O'lam's help and a little touch of magic. Now the Keeper would place the map in a trunk in a room in the labyrinth, and then bury it in a spell so powerful only one man would be able to retrieve it. The head abbot would gasp when he unrolled the breathtaking tapestry of a mythical magical bird, and would hang it in the great entry hall for all to see. And he would take the locket from Aletha and place it in a secret drawer, and she would give him instructions to pass it on to the next abbot, and the next.

Someday, the firebird tapestry would disappear from the abbey and end up hanging on the wall of a small cottage east of the city, where a fat white pig would bide his time, waiting for a sad and confused man to show up on his doorstep. The tapestry would be sold at market, and purchased by a buyer from the palace. And then the Queen, enamored with the beauty of the image, would hang the tapestry next to her bed, and it would evoke an odd mixture of emotion: joy from its beauty, but also a strange sadness that resonated like loss. At least, that was how Adin imagined it, and he knew deep in his soul there was some truth in the imagining.

Reya's words came unbidden, her voice strong and chastening: *"Heaven uses all circumstances to its advantage. Do you really think our small failures can stop the intentions of heaven? Believe me, Adin, they cannot."* Adin smiled at the memory of Reya's face and the way she had cleverly hidden all she knew. He often thought of his old nursemaid, hoping she had found joy in Sherbourne's salvation. And that she hadn't worried much when he disappeared into the past without leaving word.

Adin chuckled. He was thinking as if these things had already happened. Yet they wouldn't take place for centuries. What foolish thinking! His chuckle turned into a laugh.

Ra'nan and Jered turned back and looked at Adin, puzzled.

"What's so funny, Uncle Adin?" his niece asked.

Adin wiped the tears from his face as he tried to contain his laughter. "I am, Ra'nan." He sighed. "We all are."

Ra'nan and Jered looked at each other and shrugged, then walked down the cart road into a town bustling with the start of another ordinary day of life.

THIRTY-FOUR

REYA WALKED quietly away from Adin's side. A monk silently adjusted the headstone at the base of the newly-packed grave. Adin stood with his head bowed, his white hair trailing over his dark green robe. The other mourners had paid their respects and left hours ago, but Adin had wanted to spend some quiet moments at his mother's grave.

How odd Adin must feel, Reya mused. For so many years he had mourned his mother's death, only to find out she had been alive. The former grave had been a sham, a marker Reya herself had arranged to be placed at the head of an empty ditch. She looked at the King as he ran a hand over the carved tombstone. Adin's father, the former king, had died five years earlier and lay buried to the right of the Queen's headstone. To the left was the marker for Adin's wife, who had died peacefully in her sleep the previous year.

Reya knew how Adin's heart must be suffering. Although he had his four beautiful, sweet children and twelve grandchildren to keep him happy, he had so loved his wife. When he married a woman much like Aletha, Reya hadn't been surprised. She knew he had found a measure of happiness in the reunion with his parents and in his new family, but he never stopped missing his sister, keeping her memory alive like a second heartbeat pounding in his chest.

As Reya wandered through the abbey's graveyard, she thought about the *other* Adin—the young man who had come to her from eight years in the future. *That* Adin had helped her turn the Queen into the firebird, then went into hiding, sending her cryptic messages over the years. And then—nothing. As if he had disappeared off the face of the earth.

She looked over at her Adin, his back hunched over. He walked with a more pronounced limp now, as the years weighed on him, yet he had never let his deformities deter him from seeing the manifestation of all his dreams. He had been a fine king, a magnificent and just ruler. The people of Sherbourne greatly loved him. Now his son, Yasha, ruled Sherbourne. Adin had trained him well—not just in the ways of the monarchy, but in the affairs of the heart. Heaven had truly blessed Adin with peace and an undisturbed reign all these many years.

From time to time Adin had questioned Reya about the past, knowing she was a Keeper of the Promise. She never told him about the "man" who had come to her that night the Queen lay dying. He often wondered aloud about the stranger in the courtyard who had known his mother lived. He had also spoken in frustration about the white pig and the strange hermit who had sent him after the map. Reya thought it best not to burden Adin with the details of the strange twist of events that had sent the prince on two disparate paths. Especially since she had no idea what had happened to the "hermit." As she had learned over her many years, sometimes it was best to leave things unsaid.

Reya sat on an old stump in the corner of the cemetery, feeling the weight of her years as well. She had lived a very long time, through three kings' lifetimes. Her task had been to watch for the *pa'lat* and to help him in his *ma'gur*. She had done this faithfully and knew that heaven was pleased.

Reya sighed and looked down. A flat piece of ivory-colored stone caught her eye. Mindlessly, she rubbed the dirt away with her fingers, revealing a small rectangular marker partially buried in the ground. She leaned closer to read the name, and her breath caught in her throat. She felt along the ground to another similar stone and exposed that one as well. Her first suspicion was confirmed. Before her lay the graves of Aletha and Jered. Ancient writing covered Aletha's stone, and although Reya couldn't read it, she recognized they were the same words she had seen on the back of the twins' lockets—and the same writing woven at the bottom of the firebird tapestry.

She looked over at Adin and saw he still huddled at the Queen's marker. With more swipes of her hand, she uncovered other stones with unfamiliar names. Ra'nan, Adin, Onan. They were noted as Aletha's children. A smile came over her, and her heart warmed. She pictured her sweet Aletha with her dashing captain. Just as Adin had hoped, she had married Jered and raised a family. Reya squeezed her eyes closed, forcing tears to fall on the cold, flat marble markers, and thanked heaven for its mercies.

To the left of Aletha's grave, Reya found another marker. She strained closer to read the engraving. She put a hand over her mouth.

Aletha's brother was buried alongside her. His headstone read "He returned to find his sister and, in finding her, found peace." Next to his stone was one marked "Hirah, Adin's wife." And there were others, undoubtedly Adin's children, and grandchildren, and great-grandchildren.

Reya shook her head in wonder. She had never expected this last mystery to be solved—here, in this place, on this sad day. Yet, wasn't that just the way of heaven—to give the right comfort at the needed time? Reya lifted her eyes in gratitude. Adin had done it—somehow he had found his way back to Aletha, and had lived out his days alongside her, both of them married and raising children and starting new lives across the expanse of time. Her heart soared!

Reya stood and wiped the dirt from her hands and the tears from her cheeks. She returned to King Adin's side. His red puffy eyes began to shine, and a smile formed on his partially twisted face, a smile that lit up her heart with more joy.

He sighed. "I'm ready, Reya. Are you?"

Reya nodded and entwined her arm in his. Together they walked out of the cemetery toward the carriage that awaited them in front of the abbey. A monk held out the reins and bowed to the king.

"Your Majesty," he said. "My condolences."

"Thank you," replied Adin, his voice tender and soft. "Please convey my thanks to the head abbot for all he has done."

The monk nodded and retreated into the abbey. Reya looked over at the sharp line of mountains to the west. The sun was beginning to set, painting the sky like a canvas streaked with red and orange and pink. She recalled Adin telling of his visit years ago to a small village called Tebron, where he had found Aletha's house and her descendants.

Reya gazed at the beautiful view, picturing Aletha and Adin raising their families in a remote forest. She added them to the painting she saw stretched out before her on this canvas of time. Adin came alongside her and looked with her. They stood there for many moments in silence.

The sky lit up in flames of color, a beautiful sunset like no other, perhaps since the dawn of time. Reya heard the king's soft words drift into the air like a prayer.

"Set me as a seal upon your heart, as a seal upon your arm. For love is as strong as death; its flames are the flames of fire."

Reya stood with Adin, watching the sun's flames flicker and fade into night. She turned and saw once more the young boy with so many questions in his eyes. And then she saw the old man, now content to let heaven keep its secrets undisclosed.

"Come, Reya, I'm starving. We can make it back to the palace in time to raid the kitchen. Surely there must be a tart or a meat pie waiting for us."

Reya tousled his hair and together, laughing, they climbed into the carriage seat. Adin picked up the reins and clucked at the horses, turning them to head down the hill toward the fine, prosperous city of Sherbourne.

Epilogue

TUCKED BACK in a wooded hideaway stood a cottage—small and plain, hardly noticeable. A creek trickled over rocks alongside the cottage, filling the evening air with a soothing melody. A dozen yards away, a dirt road stretched east and west. West lay the walled city of Sherbourne. East lay distant lands, where few ever thought to venture.

The door to the cottage opened from the inside. A hairy snout poked through the opening, then pushed aside the door to make way for the rest of the pig. Winston raised his snout and sniffed the air. A smile formed on his face, making his fat jowls puff out like apples. He trotted a few steps into a clearing where he could see the sky. Streaks of red and orange spread across a backdrop of luminescent blue. Even though he could not see the sun setting over the western mountains, he could imagine it.

Already a few stars peeked out from their blanket of night. Winston sat back on his haunches, enjoying the procession of celestial bodies materializing above him. He found the Ram and the Bear. Way over on the horizon were the Twins, the *taw'ome*. His eyes followed the constellation as it crested in the night sky. He sat deep in thought, as pigs often do.

When he stood, he shook—from his fuzzy head to his corkscrew tail.

If anyone happened to glance that way—and he knew no one would—their mouths would drop open. In wonder and confusion, they would grow speechless as they watched the cottage flicker and the pig start to change. They would see Winston waver in a shimmer of light just before he vanished altogether.

Standing in his place was an old, stocky man, with a gray beard and thick mustache. The man straightened his back carefully, as if he hadn't stood on two legs in hundreds of years. He smoothed out his long tunic and trousers and wiggled his bare feet. He mumbled a few words and soft leather boots covered his toes. A dark cloak appeared on his shoulders, and a wooden staff materialized in the palm of his hand.

As he started to walk down the little stone path to the road, he fingered a silver chain around his neck. Behind him, the cottage dissolved, leaving a stand of saplings growing against the grassy hill. He looked back one last time, as if to commit what he saw to memory. He chuckled with a funny sound—part laugh, part snort.

"Well," he told himself, a look of satisfaction on his plump face. "That business is done with. So there you have it."

THE END

GLOSSARY OF THE *LAW'AZ*

a'khore: backside, rear
a'zar: gird, encompass
ab'ay'da: lost thing
ach: brother
adamah: ground
adin: delicate
ahabah: love
aletha:* true
aw'law: oath
ay'moon: faithful
ayt'saw: advice, counsel
bah'ar: stupid, foolish
bawt'sah: greedy
bay'ith: house, home
cha'mas: cruelty
d'am: blood
ga'haw: cure
ga'nab: thief (thieves)
ghed'ood: raiders, army
ghen'ay'ba: theft
ghib'bore: strong man, brave man
ha'dar: honor
hirah: noble family

ho'lay'la: madness
iv've'leth: folly, foolishness
jered: descent
ka'nan: mercy, grace
ka'rash: deaf
ka'shah: restful, still
ka'zab: liar
kah'yil: strength
ka'naph: wings
kar: ram
kef'eer: lion
keh'ber: enchantment, spell
keh'der: room, chamber
keh'leh: prison, confinement
keli'ma: dishonor
kes'eel: stupid person
kha'ta'aw: punishment
khay'fes: trick, plot
khay'fets: purpose
kheel: pain
kheh'sed: loyalty
kho'shek: darkness
ko'akh: power (of God, human strength)
ko'desh: sacred/holy
la'at: mystery, enchantment
la'shon: language, speech
law'az: strange language
ma'ar'ab: market
ma'gur: pilgrimage, quest
ma'ak'eh: low wall, parapet
ma'hath'alaw: illusion, deception

ma'veth: death
maf'tay'akh: key
makh'as'eh: refuge, shelter
makha'sha'bah: purpose, plan
mar'pe: healing
meh'lek: king
mik'dash: sanctuary
mik'vah: hope
mil'ka'ma: battle
mow'lone: lodging
mowt'sa: spring (water)
na'baal: fool
na'gheed: prince, captain
na'har: river
na'kash: serpent
na'kee: innocent, guiltless
na'thar: set loose, free
na'thib: path
naw'ame: to be beautiful
ne'buah: prophecy
o'kel: meal, food
o'lam, ow'lam: everlasting
o'yab: enemy
o'zen: ear(s)
onan: strong
oreb: raven
oro'bah: trickery
pa'lat: Deliverer
pe'ree: reward
qa'lal: curse
qowl: voice

ra'mah: to throw down, mislead, betray
ra'nan: joyful cry, to sing out
ra'pha: heal (healer)
ra'sha: wicked, criminal, guilty
ra'wah: shepherd, protector
re'sheeth: beginning
reya: friend
mil'ka'ma: a fight, battle
ro'osh: poison
sa'kar: reward
sha'arurah: horrible things
sha'har: gate
sha'kath: destroyer
sha'lach: sent forth
sha'mad: destruction, ruin
sha'ma'yim: heaven, sky
sha'qah: drink
shal'he'beth: flame
shaw'kad: be alert, watchful
shemesh: sun, sunrise
sho're: bull
ta'hore: pure, clean
ta'man: secret, hiding
taw'ome: twins
ten'uah: promise
tsa'ba: fighters, army
tsa'daq: righteousness, righteous
tsa'diyk: lawful, correct
tsa'va: commander(s)
ya'ale: goat
ya'chal: hope, wait

ya'feh: fair, handsome
ya'lak: depart, go away
ya'shane: sleep
yak'moor: deer
yasha: Savior
yo'fi: beauty
yo'shana: mystery
zar'ach: dawning, shining
z'ur: stranger(s)

*Aletha (truth) comes from Greek, the only word in the *law'az* not derived from ancient Hebrew.

The *law'az* is a liberal derivation of ancient Hebrew. All of the kingly sayings and other phrases in the ancient language are from the following books of the Old Testament: Psalms, Proverbs, Ecclesiastes, Song of Solomon, Isaiah, and Malachi.

Elements from "The Water of Life" (Grimm's Fairy Tales) and the Russian folktale "Ivan and the Firebird" provided the inspiration for this story.

DISCUSSION OF
THE MAP ACROSS TIME

THE GATES OF HEAVEN collection of fairy tales draws from Scripture, in order to help readers experience the power of God's Word and come to know our wonderful God of hope and integrity. The imaginary kingdom of Sherbourne has its roots in the ancient *law'az*, or language, based on biblical Hebrew texts. Thus, the many phrases uttered throughout the book are all Scriptures from the Old Testament, in Hebrew.

One of the reasons I explore ancient Hebrew in this story is to get a feeling for the nuances of the language, and to acquaint readers with Hebrew words. While this is not a book designed primarily to educate, the characters who delve into an ancient language parallel us as Bible students, as we dig into God's Word for deeper understanding.

Much wisdom spills from the pages of the Bible, so I seek in this series to draw from the verses that not only move powerfully within my own heart, but that lend themselves to the story being told. Here, then, are some of the Scripture passages used in *The Map across Time*, along with thought-provoking questions that can be used in group discussion or as assignments in classrooms and home schools. Other scriptural references, not included in this discussion but contained in the book, are listed at the end. Different Bible translations are used, but many of the verses are my interpretation of the Hebrew as I attempt to capture the true flavor and intent of the verse.

1) **"Love is as strong as death."** The Song of Solomon (or Song of Songs) ends with a powerful description of love. This is one of the key themes in *The Map across Time*. Portions of this passage in Song of Solomon 8:6, 7 are repeated throughout the book. The Queen utters these words to her children in her last breath. Adin, leaving to search for the firebird, tells them to Aletha. They are the words inscribed on the backs of the lockets and woven into the firebird tapestry. Why are these such powerful words, and how are they used in the book to teach what love is? How is God's love for us fulfilled in these words? How did Aletha and Adin demonstrate this kind of love?

2) Adin quotes part of Jeremiah 17:9: **"The heart is treacherous and desperately wicked; who can know it?"** to claim humans are evil and always will be. How does Reya answer him, and how does she explain the source of evil in the world? How does that compare with the Bible's explanation of the cause and end of evil? Look at the context of Jeremiah 17, and discuss why we are not to trust in humans, but only in God.

3) **"Those who are kind reward themselves"** (Proverbs 11:17). This is presented as a local saying in Sherbourne. Many of the Bible's proverbs are featured in this story as inventions of the first regent of Sherbourne, Kah'yil. How does Kah'yil's gathering of proverbs resemble that

of King Solomon? What does this proverb mean, in practical terms? Just how are you rewarded when you are kind to others, even if you are mistreated in return? (See Acts 20:35.)

4) Adin quotes Proverbs 8:11: **"Wisdom is better than gems,"** when he explains to the pig why he would choose wisdom above other gifts offered. Since wealth can open up many opportunities in life, why is wisdom better? What happened when Adin chose wisdom, and did it help him in the long run? What does God say in the Bible about searching for wisdom? (Read and discuss Proverbs 2.)

5) Another theme of the book is found in Proverbs 23:18: **"Surely there is a future, and your hope will not be cut off"** (*yesh 'achar'ith tiq'vah k'rath*). Why are these words so powerful to Adin? How does the promise of a future and a hope compel him to be true to his calling? How do God's repeated promises of hope and a future motivate you? Adin's hope was for his kingdom to heal and survive the effects of the curse. What hope do you focus on, and how does it make you feel? (Read Romans 5:1–5 and discuss how suffering and endurance lead to hope.)

6) Adin quotes Reya as having said, **"The human spirit will endure sickness, but a broken spirit—who can bear it?"** (Proverbs 18:4). Adin speaks these words from the pit of his despondency, after failing to stop the curse. He claims no one can endure a broken spirit. What does the Bible say about broken spirits (Psalm 51:17), and

why does God want us to have one? Just what is a broken spirit? How does Jesus promise to heal those with a broken spirit? (Isaiah 61:1; Luke 4:18).

7) Proverbs 1:19 says, **"Greed takes away the life of its possessors."** How is the sin of greed demonstrated by the King's behavior and attitude? What does Reya say is our problem with greed and other sins? How does sin work in us to make us incapable of doing right, without God's Spirit to help us? How can greed "take away the life" of one who indulges in it? What did Jesus have to say about greed and storing up treasures on earth? (Read and discuss Luke 12:13–21; Matthew 6:19.)

8) Jered says, **"Do not withhold good from those to whom it is due, when it is in your power to do it"** (Proverbs 3:27). How is this similar to, and different from, Jesus's command to do unto others as you would have them do unto you? What are some practical ways to apply this Scripture in our lives?

9) Another passage supporting the theme of hope in the book is taken from Malachi 4:2, which reads in part, **"The sun of righteousness will rise with healing in its wings."** Adin yearns for a day of healing and feels the truth of those words when his kingdom is saved from the curse. We, too, are under a curse—one of sin—but a day of healing is promised. How does the curse in the book symbolize the curse mankind is now under? And how does the *cure* in the book—innocent blood poured out—parallel the cure God has provided for our healing? (Read Malachi 4 and compare with Revelation 22:2.)

10) The pig tells Adin, and the Keeper tells Aletha, **"Truly there is a reward for the righteous"** (Psalm 58:11). O'lam says, "Trust heaven, Aletha, for no evil in the world can ever thwart heaven's hand. *Pe'ree tsa'diyk.* 'Truly there is a reward for the righteous.' Righteousness will prevail in the end—you will see." The *Sha'kath*, the Destroyer, is mentioned in the book as contaminating the world with evil through an initial act of betrayal. How does this compare to Adam's disobedience, as well as Satan and the demons? How has Jesus conquered evil, and how will the righteous be rewarded?

11) The pig warns Adin, **"For in wisdom is much grief, and he who increases knowledge increases sorrow."** He adds, "Scares some people away, that does." If wisdom is so valuable, and God wants us to search for it with all our hearts, why does Solomon warn us in Ecclesiastes 1:18 that gaining wisdom can cause grief? What wisdom do you think he is talking about, and how does Adin experience that bitterness when he realizes he must take Aletha away from the man she loves?

12) Adin ponders how **heaven chooses the weak and foolish to achieve great things.** How does this remind you of what Paul says in 1 Corinthians 1:27–29? How did heaven use Adin to accomplish great things? How does God use the "weak and foolish" to serve his purposes?

13) The pig paraphrases Isaiah 55:8, 9 when he tells Adin that **heaven's thoughts are not our thoughts.** Adin cannot see how heaven can accomplish something that seems impossible. Read Isaiah 55:8, 9 and discuss what

it means. How do these words comfort us when we have trouble understanding God's ways? What response should we have to these truths?

14) Discuss how Jered's rescuing of Adin is a dramatization of Jesus's **parable of the good Samaritan** in Luke 10. How do Jered's character and actions fit the type of neighbor Jesus says we should be? (Compare James 2:14–17.)

15) Kah'yil complains to Jered when discussing a traitor in their midst, "If you cannot be faithful when entrusted with the small things, how can you be relied upon to protect your brother in battle?" Throughout the book, characters are called upon to be faithful in little things. How are O'lam and Reya faithful to their appointments as Keepers? How are Aletha and Adin faithful to their kingdom, and to each other? How do you feel faithfulness is related to honor? Jesus tells us, **"He who is faithful in little is faithful in much"** (Luke 16:10). O'lam stresses this when he tells Aletha and Adin that small things matter just as much as big things. How is that symbolized by a single drop of blood bringing about the curse, as well as destroying it? Is a "small" lie, for example, not as bad as a "big" lie?

16) Reya relates the prophecy of the *pa'lat*, or Deliverer, the one destined to put an end to the curse upon the kingdom. How does this typify Jesus as our Deliverer? How did Adin react when he realized heaven had chosen him to be the *pa'lat*? What should be our attitude when God calls us to tasks?

17) The *sha'har sha'ma'yim,* or "Gates of Heaven," are set up as gates between heaven and earth—to prevent evil from getting a stranglehold over mankind. This expression is found only once in the Bible, but carries great import—when Jacob has a dream of a ladder between heaven and earth and establishes Beth'el, "the house of God." (Read Genesis 28:10–17.) He calls that place with its ladder "the gate of heaven." The Keepers are appointed to watch over these "gates" and thus ensure this promise of protection, yet, as O'lam states, they cannot control the hearts of men. Each individual must make a conscious choice to be honorable. He calls that man's blessing and curse. Why do you think he said that? What does the Bible say about our freedom to choose?

18) O'lam tells the story of the first brothers, a rendition of the account of Cain and Abel. He says, **"The voice of blood cries out from the ground"** (Genesis 4:10, author's paraphrase), explaining how the spilling of blood is sacred in God's sight, and that blood is a symbol of life. Cain was told that sin crouched at the door, but "you must master it" (Genesis 4:7). What means has God provided to help us do just that? And what does it mean that the blood "cries out from the ground"? (Compare to Matthew 23:35 and Hebrews 12:24.) Discuss how the Bible emphasizes the sacredness of blood throughout its pages.

19) Ta'man asks Adin if he has heard of the morning star, and says, "To the Keepers it is a symbol of hope, for the promise of the morning star is the promise of each day dawning anew." He mentions how this star (actually

Venus) creates a star pattern in apparent movement in the sky every eight years. This is an astronomical fact! The Bible names Jesus twice as the morning star, in Revelation 2:28 and 22:16: **"a bright and morning star."** Why is Jesus likened to a star, and how does 2 Peter 1:19 shed some "light" on this? Compare Matthew 13:43, where the righteous are spoken of as shining as the sun (which is a star). How does God's Word shine as a light in a dark place in our hearts, and how should that cause us to respond?

OTHER SCRIPTURAL REFERENCES (SOME PARAPHRASED)

Isaiah 6:11: "How long, oh how long? Until cities lie waste without inhabitants and houses without people and the land is utterly desolate."

Ecclesiastes 10:20: "Do not curse the king, even in your thoughts, for a bird of the air may carry your voice or some winged creature tell the matter."

Proverbs 18:11: "The wealth of the rich is their strong city, and like a wall in their imagination."

Matthew 6:21: "Where your treasure is, there your heart will be."

Proverbs 17:17: "A true friend is loving all the time, and is a brother born for when there is trouble."

Ecclesiastes 4:9: "Two are better than one, because they have a good reward for their labor. For if they fall, one will lift up his companion. But woe to him who is alone when he falls, for he has no one to help him up."

Proverbs 29:16: "When the wicked multiply, trouble increases, but the righteous will see their fall."

Proverbs 10:25: "What the wicked dread will come upon them."

Proverbs 9:8: "A scoffer who is rebuked will only hate you."

Proverbs 11:11: "By the blessing of the righteous, a city is exalted."

Proverbs 25:2: "It is the glory of God to conceal things, but it is the glory of kings to search things out."

Proverbs 15:13: "A cheerful heart is good medicine."

Ecclesiastes 9:11: "Like fish in a cruel net, birds caught in a snare, so men are snared at a time of calamity when it suddenly falls upon them."

Proverbs 11:14: "Where there is no guidance an army falls, but in the abundance of counselors there is safety."

Proverbs 23:10: "Do not remove the ancient landmarks that your ancestors set up."

Proverbs 25:5: "Take away the wicked from the presence of the king and his throne will become firmly established."

Ecclesiastes 3:1, 4: "There is a time for every season under heaven . . . a time to mourn and a time to laugh."